OPERATION RETRIBUTION

A Jack Stenhouse Mystery

ALSO BY FRANK A. RUFFOLO

Science Fiction Series

Gabriel's Chalice

Tres Archangelis

Xanthe Terra

Action Series

Trihedral of Chaos

Distruzione della Roccia

Mystery Series

Jack Stenhouse Mysteries

Blue Falcon

10048

Lady of the Harbor

Crime

Stuck in Traffick

OPERATION RETRIBUTION

A Jack Stenhouse Mystery

FRANK A. RUFFOLO

This is a work of fiction. Names, characters, places, and incidents are either products of the author's imagination or are used fictitiously. Certain events, locales, and business establishments are mentioned, but the characters and situations are imaginary.

OPERATION RETRIBUTION, A Jack Stenhouse Mystery, by Frank A. Ruffolo

www.frankaruffolo.com

Copyright © 2023 Frank A. Ruffolo

All rights reserved. This book or any portions thereof may not be reproduced or used in any manner whatsoever without the express written permission of the publisher, except for the use of brief quotations in a book review. For information, contact FC Literary Publishing at frankaruffolo@gmail.com.

Printed in the United States of America

First Edition, March 2023

ISBN: 979-8-9860720-0-5 (printed version only)

OPERATION RETRIBUTION

A Jack Stenhouse Mystery

PROLOGUE – ONE YEAR PRIOR

The darker the night, the better for evil to hide.

In the New Jersey Meadowlands, a black Cadillac sedan pulls into the construction site of a new hotel. The men inside are no strangers to working in the dead of night, so as usual, they keep the headlights off as they feel their way along.

When the car stops, the men walk around to the back, where the opened trunk exposes a severely beaten, gagged, and bound man.

Serge Kaspin, dethroned leader of the Patriot Guard, winces and looks up out of one eye. The other is of no use tonight; recent beatings have swollen it painfully shut.

Though the two men are much too well-dressed for their task tonight, orders are orders, and they do as they're told.

Earlier that day, their boss watched with satisfaction as others worked Serge Kaspin over for what he did to the boss' niece.

Then, when the boss had enough entertainment, he called them over and told them to roll the international arms dealer into the sedan and take him to his latest construction site.

"He's gonna become an integral part of my hotel's foundation," he told them with all the confidence of his years as capo of his New York crime syndicate.

Moaning and bleeding, Serge tries to focus on his abductors, but they've moved a little way off. He can hear them, though. They're ignoring his moans and groans while they laugh and speak rapid Italian to each other.

In the distance, the chopping sounds of an approaching

helicopter rouse Serge's curiosity. Raising his head above the lip of the trunk, he can just about make it out in the pitch darkness. *That can't be good*, he thinks, his heart pounding with the fear that's been his sole companion for the last several hours.

Another movement in the distance catches Serge's eye, so he painfully squints to get a better look. It's a car, a black Suburban SUV, and it's moving in their direction. Serge turns his head to watch for the Mafia goons' reaction, but they don't seem to know it's there.

At first, Serge is confused. Then, he understands. *They don't hear it*, he concludes, oddly pleased by their ignorance. The helicopter is almost upon them, and it's masking the sound of the car's engine.

As Serge continues to watch, the car eases forward. Then, a back window quietly rolls down, and suppressed gunfire takes out the two mafia soldiers who are completely unaware of its presence.

Serge gasps and lies back down. *Fuck! What the hell's goin' on?* he wonders, nervousness over his fate causing overworked muscles to shake involuntarily.

Soon, heavy footsteps reveal four camo-wearing soldiers from his beloved Patriot Guard looming anxiously over him.

"Take the gag off!" orders one of them.

"You all right, boss?" asks another.

Serge's good eye widens. "Holy shit am I glad to see you!" he exclaims, working his mouth after the tape is removed. "Get me the fuck outta here!"

When the men lift him out of the trunk, Serge's legs buckle. "I'm not sure I can walk," he tells them, so two of them support his arms to lead him quickly to the idling Suburban.

Disappearing into the night, Serge grimaces and his expression hardens in the safety of his supporters' vehicle.

Blinking his good eye, he bellows, "Those bastards are gonna pay for what they've done! All of them are gonna pay, and they're gonna pay dearly! Operation Retribution starts tonight!"

CHAPTER ONE

Today's weather forecast has swimwear designers and promoters of Manhattan's annual Swimfest in a tizzy. Though the premier bathing suit and sportswear fashion show features fabrics designed to get wet, the guests attending the event are not. Rain would do more than just dampen the festivities; it may even cancel them altogether.

This event is the third in a series of four held across the United States every year, so the organizers are understandably concerned that this one goes on as scheduled. The first two in Miami and Chicago were smashing successes, and the final one to be held in Los Angeles two weeks after this one is usually the best of them all.

"What rain?" ask workers sweating in the warmth of the sun currently kissing the Hudson. "The weather guys never know what's gonna happen, so why do they bother scaring us?" Mumbling and grumbling, they hurry to erect the all-important catwalk for the show in front of the Castle Clinton National Monument in Battery Park.

Outside the park, most of the city's residents are unaware of the upcoming activities. They're absorbed in their own little worlds — performing early morning jobs, making their ways to work or school, or dealing with the myriad other things that keep the Big Apple humming.

Among the crowd of people, a blue van from Apex Technologies, LLC pulls up in front of One Battery Park Plaza, and the driver, dressed in a matching blue uniform and Yankee cap, adjusts his mirrored sunglasses as he sets up orange cones to mark his territory. When he's done, he takes an oversized workbox from the back of the van and walks into the gleaming, Italian marble lobby of the thirty-five-story structure.

As a class A office tower, One Battery Park Plaza houses many of the city's influential firms, which naturally attracts the most dynamic and high-powered staff, making the building a sought-after place to work and be seen.

As the day gets started, executives and employees swipe their security cards through turnstiles to gain access to the building. A few feet away from them, the driver of the van puts his workbox down in front of the security desk.

"Mornin'," he says to the guards who look bored as they finish their coffees. "I got a work order here to repair one of the cell towers on the roof."

One of the young guards studies the mirrored sunglasses and Yankee cap, then takes the paperwork. "We didn't receive word about a cell tower problem."

"Look, pal," responds the technician, "AT&T customers are complaining, and we traced the problem to a tower on your roof. My work order is signed and approved by the building manager, so I don't give a shit whether he told you or not. If you want, I can have all the complaint calls forwarded to you, and you can deal with them yourself. It's no skin off my nose. I get paid whether I'm up there or standing down here talking to you."

The guard looks again at the technician, then takes a deep breath and activates a temporary security badge. "Here," he says, handing the ID over the counter. "This will grant you access to the roof. How long do you think you'll be up there?"

"I don't even know what's wrong yet," laughs the technician. "I'll be done when I'm done. Have a nice day."

The guard shrugs off the exchange but watches keenly as the technician passes through the turnstile, then enters one of the lobby elevators.

"Jack, I'm so excited about Swimfest. Thanks for going with me today," says Didi Stenhouse to her husband while they sip coffees at his desk at the First Precinct. "When I decided to add swimwear to the boutique, I was intrigued by the designs from Artchop. So when I learned the line's going to be there, I just had to go to see them up close."

"What's the owner's name again?" asks Jack, only mildly interested and trying to put on a good show for his wife.

"It's Ken Rodriguez. He's a collage artist who started putting his designs onto fashionwear a few years ago. Remember? I told you that he showed his fashions at Cannes."

"Oh, yeah," says Jack, nodding again.

"His show got great reviews; I'm so excited to see them in person! Hey, maybe I can even meet Ken!"

Jack could care less, but he smiles and nods. It's a slow morning, but he'd much rather be at a crime scene than a fashion show.

Jack, now a lieutenant in charge of his own unit, knows there are a number of other things he should be taking care of this morning. But Didi's so happy that he puts everything else on hold so he can indulge his wife in something important to her.

Jack's promotion is one of several changes to the First Precinct's Homicide Department in recent years. The former department head, Lieutenant Conrad, is now a captain, and after two tries, Hector Gomez made detective and is now leading his own crew.

As far as Jack is concerned, the most significant change to the department has been Allison Giancarlo's transfer to the Counterterrorism Bureau. Jack is happy his former partner is commanding her own department, but he misses her terribly.

Their daily quips took the edge off the drudgery and were often the highlight of his day.

The only position in the department that hasn't changed is sergeant. It's still occupied by newlywed John Burley, who recovered nicely from the injuries he sustained on the job a while ago.

Now that Jack's in charge of a unit, the vacant spots are one of many things he never had to worry about before, and he takes his responsibility to fill it seriously. He'd like to close the gap in his unit soon, but budget concerns are delaying that action, and he wonders if he and his colleagues will be able to keep up if things get busy.

Sergeant Burley is surprised to see Didi Stenhouse standing at the coffee maker this morning. "Hey, what's Didi doing here?" he asks Jack, his new boss. John has known Didi for many years, but she still manages to capture his attention. Today, she's wearing skinny jeans and a stretched-to-the max Guess T-shirt.

"Hey, numbnuts," replies Jack, as snarky as ever. "That's Lieutenant to you," he tells his friend with a smile. "It's been kinda quiet around here, so Conrad gave me the morning off, and I'm going with Didi to the Swimfest show at the Battery. It starts at eleven."

"Nice," says John. "I guess having a live-in babysitter helps."

"Yeah, it's great having Didi's mom living with us. But hey, I've been meaning to ask… When you gonna get Sylvia pregnant?"

John walks to the coffee machine to greet Didi and pour himself a cup of coffee. "Slow down, will ya?" he says, returning to Jack's desk. "We're still practicing. We only got married a few weeks ago."

"Hey, Jack, it's almost ten," says Didi, looking at her watch. "I want to get there before the crowd arrives. Let's go now, okay?"

Jack stands and moves his neck from side to side, the resulting "crack" a satisfying feeling. "Anything you say, babe. Let's roll."

As the couple starts to leave, John calls after them, "Don't worry about me! I'll be fine here, all alone. You two run along and have a fun day!"

When the elevator doors close on the couple, John sits down at his desk and rubs his hands together to bring feeling back into his fingers, one of several prices he's having to pay for being stubborn. He still hasn't consented to the surgery that would remove bullet fragments remaining in sensitive areas from the shooting he was involved in, so his body finds ways to let him know they're there. The surgery is risky, and he's not ready to tackle that decision yet.

When the Apex technician reaches the roof, he walks right past the cell tower he's supposed to be checking, and goes to the side of the building facing Castle Clinton. It's not too hot today — the type of blue-sky morning that makes the tourist bureau jump for joy — and he's grateful there's no strong breeze at this height.

The technician places his work paraphernalia on the rooftop and removes his equipment: a Valkyrie suppressed sniper rifle with a built-in Atlas Bipod, and a Leupold Mark 3.5 -25 x56 M5B2 illuminated scope. Moving confidently, he methodically assembles the weapon and sets up a position overlooking Battery Park.

The focus of the technician's attention today is the event taking place at Castle Clinton. The unusual-looking national monument at Battery Park was built in the early 1800s to defend New York Harbor during the War of 1812. At that time, it was known as Southwest Battery, but in 1815, it was renamed Castle Clinton in honor of DeWitt Clinton, the city's mayor.

Over the years, the structure served the citizens of New York in varied ways, none of which recalled its original intent. Among its functions, it operated as a beer hall, an exhibition center, a theater, and an aquarium. Its most notable role was as America's first immigration landing depot, predating Ellis Island.

Today, a group of photographers gather for Swimfest while workers continue to get things ready for the show. Some of the laborers are putting finishing touches on the long catwalk and setting out chairs, while others are checking the large video screens that are being used to conceal the steps leading up to the runway.

There is also a lot of activity at the rear of the castle. There, large RVs for the models' quick changes have already become the focus of model angst and fashion designer handwringing.

Jack finds a parking spot on Beaver Street, a few blocks from The Battery, then looks around for a uniformed officer. When he spots one, he puts a blue light on the dashboard and tells the man to look out for his baby. Then he and Didi walk to the castle, past the Bowling Green, the oldest public park in the city, and the Netherland Monument, a flagstaff commemorating the Dutch establishment of New Amsterdam.

At the castle, the seats around the runway have already begun to fill with eager spectators, but Jack and Didi have reservations. So while Didi goes to claim their seats, Jack stops at one of several vendors who's hoping for a good take today.

"Hey, give me two bottles of water," he says, eliciting a smile from the man behind the makeshift counter. He's one of many who are more than happy to exploit the show and the fort's attraction as a national monument and ticket booth for Statue of Liberty cruises.

"Five bucks, man," says the vendor, handing over two bottles he fished from a cooler.

Jack curses under his breath at the exorbitant price, but hands over his money. Then he joins Didi at their seats.

Before the event starts, Jack looks around at his surroundings, noting everything and everyone. It's a habit that's served him well and it never leaves him, no matter where he is or what he's doing.

The first thing Jack spots are the media trucks with their satellite towers pointing to the sky, and their presence makes him scowl. He fully expected them to be there, but the run-ins he's had with on-air personalities over the years while doing police work have tainted his opinion of them. Next, he spots several undercover police officers and Homeland Security teams scouring the crowd for pickpockets and other riffraff. Finally, he studies the faces and demeanor of nearby persons for signs of wayward activity.

While the ticketholders arrive and settle in, fashion designer Ken Rodriguez prepares his models in his rented RV behind the castle. He has plenty of time to make sure everyone is ready, as the lineup indicates he'll be the last to display his wares.

Ken is excited that his company, Artchop, will represent the United States at this event. Swimfest is an international fashion affair, drawing designers from around the world, and Ken knows he's in impressive company.

When the event begins, buyers from across the globe focus their attention on the spectacle before them. With practiced eyes, they evaluate each outfit worn by the scantily clad models strutting down the runway for potential sale in their shops.

As one of many spectators, Jack stares intently at the beautiful models, happy that his eyes are shielded behind his mirrored sunglasses. His intent is to appear aloof to the beauty before him, but he's struggling, and Didi knows it.

"They're pretty, aren't they?" she asks, leaning over to whisper in Jack's ear.

"Uh, yeah," he responds without taking his eyes off the runway.

The models come and go, and the technician on the roof grows impatient. "This is taking too long and it's getting hot as hell up here," he mutters, fine-tuning his focus on models and strangers in the crowd.

Backstage, Ken waits for his cue. It's been a long journey to get here, and he wants everything to be perfect.

"Let's join hands, ladies," he says. "There's one more thing we have to do before we go out there."

Gathering his models and staff together, they join hands and pray for a successful show. Then, there's a knock on the RV door.

"Mr. Rodriguez," says a voice, "you're up next."

Ken looks at his lovelies. "Okay, girls. Time to strut your stuff, and mine. Let's wow 'em!"

With nervous excitement, the models make their way to the stairs leading up to the catwalk. There will be one costume change for each of them, so they know they'll have to be quick after their turns in the spotlight.

When the emcee announces Artchop, the crowd welcomes the American designer, and Didi leans forward in her chair. She's heard good things about these fashions and is looking forward to seeing the one- and two-piece bathing suits, leggings, and tops for males and females in person. She wants to freshen her boutique's inventory with swimwear and beach and pool fashions and knows she needs to choose carefully.

From his position on the roof of One Battery Park, the sniper can't hear the applause and excited chatter, but he gets a good idea of what's going on through his rifle scope.

Finally, Artchop's turn ends, and he sees his target. As Ken walks onto the runway with a beautiful model on each arm and the others trailing behind him, he trains his crosshairs on the designer, watching while Ken waves and throws kisses to the crowd.

Ken is smiling broadly; he's ecstatic at the enthusiastic response his designs received. Doing his best to acknowledge the accolades, he bows for the third time, just as a splatter of blood smacks into the side of his face and he falls, pulled down by the beautiful woman he had on one arm, after a .308 round entered her head.

At first, the crowd is silent, not sure of what happened, but Jack knows. Just before gasps and screams fill the park, he pulls Didi to the ground and covers her body with his own.

On the stage, Ken does the same. In disregard of his own life, he throws himself over the other model beside him, but his action doesn't work. In an instant, a second round enters his back and exits into the woman's temple, killing her instantly.

In the crowd, panic has taken over, and while everyone runs over each other trying to exit Battery Park, police and Homeland Security officers frantically scan the area to find the shooter.

Outnumbered officers try in vain to control the crowd, but the panic spreads, and the frenzied ticketholders flee across the street, trying to get as far away as possible.

At One Battery Park, the Apex technician calmly steps out of the elevator into the lobby. With a thumbs up for the security guards who haven't noticed the chaos outside, he calmly exits the building and drives away.

At the park, Jack pops his head up to look around. "Stay here for now," he tells Didi, holding her while she cries, out of fear and grief.

When she calms down enough, she tells Jack, "I know you have to go, babe. I'll be okay; do your job. Just be careful."

"I will," he replies, moving Didi's reddish-brown hair out of the way so he can wipe the freshly falling tears from her face. "I'll get a uniformed to drive you home. Kiss Mark for me."

Jack gives Didi a hug, then jumps onto the stage and runs over to the victims. Feeling for a pulse, he's relieved to find Ken alive but unconscious. However, the two models are dead.

Jack stands to gaze through the trees at buildings bordering the area, while Homeland Security and EMTs scramble around the fallen.

"It appears to be a pro," he says to Lieutenant Allison Giancarlo, now in charge of the Joint Terrorist Task Force section of the city's Counterterrorism Bureau. "Two shots. One injured, two dead. I'm gonna call Burley."

Jack fishes his cell phone from his pocket. "Get down to The Battery," he tells the sergeant. "There was a shooting."

"At the show?" asks the shocked officer. "You okay? What about Didi?"

"We're fine, but there's an injured victim. He's unconscious right now, so get to NewYork-Presbyterian Hospital, and question him when he wakes up."

Jack ends the call and turns to Allison. "I'm gonna ask one of the uniformed guys to give Didi a ride out of here. Did you guys get any warning of terrorist activity?"

Giancarlo shakes her head. "Not any more than usual. The shot was probably from a rooftop."

"Yeah," agrees Jack. "I'll stay with your crew to scope out the area. Just let me get someone to take Didi home first."

While two EMTs try to stabilize Ken before transporting him to the nearest hospital, Jack jumps off the stage to stop a uniformed cop from the First Precinct. "Hey, Bill. Do me a favor and drive my wife home, will ya?"

The corporal nods. "No problem, Lieutenant."

Still at her seat, Didi is saying a prayer when Jack kneels next to her. "Hey, babe. Officer Thomas will drive you home. I'm gonna be a little busy."

Didi nods and rises, wordlessly embracing her husband before the officer guides her through the now-empty park.

When the media vampires make their way to the stage, the men in blue block their attempts to get close.

"What happened?" they shout. "Tell us what's going on!" They ask, even though they know the drill: the cops remain silent while the reporters do their best to glean information for their broadcasts.

Jack climbs back onto the stage while Ken Rodriguez is eased onto a stretcher. Ken is conscious now, so Jack stops the EMTs for a moment. "Mr. Rodriguez, I'm Lieutenant Jack Stenhouse, NYPD Homicide. Sergeant John Burley will be questioning you later at the hospital."

Ken is in a lot of pain, so he just nods and gives Jack a thumbs up.

"Hey," says Giancarlo, standing near Jack. "My team is checking the surrounding buildings, but I told them that you and I would help. I want to check One Battery Park. You up for it?"

"Yeah. That building is a likely place for a sniper."

"Okay, let's roll."

"Oh, no you don't," says Jack, stopping in his tracks. He's miffed at his former partner's use of a line he likes to think is his alone. "That's mine!"

Allison knows Jack well, so she merely shrugs and leads the way, forcing Jack to catch up.

While they cross the street, Detective Gomez waves his arms and shouts to get their attention.

"Conrad sent me down!" he says to puzzled looks.

Jack sighs. "Talk to me," he says, cricking his neck from the day's tension.

"Conrad wants me to work with you on this one. The Hispanic community is in an uproar, fueled by the media, of course. Their reports are emphasizing the fact that the guy who was shot is Hispanic, and they're implying that someone doesn't like the idea that his designs are doing well. Conrad says it'll look good for me to be involved. So, what do you need me to do here?"

Jack takes a deep breath, knowing that politics is an ugly part of police work. "Interview all the models and everyone else associated with Artchop. Then talk to the camera guys who were here. I'm sure they were rolling when the shots rang out. Tell them to give you a copy of their tapes."

"Okay," says Gomez.

"And while you do that, I'm going with Giancarlo to scope out the One Battery Park building. We assume it was a professional hit. I'll catch up with you later."

CHAPTER TWO

The One Battery Park Plaza building stands like a monolith reflecting the noonday sun as Jack and Allison walk into its cool, marble interior.

Jack looks at Allison nostalgically. "It's like old times," he says. "You and me together, investigating a case."

Allison's eyes twinkle in response while Jack flashes his badge at the security desk.

"I'm Lieutenant Stenhouse," he tells one of the guards, "and this is Lieutenant—"

The concerned guard interrupts him. "You here about the shooting? It's everywhere — on TV, social media — everywhere! We heard some people were killed!"

Jack looks at his ex-partner, then back at the guard. "The body count isn't your concern, bub. We need to know if you had any visitors here today other than your regular clientele."

When the wizened older guard hesitates, a younger one chimes in from the other end of the large reception desk. "There was a guy here this morning from Apex something. He said he was here to repair one of the cell towers on the roof."

"Okay," says Jack. "Has Apex been here before?"

"Uh… No, he seemed legit, though."

"Did you verify that he was from Apex?"

When the guard looks down sheepishly, Allison sighs. "Did he give you anything…a business card, a work order, anything we can look at?"

"Yeah…" the man replies, searching through a file. "Here it is. It's a work order for cell tower repairs."

Allison takes the paper. "Thanks, she says, fishing for her cell phone. "I'll check it out," she tells Jack.

While Allison Googles Apex Technologies, Jack asks the guards more questions, but they can't give him much information.

"Hello," says Allison when she finally connects to a voice with a pulse at the technology company. "This is Lieutenant Giancarlo with the NYPD Joint Terrorist Task Force. I'm calling from One Battery Plaza. Did your company send a technician here this morning?"

"Um, I'll check. Please hold."

While Allison waits, the guards give Jack two security badges so they can access the roof.

"Hello? Detective Giancarlo?" says a different voice when the call connects again. "This is Jesse Langley. I'm the manager of our contract accounts. We don't have anyone scheduled to be at One Battery Plaza today. But…and this may be relevant… one of our work vans was stolen yesterday."

"Stolen? Did you file a report?"

"Yes, I have the case number if you want it."

Allison takes down the number and thanks the manager.

"Jack," she says after hanging up, "Apex didn't send anyone here today, but one of their vans was stolen."

Jack turns to the younger guard. "Can you give us a description of the technician?"

The young man rubs his brow. "Well, not much to say… He was about six-feet, medium build. Um, oh… He was wearing blue overalls and had on a Yankee cap. And he kept his sunglasses on while we talked. You know, the trendy kind, wraparound, yellow-tinted?"

"If he was so covered up, what makes you think it was a man?" asks Allison.

The guard flushes and looks confused. "Well, I assumed… He or she, whatever, had a deep voice. But I guess it could have been a woman. We couldn't see his, um, her hair, the Yankee cap covered it all, and his, or her, shirt was buttoned up to the neck. But the guy is on our security tape. I can put a copy on a flash drive, and you can decide for yourselves."

"Okay," says Jack, stifling a smile at the guard's discomfort. "We'll pick it up after we examine the roof."

Across the street, Detective Gomez and a sergeant from the First Precinct's Homicide Department walk around the castle toward the area where the RVs are parked.

"How are we gonna know which one Rodriguez rented?" asks Sergeant Ruiz. He quickly takes it back when they spot the 'Artchop' company name and some of Ken's collage designs plastered on the side of a forty-foot Winnebago.

The door is open, so the officers peer in and announce themselves.

"Hey," says a staff member. "Do you have any information on Kenny?"

"Can we come in?" asks Ruiz.

"Yeah, yeah," says the man, waving them inside.

The officers step into a crowded space littered with clothing, makeup, photographic equipment, and other paraphernalia strewn around models and staff in various stages of fear and worry.

"He was semi-conscious when the EMTs transported him to the hospital," says Gomez. "They said his wounds aren't life-threatening."

"Thank God!" exclaim several persons, to sighs of relief from others.

"We're here to ask about the victims…" says Sergeant Ruiz, who is interrupted by a voice calling from the back.

"I just spoke to Kenny's wife, and I told her to go to the hospital!"

"All right, thanks!" replies the staff member who seems to be in charge. "Look, everyone's pretty upset in here," he tells the officers. "Can we talk outside? I can give you everyone's names and contact information so you can speak with them later."

Gomez takes in a breath. "Thanks for the offer, but Sergeant Ruiz will take down everything he needs. However, we can go outside if you want."

At the door, Gomez turns around to give Ruiz an order. "Sergeant, bag the victims' personal effects — phones, laptops, and so on."

"Will do," responds Ruiz as Gomez and the staffer descend the RV's steps.

Inside the office building, Jack and Allison walk down a hallway lined with expansive windows. Across the way, millennials decked out in Armani and Dolce & Gabbana work at sofas and desks in a large open area.

While Jack stares at the females in short leather skirts, Ally directs her attention to the men dressed in fashionable skinny suits.

"Seems to be a uniform of sorts, don't you think?" she asks, just as a well-endowed young woman notices them and winks at Jack.

"Ugh," she says, but Jack smiles with pride.

"I still got it," he crows happily.

At the end of the hall, the door to the roof requires them to use the badge the security staff gave them. Ally swipes hers, then Jack opens the door.

Inside, a staircase leads to a metal door that also needs badge verification. "Tight security here," comments Jack.

When they open this door, a blast of air greets them as they step onto the roof.

"We're gonna need one of the badges to reenter the building," says Jack, examining the lock before closing the door.

With the sun beating down on the reflective roof coating, Jack and Allison stop at a group of cell towers in the center.

"I don't know what I'm looking at, do you?" asks Allison.

"No; there's no way for us to know if he did anything to this equipment. I'm gonna look over the edge facing Battery Park."

At the ledge, Jack comments back to Allison, "Nice view from here." Then he turns away, searching the roof for anything interesting.

When Allison joins him, he's bending down to look at a spent .308 cartridge. "Any others?" he asks, removing an old Cross pen from an inside coat pocket and inserting it into the casing.

"Yeah," says Allison, retrieving another one using a BIC pen.

"Ally, I wasn't on duty when this happened, so I hope you have evidence bags with you."

"Got some," she says, taking one out of a pocket and holding it open so she and Jack can insert the cartridges.

Jack says, "The shooter must have been using a silencer. I didn't hear anything before the victims were hit. So maybe it's not a terror attack."

Allison looks over the edge. "It was probably a professional hit from a trained marksman. I'll have CSI scour this roof, but I wouldn't be surprised if they don't find anything else. Actually, I'm surprised we found these."

"I agree. Either it's sloppy work, or he wanted us to find them. Let's take a look at the security footage. And you should get some of your people to interview the folks inside at that fancy business. Maybe they saw something out of the windows."

Allison keys the mic on her portable radio to call for the forensic team. "I'll stay up here until they arrive. Then I'll question the people on the top floor myself."

Jack nods. "Okay. I'm gonna go downstairs now to see if Gomez dug up anything. We can compare notes later at the First."

CHAPTER THREE

Outside the RV, Hector sits in a beach chair opposite the senior staffer, who can't be much older than twenty-one. Gomez turns on his digital voice recorder and asks his first question while sizing up the young man. "First, what's your name, please?"

"Steve Finley."

"Okay, Steve. What do you do here?"

"I work for Kenny as a stylist and all-around go-to person. I've been with him since his fashion tour at Cannes last year."

"What's a go-to person?"

"I do all the extra things, like booking shoots and interviewing models. I even set up the catering and take Kenny's phone calls. We're a small company."

"All right, thanks. Now I need to talk to you about the two victims. Their names, please."

Steve inhales to push down tears that threaten to roll down his finely chiseled face. "Elena Guerra was shot first while she was walking down the runway with Kenny. Then Vicky Simpson was hit."

"What can you tell me about these two women?"

"Vicky was twenty-two," he begins, his voice cracking from tension. "She lived in Miami and was with us from the start. Elena was older, twenty-eight. She was an ex-playmate and joined us in Chicago."

"Do you know of anyone who would want to harm them or Mr. Rodriguez?"

Steve stares at the ground to gather his thoughts. Then he looks up. "Elena and Vicky started arguing a lot after we left the show in Chicago, but I don't know why. They even had a fight early this morning. And Kenny… He has a past that may have caught up to him."

"What about Mr. Rodriguez's past?"

"He grew up on the South Side of Chicago and was in a gang as a kid. He says some of them were pissed when he left. But that must have been at least twenty years ago. You don't think they keep grudges that long, do you?"

"Why were they pissed?"

"I don't know. Kenny never said, and I didn't ask."

Were there any threats to Mr. Rodriguez or the models?"

Steve shakes his head. "Not that I know of."

Gomez shuts off the recorder and stands. "I'll need the personnel records of Ms. Simpson and Ms. Guerra so we can notify their next of kin."

Steve stands as well. "I'll have to call Ken's wife; she handles all the office stuff. If you ask me, she's the real boss around here."

"What's her phone number? I'll want to talk to her as well. And Steve, we'll be in contact with you and the others again. This was just a preliminary discussion. There will be more questions later."

In the lobby of One Battery Park Plaza, Jack stops at the security desk to pick up the promised flash drive containing CCTV footage of the suspected shooter. Then he heads outside to Battery Park.

Within minutes, he's back at Castle Clinton, deserted now except for some remaining police presence, lots of yellow tape, and a group of city workers waiting for the CSI crew to clear the crime scene.

Jack stops a passing officer. "The media finally had their fill?" he asks derisively, noting how most of the satellite trucks have left the area.

"Yeah," replies the officer. "They must be falling over themselves to get this on their news stations before their competitors."

"You know it," agrees Jack. "But I don't have any sympathy for them. I only care about the poor bastards waiting to remove the chairs and dismantle the runway and other equipment. It's gonna be a while before they can go home today."

Jack finds Hector behind the castle. "Hey," he says. "I gave the CSI gurus a couple of spent .308 casings from the roof, and I have footage of the suspected shooter from the building's security cameras."

Hector asks, "Where's Giancarlo?"

"She's interrogating possible eyewitnesses on the top floor. What's the skinny down here?"

"I got the names of the two victims, and Ken's wife will get me their files. She's with her husband now, so it may take some time. But I found out a couple of interesting things. There may be something to them, maybe not."

"Yeah? What do you have?"

"The two women who were shot didn't seem to get along with each other. And Ken pissed some people off from a gang he was in when he was growing up in Chicago."

Jack cricks his neck to relieve a sudden pain. "When he was a kid? That's a long time ago. Look, I'm heading back to the First to view this flash drive. Then I'll get the crime lab to print an image of the possible shooter."

"Okay; I'll hook up with Ruiz and meet you back there."

Before Jack leaves, he takes off his sports jacket and drapes it over his shoulder. "Damn, it got hot all of a sudden," he complains to Hector. "This shirt's gonna be soaked before I get to my car. I thought I left the heat in South Florida."

"Mrs. Rodriguez," says John, flashing his badge and ID at Ken's wife in a hospital waiting room. "I'm NYPD Sergeant Burley. I need to ask you some questions."

Cindy Rodriguez is waiting for an update on her husband's condition, and she's worried. With a half-smile, she waves her hand at the next chair. "Sure," she says. "But I don't know what I can tell you; I wasn't there."

"I know," says John, taking the seat. "But you may have information that can help our investigation."

"Okay… What do you want to know?"

"You're involved in your husband's business, correct?"

"Yes, I manage the books and the office stuff."

"Have you had any problems paying bills recently?"

"Uh, no… It's tight, but we can still keep up with everything."

"All right. Now what about your husband? Is there anyone who may have a vendetta against him or the two models who were killed? We know that Ken was involved in a gang when he lived in Chicago."

Cindy blinks rapidly, then stares at the sergeant with wide eyes. However, before she can respond, the doctor in charge of the ER approaches them with news.

"Mrs. Rodriguez? Your husband is awake and resting comfortably. He lost a lot of blood and is rather weak, so we're going to keep him here for a couple of days. But I'm confident that he'll be released by week's end. You can go in and see him now."

The doctor, an Asian man in his early thirties, turns his attention to Burley. "Sergeant, it's against my better judgment, but I know you have a job to do. So you may see Mr. Rodriguez as well, but please keep it short. Tomorrow's another day."

Burley and Cindy rise just as a call comes in over Burley's radio. "I got a 10-71 at the compost yard at East River Park. Need assistance."

Burley listens, then lowers the volume and follows Cindy to Ken's room.

"What's a 10-71?" she asks.

"It's a car fire. Ah, here's the room."

Jack drapes his sports jacket over his desk chair, then heads to Forensics so he can view the flash drive.

"Jack," says Captain Conrad, catching him as he passes his office. "An Apex work van is on fire at the East River compost yard. The plate matches the van that was reported stolen."

"Fuck," growls Jack. "Allison and I are fairly sure it was a professional hit. Whoever it was is wasting no time getting rid of evidence."

Ken Rodriguez is doped up on painkillers and bandaged like a mummy when Cindy sees him.

"You know me," he tells her weakly. "Gotta get all the attention."

"I know," Cindy replies, patting her husband's hand. "But you could have picked a better way to do it."

Turning her head, she acknowledges Burley standing

behind her. "Honey, there's a police sergeant here. He needs to ask you a few questions. Are you up to it?"

Taking the cue, Burley approaches the bed while Ken tries to put him into focus.

"Mr. Rodriguez," says Burley, "I know you're a little woozy, but I need to ask you some questions." Ken nods, so he continues. "Can you think of anyone who may have a beef with you or your models?"

Ken takes a moment to think. Then he says, "Well, I'm from South Chicago, and when I moved away, some of the guys there weren't happy. It was a long time ago, but they don't like it when a homeboy leaves. I haven't heard from any of them in years, and anyway, this isn't their style. So no, I don't know who could have done this."

"And the models?"

"Well, they had a falling out and were constantly at each other's throats. I even had to separate them this morning. But as far as I know, it was just between the two of them. I don't know what was going on, but I couldn't take it anymore, so I was going to let them both go after today's show."

"Did they know you intended to sack them?"

"No, I didn't tell anyone."

Cindy looks at Burley. "I always thought they had man troubles. They fought like cats and dogs."

Ken closes his eyes as a sudden wave of pain washes over him.

Cindy asks, "You want me to call someone?" She's concerned by the look on Ken's face.

As if she were telepathic, a nurse walks in. "Mr. Rodriguez needs to rest now, so I'd like to clear the room," she announces firmly. "Sergeant, you're going to have to leave."

The nurse turns to Cindy. "You can stay if you promise to let him sleep."

Cindy looks at her husband. "He's in pain," she says.

"I'll take care of it," says the nurse.

Burley hands his business card to Ken's wife. "I'll be in contact with the hospital to make arrangements to speak with your husband again. Please call me if there's anything you can tell me before then."

Cindy takes the card while the nurse pulls the curtain around Ken's bed and starts to fiddle with equipment at his head.

While she watches, her phone rings, so she reaches into her shoulder bag and looks at the screen. "It's Steve Finley," she tells Ken.

The First Precinct's crime lab looks like it might have come straight out of the latest sci-fi movie. The space is dotted with computers, electronic test equipment, microscopes, and other devices, many of them manned by technicians in white lab coats. The room is quiet, save for the hum of equipment and the occasional tapping of computer keys. Yet, every one of the technicians is busy, each of them tasked with gleaning as much information as they can from all types of evidence.

Tucked away in a corner of the room, Jack is also silent. He's been studying the security footage of the suspected shooter for the past half hour, going over and over it to make sure he doesn't miss anything important.

Finally, he looks up at the technician standing next to him. "Whoever it was, never looked at the camera," he says dejectedly. "Maybe your crew can get something from the van or one of the shell casings. Call me if you get anything."

Leaving the technician to his work, Jack heads to the elevator somewhat reluctantly. He likes visiting this floor because it's quiet. There are no suspects or criminals to manage here, only silent evidence to sift through.

Jack hits the 'up' button and steels himself for what he knows is waiting for him at Homicide — organized confusion.

The solitude is gone as soon as the doors open, only turmoil reigns in this department. Cops mill about, some taking statements from victims and perps, while others try to calm angry and fearful persons screaming about rights and justice.

With a deep sigh, Jack starts across the office as a working girl from the streets, a buxom twenty-something looking older than her years, passes him on her way to the elevator.

"Jack?" she asks, stopping as recognition dawns on her. "Hey, Jack!"

Hearing his name, Jack turns around.

"Remember me?" she asks. "You busted me on Beaver Street a couple of years back."

"Oh, yeah," he says, looking up and down at all her good parts. "I thought you said you wanted to go 9 to 5."

The woman steps inside the elevator and shrugs. "Rent is too high," she replies, just before the doors close on her smiling face.

Jack reaches his desk, sits down, and pushes aside a mound of paperwork. "What did you guys find out?" he asks Sergeant Ruiz and Detective Gomez.

"We got the name of the hotel the two victims were staying at," says Gomez, "and Jimmy here, thinks he found a common thread between them."

Ruiz looks askance at Hector. "I'd like to be called James. Only my family calls me Jimmy."

Hector and Jack exchange surprised glances. Then Jack gets a twinkle in his eye. "So, what did you find out…Jimbo?" he asks with a devious smile.

James lets out an exasperated sigh. "I guess it was a pipedream to think my colleagues would be more professional. So, okay, I get it, have your fun. I'm the new guy, right?" James rolls his eyes and lets out a breath. "Meanwhile, I searched their phone contacts, and they both list a guy named Russell Holden. I also looked at Elena's tablet. She never logged out of her social media page, so when I looked through it, I found photos of her with a guy named Russell."

"Sounds like we need to look into this guy—" starts Jack before he's interrupted by James.

"There's one more thing. I found a folder labeled Patriot Guard on the tablet. It's password protected, so I can't open it. I'll give it to Forensics to see if they can unlock it."

Jack's eyes widen at the mention of the familiar name. "They're back?!" he asks, astonished to hear that name again.

Ruiz notes Jack's reaction. "I thought that group sounded familiar. That's the one you helped bust up, isn't it?"

"Your lips to God's ears, Jimbo. We didn't get them all. Check with the FBI to see where they're at with their investigation; I know it's ongoing. Let them know what you found. Meanwhile, I'll check out Elena's hotel room."

"Hold on," says Gomez. "I forgot to tell you that Rodriguez's assistant, a guy named Steve Finley, said the two victims were arguing pretty fiercely before the show."

Jack laughs. "Maybe they were fighting over that Holden guy. Ruiz, see if you can get a lead on him; try giving him a call. Gomez, come with me."

CHAPTER FOUR

"Commander," says a uniformed soldier in an A-frame cabin in western North Carolina, "the problem with Elena Guerra has been resolved, and Cindy Rodriguez was given a warning."

Serge Kaspin's mouth twitches as he stares out the window at the wilderness surrounding his isolated hideout. "Any problems?" he asks.

The soldier clears his throat, afraid to answer. "Well, sir," he says hesitantly. "There was collateral damage."

"Civilian or law enforcement?"

"Civilian."

"Fuck it all!" replies Kaspin angrily. "Tell Colonel Powell that I want to see him. We need to finalize our strategies."

Jack and Detective Gomez walk up to a young clerk staring vacantly across the lobby of a small hotel near Castle Clinton. As they approach, the woman makes eye contact with the detective, and her face lights up with a wide smile.

"Hello," says Hector. "I'm Detective Gomez, and this is my partner, Lieutenant Stenhouse. We need to get access to the room occupied by Elena Guerra."

"Do you have a warrant?" asks the clerk, flicking her hair back seductively.

Jack blows out a breath and eyes the woman's ID tag. "Miss Castro," he says, "we're investigating a homicide. Your guest was murdered this morning. Can we get a key to her room?"

Stunned, the clerk takes in a sharp breath and seems to freeze in place with her mouth open.

"HEY! Now, please?" says Jack, breaking her trance.

"Um, I'm not supposed to allow you to go in without a warrant," stammers the clerk.

"Miss," says Jack, "the woman who was staying in that room is dead, so we need to look around to see if we can find any reason for that. Will you cooperate and let us in?"

"Oh. Yeah, yes," she says, fumbling to activate a new key card with trembling hands. "It's Room 510," she says, handing the card to Jack.

Hector thanks her, then points to a hallway. "Elevator that way?"

"Yeah," she replies, still flustered.

Inside the elevator car, Hector punches the button for the fifth floor, then turns to Jack. "You must be getting old. She made eyes at me, not you," he snickers.

Jack rubs his middle finger against the side of his nose. "What's the matter, Detective? Hasn't a pretty girl ever flirted with you? Do I need to give you some tips?" he asks mockingly.

Just then, the door opens on their floor, and Jack pushes Gomez out.

Following the signs, the pair turns left, then looks for Room 510.

"Ugh. Smells lovely," grumbles Jack, trying not to breathe in too deeply.

"Smells like carpet cleaner and air freshener," says Hector after passing a housekeeper pushing a cart full of bed linens, towels, and sundries.

When they reach Elena's room, Jack swipes the card and waits for the green light to confirm the door is unlocked.

Inside, the men see the typical assortment of suitcases,

shoes, and clothing.

Jack looks around. "Nothing unusual so far."

Hector sorts through toiletries in the bathroom while Jack unzips one of the suitcases and moves things around.

"Huh, what's this?" he mutters when he finds an envelope under a pile of blouses. The envelope is unsealed, so he reaches in and pulls out its contents.

"Hmm, let's take a look," he mumbles at a bunch of photographs in his hand.

He starts rifling through them, but nothing stands out, until he sees one in particular. Then he gasps when he looks at the next few.

"What's wrong?" asks Gomez, exiting the bathroom. "You look like you've seen a ghost."

Jack hands the photos to Gomez. "Take a look at this shit," he snarls.

"Holy crap! That's Serge Kaspin, and the date stamps are recent! He's supposed to be dead!"

Jack moves his neck slowly side-to-side, an action he performs when his muscles tighten from tension. "If the dates on those pictures are correct, we're in deep shit," he tells Hector dejectedly. "It's just a matter of time before Kaspin takes revenge for what we did to him and his groupies in Brooklyn last year, and all of us are in his ten-range."

"Do you think he had something to do with the shooting at the fashion show?"

"I wouldn't be surprised. Maybe he knew the girls."

Jack takes the pictures back, then walks toward the door, followed by Gomez.

"Didn't the feds shut down his little army?" asks Hector, closing the door behind them.

"They disabled it, but he must be gearing up again."

"Looks like we better take a deep dive into Elena's tablet," muses Hector. "Maybe it'll shed some light on this crap."

Jack scoffs, "I've always said I love my country; it's the government I'm afraid of. The feds should have shut that group down completely when they had the chance. Now we gotta let Giancarlo and Assante know they better watch their sixes. Who knows what that maniac is planning now?"

"Russell is on his way in to see us," announces James Ruiz when Jack and Hector arrive back at the First.

Jack rolls his eyes. "I don't think Russell's involved with the murders unless there's some other information about him in the protected file. I have an idea who did this but I'm still working out the details."

Allison Giancarlo knows how determined Jack gets when he thinks he's solved a problem, so she starts forming a question. But Jack cuts her off.

"Hold on, Ally. It's Kaspin. Your family fucked up, so he's still around and we're all in his crosshairs."

Allison is shocked. "What do you mean—he's around?"

"We found photos of him and Guerra, and they were taken recently. Kaspin's responsible for the shootings, I'm sure of it. And the other mafia fuck up is Larry Grimes. Your family never touched him after he stole their gold before the Trade Towers collapsed."

"Don't worry about Grimes, Stenhouse," says Captain Conrad, overhearing the conversation. "I haven't had a chance to tell you yet, but Grimes' body was found in a landfill in Pompano Beach. That's in Florida, in case you forgot."

Jack snaps his head around to face the captain. "When did they find him?"

"Yesterday. There was a bullet hole in the back of his head and a statuette of the Twin Towers shoved up his ass.

Now, what's this shit about Kaspin?"

"Holy shit! Poor Grimes," whispers Allison.

Jack lifts a brow at her, then turns to the captain. "We found recent photos of him with Elena Guerra. Here, take a look."

Jack hands the envelope from the hotel room to Conrad. As Conrad goes through them, he passes them to Giancarlo.

"It pains me to say this," Jack tells his boss, "but you better get the feds in. Kaspin's gonna want revenge for what we did to stop him and his Patriot Guards. We're number one on his list. Mark my words, Captain."

The next moment, an explosion rocks the building, and everyone ducks for cover.

When silence finally returns, Jack bolts toward the elevator, shouting, "My baby better be okay out there!"

On the ground floor, Jack exits the elevator to chaos and destruction near the building's entrance. Outside, glass debris covers the ground and sidewalk, with blood splattered on the wall of the building.

As the sound of sirens creeps closer, uninjured police officers run around, helping fallen comrades and innocent citizens as best they can.

"Help!" calls a woman when she sees Jack weaving his way through the mayhem.

Jack wants to check his ride, but he stops when the woman tugs his arm. Stooping down next to her, he inspects her wound.

"Doesn't look bad," he announces, and motions to an officer with a first aid kit. "He'll help you, ma'am," he tells her.

Then he stands up and looks to where he parked his beloved Road Runner. Finding it untouched, he breathes a sigh of relief, then turns around to help someone else.

"What the hell happened here?" he asks a passing

uniformed officer.

"A black SUV drove up, the back window dropped, and someone stuck out an RPG."

Jack spots Captain Conrad in the rest of the crew from Homicide. "It was Kaspin's men," he declares firmly. "They delivered his calling card — an RPG."

Giancarlo pulls Jack aside. "Before you got back here today, we did a background check on Cindy Rodriguez. Get this...she's an Army vet, deployed in Afghanistan in the same unit as our friends from the Patriot Guard case, and she was there the same time Kaspin and Black Horizon were active."

"FUCK!" shouts Jack. "That means the targets in the Swimfest shooting were Ken and Elena! Ken wasn't collateral damage; Vicky was! She was just someone who got in the way. Get Cindy Rodriguez in here — STAT! She may not be just a concerned wife after all."

While ambulances arrive at the First Precinct, a black Suburban vehicle turns onto the street occupied by Didi's lingerie boutique.

"There it is," says the front-seat passenger. "Slow down."

When the driver complies, the passenger snaps multiple photos with a digital camera. "All right, let's go," he says after he's taken enough.

CHAPTER FIVE

Providentially, three police cruisers parked at the front entrance took the brunt of the RPG, or the damage would have been much worse.

The cars are now on fire, so while firefighters work to put them out, EMTs scurry around tending to human casualties. Unfortunately, several patrolmen died in the blast and others were injured, along with citizens who happened to be in the wrong place at the wrong time. The building facade also sustained damage — several windows were blown out. Miraculously, no one inside was injured.

Later, the Homicide team returns to their floor and gathers in Conrad's office.

"Kaspin won't stop until he gets retribution," says Jack, thinking while pacing the floor. "So in a first for me, I think we should call in the feds. We may be cops, but we're at war with a paramilitary unit, and we're gonna need help with this one."

A knock on Conrad's door announces a uniformed officer who pokes his head in. "Mrs. Rodriguez is in Interrogation Room Two."

Jack sets his mouth in a hard line. "I'll take this," he says. "But Captain, all of us need to think about our families; we're gonna need protection 24/7. This ain't gonna go away fast. Allison, you better let Lucchese know that Kaspin is active again. I bet he won't be happy that you know he let him get away."

Jack exits the office, making a beeline for Interrogation Room Two.

Opening the door, his jaw clenches tightly. *Hmm*, he

wonders when he sees Cindy wearing yoga pants and a T-shirt fashioned by Artchop, her husband's company. *Does that mean she cares about Ken, or is she just putting on a show for us?*

Jack closes the door and takes a seat opposite Cindy. "As you probably noticed when you got here, the precinct was attacked this morning. What do you know about Black Horizon and Serge Kaspin?" he asks abruptly.

Cindy stares at Jack with her mouth open. It seems he caught her by surprise. Then her expression changes and she looks up at the ceiling with tears in her eyes.

"Did I hit a nerve?" asks Jack, noting her reaction. "Mrs. Rodriguez, yesterday's attack at the fashion show was done by a pro. We believe Elena Guerra was one of the targets and that Ken's hit was a message to you. So tell me, what's going on?"

Cindy takes a minute to answer, trying to weigh her options. Then she asks, "How do you know about Kaspin?"

"Really?" snaps Jack, narrowing his eyes in warning. "That's not important. Answer the question. What do you know about him and Black Horizon?"

Cindy sighs and lets her eyes roam the room. She struggles to focus on anything but Jack because the detective's stare is piercing and uncomfortable. When she can't find respite, she sighs again and says, "Look, all I know is that when I was deployed in Afghanistan, Kaspin was running opium out of the poppy fields there, and he wanted me in on it. When I refused, he threatened me. He told me to keep my mouth shut or he'd do something nasty to me or my loved ones."

"Huh," says Jack, absorbing the information. "Did he contact you when you got home?"

"No, but I kept looking over my shoulder. He's a bad dude, and I never felt safe until I heard he was missing after a gunfight at the Red Hook Terminal."

"You heard that on the news?"

"Yeah."

"So what do you think happened at the fashion show?"

"I think he finally decided to act. I never said anything to anyone, but I found out that Elena had an affair with Kaspin, and he really got under her skin. She talked about him a lot, and who knows how many people she confided in? She was devastated when she thought he might be dead."

"But you were happy."

"Damn right, I was happy. But the bastard wasn't dead! He recently sent me a text message to remind me to keep quiet, and I think he shot Elena because she blabbed too much."

"What about your husband?"

"I think he shot Ken just because he could. Lieutenant, you better get him before he does something else."

Jack stands. "Does your husband know what you just told me about your relationship from Afghanistan?"

Cindy cries, "No! He thinks the shots were directed at the models, but he doesn't know why. What am I to do, Lieutenant? I know Kaspin won't ever leave me alone!"

Jack rubs his neck and looks down at Cindy. "FBI and Homeland Security will be getting in on this, so you'll have to deal with them. We can keep you here until they arrive, and I'll post a guard outside your husband's hospital room. How's he doing, by the way? I thought he was going to be discharged soon."

Cindy wipes her eyes. "He has a slight fever, so they're giving him antibiotics, and they say he has to stay until the fever's gone. They think he'll be there at least another twenty-four hours."

"Okay. Look, I have to leave now, but I'll send someone in to make arrangements for you."

Outside the room, Allison Giancarlo stops Jack in the hallway. "Russell Holden called. He saw the news report about the attack and asked if we still wanted him to come in. I told him to stay in town, and we'd call him back."

Jack sighs, frustrated by the twists in the case. "That explosion may have put a ding in our investigation, but it won't stop it."

"I know, but that was way too close to home for my taste. Listen, I'm gonna speak with Uncle Vito. But before I do, I'm moving my family to my husband's aunt's house upstate. I don't want them anywhere around here while we deal with Kaspin. What are you gonna do about your family?"

Jack shakes his head. "I don't have a fucking clue. Look, after you speak with Lucchese, pay a visit to Russell. We shouldn't wait too long to talk to him. Meanwhile, I'm going to Forensics to see if they got anything off the security camera or the van and rooftop."

Mob boss Vito Lucchese is in the back room of Ristorante di Cosenza, his new restaurant on Mulberry Street, sipping a cappuccino with his son, Michael.

"*Michele*, a little birdie told me that someone attacked the First Precinct earlier today. Get with our people on the street to find out what happened. I want to know what's going on in my city."

Michael nods and rises just as the bartender walks into the room.

Bowing slightly, the barman declares, "*Signore*, Allison Giancarlo is here to speak with you."

Vito's brows snap together in surprise. "Where is she?" he asks.

"I told her to wait at the bar."

Vito dismisses the bartender and turns to his son. "Michele, bring her in and stay with me while I find out what she wants."

Michael nods and heads for the bar area.

"*Cugina!*" he says, greeting Allison with a smile and a kiss on both cheeks. "It's so nice to see you! Come with me; my father is happy you're here."

Allison walks ahead of Michael into Vito's private room, where her uncle conducts much of his business. She greets him with a kiss on his cheek, saying, "Hello, Uncle Vito."

The smile Vito had fades when he sees Allison's expression. "You are not here for a social call, are you?"

Allison pulls out a chair and sits down while Michael takes up a position behind his father. "Uncle Vito, this is a courtesy call, not really business," she says. "Your sources probably informed you of the attack on the First Precinct this morning."

"I have heard of it, yes," says Vito warily.

"Well, we believe Serge Kaspin orchestrated it."

Allison doesn't have to wait long for a reaction to her comment. As soon as Vito hears the name Kaspin, his face contorts with suppressed rage.

"Calm down, Pop," says Michael, knowing how his father feels. "Your heart."

Vito waves a hand to dismiss his son's concern. "Why are you telling me this?" he asks his niece.

"*Zio*, we're not as stupid as you think," she says. "We know you grabbed Kaspin off the dock at the Brooklyn Red Hook Terminal when his New Patriot Guards were offloading that shipment of weapons, and we were willing to overlook it because we wanted Kaspin gone as much as you did. But he didn't stay gone."

Vito is outraged that his soldiers failed him and that he didn't know about it. But he won't give Allison the satisfaction of knowing how upset he is. So he makes his face impassive and listens quietly.

"Somehow, Kaspin stuck it to your soldiers, and now he's back."

Allison studies Vito to see if he knew about the failure to get rid of the mercenary, but his face is a blank canvass, so she keeps talking. "Kaspin's a vengeful bastard, so he's going to find a way to get revenge on everyone who thwarted his plans. Remember his goal? It was to use those weapons to cause chaos and make the government listen to his demand to stop moving the country away from the original intent of the Constitution. Well, nothing has changed with the government, so you won't be excluded from his hit list."

Vito looks at her vacantly, so Allison presses on. "There was also a shooting at a recent fashion show at Castle Clinton; you may have heard about that, too. If you and your sources have any information about that shooting, or if you know where Kaspin is, we'd appreciate you letting us know. Our job is to protect all the citizens of New York, and that includes you."

This time, Vito gives Allison a wry smile. However, he still doesn't say anything, so Allison declares, "I suggest you enhance your security detail. Mark my words, Uncle, he's coming for all of us."

When Vito still doesn't respond, Allison stands and pushes her chair up to the table. "I'll be on my way now," she says, "...unless you have something to tell me."

Vito remains impassive, so Allison sighs. "You have my number," she says, then turns to leave.

"*Aspetta*," says Vito, rising from his chair.

Allison turns back to see Vito approaching her with his arms held out. He encloses her in an embrace and whispers something in her ear. Allison listens, then pulls away and stares at her uncle.

"Come on," says Michael, grabbing her arm. "I'll show you out."

On the sidewalk in front of the restaurant, Michael

moves Allison away from the door so he can speak privately. "Look," he says, lowering his voice conspiratorially, "we know a hitman came into town a few days ago. He stole a van, and we think he's still in the city."

Michael imparts that bit of information, then looks meaningfully into Allison's eyes, turns around, and reenters the restaurant.

Jack rewards himself with a fresh cup of coffee after completing some of the paperwork that has backed up on his desk. Happy that some of it is done, he stretches his back and says to Burley, "Hey, I'm going down to Forensics."

"Okay," says John with a light wave.

Jack sips his coffee on the way down to his favorite floor, then almost spills it when the doors open. "Jacob!" he calls out. "Where the hell you been, man?"

FBI Special Agent Jacob Assante turns when he hears Jack. "Hey, buddy!" he responds. "Good to see ya! We heard Kaspin's back from the dead."

"Yeah, and he's up to no good — as usual."

"The Bureau's been keeping tabs on the New Patriot Guard ever since the Red Hook incident, but we haven't heard anything about Kaspin. They've been keeping a low profile until two weeks ago, when NSA started picking up some chatter."

"I'm glad you're here," says Jack. "Come with me into Forensics. You saw the calling card Kaspin left outside? Well, he also left two bodies on a catwalk."

"A catwalk? What are you talking about?"

"A few days ago, a sniper hit three people at a swimwear fashion show down at Battery Park. Two of them died, and the other is still in the hospital."

"What does that have to do with Kaspin?"

"The wife of the guy in the hospital was in the same Army unit as our friends from the Lady Liberty case. You know, the one that Serge recruited from?"

"Yeah, I remember. But we thought Kaspin got whacked by the Mafia!"

"So did we. We figured he was a goner when Vito Lucchese's goons kidnapped him from the Red Hook Terminal last year. But I guess Vito's people screwed up."

"Wow, that's weird," says Jacob, scratching his chin in thought. "It's not every day that someone escapes from the Mafia. Hey... You don't think they made a deal, do you?"

"Oh, god, I hope not!" exclaims Jack, horrified by the thought.

"Sheesh! Have you talked to Vito yet?"

"Giancarlo's down there now. Her uncle's new hangout is a restaurant he opened on Mulberry Street."

"Should be an interesting conversation," states Jacob, knowing how much Allison dislikes the fact that she's related to a crime figure.

"Yeah. Either the goons screwed up, or maybe you're right.... Vito and Kaspin are planning something together."

Jack holds the door open as the pair enters the crime lab.

"Stenhouse," motions a man seated at a computer terminal. "We got something."

The experienced specialist adjusts his glasses as the men approach his work area.

"What did you find?" asks Jack. "By the way, this is FBI Special Agent Assante."

The specialist nods and opens a computer file containing video footage from the lobby at One Battery Park Plaza. "This is from the morning of the Castle Clinton incident."

"Yeah, I already looked at it," says Jack. "Did I miss something?"

The specialist points at the screen. "Watch. The Apex technician is trying to hide his face as he approaches the elevator."

"Right..." says Jack, unsure of why the technician is interested in this particular sequence.

The man continues as if Jack didn't say anything. "I'll stop it here. There, can you see it?"

Jack and Jacob bend down to take a closer look at the screen, but neither of them sees anything. Then Jacob says, "Oh, wait... I see an image reflected in the polished brass on the wall."

The specialist puffs out his chest. "Yeah, that's it! We enhanced the image and put it through our facial recognition software, and we got a hit. It's Stefan Coleman. He's a former black-ops expert who was working with Black Horizon. Now, he's a contract hitman on the most wanted list with Interpol and you guys," he points at Jacob.

Jack takes out his phone and calls Giancarlo. "Where are you?"

"On my way back; should be there in five. What's up?"

"Our killer is an international hitman named Stefan Coleman."

Allison's eyes widen. "Michael Lucchese just told me that they heard there was a hitman here in the city, and they think he's still here."

"They're right," says Jack, ending the call. Then he looks at Jacob. "We got work to do, amigo. Let's roll."

***

"I still can't understand why he uses this outdated shit," says James Ruiz, shaking his head at Jack's refusal to give up on methods the younger officer considers hopelessly old-fashioned.

Hector Gomez chuckles, "It works for Jack. He says it helps him connect the dots better when he can visualize what he's thinking."

Ruiz studies Jack's whiteboard, where the veteran cop is keeping a timeline of the dates and times pertaining to the case, the names of the players they've identified so far, and the photos they've gathered. Under all of them are black lines crossing each other in a crazy zigzag pattern.

"To me, this is confusing as hell," says James, scratching his head.

Behind them, John Burley asks, "What are you guys looking at?"

Hector chuckles. "It seems Jack's whiteboard doesn't measure up to our boy's standards," he responds, playfully punching James' arm. "He thinks Jack should up his game and go digital."

"Nah, that works for Jack," says Burley, eliciting another chuckle from Hector.

"That's what I sa—" begins Hector, until Burley cuts him off.

"Hey! What the hell is Kaspin's name doing up there?" shouts John, pointing his finger at the board.

"Oh, haven't you heard?" answers Gomez. "The bastard's back. Seems the Mafia didn't get rid of him like we thought they did."

"Holy crap!" shouts John, raising both hands in anger and frustration. "I still ache on cold mornings because of that asshole!"

"What do you mean?" asks Ruiz, looking over John with a critical eye. "You seem well enough to me."

"Yeah, maybe on the outside," says John. "But inside...

Those bullet fragments are still in there, and every now and then, they find a way to remind me."

"You ever think about the shooting?" asks James. "I don't know how I'd deal with it."

Burley looks off into the distance. "Yeah, I think about it sometimes… But Allison Giancarlo was also shot that day… And it was all because of Serge Kaspin!" The mercenary's name spits off his tongue in disgust.

The group turns when Captain Conrad joins them.

"I just got off the phone with the mayor," he says. "He wants this case over and done with. So Ruiz, I'm assigning you to Stenhouse until we wrap this up. And guys, we're working with the FBI again."

"What about our families?" asks John. "They could be in danger."

"So are we, so you should move them out of town. If you don't have somewhere for them to stay, we'll pay for a hotel. Meanwhile, we're going to station uniformed units at your homes, and at Jack's wife's boutique. We're gonna use every resource at our disposal to keep them and everyone else safe; no expense spared. This is our house, and we're not gonna let that asshole hurt us again!"

"You got that right!" shout the men, determined to prevent another incident involving their precinct.

"So, let's get to it, people!" agrees Conrad. "Now, I gotta leave you to it. I'm due at a press conference, one of my least favorite tasks," he frowns. "The bullshit of those media folks is sometimes enough to choke a horse!"

After Conrad leaves, the group returns to their desks. Then after a while, Jack and Jacob enter the floor, waving their arms.

"We got the shooter's name!" they shout.

"Yeah? Who is it?" asks John.

"It's a guy named Stefan Coleman."

"Coleman?" says Gomez, raising a brow in surprise. "I know that name! Didn't he work for Black Horizon?"

"Yeah," says Jack. "He was black ops, and now he's a hitman."

"Huh. I'm not surprised," says Gomez. "My Seal unit ran into him when I was in Qatar, and he was always bragging about what a great shot he was. He thought he was hot stuff. Always acted like his shit don't stink."

"Well, we're gonna take him down quite a few pegs," says Jacob. "I'm gonna circulate his photo and service info around and advise TSA to keep a lookout for him at all the transportation hubs, 'cause he may still be in the city."

Jacob stops and looks at each member of Jack's team. "But TSA is a huge agency, and you folks are on the ground. So I'm gonna ask you all to work closely with the city's transit authority and department of transportation; they need to monitor all the exits from the city. While you're doing that, I'm going to coordinate with NSA. They can check the phone and credit card activities of Coleman and the Patriot Guard members we've been watching."

"All right, buddy," says Jack. "We'll get right on it."

"Great. I'll catch up with you later."

Jacob gives a short wave to the team and leaves the floor. Then Jack turns to his colleagues.

"Burley, let Sylvia know what's going on and get her out of town. Ruiz, your family is okay. You weren't involved in the Lady of the Harbor case, so Serge Kaspin has nothing against you."

"What about you, Giancarlo, and the others on the task force?" asks Hector.

"Captain Conrad's going to talk to the others, and Ally already has a plan. I hope she's working on it."

Jack looks at his fellow detective. "Hector, you're lucky you're not dating right now."

Hector frowns. "That's one way to look at it," he says, until he catches a side-eye from Jack. "I know, I know," he adds. "I'm tryin'. But what about you?"

Jack takes in a breath and runs his fingers through his hair. "I don't know yet," he says, aware that he needs to come up with a plan. "Whatever I do, I gotta do it quickly. If Kaspin has the balls to attack the First, there's no limit to what he'll do next. So the first thing we hafta do is get our families settled. Then, we can concentrate on this case."

While the group talks together quietly, Allison Giancarlo sits suspect Russell Holden down at an empty desk, surprising Jack.

"Ally," he calls, crooking his finger at her so she'll join him some distance away. "What's he doing here?"

"I thought it'd be better if we talked to him sooner rather than later, so I told him to come down to the station. I didn't have time to put him in an interrogation room."

Jack sighs. "All right, but I have some news for you. We know the shooter; it's a hitman named Stefan Coleman."

"You got that already? That's good police work, Stenhouse!" praises Allison.

"Yeah, yeah," affirms Jack. "But it was Forensics, not me. Anyway, is your family going out of town?"

"They're packing now, grumbling the whole time."

"Better safe than sorry. Kaspin could be around any corner."

"Don't I know it," responds Allison, rubbing the arm where Kaspin's men shot her. "So let me get back to Holden."

"Um, why don't we let Gomez deal with him? You're gonna be busy with your team; we're gonna need your help catching this sonuvabitch."

"Hmm... Good point," says Allison, then she leans in toward Jack. "Vito said a couple of weird things to me just before I left. He pulled me aside and apologized for letting Kaspin get away. Then he said he's gonna 'deal with him,' and warned me to watch my back."

"What do you think he means?"

Allison shrugs. "I haven't a clue, and I didn't have time to find out because Michael pulled me out of there in a hurry."

Hector knows Jack and Allison are talking about the case, so he decides to take charge of their person of interest. "I'll take him to a room," he tells them, indicating Russell. "Jim, come with me. You can observe."

While James Ruiz stands before a one-way mirror in the adjacent room, Hector takes a seat across from the POI at a metal table.

"Let's start with your name," begins Hector.

"Russell Holden."

"Mr. Holden, how do you know the victims, Vicky Simpson and Elena Guerra?"

"Uh, I met Elena in Kabul. We were there together, and we kept in touch after we were discharged. I met Vicky at a cocktail party; she was with Elena."

"Do you know Serge Kaspin or Black Horizon?"

Russell frowns and looks down at his hands, not sure he wants to answer.

Hector sees the reaction, so he asks again, "Do you know them?"

A minute of silence passes, then Russell looks up. "Yeah, I know them," he says. "But I can't say anything. I don't want to end up as worm food."

Gomez rises from his chair, then leans down over the table, causing Russell to flinch at his nearness.

"The feds can supply you with protection," states Hector

decisively. "What do you know?"

Russell leans as far back in his chair as he can, trying to put space between himself and the detective. "I need to speak with my lawyer," he says. "His office is out of state, but he has colleagues here in the city. I won't say anything else until I know I'll be protected. My momma didn't raise no fool."

Gomez turns his head to look at the mirror. Then he straightens up and waits for Ruiz to join him.

"Keep Mr. Holden company while he calls his lawyer," Hector tells the sergeant when he steps into the room. "I'll call Assante to arrange for protection."

As the afternoon progresses, thunderstorms roll in on this typical summer day, and the temperature in the Big Apple peaks in the low eighties. With the sky darkening, pedestrians begin to notice the gathering clouds.

In her office at the back of her lingerie boutique, Didi orders more inventory while Sonya, her friend and assistant, rings up a customer at the sales counter.

"Hi, Jack," says Sonya, when the bell at the top of the door jingles to announce a visitor. "Everything okay?" she asks, noticing his expression.

Jack heads for the office. "She in the back?" he asks, not waiting for a reply.

When Jack appears in the doorway, Didi takes one look at him and knows he's not there for a booty call.

"What's wrong?" she demands.

Jack closes the door, then leans down to kiss his wife on the cheek. "There's a problem," he says, sitting in a chair opposite Didi's desk. "Serge Kaspin is the one who orchestrated that hit at the fashion show, and he also attacked the First Precinct this morning."

Didi gasps, and her hand flies to her mouth. "What happened?" she asks, wide-eyed with fear.

"RPG, his signature move."

"Oh, my god!"

"Yeah, and we think, well, we know, that he won't stop at that. He's probably going to go after all of us for what we did to him during our last encounter. Does your mom still own that vacation place in Pennsylvania?"

Didi doesn't hear the question. She's upset and can only think to ask, "What the hell are you gonna do, Jack?"

"Does your mom still have that cottage?"

"Why? What does that have to do with a guy who wants to kill you?"

"I want to get you, Mark, and your mom out of town while we try to stop him. There's no guarantee he won't go after you, too. So, does she still own that cottage?"

"No, she sold it a couple of years ago. I told you…" Didi says, before becoming too upset to continue.

Following orders from Captain Conrad, a police cruiser parks near Jack's Road Runner in front of Didi's shop. "Unit 18 reporting in," he radios, then tries to make himself comfortable for the long shift ahead.

As he does, an unmarked van slows down in front of the boutique, and the side door slides open with a man standing in front of the open door. On his shoulder is an RPG he aims at the boutique.

Seconds later, the whoosh of the projectile flying past the officer is followed by a loud explosion, and the van speeds away, unscathed.

"Holy crap!" shouts the uniformed cop in the cruiser, ducking as the explosion rocks his vehicle. "What the fuck?!"

While the officer calls for help, Jack and Didi lie on the floor of her office, covered in debris. Both are alive and unconscious, but Sonya and the customer, who were in the front of the store, are dead.

"Hello?!" calls out the officer, entering the store through a gaping hole in the building. He's hoping for survivors as he wedges himself into the tangled mess of the lingerie boutique.

"Shit!" he says, spotting Sonya lying face down under part of the shattered glass counter. He can see that she's dead, but he checks for a pulse anyway. Then he finds another body and pronounces that one dead as well.

When first responders arrive with multiple trucks and police units, the police officer shouts, "There's a cop in here somewhere! This store belongs to Lieutenant Stenhouse's wife, and his car is outside! His wife must be in here, too!"

At the rear of the building, Jack slowly awakens inside the damaged office and pushes himself off Didi. When the blast hit, he threw himself on top of her like a protective blanket, but she doesn't look good.

"Dee!" he yells at her more loudly than necessary because of the thunderous ringing in his ears. "Babe, wake up!"

When Didi doesn't budge, Jack turns her over and finds blood gushing from a large gash on her temple.

"Oh, my god!" he moans, ripping off his shirt to press against the wound. "Help!" he yells into the darkness. "Somebody, help!"

"Who's there?" answers a muffled voice, followed by first responders pushing the damaged door aside to enter the office.

Jack screams at them, "She's unconscious and bleeding!"

"Okay, we got her!" replies an emergency technician who kneels next to Didi.

While the EMT assesses Didi's condition, another EMT begins to examine Jack. "I'm fine," he says, pushing the man away and getting to his feet. He tries to take a step, but his legs buckle under him, and he collapses against Didi's desk.

Jack is alarmed to see that the EMTs haven't been able to revive Didi.

"How bad is it?" he asks, afraid of the answer. No one responds, so he watches quietly as they insert an IV and take his wife out on a stretcher.

"I gotta go with her!" groans Jack, still dazed and unable to walk on his own.

"You got it, buddy," says a firefighter, grabbing him under an arm and helping him through the rubble.

When Jack emerges into sunlight, a medical technician spots him. "We're taking her to the hospital, and you need to come, too," he tells him. Jack makes no reaction, so to assess his mental state, he asks, "Do you understand what I'm saying?"

Jack nods dumbly and climbs into the ambulance next to his wife. Sitting on the bench, he grabs Didi's hand and strokes it gently, calling her name over and over, hoping to awaken his unresponsive princess.

CHAPTER SIX

While a steady crowd of blue and black files in and out of the largest visitation room at Eastwood Crematory and Funeral Home, an unusually chilly summer rain falls across the Big Apple.

She had many admirers, muses the funeral director, his expression a mask of professional attentiveness.

From Jack's seat in the first row, his eyes never leave the closed coffin, even as a continuous line of people stops to express their condolences.

He listens to their words of comfort and nods in appropriate places, but he doesn't really hear them. To keep himself from breaking down into heaving sobs, he holds tightly onto Mark, partly for his own comfort and partly to keep the boy from fussing in the unfamiliar circumstances.

However, as much as Jack tries, Mark refuses to be pacified. As children often do, he senses his father's grief and begs his grandmother for solace. Though she's just as heartbroken, she takes the little boy from his father, knowing that he needs just as much comfort as she does.

"Jack," says Jacob, stepping in front of the widower's unseeing eyes.

"Oh. Jacob," replies Jack, mechanically rising to embrace the younger man.

Jacob begins as do so many others when they don't know what else to say. "I'm so sorry…"

Jack sighs and silences his friend with a long hug.

When the men separate, the FBI agent whispers

something into Jack's ear that causes Jack to turn to his mother-in-law. "Mom, I, ah, need to talk with Jacob," he tells Sharon, who is doing her best to keep Mark occupied while she cries softly. "I'll be right back."

As the pair walks toward the back of the room, Jack nods to his team, seated in the rows behind him. The room is almost full; it looks like all of the First Precinct has shown up. It seems that everyone knew and loved Didi, a detail that isn't lost on Jack.

Jacob leads Jack to a small waiting area outside the visitation room where Captain Conrad and Inspector Rawlings are conversing in low voices.

When they join the two men, Jacob tells Jack, "The Bureau made arrangements to move Mark and Sharon to a safe house in Ellicott City, a small town north of Columbia, Maryland. I know it isn't close, but they'll be safe there until this shit's ver."

"Thanks," says Jack stoically. "The sooner they get there, the better. I won't be able to get back to hunting Kaspin until I know they're settled."

"I understand," says Jacob, nodding sympathetically.

To change the subject, Jack asks, "Any news on the shooter, Stefan Coleman?"

"The NSA picked up some phone traffic. He's using a burner, no surprise there. But they also got a couple of pings from an unregistered phone off cell towers in the Bowery area, so we're checking local cameras. We'll get him, Jack," adds Jacob reassuringly. "Just concentrate on your family now. We got this."

Inspector Rawlings places a comforting hand on Jack's shoulder. "Take as long as you need," he says. "When you come back, we want you at one hundred percent."

Jack looks past the men around him at the closed coffin in the next room. "I want to thank all of you for your condolences and support," he tells them sincerely. Then he lowers his eyes and says, "I know Didi would say…"

Jack's voice begins to tremble, and he can't continue. He has to stop himself because fresh tears threaten to overwhelm him. "I won't forget any of it," he says quietly. "But I can't afford to take time off; I'll be back tomorrow."

"Stenhouse—" warns Captain Conrad, knowing how stubborn his detective can be. But Jack is shaking his head decisively.

"Nothing's gonna stop me from ending this shit once and for all," he vows, and this time, his voice is clear and unwavering.

Meantime, the mountains of North Carolina are exceptionally pretty during these lazy days of summer. The lush vegetation and iconic haze that gives the Smoky Mountains their name attracts thousands every year. However, not all areas of the state are busy with an influx of tourists. Some places are still rural and sparsely populated.

That's one of the primary reasons Serge Kaspin chose to build his A-frame retreat in this particular spot. The tranquility of the region is the perfect cover for the illicit arms dealer to conduct his business, especially now that he's committed to exacting revenge on the people who foiled his plans to move the country back to its founding ideals. He's determined to get what he wants, and the irony of his methods — using violence and deadly weapons to make his point — is completely lost on him. His focus is laser straight on his goal.

The room of the house that Serge spends most of his time in is dominated by a large window overlooking a lazy river. Serge prefers this room to others because the view seems to settle his mind. Today, he's sitting on a large sofa, waiting for one of his Patriot Guard collaborators.

"Sir!" announces an older man with peppered hair when the door opens.

"Yes, Colonel. I've been waiting for you. Give me an update on what's going on."

The man's face lights up with good news for his commander. "We handled Stenhouse, sir!" he declares happily.

"So he's dead?"

"No, sir. But we hit him where it hurts the most! We got rid of his wife!"

The colonel's face drops when Kaspin doesn't react the way he expected. He takes a step back, knowing the hot-tempered arms dealer is capable of anything.

"You did what?!" bellows Kaspin, jumping up from the couch with his face a deep shade of red.

"Uh, Stenhouse's wife is dead, sir."

Kaspin clenches and unclenches his fists menacingly, fixing his beady eyes on his subordinate. "I heard you!" he hollers at the confused man.

The colonel wonders what will happen next while Kaspin seethes, his face getting redder and redder.

After an uncomfortable length of time, Kaspin sighs and walks over to the large window. "Let me think about this," he declares, chewing over this latest development.

With his back to the colonel, he says, "Killing the wife will make Jack more determined than ever. However, he'll also languish in sorrow and guilt for the rest of his life. So, I'm satisfied. Good work, Colonel."

The colonel relaxes and waits to be dismissed. But Kaspin is still thinking.

Facing the river, he avers, "Things are progressing well. We've taken care of Elena Guerra and sent warnings to Cindy Rodriguez, the First Precinct, and Jack Stenhouse. But there are still a couple of targets on my list, so let Coleman know that he needs to stick around."

"Will do, sir!" snaps the colonel. "May I ask who will be next?"

"Yes, you may," says Kaspin, turning around. "It's Vito Lucchese."

While friends and colleagues file out of the funeral home, Allison Giancarlo and her husband walk over to Jack for a private moment.

"It was a great turnout," Allison declares, not knowing what else to say to her longtime friend.

"Yeah. I think everyone from the department showed up, and I really appreciate it," replies Jack absentmindedly. His attention is on Sharon as she takes Mark out of the room for a diaper change. Since Didi's passing, Jack has found that he needs to know where his boy is at all times.

Allison follows Jack's eyes and tries to change the subject. She knows how sad her friend must be. "Um, we're going to grab a bite to eat," she says. "You wanna join us?"

Jack turns his head to look at Allison. "Thanks for asking," he says," but we should get home. We have a lot to do, and Mark must be tired by now."

"All right," says Allison, grabbing her husband's arm. "I guess we'll—"

"By the way," Jack continues dully. "The FBI set up a safe house in Maryland, and I'm gonna send my family there later tonight." To Allison's husband, he says, "I thought you were already out of town, Vinnie."

Vincent replies, "I was. The kids are there, but I had to come back when I heard about…"

Awkwardly, Vincent lets his thought trail off. Then he says, "They're at my uncle's place near West Point."

Jack is pleased. "Good," he says, hugging Vincent and Allison. "Get yourself back there, pronto. Thanks for coming."

When Sharon returns with a freshly changed Mark, Vincent waits for Allison at the funeral home door while she opens her umbrella. The rain that started the day off still hasn't let up.

"Is that the last of them?" asks Sharon, as several people run out to their cars.

Jack doesn't answer. His mother-in-law's question brings home the realization that he's now the only parent his son has left. "Mom," he says, "the FBI will be at the apartment tonight. They're gonna take you and Mark to a safe place in Maryland, so you'll have to pack as much as you can for the both of you. I can't have you guys here while I sort things out."

Sharon pats her son-in-law's arm. "Okay," she says. "Whatever you think is best. And please don't worry about us; I'll take good care of this boy here."

Jack chokes back tears. "I'm so grateful you're here, Mom."

Jack and Sharon walk over to the closed coffin for one last goodbye while John and Sylvia Burley step beside them.

"Hi," says Jack, noticing their presence. "I thought everyone left."

"We're heading out now," states John, "but before we go, I wanted to tell you not to rush back to work. You can take all the time you need; we got your back."

Jack narrows his eyes at his colleague. "Just make sure you get Sylvia away from this shit. Kaspin will stop at nothing."

The couple is silenced by Jack's declaration. Then Sylvia declares, "Actually, Jack, I'm going to be out of town for a few weeks. My company is sending me to Brussels on an insurance fraud investigation."

Jack raises a brow. "That's great timing," he says, "although I bet your husband didn't plan on you being so far away," he adds, looking at John.

John grabs Sylvia's hand. "Well, as you said, the timing is good." Then he adds, "Look, I'm available for you, Jack. Whatever you need, just call."

Jack is grateful for the kind words. "Thanks, buddy," he responds quietly.

"Okay, we'll be off then," says John. "And don't forget… anything at all."

"I know. I got your number."

After John and Sylvia leave, the little Stenhouse family is the only one left in the visitation room, so the funeral director approaches them.

"Mr. Stenhouse," he says politely, "we're going to move the coffin now. The crematorium is this way."

It's now early evening, and the rain outside is hanging on like a bad cold.

While Jack entertains Mark by bouncing his son on his knees as he sings Pony Boy, a children's song he learned from his mother, Sharon and a couple of FBI agents place several pieces of luggage in front of the freight elevator.

"We're ready," announces Sharon.

Jack reluctantly stops the game and hugs his son tightly.

"I'm gonna miss you, kiddo," he mutters into the boy's neck as fresh tears flow down his cheeks. Jack was never one for tears before, but now, everything is different.

Standing by, Sharon waits quietly, knowing how important these moments are for the grieving father.

When Jack is ready, he kisses his son, then hands him off

and wipes his eyes. "You look so much like Didi," he mutters to his mother-in-law as she joins the agents in the freight elevator. "I guess I'll never get used to her not being here."

Sharon takes in a sharp breath against the pain of losing her only child. "We love you," she says to Jack. "You gonna visit soon?"

"I'll try," he answers into the space between the elevator's closing doors. His family is leaving, and now he'll be alone.

When the bell dings to announce the elevator's descent, Jack exhales and turns his neck to relieve the pressure that had been building all day.

The sudden silence of the apartment is oppressive. "Where the hell is that bottle of single barrel?" he mutters to himself.

Nine a.m. the following morning, Jack walks into the precinct wearing his mirrored sunglasses under the harsh fluorescent lighting. One hand holds a cup of steaming black coffee, while the other grips a can of Coke.

John Burley looks up from pouring coffee into his mug from the carafe at the office coffee machine, only mildly surprised to see the man who just lost his wife already back at work.

"Salute! Good morning," he says, holding his mug up in greeting. "I was hoping you'd take at least a few days off."

The previous evening, Jack finished off half a bottle of single barrel whiskey in a couple of hours, then spent a restless night on the couch. But he made it into work anyway. However, his tongue is asleep, his teeth itch, and it's an effort to make a fist tight enough to hold anything.

Jack places his drinks on his desk, then pulls out the

chair and sits down, wincing as he does. "I was thinking," he says slowly. "Since Sylvia's gonna be away for a while, why don't you crash at my place? Kaspin is probably done with me for now, so you may be safer there."

Captain Conrad hears Jack's voice and walks over to join them. "I knew you'd be here today," he says, shaking his head at his detective's stubbornness. "I have news, but first I want to tell you that if you feel things getting to be too much, don't think you'll let anyone down if you go home early for a while. There are plenty of people around here who can take up the slack."

"Thanks, boss," says Jack, squinting up at the captain. "I'll keep that in mind. But for me, the best way to heal is to get that bastard behind bars. I won't be able to rest until that's done."

Conrad sighs, knowing the fight he's going to have with the police psychologist about pressing Stenhouse into counseling. To get his mind off that problem, he changes the subject.

"We got the coroner's report on Elena Guerra," he says, sitting on the corner of a nearby desk. "It says she was pregnant."

Jack waves a hand at the news. "One more thing to consider," he says wearily.

"Yeah. I don't know if it's relevant, but keep it in mind. Listen, Agent Assante will be here this morning. He wants to share some FBI info on our shooter."

Conrad takes a closer look at Stenhouse. "You sure you're okay, Jack? You look like something the cat dragged in."

Jack shrugs and rubs the side of his nose with a middle finger. "I got friendly with a bottle of whiskey last night," he says matter-of-factly, taking a swig of his Coke, belching loudly, and rising slowly to his feet. "Gotta see a man about a horse," he announces, and heads for the restroom.

Conrad turns his attention to John. "Be on the lookout," he tells him. "You could be in Kaspin's ten-range."

"No problem, Captain," replies John. "Stenhouse asked me to bunk with him while Sylvia's out of town, so I'm gonna take him up on it. I think he wants company, but he won't come out and say it."

"Did you send Sylvia somewhere safe?"

"You could say that. She's going to Europe for work, so she'll be out of the way for a couple of weeks at least. She's on a new insurance fraud case for Liberty."

"Sounds like a plan," says Conrad, giving the sergeant a thumbs up. "Let me know when Assante gets here."

When Jack returns from the restroom, he sits down heavily. "Bring me up to speed," he tells John. "What's the skinny on Russell Holden? And have we made any progress on finding Kaspin or the shooter... What's his name again? Stefan something?"

John nearly chokes on his coffee. "Damn, Jack, you don't waste any time, do you?" John takes a minute to wipe his chin, then says, "Okay, the shooter is Stefan Coleman, and like Conrad said, Assante should have an update on him. Regarding Holden, turns out he knows Kaspin. He was in the Patriot Guard before the shit hit the fan last year in Brooklyn. He said he thinks the guy's somewhere in North Carolina, so that's a start."

John takes a closer look at Jack. "How you doin', man?" he asks sympathetically.

Jack stares through his shades at nothing in particular and cricks his neck. "I try not to think about it; that's why I'm here. I want Kaspin, and I don't care how I get him; he could be dead or alive. Makes no difference to me."

The Big Apple is a beehive of activity when mid-morning rolls around, just as it is on almost any day of the week. Vehicles of all kinds clog the arteries with New Yorkers working, and visitors playing. In contrast to much of the city, Mulberry Street in Little Italy is semi-quiet. Some of the restaurants on the street aren't open yet, so Michael Lucchese and his father take advantage of the lull to have a leisurely breakfast. While they eat, they talk about business and family.

"I like this location, Pop," says Michael. "This new place is right in the middle of the action."

Michael and his father are in a private room at the rear of Ristorante di Cosenza, Vito's latest acquisition. As usual, Vito insisted on ordering the meal, so today they're both having eggs in a basket with sides of sausage and potatoes, washed down with cups of strong espresso coffee.

Vito swallows a generous forkful of sausage, then asks, "Is Allison's family settled in at their safe place?"

"Yeah, Pop. Our guys are keeping an eye on them. I also put men on the roof here and at your other businesses. I want to be ready in case that *coglione* shows up."

Vito nods and spears another forkful of sausage.

While the two continue to talk and eat, a white and blue telephone company van makes its way down the street. The logos on the vehicle are well known, so it draws no attention from passersby or the men on the roof. And that will prove to be a grave mistake.

A split second after the vehicle comes abreast of the restaurant, the side door slides open and the barrel of an RPG-7 grenade launcher pokes out. On the roof, Vito's men don't react until the weapon fires at the front of the restaurant and all hell breaks loose.

The grenade's explosion is so powerful that Michael and Vito are knocked unconscious, even though they're at the rear of the building.

When the guards finally respond to the blast, everyone on the street and in surrounding buildings are either hunkering down wherever they are or scattering around a pair of garbage trucks that have suddenly appeared at each end of the block.

The rapid fire of the guards' automatic weapons continues until the familiar wail of sirens attracts unwanted attention. As the sounds draw nearer, the shooting stops and the garbage trucks disappear around the corners, as if they were never there.

When the responders arrive, they immediately swarm the area like marauding grasshoppers. Some check the van while others assess the damage to the restaurant.

"No survivors!" shout the ones checking a couple of dead men in the bullet-riddled van. Others bent on putting out a blazing inferno fueled by leaking gas lines, wave frantically. "Get those hoses over here!" they yell.

At the back of the building, Michael and Vito Lucchese are still unconscious. They're lying on the ground, covered by ceiling tiles and bent crossbeams amid swirling dust and thick smoke. They're alive, but the dust and smoke are slowly choking them.

"Get them out!" shout Vito's soldiers, frantically pointing firefighters to a rear entrance tickled by smoke and flames.

Following the men's directions, the firefighters disregard their own safety and break the door down. Then, they quickly locate the limp bodies of Vito Lucchese and his son. There are more victims inside, however, the firefighters know the routine: the others must wait until these two are saved.

While detectives in New York investigate the explosion, a phone rings in North Carolina.

"So?"

Serge listens to the update of his latest order while eating his solitary breakfast. The local specialty has become his favorite — fried livermush with a side of grits.

CHAPTER SEVEN

After finishing his coffee, Jack finally feels like he can remove his mirrored sunglasses. But his head still throbs, so he shakes two pills from the bottle of Naproxen he keeps in a desk drawer for this precise reason.

While he waits for the painkiller to do its work, he reaches reluctantly for the top form on a pile of paperwork and starts to fill it out.

He only completes a few lines when a shout from the elevator stops his pen over the next section.

"Someone hit Lucchese's restaurant just like Didi's boutique!" shouts Jacob Assante, flailing his arms while making a beeline for Jack.

"They dead?" asks Jack, not looking up from his work.

Wow, that's a weird reaction, thinks Jacob, frowning down at the detective, who's still writing as if his announcement meant nothing.

"Vito and Michael were injured, but there's no word on their condition yet," continues Jacob. "They're at New York-Presbyterian."

Jack still seems unimpressed, so Jacob turns to John Burley, hoping for a better reaction. "It was an RPG attack from a stolen phone company van, so it had to be Kaspin. There are other victims, and much of the building is gone."

John opens his mouth to comment but closes it quickly when Jack pipes up. "I feel bad for the other victims," he says in a voice so low that it's hard for others to hear.

However, Jacob hears and sighs at Jack's strange

reaction. Then he walks over to the coffee machine and pours himself a cup. Looking back at Jack, he raises his voice over the office hubbub so he can be heard. "My parents send their condolences."

Jack winces at the comment. The last thing he wants is to be reminded of his pain, so he swivels his chair around, lowers his eyes, and takes in a couple of deep cleansing breaths.

However, he knows Jacob means well, so when the agent returns, he responds to the sentiment, keeping his eyes on the ground. "Thank your parents for me," he says quietly.

Jacob nods his head. "Guess I'll be on my way now," he declares. "They're gonna need help at the scene."

When Jacob walks back toward the elevator, he passes Detective Gomez and Sergeant Ruiz, who nod hello when they see him.

While life in the First Precinct goes on all around Jack, he stares blindly at his old-school whiteboard; his attention so focused that he's oblivious to the never-ending dance of handcuffed suspects and damaged victims swirling around the precinct floor like a second-rate, off-Broadway performance.

Hector knows Jack is hurting, so he places a comforting hand on his friend's shoulder. "I expected you to take a couple of days off this time," he says, referring to Jack's determination to return to work no matter what else happens.

Jack blinks at Hector's touch but doesn't take his eyes off the board. "Gotta distract myself somehow," he responds dully. "Too many memories at my place."

Hector is worried by his friend's tone, and tries to cheer him up. "I want to be there when you nab that dickhead," he declares, more forcefully than necessary. "Then, when he's good and fucked, we'll go out and get plastered!"

As a smile forms on Jack's lips, a noise at the elevator causes both men to turn around to see what's going on. It's

Jacob, exiting the elevator at a run. "I was just about to get into my car when I got a call!" he announces excitedly. "We got Coleman! He's inside a small hotel in the Bowery! We got agents surrounding the place!"

That's exactly what Jack needs to hear. Jumping out of his chair, he grabs his jacket off the back and sets off. "Let's go!" he shouts to the others. "I've been waitin' for something like this!"

Ten minutes later, Jack parks his Road Runner behind a POS government-issued sedan, and four men pile out.

A female FBI agent at the scene tells Jacob, "We have all the exits covered, and he hasn't seen us. He's at a kiosk just inside the entrance."

Jack enters the hotel's revolving door, followed by Hector and Jacob.

"That's him in the gray suit," whispers Hector when he spots his former military acquaintance paying for a cup of coffee.

"Okay, he's all yours," says Jack.

Drawing their guns, the three approach Coleman as he turns around while pocketing his change.

Coleman looks at the three barrels facing him. "Well, well, well. I'm impressed," he snickers while casually sipping from his cup. "They sent three of you to get me?"

Then he lowers his cup. "Hey, I know you," he says, pointing a finger at Hector Gomez. "Long time no see, buddy. But why all the backup? Guess what they say about the Navy is true — they can't do anything alone!"

Though Gomez tries to let the disparaging remark about his time in the Navy roll off his back, it bothers him. "Stefan Coleman, you're under arrest for the murder of Vicky Simpson and Elena Guerra," he says grimly. "You have the right—"

"Yeah, yeah," mocks Coleman, cutting Gomez off mid-sentence. "I know…I have the right to silence and shit. But hey, how about we do this mano-a-mano, Navy-man, without your buddies' help? I always wanted to kick a Navy Seal's ass."

Now, Gomez is angry. He looks for the others' reactions, but they merely shrug and lower their weapons.

Gomez is ready for a fight. "Let's boogie," he says.

Coleman rests his coffee cup on the counter while nearby hotel personnel and guests scatter.

Hoping for a quick ending, the hitman charges first. However, Jack stops him with a well-placed bullet to the left thigh that shatters his femur and sends him face down to the granite floor.

"Hey! What'd ya do that for?" shouts Gomez, upset at being deprived of a means of repairing his bruised ego.

Assante ties his belt around Coleman's leg while Jack waves Gomez over to him. "This ain't the Old West," he tells him. "We don't settle things with fistfights anymore."

"But you didn't stop me—"

"Shut up, Gomez," says Jack.

When the FBI agents take over, Jack walks over to Jacob. "I need a favor. Tell the EMTs not to bring him to Presbyterian. He should go to a more secure facility. Rikers would be a good choice."

"Rikers is a prison, and it's closed now."

"Yeah, the airport expansion closed the prison, but the hospital wing is still open. So I recommend you send him there. That way, we know he can't get out. Well, not as easily."

Jacob considers the request. "Okay, we can do that," he replies, then dials a number on his phone.

While Jacob talks, Jack leans down next to Coleman, and in a menacing whisper, says, "If I find that you had anything to do with what happened to Didi, I'll cut your balls off and shove them down your throat. You have my word on that, asshole."

Then he straightens up and crooks his finger at Burley. "Come with me," he says. "We're going to Presbyterian to talk to the Luccheses — if they're still alive."

Inside and outside the hotel, people snap pictures and record what they've seen, scooping the local TV stations again. When the reporters arrive, they aren't pleased to see them, but they go about their business anyway. The news media knows that cell phones are making them irrelevant, so they do whatever they can to spice up their stories. More than ever, their coverage needs to be interesting for viewers to tune in.

Meanwhile, John follows Jack to his Road Runner. "You know, you're gonna hafta deal with PD bullshit because of that leg shot," he says.

Jack doesn't care. "You have obviously mistaken me for someone who gives a shit," he replies, sarcastic as usual.

The weather in the Smokies is pleasant today, so Serge Kaspin sits on his back porch overlooking the river to sip a tall glass of sweet tea.

Down below, groups of tourists float by the cabin on rented inner tubes, appearing periodically to Serge through gaps in the trees and bushes. Serge is close enough to hear them chattering and laughing happily, and some wave when they see him.

Unexpectedly, Serge is in a good mood today. The solitude and cool mountain breeze are soothing; they've done wonders for his mindset. So he puts aside some of his natural aloofness and waves back.

However, nothing lasts forever. When an aide coughs politely at his elbow, his countenance changes dramatically.

"What is it?" he asks gruffly.

"Sorry, but there's some bad news."

Serge sighs and puts his glass down on the table next to him, returning to his former self. "Tell me," he commands.

"Yes, sir. Our shooter, Stefan Coleman, was arrested."

Kaspin is livid. "Damn it to hell!" he barks, hitting the table so hard that his glass threatens to fall over. Then he sees his aide's expression. "There's more?" he asks angrily.

"Unfortunately, there is, sir."

"Well, spill it, man!"

"Um, yes. The crew that hit the Luccheses didn't fare well. All of them died at the scene, sir."

Kaspin inhales and exhales rapidly, then turns back to the serenity of the river. "Casualties of war," he responds flippantly. The deaths are inconsequential to Serge's overall mission, so he dismisses them as casually as if he were stepping on ants on a sidewalk.

"Here, take this," he says, holding out his glass. "Grab your video camera and bring more tea. I'm going to send a message."

"This place is crazy busy," declares Detective Burly while Jack parks his ride behind an ambulance at the entrance to New York-Presbyterian Hospital's Emergency Department.

"Yeah, must be the victims from the attack at Vito's place," states Stenhouse, watching people streaming into the facility.

The blue light is still spinning on the Road Runner's dash while Jack and Burley flash their badges at the security desk.

"Excuse me," says Jack, popping his head into a small room where a nurse is taking information from a new patient.

"We're looking for Vito and Michael Lucchese. They were brought here earlier today."

The nurse looks up, shaking her head at the interruption. "I'm with a patient. Please wait outside," she declares firmly." Then she looks back at her computer and returns to asking questions of the man in front of her with one hand wrapped in a bloody towel.

"I asked you a question," declares Jack, standing in front of the man in the chair.

From the doorway, John mouths, 'Sorry,' but doesn't stop his fellow officer.

"Buzz us in now," Jack orders in his most commanding voice.

Stunned by the officer's rudeness, the nurse presses a button, unlocking a connecting door.

"Now that wasn't so hard, was it?" asks Jack as he and Burley leave the nurse and the man with the bloody hand looking after them with their mouths open in shock.

Inside the door, organized chaos prevails as nurses, doctors, and technicians run around, tending to the trauma cases. When a nurse rushes by, Jack grabs her arm. "What's the status of the Luccheses, Vito, and Michael?"

"Uh, I'm not sure," she replies and tries to get away, but Jack's grip is too tight. "Um, let me get you the attending physician," she says. "Wait here."

The nurse pulls her arm out of Jack's grip and enters a nearby room where the officers can hear her talking. A few minutes later, a doctor comes out.

"I'm Dr. Dayal," he says. "Can I help you?"

"Yes, I'm Lieutenant Stenhouse, and this is Detective Burley. We're looking for Vito and Michael Lucchese. It's important that we speak to them."

The doctor pauses, then says, "Lieutenant, I'm sorry to

tell you that Vito Lucchese did not survive his injuries. But Michael is in Room 6. You can see him now if you like. But he's scheduled for an MRI, so he'll be taken down for imaging when the machine is up and running again."

Jack is stunned by the news. So John says, "Thanks," and pulls Jack away and down the hall before he can get them into any more trouble.

John can't help voicing his surprise as they walk.

"Vito's dead?!" he asks, glancing at Jack for his reaction. But Jack's face is impassive. "Did you hear what I said?" he asks.

"Yeah," replies Jack.

"I thought you'd be happy."

"I am," he snarls.

When they round a corner, they see two burly men standing outside a room at the end of the corridor.

"That must be it," says John.

Jack shows his badge to the men, then pulls a corner of his jacket away from his holstered Glock. "I'm Stenhouse, and this is Burley," he thumbs. We're here to speak with Michael."

Without a word, one of the soldiers enters the room and closes the door. When he returns, he stands nose-to-nose with Jack. "You got five minutes," he states coldly.

"Hmmph," huffs Jack as he shoves the man aside and pushes at the door.

Behind him, the second man raises a hand to stop Burley from following. "Not you," he says. "Just him."

Jack stops and turns his head to catch John's eye. Then he continues to go through the door.

While John waits outside, Jack approaches the bed holding Michael Lucchese. The mobster's son looks weak; his head and one of his arms are wrapped in bandages, there are wounds on his face, and an IV line is dripping something into a vein.

"Sorry for your loss," says Jack, moving a chair next to the bed. "We're trying to find Serge Kaspin. We think he's responsible."

Michael licks his dry and cracked lips. "This was our fault, so we'll take care of it. We didn't make sure he was dead."

Jack doesn't reply. He's surprised to hear Michael admitting to a crime.

Michael coughs weakly. "I heard about your wife. That shouldn't have happened."

Jack sighs deeply. "Well. We both have skin in the game now, so maybe we can work together. How about this? If I look the other way while you try to avenge your father, will you promise not to interfere with what I hafta do to fuck this guy my way?"

Michael looks Stenhouse in the eye. "Seems fair," he says, reaching out his uninjured hand.

As the men shake on their agreement, an orderly announces, "Mr. Lucchese, Imaging is ready for you."

When Jack reenters the hallway, one of the large men at the door "accidentally" bumps into him as he passes, which doesn't sit well with Jack.

Turning around, Jack quickly walks up to the man and purposely steps on one of his highly polished snakeskin shoes, scuffing the top. "OOPS," he says theatrically. Then he leans in and whispers, "*Sei uno stronzo!*" and turns to leave.

A few feet away, John asks, "What did you say to that goon?"

"I called him an asshole in Italian. I figure it's something he hears often."

John snaps his head around and looks at Jack dubiously. "You speak Italian?"

"Nah, mostly the cuss words."

Rikers Island is now a ghost town. When they decided to expand a runway at LaGuardia Airport, they shut the correctional and mental institution down and transferred most of the detainees and staff to other facilities. However, a few prisoners remain; they're in the hospital wing and can't be moved until they're cleared for transport. As soon as that happens, the entire Rikers jail complex will be scheduled for demolition.

One of the island's last detainees is Stefan Coleman. At Jack's suggestion, Jacob recommended that his FBI superiors move him there, and now, the suspected shooter is in surgery to have a rod inserted into his femur to strengthen the leg Jack shot.

Hector Gomez and James Ruiz wait in the hallway outside one of the jail's old isolation rooms. The entire building is cold and dank, and unpleasant odors of mold and disinfectant permeate the area.

"This place gives me the creeps," says James, wrapping his arms over his chest after a sudden blast of cold air chills him to the bone. "Did you feel that?" he asks. "I heard stories about the ghosts of prisoners hanging around places like this. I wish we weren't here," he adds bleakly. "Why do I always get the shit jobs?"

Gomez looks down the dreary hallway. "I don't like it here, either."

Beside him, Ruiz shudders. "I could have sworn someone just walked by," he says.

"Shut up, will you," demands Gomez, more gruffly than necessary.

A noise at the end of the corridor suddenly makes both men brace for a possible otherworldly encounter. But it's just a corrections officer and a nurse walking toward them.

"Did you two see anything down there?" asks Ruiz, shaken by a strange tingling up and down his arms.

The guard eyes him and sets his mouth firmly. Then he turns to the nurse.

"One of our inmates just passed away," she responds, "so, well, you know..."

The guard and nurse continue to the nurse's station as two orderlies enter the dead inmate's room to process the body.

"I don't like this place," says Gomez.

Moments later, the wobble and squeak of a hospital bed reverberates down the hall as a gurney is wheeled into an empty room.

"There he is," says Hector, tapping James' arm to get his attention.

The officers walk down to the room with the new patient. As they watch, an older nurse hooks Coleman up to an IV pump and locks the bed's wheels in place.

"He's pumped up with morphine, and he's still groggy from the anesthesia," she tells them. "You can try to talk to him, but don't expect much. Stay as long as you like." Then she leaves, chuckling as she closes the door of Coleman's room.

Ruiz is still jumpy. "Let's get this over with and get the hell out of here," he says.

Coleman is awake but doesn't seem too aware of his surroundings.

"Hey, ghost man," says Hector, leaning over the bed. "You with us? We need to talk."

Coleman works to put his visitors in focus. "Well, if it ain't the frogman and his little tadpole," he says, his words slurred from the remnants of anesthesia.

"Cut the crap!" snaps Gomez, irritated again by another jibe. "Between the FBI and Interpol, you won't see the light of day until you're a wrinkled old man unless you give us some info. Then, maybe, you could catch a break."

Coleman laughs and looks toward the window.

"Where's Kaspin?" asks Hector.

"Maybe I'll tell you something, but how would you know if it's the truth?" snickers Coleman. "I can say anything I want right now, just to make the insides of your asses so smoky you'll be farting rings."

"Yeah, he's full of drugs, you know," says James.

Gomez narrows his eyes and clenches his fists. He'd like nothing better than to take a swing at this asshole's smiling face, but instead, he grits his teeth and tries to calm down.

"What did you say?" he asks, daring Coleman to repeat his insult.

Wisely, Coleman resists the bait. "I'm not gonna tell you squat about Kaspin, not even if you give me a sponge bath with a surprise ending."

Hector's expression hardens, and he looks like he's going to strangle the guy. "I don't play that way. I'm—" he starts, until Ruiz pulls at his arm, leading him to the door.

"We tried," says James. "Let's leave this prick to whatever fate awaits him."

"Wait," says Coleman with a moan. "I'll only tell you one thing, and then I'm done with you two clowns. I had nothing to do with the assaults on your police station, the mob's food joint, or Stenhouse's wife. I took care of all my targets, except you, Giancarlo, and Burley," he says, looking directly at Hector. "So I guess Kaspin's gonna replace me now. He was pretty clear about wanting all of you dead."

Hector stares daggers at Coleman, wishing he could take that swing at him. "Seems like you're pretty lucid now."

Coleman looks back with a lopsided grin. "That's all I'm gonna say, so don't let the door hit your asses on the way out."

At that moment, a doctor enters to check on his new

patient.

"How long will he be kept here?" asks Hector.

Dr. Rakesh Chabra looks at Coleman's chart. "Well, as you know, this place is shutting down next week, and he's one of only four, ah, three patients here now. We'll keep him here for forty-eight hours, and if all goes well, he'll be released into FBI custody. They've arranged for him to be transferred to the Metro Correctional Center."

"Thanks," says James, pushing Hector out the door.

As the officers exit the facility, Gomez's phone buzzes. "Yeah, okay," he says and ends the call. "That was Stenhouse. He wants us to meet him at that burger place near the First, his treat. Giancarlo, Burley, and Assante will also be there."

The burger restaurant Jack chose to meet with his colleagues is one of the few places he never took Didi. That's why he asked the others there, hoping there'd be less memories to sadden him.

However, visions of his wife cradling the son she'll never see grow up have a way of popping up at the most inopportune moments, even though he tries to contain them to times when he's alone.

Jack sighs and shakes those thoughts off. "All right," he announces, holding onto his Guinness for dear life. "I asked you here so we can discuss the status of our investigation away from the distractions at the precinct."

"And because you want to keep us alert and well-fed, right?" jokes John, sipping an Arnold Palmer.

"After this meal, you may be the only one who'll be alert enough to remember what we discussed," Jack jokes back, nodding at John's drink. "Still on the meds?"

"Yeah," sighs John. "Sometimes, the pain from those

bullet fragments sneaks up on me, and my meds don't mix with booze. So I'm on the wagon for the foreseeable future."

James quips, "Well, at least we know we always have a designated driver!" Then, when he notes the blank stares of Allison, Hector, and Jack, he retracts his comment. "Sorry," he says. "It sounded funnier in my head."

John responds, "No prob, Jim. It is what it is."

Jack takes a sip of his drink. "Let's run down the facts of the case. You all know Jacob and the feds have taken over the search for Kaspin, and the catwalk killer is in custody. So, as far as the captain's concerned, he wants us on other things. He says our involvement is over. However, all of you — Allison, Hector, John, and Jacob — all of you need to stay vigilant. We know Kaspin isn't done yet. And while this town will surely provide us with more murders we'll hafta solve, we definitely don't want them to be yours."

The group goes silent, and Jack looks out the window.

To break the silence, Jacob states, "We're continuing our investigations into the attacks at Didi's, the First, and Vito's restaurant."

Hector pipes up, "That reminds me. What's the latest on the Luccheses?"

Jacob looks to Jack.

"Vito's dead," he declares colorlessly.

The crew gasps: they didn't expect that news, and they look from Jack to Allison for their reactions.

Jack is silently sipping his drink, so Allison speaks up. "I know he's my uncle, but one less mob guy is okay with me. So… I guess we better start prepping for takeover battles."

"Not necessarily," maintains Jack, returning to the conversation. "Michael's already out of the hospital. His main injury was a concussion, so I'm sure he's been issuing orders to quell notions that he's not ready to assume the crown."

"In addition," interrupts Jacob, "we believe the Patriot Guard conducted all the attacks under the supervision of our friend, Serge. So we alerted our operatives in the North Carolina and Tennessee areas."

When the food orders arrive, the conversation stalls, and when Jack picks it up again, the mood is noticeably darker.

"Jacob, let me know when you track down Kaspin's hideout," Jack contends, stabbing a French Fry with more force than necessary.

Gomez swallows and lifts his fork for attention. "Coleman didn't say squat when we talked to him."

"Well," clarifies James, "he did say that he's out of commission now, so he thinks Kaspin will hire another hitman to continue his revenge attacks."

Jack shakes his head. "No way," he insists. "He'll probably get someone from the Patriot Guard this time. He knows he can control them."

Jack takes a large bite of burger, then downs a healthy swig of beer and looks across the table. "Jacob, we're counting on you guys to get us everything you can on that dammed Guard."

Allison clears her throat. "You know, my team is primed and ready to take them on. They're essentially domestic terrorists, right?"

"Yeah, that's true," says Jack, nodding thoughtfully. "Go ahead and do your thing, Ally."

CHAPTER EIGHT

As another day dawns in the Big Apple, the predictability is comforting. But as usual, Jack is awake before Burley enters the shower. He hasn't been sleeping well, so when he hears someone else in the apartment, it's reassuring, even though John isn't family.

When the water turns on, Jack sighs and throws the covers off, trying not to look at the undisturbed part of the bed previously occupied by his wife. He pulls on a pair of jeans, then walks to the window overlooking Suffolk Street to reassure himself that the patrol car Conrad ordered is still there.

When John exits the bathroom, he calls out, "How do you like your eggs?"

When he hears 'over easy,' Jack's sense of humor returns for a brief moment.

"Okay, scrambled it is," he sings out and walks to the kitchen to prepare eggs and bacon for their breakfasts.

"You seem better today," says John, now dressed and strolling into the kitchen with slightly damp hair.

"Well, life goes on, and I'm sure the city will have something for us to do. So we may as well get to it," replies Jack. "Coffee is ready and so are your 'over easy' eggs."

Jack's phone rings just as the two start to eat. "See, what did I tell you?" he says, clicking on the call. "Stenhouse, here. Yeah? Fuck. Okay, where? Got it."

Jack ends the call and picks up a piece of bacon. "Finish up; we gotta boogie," he tells John. "Russell Holden was found floating in the East River. They think he jumped."

Jack and John arrive at the scene of Russell Holden's alleged suicide amid a sea of blue lights shining off the nearby Battery Maritime Building.

"Back here!" calls an officer when he sees the men approaching from the street.

Down at the pier, a team of divers is loading Russell's body into a metal cage. When it's secure, officers lift it from the water and place it on the dock's edge.

Watching the activity, John asks, "Wasn't the FBI supposed to be protecting Holden?"

"Just another government snafu," smirks Jack. "I don't know how Assante puts up with it."

Just then, Jack hears his name and turns to see Agent Assante approaching from the rear. "Nice job protecting our witness," Jack snipes. "What the hell happened?"

"Fuckin' Holden, that's what. He overpowered the agent who was watching him at a safe house in Little Italy."

"Sheesh! How'd he do that?!"

"He unscrewed the shower head and knocked the agent out with it. When we couldn't contact our guy, we rushed to the safe house, but Holden was gone. He left a note, though. Said he was afraid of the Guard."

Jack looks at Holden's body. "How's your agent?"

"There's a nasty lump on his head. We sent him to get checked for a concussion."

Jack kneels beside Holden. "Holy crap," he says and rises quickly. "Check ballistics on the bullet. Holden was shot in the right temple, but he was a lefty. This was a hit, Jacob. You guys better get your shit together and fast. You, me, and a bunch of my friends are still in Kaspin's crosshairs, and I don't want to be going to any more funerals. Nothing against you, but the

Federal Government can screw up a one-car funeral."

While Jacob bends down to check the body for himself, Jack says, "I'm still part of this, Assante, and I want the Bureau to keep me in the loop. Fill me in on anything you get off the body and the security cameras on the dock."

"What are you gonna do now?" asks Jacob worriedly.

Jack looks out over the water. "This shit *has* to end. C'mon, John. Let's go down to the JTTF. I wanna talk to Giancarlo."

Earlier that morning, an unmarked police sedan picked Allison up from her temporary digs at a hotel in Chinatown, a few blocks north of her Joint Terrorist Task Force's headquarters.

The unmarked unit is one of the security layers Captain Conrad put into place to protect his team from Kaspin's wrath. However, that layer may not be working as well as he intended. When Allison and her driver left the building, a man in a car parked across the street took photos of them.

Unaware of the man, Allison arrived at JTTF as usual and immediately got to work reviewing the constant stream of data coming across her desk. Hours later, a light knock at her office door causes her to look up in surprise.

"Hey," says Jack, slipping into the room ahead of Sergeant Burley. "Sorry to barge in, but Kaspin struck again."

Allison lays her papers on the desk. "What now?" she asks, ready to listen.

"A team just fished Russell Holden out of the East River."

Allison narrows her eyes. "Fucking feds!" she spits out in a voice layered with disgust. "Sometimes, they're a big help, but other times, not so much."

Allison shuffles through some papers, then holds one up.

"I'm glad you're both here. I was just reading a report about suspicious activity."

"Yeah?" replies Stenhouse, taking a seat while Burley stands.

"My counterparts upstate say paramilitary groups are training near the Mario Cuomo Bridge in a small town called Blauvelt. They also found them in Rockefeller State Park Preserve, a park some distance from there. Ever hear of either of those places?"

"Nope," the officers reply.

"Me neither. Anyway, I sent one of my guys up there to check them out. He's scheduled to report back in two days."

"Okay, sounds good," says Jack.

"Meanwhile," resumes Allison, twirling a pen between her fingers, "how the hell did the FBI lose Holden?"

Burley responds smugly, "He knocked his nanny agent out at the safe house and took his gun."

"So much for their 'safe house,'" frowns Allison.

Jack agrees. "Someone was watching, and it must have been a hitman. There's a bullet hole in his right temple."

"Not suicide?" asks Allison, referring to a report on her computer.

"No, Russell couldn't have shot himself," says Jack. "He was lefthanded. Listen, Ally, stay vigilant. We know Kaspin will try anything — he'll do anything to anyone, anywhere. So no matter what you think of the FBI, you're gonna hafta keep them in the loop. We can trust Assante; he's one of the good ones. So after your guy makes contact again, set up a meeting for all of us. Okay?"

On the way back to the precinct, Jack notices that the same car has been behind him for a while. "We got a shadow, a blue Camry," he tells Burley.

Burley turns to look out the back window. "You sure?"

At the next light, Stenhouse and his shadow are boxed in by a line of cars, so Jack decides to find out who the guy is. Putting his car into park, he bounds out of the Road Runner and approaches the Camry with his gun hidden behind his back. In line with the driver's window, he pulls the weapon out and aims it at the driver's head. "Exit the car standing, or get carried out," he orders. "Your choice."

The driver blinks, then moves one of his hands toward the gap between the seats. But Burley is on the other side of the car. "FREEZE!" he shouts, breaking the passenger window with a spring-loaded automatic center punch.

Knowing he's outmaneuvered, the driver clasps his fingers behind his head.

"Exit the vehicle!" commands Burley.

Jack steps back to clear the door while keeping his gun trained on the man dressed in camouflage pants and T-shirt. "Keep your hands on your head and get down on your knees!" he barks when the guy is free of the car. Then he shouts, "Kiss the pavement!"

While Jack takes custody of the driver, Burley opens the passenger door and finds a digital Nikon camera and a 9mm Ruger wedged between the seats. "Well, lookie here," he says to Jack, holding up the camera. "Wonder what's on it?"

"Take a look," says Jack, putting his knee into the small of the camo man's back and handcuffing him.

Burley fiddles with the camera while Jack calls for backup.

"Hey, look at this," says Burley, flipping through the photos stored on the camera. "Looks like we have our own personal paparazzo," replies Burley, showing him the camera with photos of Allison Giancarlo, Jack, Jacob, and himself.

"Fuck," says Jack, turning to the suspect. "Who sent you? Serge Kaspin?"

"I'm not sayin' shit," he states defiantly.

Jack sighs. "Let's bring him to the First."

"Uh, what are we holdin' him for?" asks Burley. "We got nothin' on him."

"We got something — his camera, his fingerprints, and his gun," responds Jack. "That'll do for a while."

Later, Burley and Stenhouse watch the freelance photographer through a two-way mirror at the First.

"His name is Cameron Taylor," says Jack, reading from a report. "There are no priors on his Ohio license and no outstanding warrants or other criminal activity." Reading further, he says, "Wow, he's ex-military — Marines — and was employed by Black Horizon. His social media references the Patriot Guard and has the typical pro-gun, rah-rah shit. Oh, and his car is rented from Charlotte airport."

"What about his gun?" asks Burley as Jacob, Sergeant Ruiz, and Allison Giancarlo join them.

"Let's see... He has a carry permit from Ohio, so it's illegal here."

"We looked at his camera," says Jacob. "There are photos of all of us on it, including Russell Holden. Does your report show where he drove the rental?"

Jack shakes his head.

"Well, we checked. Taylor's been busy. He rented the vehicle three weeks ago, and he's driven it over three thousand miles. We're checking his credit card history now."

"Guess it's time to chat with Mr. Taylor," says Jack, motioning to Jacob and cricking his neck.

When the pair enters the interrogation room, Cameron Taylor looks up and leans his chair back on its rear legs with a wide smile on his face.

"Hey, we like a good joke," says Jack. "Is something funny, Taylor?"

Taylor brings the chair down with a thud. "This is how you treat tourists in your fair city?"

Jack's eyes narrow into slits. "Tourists don't go around taking pictures of cops and dead people," he growls. "You came from North Carolina, right? Did you see a guy named Serge Kaspin there?"

Jack waits for a reaction, then grins when he sees a slight twitch in Cameron's right eye. *Gotcha*, he thinks.

But Cameron's face quickly goes blank. "Who?" he asks. "I don't know anyone named Kaspin. Is he a friend of yours?"

At that moment, a forensic technician walks into the interrogation room with photos he hands to Jack. Jack looks at each one, then passes them to Jacob.

"Cameron Taylor, we're arresting you for an attack on a government facility, two cases of murder, and five cases of attempted murder," Jack declares briskly. "And the feds will probably charge you with terrorism as well."

Taylor lifts his brows in surprise, so Jack asks, "What's the matter, Cameron, my man? You're not smiling anymore. You have anything to say now, asshole?"

"Yeah, fuck you!" roars Taylor. "I want a lawyer!"

Jack turns toward the mirror. "Burley, you want to come in here and read him his rights? After that, you and Assante can take him to Central Booking."

Jack turns back to Cameron. "You gonna cop a plea, now, Taylor? Have a nice day, asshole, and welcome to New York."

In the hallway, Jack walks over to Ruiz and Allison, who are waiting for him. "What'd I tell ya?" he says to Allison.

"Kaspin's been watching you. He already has a bead on ya."

CHAPTER NINE

Everyone at the station knows that if you're called to the inspector's office, it's either because you did something particularly well or something exceptionally horrible. There's no in-between.

So that's why Jacob, Captain Conrad, and some of the members of Jack's team are nervous today. They don't know why they're sitting at a long conference table with Inspector Rawlings at the head, and he's even acting strangely. It's disconcerting. The man they all know as almost incapable of showing emotion, is repeatedly sighing, and pacing the floor nervously.

While they stare at each other uncomfortably, Rawlings suddenly stops and grabs the back of his chair. "I know you're all wondering why you're here," he begins. "I have bad news for you, and I know it's going to be hard to hear. So I'm just going to come out and say it."

The inspector looks around at the expectant faces before him, wishing his upcoming retirement was already behind him. Then he launches into his news. "If you notice, Hector isn't here today. When we radioed his security detail this morning for our usual check-in, our officer didn't respond, so we sent backup, and when they arrived, they found our guy sitting in his patrol car with a bullet hole in his left temple. Following protocol, they went up to Hector's apartment and found the door ajar with signs of struggle inside: broken furniture, shattered glass, and blood stains. CSI is scouring the apartment now, and they believe Hector was abducted. Based on what's been going on, we think it could be the Patriot Guard."

Rawlings lets the team blow off steam, then holds his hands up for quiet. "Special Agent Assante, we're gonna need the full cooperation of the FBI and every other federal agency you can recruit to stop this madness. I'm tired of this vigilante organization of fucking assholes attacking my men and this city. So, Lieutenant Stenhouse, I want you to drop everything and concentrate on cleaning up this fucking mess."

"You bet I will," shouts Stenhouse, slamming his fist on the table to shouted agreements from the others.

"You know what to do," says Rawlings, "now get out of here. I have more people to contact with this bad news."

When everyone is in the hallway, Rawlings slams the door on them.

"I've never seen him so pissed," comments Conrad, turning to Jacob. "Come to my office; we need to talk." To the others, he says, "Hang around until Jacob and I are done. We need to formulate a plan."

No one wants to move; no one wants to speak. So Jack and his team remain in the hallway. They're all worried about Hector.

Suddenly, Jack startles everyone when he punches the wall. "Sounds like Gomez kicked some ass!" he mutters loudly. "It's clear they took him for a reason! If they wanted him dead, we would have found his body!"

Burley shakes his head anxiously. "If Kaspin has him, he's gonna need every bit of his Navy training. They're gonna put him through some heavy shit."

While the team gathers round to discuss the problem, Jack gets a faraway look in his eyes. Allison has seen that look before, and she's worried.

"Jack?" she says, calling his name to bring him out of his trance.

But Jack says nothing. Looking on, Ruiz and Burley notice that he looks like a volcano ready to explode. Neither of them has seen Jack this intense, and they don't know what to do.

While Jack seethes, the men turn to Allison for guidance. "You know him best," they tell her. "Can you calm him down?"

Allison nods and walks over to her former partner. "Take a breath, buddy," she says, running a hand over Jack's back. "Remember what I said the other day? One of my guys is getting cozy with the Guard right now, and I should have a report from him today. So let's approach this together, okay? We make a great team, right, Jack?"

Jack hears what Allison is saying, however, none of it is registering. He continues to stare off into space.

Then, he turns and looks at them. "First, it was the precinct, then it was my wife, and now, it's Hector. He even got your uncle," he says, looking intensely at Allison, "and all of us are worried we could be next. So there is nothing, nothing! that's gonna stop me from killing that bastard with my bare hands — badge, or no badge! And I'm gonna make damn sure he feels every bit of the pain he's putting us through!"

Jack turns and stomps toward Conrad's office, stopping halfway down the corridor.

"You comin', or what?" he thunders, looking back at the others. "This is it, folks! Follow me now, or get the fuck out of my way!"

Jack storms into his boss' office while Jacob is speaking.

Disrupting their conversation, he roars, "Kaspin is mine, no matter what!"

Conrad understands that Jack is coming from a bad place right now, so he takes a deep breath before speaking. "We know you have it in for him, and we sympathize with your pain," he states calmly. "However, we're all officers of the law, and we're not gonna stop until we take that fucker down! I guarantee that nothing is gonna stop us from rescuing Gomez!"

Jack looks at Agent Assante, seeing only the face of

the agent's sister. "We failed Maria; we cannot fail Hector!" he declares, passion for a good friend's demise eating at his memory. "I thought the feds took care of the Patriot Guard! What's the matter? Is your office too busy being politically correct to do what needs to be done? There's a training camp just north of this city! What the hell are you guys doing about it? How the hell are you going to protect the rest of us and yourself, Jacob? This is turning into another FUBAR operation by the government!"

Assante is incensed by Jack's comments and rises from his chair so rapidly that it tips backward. "Are you saying the FBI had a hand in my sister's death?!" he bellows, clenching his fists and going nose-to-nose with Jack.

"Whoa!" declares Conrad, jumping out of his seat to push the two men apart. "Go home, Jack! That's an order! Take time off to find yourself! You need a break!"

Jack pushes Assante away and storms out of the office as Conrad's phone rings.

Halfway out the door, Jack stops. He's not done yet. Inhaling deeply, he turns around to confront his boss.

But Conrad isn't in the mood for Jack's shit.

When Jack storms back in, Conrad takes control before Jack can get a word out. "Shut the fuck up, Jack!" he declares hotly. "That was Kaspin on the phone! He has Gomez, and he said he'll send us a photo to prove it!"

That stops Jack in his tracks.

"Get me the details of that call," says Assante. "I'll find out where it came from." Then he turns to Jack. "No hard feelings. You're always welcome on my team."

Jack laughs sardonically. "Naw, me and the feds are like oil and water," he states firmly. "I thought we could work together, but it's always the same with you G-men. Boss, I want to speak with Stefan Coleman alone — my terms. I'll get him to talk! I want to see him before the feds get their hooks into him."

"Again, Jack?" interrupts Assante. "I can't let you do anything that will hurt this case. If you do anything irregular, his lawyer will get him released, or he could even sue us. What the hell are you thinking?"

Jack stands firm. "You're not like your sister at all," he states harshly. "She had bigger balls than you! Fuck this PC bullshit! Fuck the FBI, and if you stand in my way, fuck you, too! I'm going to Rikers! Let them know I'm on the way!"

Conrad tries to stop him, so Jack asks, "What are you gonna do, Captain? Fire me? Hah! That will just take my constraints off! At this point, I don't give a fuck about anything but giving that piece of shit his due! Let's go!" he adds, motioning to Sergeant Burley, who's been watching from the doorway.

Behind Jack's back, Conrad points a stern finger at Burley. "Watch his ass!" he orders him. "Make sure he doesn't do anything stupid."

Burley chuckles in reply. "I'll try, but who's gonna watch my ass?"

John catches up to Jack just as he unlocks the bottom drawer of his desk and pulls out a blackjack, an old Yellow Pages phone book, and some ammonia capsules.

Burley smiles. "More old-school shit?"

"I call these attitude adjustment tools," he responds, stuffing the capsules into a pocket and patting it affectionately.

Stefan Coleman is the only patient remaining in the Rikers jail complex, and in anticipation of its closing, the staff has been pared down considerably.

"Hi," says Jack to the only nurse at the nurse's station. "You look lonely. Isn't there anyone else here?"

"No, we're closing down for good next week, so it's just

one doctor and me. What can I do for you?"

"We're here to speak with Stefan Coleman. I'm Lieutenant Stenhouse, and my partner here is Detective Burley."

"Okay," she replies, eyeing the bag Jack is carrying. "I was told you were coming. Did you bring our guest a gift?" she asks, grinning slightly.

"Uh, yeah," says Jack. "It's something personal."

Jack is concerned the nurse won't let his "gift" pass, but he needn't have worried. She's seen it all in her forty years on the job and is pretty certain her patient won't appreciate the bag's contents.

"All right," she states. "He's in 124; that's down the hall on the left," she points. "You guys go on. I'll leave you alone so you can visit privately."

Jack tips an imaginary hat and leads the way to Coleman's room.

"I bet she can't wait till this place closes," comments Burley. "Seems like she's been here way too long to care anymore."

When they reach Coleman's room, Burley closes the door behind them and leans against it to prevent anyone from entering.

When the men arrive, Stefan looks up from an outdated magazine. "What are you doing here?" he asks, propping himself up in the bed and shifting his injured leg uncomfortably. "No one told me I was having visitors today. Should I call my lawyer?"

"No call needed," Jack responds.

Coleman watches with increasing unease as Jack slowly removes the phone book and the blackjack from the bag.

"What's that for?" he asks nervously.

"Well, you see, it's like this. We're pretty sure your

buddy kidnapped our friend, and we're not happy about it. So I thought I'd bring over some items that might help jog your memory. You didn't have much to say the last time we met. We need answers, Coleman, and we're not leaving until we get them."

Jack takes out his handcuffs, and Burley walks over with his own. Together, they cuff Coleman's hands to the bed railings.

Now, Coleman is scared. "Do what you want, assholes!" he shouts. "I'm not tellin' you shit!"

"We'll see," grins Jack. "I'm gonna ask you some questions now, and depending on your answers, you may get to meet these items here." Jack looks at Burley. "You ready, John?"

"Yup."

"Okay. So, let's get on with it. We know Serge is in North Carolina, but we don't know where. Where is he, Coleman?"

Coleman shakes his head. "I wouldn't tell you, even if I knew!"

"Wrong answer," frowns Jack.

Burley grabs Coleman's head and turns it to face him. "Okay, fucker, this is helpful step one," he says.

While Burley holds Coleman's head steady, Jack lays the phone book over the hitman's cheek and smacks it with the blackjack.

Dazed by the blow, Coleman shouts, "What the fuck! You guys are crazy!"

"Next time, it'll be even harder," states Jack. "Where's Kaspin?"

Coleman spits out a verb and a pronoun, and the sequence starts again but more forcefully.

The new blow leaves Coleman confused and in danger of passing out. So Jack removes the phone book and takes a small capsule out of his pocket.

Holding it under Coleman's nose, he breaks it open, and the prisoner jerks awake.

"Ready for round three?" asks Jack, holding up the phone book.

Stefan responds in a shaky voice. "No… Wait. Kaspin could be in Charlotte or the Smoky Mountains; maybe Cherokee. He has places in both locations, but I know he likes to gamble in Cherokee."

John raises a brow. "Gamble? How does he have time to gamble while he's kidnapping people and killing them?"

"Where is Kaspin hiding?" asks Jack.

Coleman shakes his head, wincing at the pain in his face. "I don't know."

Jack sighs heavily and moves the book to Coleman's face. "Round three, comin' right up!" he says.

"Wait, wait!" yells the helpless patient. "You win! I'll tell you what I know!"

Jack doesn't believe him, so he keeps the Yellow Pages in place and plays bongos on Coleman's face.

The men have to revive him again and wait for the cobwebs to clear.

When Stefan's eyes flutter open, Jack asks, "You ready now, ghost man? Spill it before I really go to town on you."

Coleman is groggy from the repeated blows, so he speaks slowly. "From…what I…found out… He has two…locations. One near Cherokee…and another one…near, um…Charlotte. I don't know…exact…locations… I swear."

Burley looks over at Jack. "He don't look good, boss. Maybe he has a migraine."

"Yeah, he must have a bad headache by now. Let's uncuff him."

Jack puts the phone book and the blackjack in his bag.

"We'll tell the nurse to check you out. Thanks for the info."

At the nurse's desk, Burley points toward Coleman's room. "He's a little groggy. You should go down there now."

"Groggy, huh?" she smirks. "Didn't he like what you brought him?"

At three in the morning, a black SUV turns onto a dirt road overlooking the Tuckasegee River in the western North Carolina mountains. When it enters a gravel driveway, it creeps to a stop, and two men exit from the front.

The one on the passenger side opens the back door and pulls a hooded and handcuffed person from the back seat.

Semiconscious from a sedative, Hector Gomez drags his feet along the gravel as the two men carry him up to a house, one under each arm.

Under a bare outside light, one of the men opens a door to a hallway facing another door. This one opens onto a ten-foot square cement room with an army cot, a toilet, and a sink.

Holding Hector steady, the other man removes Hector's hood, then pushes him inside, where he falls onto the floor.

When the iron door is latched closed, the room becomes pitch-dark. Hector feels around with his hands but finds nothing, so he tries to get to his feet.

His legs won't support him. "Oof," he mutters, and lays back down.

On the other side of the door, Serge Kaspin slides a small window open and chuckles.

Hector flashes half a peace sign at the eyes staring back at him. "Is that you, Kaspin?" he shouts. "You think you're gonna get away with kidnapping a cop? Every law enforcement agency in the nation is gonna come after you now!"

CHAPTER TEN

When another sunrise awakens the city from its overnight respite, Stenhouse and Burley are already at the First. Neither of them could sleep, so they decided to get a jumpstart on the day's work.

However, the lack of adequate rest has made Jack more ornery than usual. When the time comes for most of the officers to be at work, he checks the clock on the wall for the third time, and frowns.

"Allison and Jacob should have been here by now," he grumbles at John. "I bet they don't have a single thing new. I'm pissed, Burley! Serge and his fucking gang are doing whatever they want, and what the hell are we doing to stop them?"

At the other end of the department, Captain Conrad throws open the door to his office and bellows angrily, "STENHOUSE! What the hell did you do to Coleman?!"

Jack replies in a voice dripping with sarcasm. "Whatever do you mean, Captain? We had a nice chat."

The captain storms toward them with his face an ugly red color. "Nice chat?! The man has a concussion, dammit, and he swears you gave it to him!"

Burley raises a hand to offer his own take. However, Conrad turns on him, too. "What the hell did you two do?"

"We didn't do anything unusual, sir," responds John, hoping his voice sounds sincere. "We questioned Coleman and he decided to cooperate. He told us Serge has two locations in North Carolina, one near Cherokee and another near Charlotte."

Jack rises and inhales deeply. "I don't know what he told

you, but it's our word against his, sir. Who are you going to believe? Maybe he tried to get off the bed and fell and hit his head or something. His leg is still messed up."

Conrad looks from one man to the other and sighs.

To change the subject, Jack asks, "By the way, where the fuck are Assante and Giancarlo? One of our own was kidnapped, and we're sitting here with our thumbs up our asses!"

Conrad knows all of Jack's tricks and won't be distracted. "Fuck it all, Stenhouse!" he growls. "Your little stunt better not get me in trouble!"

"No trouble, sir. Just business."

Conrad sighs again. Stenhouse's methods are sometimes unorthodox, but he's one of the best detectives in the department, so the captain tends to give him more leeway than others. Narrowing his eyes, he says, "Assante was called to D.C. about the Patriot Guard, and Giancarlo will be here shortly. She called me first thing this morning and said she was gathering the latest intel from the compound in Blauvelt."

Conrad turns, then looks back at Stenhouse and Burley. "Get rid of the phone book, you assholes," he orders.

While Jack waits for Allison, he looks absently across the floor at cubicles filled with victims and perpetrators.

Not far away, several handcuffed high-class call girls still in their working clothes, are being led off by a couple of officers. As they pass Jack, one of the group notices him looking at their good parts and winks at him. "I work well in cuffs, and mine match my collar," she says, flipping her hair flirtatiously.

Jack gives the woman a thumbs up, but doesn't return the wink. Instead, he looks away and tosses the remainder of his current brew into the nearest trash can. "I need another coffee," he tells Burley. "I hope Allison brings donuts."

Jack walks over to the coffee pot to refill his cup just as Giancarlo strolls in. "So glad you could make it," he calls out.

"Coffee?"

Jack lifts the pot in Allison's direction, but gets no response.

"I got info on the Guard," she says when Jack joins her. "A small group of about fifteen men meets at Rockefeller State Park every Saturday, and my guy joined them there. They took him right in, so tomorrow, we'll crash their party. Any word on Gomez?"

Stenhouse sits down at his desk. "Serge is probably holding Hector at one of his houses in North Carolina, near Cherokee or Charlotte."

"Where'd you get that info?"

"From a little birdie named Stefan Coleman. So now that we have a better idea of where Hector may be, John and I are going to North Carolina after we join your raid."

Allison responds in a faint voice. "You taking Ruiz with you? Hector was his partner, you know."

"Right," says Jack. "I forgot about him. Yeah, him, too."

Jack turns around when he feels a presence behind him.

"You have something to tell me?" asks Captain Conrad, always suspicious when he sees whispering going on.

Jack's brows arch high on his forehead. "Damn, sir, you got this area bugged? I was just telling Giancarlo that Kaspin is in North Carolina and that I'm going down there to have a look around."

Conrad knows that even though North Carolina is way out of their jurisdiction, he won't be able to keep Jack from going there, so he doesn't even bother to voice his opinion. Instead, he says, "I'm going to call Cindy Rodriguez back in for questioning. Maybe there's some info she hasn't shared yet. I'm sure her husband isn't happy with her right now. Ken must have found out by now about her relationship with the guy who ordered his shooting." Conrad looks squarely at Jack. "You two dodged a bullet, you know. Coleman isn't going to press charges. No more of that shit. You hear me?"

Behind Conrad's back, Allison narrows her eyes at Jack. "Get rid of that phone book," she mouths gravely.

Jack takes one look at her serious expression and bursts out laughing. "Oh, no, not you, too?" he asks, raising his hands in feigned innocence.

After a couple of hours of shivering on the cold floor, Hector finally fell asleep, still dressed in his wrinkled suit and tie. So when the sound of the door unlocking awakens him, he struggles to wipe the meager amount of sleep from his eyes.

Blinking against the unexpected light, he watches with a wary eye as Serge Kaspin and an armed associate enter the enclosure with a tray.

The assistant lays the tray on the floor, then backs away and unholsters his .45 while Serge waits.

"Master Chief Gomez," says Serge smugly, "I'm willing to uncuff you if you promise to be nice. However, if you decide to be a bad boy, you'll be shot on the spot. Copy that?"

Glumly, Gomez nods, so Serge motions for him to stand, then turns him around and removes the handcuffs.

Rubbing his wrists, Hector faces his captor. "Why the fuck am I here? And why the fuck aren't I dead yet?"

Serge laughs at Hector's bluntness. "Right. Let's get to the point, shall we? For now, you're worth more alive than dead. But that may change at any time. So, why don't you enjoy your breakfast, then clean yourself up a bit? There are wet wipes on the tray. You're gonna be in the movies, Navy."

With no more to say, Serge and his goon return to the hall and the door clangs shut, leaving Hector once more in the dark. This time, a light in the hallway lets in a little illumination, so it's not as gloomy as before.

Squinting in the shadows, Hector pokes around on the tray. "What the fuck do they feed prisoners around here?" he mumbles unhappily. "Oh, shit. Powdered eggs? I hate powdered eggs!"

Ken Rodriguez starts complaining as soon as Stenhouse and Burley open the door to the interrogation room. "How long do we have to stay in New York?" he whines, looking for agreement from his wife. "We need to get back to South Florida! We already missed one fashion show because we've been here too long!"

Jack takes a seat while John remains standing. "We only called Cindy in," he says.

"Yeah, well, I gotta find out what's going on, don't I? Seems like my wife has a history of keeping secrets."

Cindy Rodriguez winces at the comment but doesn't dispute it, and the officers wonder how much she told Ken.

"How are you feeling?" asks Burley, knowing something about being shot. The men notice Ken using his free arm to protect the other one resting in a sling.

"Like I got hit by a truck."

Burley sympathizes. "I know what you mean, so we'll try not to keep you long. You want anything to drink before we start? Coffee, water, soda?"

Cindy hasn't said a word yet, but that question gets her attention. "A couple of Diet Cokes, please," she answers, speaking up for the first time.

"Okay," responds Burley. "Be right back."

When the door closes behind John, Jack turns to Cindy. "You knew Kaspin fairly well. Do you have any idea where he may be hiding now? A source told us he has some houses in

North Carolina."

Cindy looks Jack in the eye. "Well…," she says, "he once told me he likes the mountains. He grew up in Franklin, a small town in that state."

Jack makes a note on a pad, then looks up with narrowed eyes. "Why would our boy kidnap a law enforcement officer?"

Cindy's mouth drops open. "I have no idea," she responds with a firm head shake. "He kidnapped someone?"

"Mrs. Rodriguez, Detective Hector Gomez is missing, and we have solid reasons to believe Serge has something to do with it."

"Oh? I don't know anything about it!" replies Cindy, glancing at her husband to make sure he heard her. "I really don't know," she insists.

"But you do know Hector, right?" asks Jack, stopping while Burley hands out the sodas.

Cindy pops open her can. "Yeah. I saw him around here and recognized him from Afghanistan. But I don't know much about him, only that he was a Seal. I didn't know he became a cop."

Burley jumps into the conversation. "You had contact with Kaspin overseas, correct?"

"No, not really. I didn't want anything to do with him in Afghanistan and I let him know it, ah, rather forcibly."

"Yeah," says Ken. "She ruptured one of his balls with a well-placed kick," he reveals, gesturing dramatically in the general area of his groin.

Cindy casts Ken a sidelong glance. "I remember Kaspin saying he ran into some Seals in Afghanistan, and they gave him a problem. Maybe one of them was Hector. Everyone knew Kaspin held grudges, so maybe that's why he's hassling your detective."

"Hmm… maybe," responds Jack. "Thanks for the info;

it's helpful. You have anything else, John?"

"No, we can check that angle."

"All right," says Jack. "You guys can go now, but watch your sixes in case Kaspin 'reaches out to you' before we can catch his ass."

Cindy grabs her handbag. "You won't catch him. He doesn't want to be caught. You're gonna have to kill him."

Jack licks his lips. "We can certainly arrange that, no problem," he replies.

Returning to their desks, Burley stops and pulls Jack aside for a minute. "Kaspin has a ruptured ball sack?"

Jack cringes with imaginary pain. "Guess so," he winces.

"No wonder he targeted them. That Cindy sounds like one tough broad. If I were Ken, I wouldn't even dream of cheating on her!"

"Ya know it," smirks Jack.

Jack's cell phone rings, so he pulls it out and checks the call screen. "Hey, excuse me," he tells John. "I gotta take this; it's my mother-in-law. Meanwhile, when you get back to your desk, call Giancarlo and get the particulars on the raid tomorrow."

"Will do," says John, leaving Jack to answer his video call.

"Hi," says Jack, smiling at the face on the screen. "Yeah, I'm okay. How are things with you guys? Yeah? Is he there?" Jack's eyes light up when his son's face appears next to his grandma. "How's my little man!" he asks the toddler. "I miss you sooo much! Are you having fun with grandma?" Jack waits while Mark holds up a toy car. "Oooo, is that a new car? What sound does a car make?" he asks, delighted that he's talking to his little son. "That's right!" he responds after Mark makes a vroom-vroom noise. After more conversation, Sharon prompts Mark to say goodbye to his dad. "I can't wait to see you guys!" he says, waving at the screen.

When the call ends, Jack wipes a tear from his eye. Then he stiffens and walks to his desk.

"I love talking to my nieces when my sister calls," says Burley, coming over to give Jack some news. "Video calls are the best with little kids, aren't they?"

"Yeah, I just miss him so much," agrees Jack.

"I know. But listen, we're gonna meet at JTTF headquarters tomorrow morning at seven. The FBI will also be there, and we'll all head up to Rockefeller Park."

"Thanks," Jack responds.

In North Carolina, mercenary activist Serge Kaspin sits on his back porch, waiting for his cue. When it comes, he says to a video camera, "Good morning, Lieutenant Stenhouse. I would like you to meet my new house guest, someone you know quite well, Master Chief Petty Officer Hector Gomez, your good friend and fellow detective."

Jack is antsy. "Hey, you wanna go out?" he asks John, shrugging into a jacket as he briskly walks into the living room where his housemate is flipping through television channels.

"Go out? Now? We got that raid early in the morning!"

"I know, but I gotta get outta here for a while. There are too many memories haunting this place, and I can't seem to get rid of any of them tonight. You gonna come?"

"Um, yeah. I guess so. Where we goin'?" John asks, grabbing his coat from the back of a chair.

"There's a small cocktail lounge up the street. You can keep me from overdrinking."

"Yeah, right," laughs John, clicking the TV remote off.

"Okay, let's roll."

The night is cool, so the pair are happy they grabbed their jackets.

When they arrive at the bar, it's packed full of a Friday night crowd, well on its way to getting oiled.

"Busy place!" shouts John, raising his voice over the noise.

"Yeah!" Jack responds, pushing his way through tightly packed people. "I know the bartender!" he shouts back.

Eddie is happy to see Jack again. Stenhouse is one of his regulars, but he hasn't been to the bar since Didi died. "Hey, Jack!" he shouts, greeting his good customer with a fist bump. "Condolences, buddy. First round is on me. How's your son doin'?"

Jack sighs. "He's with his grandma right now. They're away for a while until I can get things sorted out. So my friend and I will have single barrels on the rocks, and make mine a double. Thanks for the drinks, Eddie."

Eddie calls to one of the barmaids. "Hey, Laura! Set up a small table in the corner for my special friends and treat them right."

The well-endowed woman is an expert in getting customers to part with their money. Working for tips, she grins widely, lowers the zipper of her tight sweater, and sets up the table.

"Here ya go," says Eddie, handing the men their drinks. "That table is for you," he says, motioning to Laura. "I told her to take good care of you." Jack and John look over at the barmaid, who's wiping down a table in a short tartan skirt.

When she's done, she takes Jack's arm and leads him to the table. Turning his head back to Burley, Jack shrugs as John follows them.

Laura pats Jack's arm sympathetically. "We all heard

about Didi," she tells him. "So sorry, Jack."

At the table, the officers sit opposite each other, drinking and watching the bar fill up.

Jack looks down at his glass. "Bottoms up!" he says, downing half of it in one gulp. "Memories are here, too, but not as many."

John doesn't reply to Jack's comment because he's too busy staring at Laura while she takes care of other customers.

Jack wonders why his friend is silent and follows John's line of sight. "Hey, you're a married man now," he laughs. "What the hell are ya doin'?"

John grins mischievously. "Like you always say, window shopping is perfectly acceptable."

"Yeah, well, just don't go making love to one of your socks tonight. Sylvia may not be here right now, but that ring says she may as well be."

John laughs, then gets serious. "It's been a couple of weeks since, you know. How you holdin' up, Jack? Sometimes, I see you walking around the loft like you're in a trance."

Jack finishes his drink and catches Laura's eye to signal for another. "I miss her, a lot. And with Mark away, it's awfully quiet around the house."

When John opens his mouth to speak, Jack adds, "You know what I mean. I appreciate you being there, but it's not the same. I can't wait till I get my hands on Kaspin. I'll have no problem killing that bastard."

John inhales deeply. "Don't jeopardize your career, man. You need to let this play out legally."

Jack snaps. "Fuck my career, and fuck the NYPD! I have pensions coming from Fort Lauderdale and this place. So I don't need this shit anymore. Maybe I'll switch to a P.I. job, or hell, maybe I'll even write a book. I'm tired of this crap. I wanna be with my wife tonight, but I can't. So maybe I'll tap Laura."

John's eyes widen, and he starts to speak again, but Jack stops him. "Promise you'll watch my six to make sure I don't," he says. "Now, finish that drink, and get another."

CHAPTER ELEVEN

The previous night was fun, and despite asking John to prevent it, Jack overindulged. And so did John. So now they're both paying the price.

When the pair walks up to the JTTF entrance, a black MRAP pulls up carrying Jacob Assante and his crew, so they wait for them before entering the lobby.

"You too?" asks Jacob, eyeing John. "You guys gonna be all right for the raid?"

Jack and John hold up cups of steaming black coffee as if they alone are enough to remove their massive hangovers.

"Whatever," comments Jacob, holding the door open for them.

JTTF headquarters is in a sub-basement of a nondescript building with restricted access, so they look around for Giancarlo, who has to give them access.

"Oh, great," they hear as Allison walks toward the group. "You spreading your nasty habits around again?" she asks, frowning at Jack and the mirrored sunglasses neither he nor John have removed. "Well, since all the J's are here, we may as well get started. Follow me."

Allison leads the way to an elevator, where she holds her palm up to a reader. "We're gonna have a brief meeting downstairs to make sure we're all on the same page. And Jacob, I want to personally thank you and the FBI for allowing the NYPD in on this raid. Our guy is also up there....so thanks."

When the doors open, Allison steps in and side-eyes her former precinct colleagues. "I have Naproxen if you want it."

John looks grateful. "Thanks," he replies. "I could use some, but Jack would do better with morphine."

The elevator plunges downward for some time, then opens onto a platform overlooking a darkened room below. Behind a wall of bulletproof glass, the men look down on a vast control room filled with people focusing on monitors and screens scanning key areas of the Big Apple.

Jack and John turn to Allison with heightened respect.

Amazed by what they're seeing, Jack says, "This is the Joint Terrorist Task Force, and you're in charge of all of it?"

"This is it," beams Allison, stepping onto a metal staircase. "The conference room is one floor down."

Jack allows the others to go ahead of him so he can take another look at the sophisticated gadgetry in the room. Then he steps on the stairs. "George Orwell wrote a manual for this shit," he mumbles.

In the conference room, Allison directs the men to sit around an oak table with file folders at each place.

"The Patriot Guard has been meeting at Rockefeller Park Preserve for the past five months," she begins. "They rent a little-used section of the park where they set up obstacle courses and hold martial arts classes. They also hold monthly weapons training in an indoor shooting range in Nyack called Westchester Pawn and Gun. Our main team will assault the park while the FBI investigates the shooting range. You got the search warrant, right?" she asks Jacob.

"Yeah, it's done."

Allison nods. "Our close relationship with the FBI makes things so much easier. Now, our intelligence estimates that approximately fifteen to twenty Guard members will be at the park today. We think the group totals twenty to twenty-five, but not all of them attend every week. There's an overview of the park and a photo of Frank Scalise, our undercover agent, in your folders."

Allison continues while the men leaf through the folders' contents.

"The park is in Pleasantville. We're going to tag along with the FBI and enter off Phelps Way, then continue to the northeastern corner. It's approximately thirty-five miles from here and should take an hour or so to get there. So we'll leave in five minutes. Any questions?"

"I assume the Guard will be armed," states Jacob.

"Yes, we're going in hot."

"There's only one road in and out," says Jack, looking at the map provided. "What about other people who may be there?"

"Good question," states Allison. "The Guard takes over the back of the park, so we'll do our best to keep others away from that area when we see them. However, the Guard posts personnel to keep that area private. As for the one road in and out, local police will block off the entrance after we get there, so no more civilians will be able to enter."

"All right, let's do this," says Jack.

"How may I help you?" asks the desk sergeant when a young bicycle courier enters the building.

The nineteen-year-old leans his bike against one wall of the First Precinct lobby, then reaches into a leather case over his shoulder for a large brown envelope and a leather-bound ledger with his company's name on the front.

"I have a delivery for Lieutenant Stenhouse," he says, sliding the envelope and his ledger under the window. "Please sign the form on the bottom line."

Hector doesn't know how long he's been in the dark room. After Serge's visit, he checked the place thoroughly and found nothing suspicious. But that's no guarantee there's nothing there. He also looked through the bars in the center of the heavy door but couldn't see much beyond the wall in front of him.

Resigned to his situation, he parked himself on the cot, and with nothing else to do, has been staring glumly at the concrete walls. The room he's in is built solidly, so he concludes there's no escape from this place, other than overtaking the men who enter with his food. He assumes they're going to feed him, and figures that would be his best shot.

As Hector runs through ways to get out of there, the lock in the middle of the door suddenly clanks open.

"How ya doin'?" asks Serge, striding into the room with a smile from ear to ear. "Just so you know, your service as a Seal is the only thing that's kept you alive so far. You're my insurance, whether you like it or not. Even though you were a pain in the ass in Afghanistan, and you haven't changed now that you're a cop, a bargaining chip is a bargaining chip. Ya know what I mean? So I have a proposition. If you promise not to cause any trouble, I could be convinced to give you a little more freedom."

"A little more freedom, huh? I don't know about that," argues Hector. "I don't plan to be here much longer. Somehow or other, I'm getting' out of here. So you can wipe that shit-eating grin off your face."

"Ooorah!" exclaims Serge. "I guess I should have expected nothing less. All righty then," he sighs. "Have a nice stay, Navy. I hope you enjoy the view."

When the door closes on Serge's echoing laugh, Gomez jumps off the cot and puts his face up to the bars in the door.

"Ha. There it is," mutters Gomez. "My way outta here."

Hector saw the light from outside shining into the hallway when his captor opened an exterior door just out of view.

Walking back toward the cot, he drops to the floor and begins doing pushups to prepare for his getaway.

It's nearly 8:45 a.m. when two black MRAPs of the assault team, one from NYPD and the other from the FBI, head down one of the narrow carriage trails to the rear of Rockefeller Park Preserve.

"What the hell?" they hear shouted at them by a group of people setting up for a day of fun. The sight of the unlikely caravan causes the parkgoers to whip out their cell phones to capture images of the event.

"Gotta keep an eye on them," Allison radios to the group leader.

"Roger that," he replies.

Allison returns her attention to the screen showing what the drone flying over the Guard is seeing. "Hold up," she orders.

The caravan stops about three hundred yards from their target. They haven't been seen yet, and Allison wants to keep it that way.

"Meet me outside my car," she radios to Jack, John, and Jacob.

Allison looks worried when the group gathers at the rear of her NYPD vehicle.

"What's wrong?" asks Jacob.

"We got a slight problem. Seems our intel was flawed. There are about fifty people at the encampment today, not the fifteen to twenty we were expecting, and at least ten of them appear to be armed. I can't tell if any others have weapons."

Jack rubs his chin. "Did you try contacting your man inside? What's his name? Scalise?"

"Yeah. He doesn't answer. There's also a large tent, so who knows what's inside that."

Jack's eyes narrow in thought. "Well, it's not a birthday party. Look, we gotta go in, no matter what. Hopefully, they won't put up a fight. If they're locals, they're probably family men and women. The original Guard, not so much."

Allison goes on with her observation. "There's a pickup at the entrance to their camp with a man standing outside it, and he's armed with an AR. The drone doesn't show any other parkgoers in the general area, so we can barge in on their picnic just as we planned. I'll take the lead. The guy on the turret can neutralize the guy with the AR if necessary."

"Let's go," says Jacob, waving a hand over his shoulder.

Up ahead, the trail widens, and the two MRAPs lumber side-by-side down the tree-lined road. Above them, birds squawk their disapproval of the noisy machines invading their territory.

About thirty feet in front of the lone guard, an agent aims a rifle out of a window. "This is the FBI!" he shouts. "Lay down your weapon, put your hands on your head, and clasp your fingers together! Then walk slowly toward us!"

The camo-wearing-soldier-wannabe seems frozen in place beside his elevated Ford F150 with his mouth open in shock. He stays that way until he spots the SWAT sniper with a bead on him in the MRAP's turret.

"Holy shit!" he exclaims, suddenly wanting to change his underwear. "Okay, okay!" he shouts, laying down his rifle and ambling toward the vehicles, his hands clasped tightly behind his head.

FBI SWAT officers take the man into custody while Allison grabs her radio. "We have to assume he notified the compound," she tells the FBI commander. "The drone feed shows most of his friends assembling in the tent, but some are running into the woods. So we have to assume they're taking up defensive positions. This isn't going to go well."

Allison, Jack, and Jacob approach the wide-eyed man, who is now shaking with apprehension. "Am I under arrest?" he asks nervously.

"Not yet," replies Jacob. "I'm FBI Special Agent Assante. "Did you notify the compound of our arrival?"

The man looks worried. "Hey, I'm... I'm just a car salesman with a wife and two kids," he declares, tumbling over his words in his haste to comply. "I, I don't need any of this shit! Yeah, I called them when I saw you through the trees!"

Jacob frowns. "Where's your radio?" he asks.

"There's a handheld in my truck."

Jacob finds the radio in the parked pickup and keys the microphone. "This is FBI Special Agent Assante," he intones. "We blocked your only exit, and we're watching your camp from above. So I suggest you tell your people to walk out of there slowly and quietly without their weapons and with their hands in the air. If they don't, we can get pretty aggressive. You have three minutes before we come in to get you. Do you copy?"

Jacob waits for a reply, which takes forever. Then, he finally hears a loud "10-4!" and returns to the group. "I gave them three minutes to surrender. Now, we wait."

"I'll watch the drone feed and let you know what they're doing," says Allison, entering her MRAP.

A minute later, she calls out, "Looks like most of them are starting to leave! A large group is walking toward us, but about five are ready for a fight. Many of them are unarmed, but not all!"

Then Allison spots a man aiming at the drone and opens her mouth to speak, but her screen goes black too fast to call out a warning. "SHIT!" she shouts, jumping out of the vehicle. "They shot the fucking drone!"

Ahead, the pretend soldiers make their way toward the assault team. Most are men, but a few are women, and all are dressed in camo gear. When they're close enough, SWAT team members take them to the back of the vehicles, where they're searched and restrained with zip cuffs.

The three minutes have now passed, so Jacob activates the guard's radio. "Time's up!" he informs whoever's listening. "Unless you're willing to risk your lives for Serge Kaspin, I suggest the rest of you come out now and lay down your weapons!"

"Fuck You!" Jacob hears in reply.

"Wow," he mumbles, shaking his head sadly. Then he gives directions to Jack and Allison. "They're hunkering down, so we'll use the MRAPs in a frontal assault. Allison, circle your team around the camp on the left. Mine will go to the right. We'll drive the MRAPs in when everyone's in place."

"What about them?" asks Jack, nodding at those who already surrendered.

Jacob looks over at the group. "I'll keep two men behind to watch them," he states confidently.

When the two squads enter the wooded area, Sergeant Burley grabs an armored vest. "I'm going with them," he declares.

"Wait," says Jack, slipping on another vest.

Jack looks past the parked pickup. "When the MRAPs go in, I'm gonna follow behind them on foot. I'm not sitting this one out, either. You wanna come with me, Burley?"

"Yeah," answers John as Jacob and Allison grab vests for

themselves.

"All right, we'll come with you, too," says Jacob, unholstering his handgun.

Allison and Jacob listen to the chatter of the SWAT officers as they stage in the trees. When they hear, "We have them in sight!" Allison motions to the MRAP drivers. "Let's do this!" she orders, moving to the rear of the vehicles.

As the trucks creep forward, the four compadres follow behind, handguns drawn and ready.

Minutes later, the compound's obstacle course and tent become visible in a clearing, and an amplified voice booms out of the FBI vehicle. "This is the FBI! Your group is surrounded! Abandon your positions and surrender your weapons! This is your last warning!"

Instantly, one of the guardsmen hunkered down around the compound, pops up, and raises his AR rifle above his head. Holding the gun aloft, he walks toward the MRAPs and lays it on the ground. Then he drops to his knees with his hands on his head.

"Lay down and crawl closer to us," commands the amplified voice.

But the man doesn't move.

For a moment, Jacob wonders, *What the fuck?* And then it occurs to him. "Don't send anyone out there!" he orders the agents in the truck. "The rest of them must be waiting to pick us off!"

Understanding the situation, the vehicle in front of them lurches forward to separate the man from the wooded area. But as soon as it does, the guardsman's unseen comrades open fire, and answering gunshots erupt from the neighboring SWAT team.

While the firefight lasts, birds fly from the trees, and small mammals scatter from the area.

Then, all is quiet, and Jack sneaks out from behind the truck. "I love the smell of gunpowder in the morning," he declares cynically, swinging his gun around in a wide arc lest anyone wants to take a potshot at him.

From their positions in the woods, the SWAT teams proceed with caution to their assigned targets. "Heading in," informs the leader.

Without warning, a large explosion erupts from the tent in the nearby clearing, sending out a concussive wave that knocks everyone to the ground, including Jacob and Allison, who were walking back to the man who refused to move.

"Fuck!" screams Jack, dropping to his knees and covering his ears. The loud blast temporarily deafens him and everyone else who isn't wearing ear protection.

When the officers regain their composure, some tend to their wounded and dead while others search the area for more victims.

Looking around, Jack spots Jacob scrambling to his feet, but lying near him, Allison isn't moving. "Allison's down!" he mouths to John, who is rubbing his ears in pain.

Giancarlo is in bad shape. She's unconscious, and a one-foot section of metal tent pole is protruding from an area not covered by her armored vest.

"Holy crap," breathes Jack, terrified for his friend.

A SWAT officer kneeling next to her says, "I got a pulse, but it's weak."

When EMTs arrive, they take control of the situation, pushing everyone away from the injured so they can get to work.

"What's the damage?" asks Jacob, spotting the FBI team leader coming out of the woods.

"None of the Patriot Guard members who fired on us survived," he says. "I haven't heard about the ones in the tent yet."

Enraged by the unnecessary carnage and Allison's injury, Jack grabs the shirt of the man who surrendered and throws him against the side of one of the trucks. "If my friend doesn't make it, I'm coming after *you!*" he growls, angry veins popping from his neck.

But Jack's threat doesn't faze the guardsman. "Casualty of war," he shrugs, still in Jack's clutches. "You can't touch me, lawman."

Incensed, Jack jumps on the man and repeatedly pummels him until Jacob and John pry him off.

Jack seems out of control. The last few weeks' events have finally erupted in his mind, and the men have trouble keeping him from attacking the hapless man again.

Seeing them struggling to hold Jack at bay, two SWAT officers help them, and together, they all drag Jack from the downed man.

But Jack isn't ready to stop yet. "FUCK YOU!" he screams, clawing at the officers to return to the man, who's now out cold.

Later that day, Allison is wheeled into surgery, and John and Jack are directed to the nearest surgical waiting room.

They're the only ones there, so they plunk themselves down in the chairs nearest to the door.

"I can't leave here until she's out," declares Jack, nervously twisting his fingers into a knot.

"Me, neither," states John, biting down a ragged nail that broke during the scuffles at the park.

After exhausting all the chit chat they cared to share, Captain Conrad and another officer pop in, relieving their boredom. "What have you heard so far?" their boss asks, noting the tension in his subordinates' faces.

Jack purses his lips. "She's still in surgery. They told us she lost a lot of blood and has at least one broken rib and a punctured lung."

Conrad sighs and introduces his colleague. "This is JTTF Captain Adderley. Before we left to come here, he contacted Giancarlo's husband, and he's on the way with their kids."

Conrad takes a seat and looks hard at Jack. "I heard about your outburst, Stenhouse, and it's just what I feared would happen if you didn't take time off."

"I lost my temper. No big deal."

Conrad frowns at his troublesome employee. "It *is* a big deal, Jack. So I'm ordering you to take a break, and I scheduled counseling for you starting next week. This is mandatory, Stenhouse. Neither Rawlings nor the commissioner wants you around until you're in better shape."

Jack doesn't look pleased, but the captain knows he got a good deal. "They're being extremely generous in only requiring counseling. It could have been much, much worse."

"Aww, did the poor baby have his feelings hurt?" asks Jack, as impertinent as ever. "Did he file a complaint?"

"You know he did, Stenhouse. What you did to him was way out of bounds, and I'm surprised the higher-ups are settling for such a light punishment, if you can even call it that. So there's no question… You have to get away from here. Take the weekend to play with your son and cool off. Maybe you'll be yourself again when you come back. Capeesh?"

Jack frowns and starts to refuse, but Conrad stops him. "No buts, Lieutenant! The FBI has already arranged a round-trip plane ticket for you to Baltimore! The flight leaves tonight, and a driver will take you to the safe house. You'll fly back to the city Monday morning, and you'll meet with the counselor that week. The tickets are at Southwest check-in. A uniformed is waiting outside to take you home to pack."

Jack draws in a breath, then exhales slowly. There's no sense protesting; everything's been arranged. However, he does have a couple of requests. "All right, I'll go. But I want to wait until I find out about Allison. And when I come back, I want to speak to that mercenary I introduced to my fist."

"I don't know about tha—"

"Are you here for Allison Giancarlo?" interrupts a surgeon, still dressed in surgical scrubs.

Jack jumps to his feet. "Yes!" he says, answering for all of them. "How is she?"

The surgeon removes his surgical cap wearily. "Are you family?"

"No," responds Captain Adderley. "They're on the way."

"Well, I can't say much if you're not family. All I can tell you is that Officer Giancarlo is in ICU recovery."

That response doesn't satisfy Jack. "Is she okay?" he asks again, doggedly searching for more details.

The surgeon sighs. "If that pole had been a centimeter deeper, it would have punctured her heart."

"Shit!" responds Jack and the others, shuddering with what could have been. "Can we see her?"

"No, only family in the ICU." His obligatory report completed, the surgeon turns around and heads for the nursing station.

"Crap," mutters Jack. "That woman better pull through."

"You got that right," agrees Adderley. "She's one of the good ones."

Conrad catches Jack's eye. "So, you got your update. Now you gotta head out."

"But he didn't tell us anything," Jack protests, trying for more time.

Conrad is adamant. "That's all you're gonna get, Lieutenant. We'll have to wait for Vincent and the kids to get here."

"Okay, I'll go. But one of you better call me when you get more info, or all of you will be on my shit list. Capeesh?" he stares at Conrad.

By 7:30 that night, Jack is finally in Ellicott City, Maryland, courtesy of the FBI's D.C. branch.

"How much longer?" he asks his driver.

"The safe house is a couple of blocks away."

"Okay," says Jack, clicking a button on his ringing cell phone.

"You have an update?" he asks, hopeful for good news about Allison.

"Yeah," John tells him. "Vinnie says they had to re-inflate her lung and repair other damage, and all that went well. But man, there's some bad news."

"Crap. What happened?"

"She suffered a stroke during surgery. The doc says she should recover from her injuries, but there's some weakness on her right side. Her face is drooping a little, and her speech is slurred. They're optimistic that she'll recover after some physical therapy. But she's gonna be out of service for a long time."

"Ahh, that bites," says Jack sadly. "But I know she'll bounce back. She's too strong to stay down for long. Anything else?"

"No, I'm goin' home. Been a long day."

"Right. Thanks for the call, pal."

"You're welcome, buddy. Hug Mark for me."

When Jack hangs up, the driver turns into a wide driveway in front of a two-story house and lets Jack out with his overnight bag.

The sedan backs out onto the street while Jack's mother-in-law strides up to him, holding Mark in her arms.

Jack smiles. *There's my family*, he thinks happily, releasing pent-up stress with a deep, cleansing breath.

In North Carolina, things aren't going well. Colonel Powell has just delivered his report about the FBI raid at the park, and Serge is seething with anger.

"Fuck, fuck, FUCK!" he screams, throwing his phone over the deck railing, right into the Tuckasegee River. "How the hell did NYPD and the fucking FBI bust up our group? Get the remaining crew together in Charlotte, and bring them out here, STAT! Then get hold of Josie and tell her to bring some friends. We need more recruits, dammit!"

"Will do, boss," says the colonel. "But remember the good news... We got Giancarlo. And word has it that she suffered a stroke."

Serge cocks his head at his number two. "Why the hell didn't you tell me that in the first place, Powell? That means I can check another one off my list!"

Hector hears the familiar nightly music seeping through the ceiling and knows that it's now or never. He's been keeping track of his jailers' daily routines and knows the music means they've begun their evening revelry. So it's time to put his plan into action.

To start, he pulls out a long, thin wire from the seam of his shirt cuff. Then he strides to the door, shouting, "Hey! Where's my dinner?" and bangs on it loudly to catch the attention of the lone guard. "Get me some of that party food from upstairs!" he yells.

"Shut the fuck up!" replies the guard, tucking his weapon into his waistband. "You'll get what I give you!"

The man disappears, and when he returns, he's carrying a tray of the same field rations Hector's been eating since he got there.

"Step back!" he orders, inserting his key into the lock.

Hector retreats and tenses his body. His plan is to overtake the jailer the moment he steps into the cell.

"Here's your fuckin' dinn—" the lookout begins, until Hector pounces, and the metal tray flies out of his hands, crashing against the concrete wall. "What the fuc—?" is all the guy can get out before Hector wraps the wire tight against his throat.

Though the man struggles mightily, Hector keeps the line taut until the man's hands fall limp at his side. When the guard slips into death, Hector releases his grip, and the body falls to the floor.

"Thanks for not tidying up around here," he says, re-inserting the wire into his shirt and taking the man's keys and 9mm handgun.

Outside the room, Hector approaches the exterior door. Fumbling with the keys, he finds the right one and inserts it into the lock, hoping no one suddenly appears from upstairs.

The door creaks open onto a cool Smoky Mountain night, but Hector doesn't linger. Shutting the door with a soft click, he lets his eyes adjust to the darkness, then ducks below the windows and runs down the dirt road toward freedom.

Early the following morning, Kaspin and Colonel Powell stand over the dead guard. They were alerted to the situation when someone noticed that no one had claimed the prisoner's breakfast.

"Oh, how I hate those fucking Seals!" spits Kaspin, angered by the loss of his primary negotiating asset. "Have the men get rid of this body!"

"We'll have to work fast," says Powell. "Gomez must be far gone by now. Hell, he may even have caught a ride into town, so the cops could already be on the way!"

"Right. That's a real possibility, so let's get outta here. We're gonna hafta leave this place. Pack up any incriminating evidence."

"What about Charlotte?" asks the colonel.

"Yeah, we're gonna hafta close Charlotte as well. Gomez may have overheard something. Dammit all to hell!" bellows Serge, stomping out of the cramped room. "That fuckin' Seal is screwing up my plans! I have a backup, but I'm pissed that he's making me use it!"

"You have an alternate location?"

"Yeah, I have friends in Cherokee, so we'll go there. Dammit! It's gonna take me a few days to iron out this mess!"

Late Saturday morning, Sharon has to go shopping. "I need a few things, so I'm going to the Columbia Mall," she tells Jack. "You need anything while I'm out?"

"Nah, I'm good," he replies. "Have a good time at the mall."

Jack isn't concerned that his mother-in-law is leaving the safe house because he knows her FBI shadow will keep an eye on her.

"I'll take care of this guy," he says, tickling Mark's belly to make him laugh.

Sharon watches for a moment, smiling at the interaction. Then she grabs her purse and heads out the door.

In the living room, Mark is scooting around the tiled floor. "Look at you!" laughs Jack, charmed by how fast the boy can get around on his hands and knees.

Jack sees Didi in his young son's eyes and is grateful for the reminder that his wife will always be with them somehow.

"I should record this," he says, pointing his cell phone at Mark just as the boy grabs a table and raises himself on wobbly legs.

"Hey, you gonna try to walk, buddy?" he asks, still recording.

"Mama," the boy mumbles, taking hesitant steps toward his father. Jack records his son's first steps until Mark grabs onto his legs.

"You did it!" he says, happily hugging his son. "I'm so glad I got that on tape! But ya know, we're gonna hafta work on your vocabulary, buddy. I'm dada," he says, lifting his son high above his head.

That's when the unmistakable odor of a full diaper makes Jack wrinkle his nose. "Oof! That's ripe!" Jack holds the boy out at arm's length. "I thought I was getting away from shit when I left New York!"

Holding his son gingerly, Jack heads for the changing table upstairs, beaming with pride at his son's accomplishment. "I can't wait to show everyone your first steps!"

Then it occurs to him that Sharon wasn't there to see it. "Oooo, your grandma's gonna be so upset when she gets home!"

When Monday morning rolls around, Jack steels himself not to cry, and he doesn't. At least not in front of his family.

"I don't like leaving home either," says his driver, hearing

Jack sniffling in the back seat. "Especially when it's gonna be a long assignment."

"Yeah, it's tough," he replies, wiping his nose on a sleeve.

After Jack's flight lands, he's surprised to see his boss at La Guardia's baggage claim area.

"What are you doing here?" he asks, worry for his injured friend knitting his brows together in a frown. "Is it Ally?"

Captain Conrad responds cryptically, "I'll tell you on the way."

Jack dislikes evasiveness. So to prevent himself from insisting on an answer, he makes stilted chitchat while searching for his luggage.

"Here it is," he says, relieved that it was one of the first bags out. Grabbing the duffel bag, he asks, "Where's your car?"

"I have the sedan," says Conrad, pointing to a chauffeured vehicle sitting at the curb. "Put your bag in the front and sit in the back with me."

On the way out of the terminal, Conrad turns toward Stenhouse. "First of all," he says, "the mercenary you beat up in the park isn't pressing charges, so you're off the hook — again. I don't know how you do it."

Jack shrugs. "What about Allison?"

Conrad turns his head to the window. "She's going to need extensive physical therapy. One side is weak, and she may walk with a limp for the rest of her life. So, she decided something, and you're not going to like it."

"What is it?"

"She decided to take early retirement."

"Crap! It's that bad?" asks Jack, raising his brows in

surprise.

"It is for her. She says she's had enough and wants some peace and quiet."

Jack mumbles in a low voice, "I know the feeling."

"Huh? I didn't catch that," says Conrad. "What did you say?"

"Uh, it's nothing," answers Jack, looking out the window.

Conrad gazes at his lieutenant for a long time. He suspects something's up but decides to pursue it later. Instead, he says, "Okay. Well, that's it for the bad news. Now, for the good news. Hector escaped! He made it to Sylva, North Carolina, and contacted us through the local police department. The FBI picked him up there and brought him back."

"Ha, that's my guy!" responds Jack, slapping a thigh in relief. "I knew he'd get out of there!"

"Well, it was touch and go for a while, but he made it out. Now, the FBI is monitoring Kaspin's place, and they're gonna raid it in forty-eight hours — after they get enough personnel and equipment there from Charlotte. Everything has to be flown into a small regional airport in Asheville, about forty miles from Kaspin's location. Hey, you like the Smoky Mountains?"

"Yeah, I guess so. Why?"

"I know you just got back, but I'm sending you up there tomorrow. Be at the First bright and early in the morning. You have a ticket on Delta."

CHAPTER TWELVE

At seven the next morning, Jack finds a large envelope on his desk at the First. "What's this?" he asks John.

"A courier left it for you. Did you order porn while you were away?"

"Yeah, right," huffs Jack, turning the envelope over to check the postmark. "It's from North Carolina. Isn't that where Hector was?"

"Yeah."

Jack rips the envelope open and turns it upside down to shake out the contents. "What the hell?" he remarks when an unmarked DVD slides into his hand.

"You sure it's not porn?" asks John with an impish smile.

Jack clicks his tongue in annoyance. "Shut up, Burley. Let's see what this is. Put it in your laptop, will ya?"

Minutes later, the pair's eyes widen as Serge Kaspin says good morning and tells them Hector is his "house guest." When the camera pans to the left, the weary, disheveled-looking detective peers sleepily into the lens.

The camera swings back to Kaspin, smiling wryly. "I hope you've been enjoying my calling cards. We're at war, you know. Nothing has changed; the government is still corrupt and bent on wrecking our country. So be prepared for a lot more collateral damage. I'm taking revenge on everyone preventing us from carrying out our mission, and I won't stop until my retribution is complete. Make no mistake, Lieutenant, this isn't a warning; I'm simply stating a fact. I hope to meet you on the battlefield soon, Stenhouse!" Kaspin gives a little wave and then the picture fades, and the national anthem plays over a black screen.

"What the hell was that?" asks John.

"Get that fuckin' thing over to the FBI!" orders Jack, walking back to his desk to answer his ringing telephone.

Jack plops down in his chair and sighs before picking up the receiver. "Stenhouse!" he answers angrily.

"Whoa, you don't sound very happy," says a familiar voice. "Don't bother tracing this call, Stenhouse. I'm on a burner. I assume you've watched my video by now, so there's a few more things I thought of after I sent it." Jack mouths "Kaspin" to John as he listens. "Did you figure out yet that I'm the reason Giancarlo is so messed up? I heard she's retiring, and that tickles me to no end. So I'm crossing her off my list. But my former guest is still in my crosshairs. He chose to leave before I could complete my plans for him, so tell him to watch his six. Now, I figure it won't be long before you descend on this place, so you should know that I'm leaving here. But be sure to tell Burley he's next on the list, and let Cindy know she's not off the hook yet."

Kaspin pauses for a moment, giving Jack an opportunity to jump in. "You sonofabitch," he growls, "I'm gonna get—"

"Yeah, yeah, I know," Kaspin continues, unshaken by Stenhouse's tone. "You're gonna stop me, hurt me, blah, blah, blah. Does Burley know how much Sylvia is enjoying Brussels? You should tell him to visit her soon because I'm not sure she wants to come home. She seems to be having a really good time there without him. And by the way, I so enjoy watching Sharon and Mark! That boy is the spitting image of your wife, Stenhouse, and Sharon's doing a great job with him! See ya 'round, big guy!"

The line goes dead, and Jack slams the receiver down. "That was Serge!" he shouts wildly. "He won't be in Carolina, not where he was holding Gomez, anyway! He's leaving there, so who knows where he's going now! Fuckin' shit!" he says, pounding the desk. Then he looks at John and softens. "He said you were next, bro, and he knows Sylvia's in Brussels. He also threatened Gomez and Cindy Rodriguez, and he's been spying on Mark and my mother-in-law!"

John's mouth is open, and his face is purple with rage. "He's watching Sylvia?! What the hell am I gonna do now?"

"Don't worry; I'll tell Assante to put a team on her."

"What's an FBI team gonna do against that guy?"

"What do you need our men for?" asks Jacob, approaching from the rear with Hector at his side.

Jack explains wearily, "I got a DVD from Kaspin, and he also called me. I just got off the phone with him."

Hector is wary. "He called you?" he asks dubiously. "What the fuck did he want?"

"He said he was leaving his location and told me to let Burley and Cindy Rodriguez know they're next. The bastard's laser-focused on taking revenge on all of us, and he won't stop till each of us is either dead or out of the picture!"

Jack points at Hector. "And he's not happy about your escape!" he adds, eliciting a smile from the detective. "He also knows where Sylvia is, and has eyes on my family!"

Hector's smile fades fast. "Fuck!" he shouts crossly. "We thought we got them to safe places!"

"Fuckin' guy's everywhere!" yells Jack.

Jacob raises a finger to get their attention. "Several guys have been assigned to this case at our field office in Charlotte," he tells them. "One of the Patriot Guard still in custody says they occasionally use a house north of the city, near Mooresville. But from what Jack just said, it's probably abandoned by now, along with that cabin by the river Kaspin seems to like so much. In any case, we'll still send forensic teams to both locations."

Jack looks at Assante. "Remember Sam Anderson?

Where is he now? We should talk to him again."

Jacob is puzzled by the name for a second, but then a lightbulb goes on in his head. "Oh, yeah, the guy who wanted to nuke Manhattan for Kaspin. His execution's on appeal, so he's still in solitary at Leavenworth. Damn, Jack. How did you remember his name? That case was closed a year ago."

Jack cricks his neck. "He was in charge of the Patriot Guard and close to Kaspin, so there may be information he hasn't shared with us yet. Can we offer him a prize or something?"

Hector and Jacob are amazed that Jack would consider rewarding the bomb-loving prick for details he should have revealed by now, but John doesn't care. On the contrary, he's eager for anything that could help. "Look," he says. "I need to make sure my wife's safe from anyone who could hurt her, so I don't care what we have to do to get that done."

"You're right," says Jacob, knowing how worried Burley must be. "We'll tighten up our involvement with Interpol and the CIA, and I'll arrange to get you over to Brussels as soon as possible." Jacob turns to Conrad, who has joined the group. "Is that okay with you, Captain?"

"Absolutely. We need to take care of our own."

"Sounds like a plan," says Jack, dangling his car keys on a finger. "I'm gonna visit Ally now, and after that, you and I need to go to Leavenworth," he says, eyeing Jacob. Then, shifting his gaze to Hector, he says, "While I'm gone, call the Rodríguezes, and tell them what Serge said about Cindy. Then get ahold of Sergeant Jorge Octavio at the Sunrise, Florida police department. That's where Cindy and Ken live, so we need to give the boys down there a heads up."

Jack's footsteps blend into the hustle and bustle of the hospital as he walks toward Allison Giancarlo's room with a bouquet straining to stay upright in a gaily ribboned vase.

At the door, he inhales deeply and steels himself for the visit. "Hey, lady!" he says, stepping briskly into the room. "Where's your family today?"

Allison gives Jack a half-smile. Her face is lopsided, and her mouth twists slightly.

Jack puts the vase on the table next to Allison's bed, and turns it so she can see the roses, carnations, and baby's breath in the best light.

"So when are you coming back to work?" he asks, trying not to react to his friend's changed appearance. Jack knows what Allison decided but asks nonetheless, hoping she changed her mind.

Allison shakes her head and answers as best she can. "I'm...done... Doctors say...I'll have...a...permanent limp. I need to...be with family...now. Thanks for...the flowers."

Jack nods sadly. "I understand. But promise me you'll keep the option open in case you prove all the experts wrong. You're a fighter, Ally."

Allison grins unevenly. "How is...Mark?"

"I went up there for the weekend. He took his first step, and I was the only one who saw it! Thank God I was recording him at the time! Here, let me show you!"

The proud father takes out his phone and starts the video.

"Aww, they're...so cute...at that...age," grins Allison. Then she says, "Vinnie and...the kids...went for...lunch. They should be...back...soon."

"Oh. Well, I can't stay; Assante and I are going to Leavenworth to speak with Sam Anderson. We're gonna get Kaspin, Ally, and he's gonna pay for all this shit!"

Jack leans over to kiss Allison's forehead and as he does, Allison responds, "No prisoners...Jack."

"You got it, babe," he winks and heads for the door.

When he's out of sight, Allison mumbles, "Kaspin...is...toast."

That night, CIA operative Frank Sansone is awakened by his cell phone in a small hotel room in Brussels, Belgium.

"Yeah?" he answers sleepily.

"Is this Frank Sansone?"

Frank bolts upright, instantly alert at an unfamiliar voice knowing his name. "Who wants to know?" he demands.

"My name is FBI Special Agent Jacob Assante. I'm Maria Assante's brother. I believe you knew her. The FBI needs your assistance, Frank."

The next day, Cindy and Ken Rodriguez are at home in a gated community near Sawgrass Mills, a large shopping complex with restaurants, high-rise condos, and the home stadium of South Florida's professional hockey team. They haven't worked much since returning from the New York fashion show, and the bills are beginning to pile up. Ken's work in the fashion industry has afforded them this modern home. However, without his income, it's getting harder to pay for it.

"You exercising that arm?" calls Cindy from the kitchen.

"Yeah," he answers, grimacing as he raises and lowers his wounded appendage. "I think it's getting better!"

Cindy is about to respond when car doors slam in the driveway.

"You expecting someone?" calls Ken.

"No, I'll see who it is." Cindy pushes aside the curtains at their front window and gasps. "It's two police cruisers and an unmarked sedan!"

Outside, City of Sunrise Sergeant Jorge Octavio is heading to the front door with his badge, 9mm, and small radio visibly fixed to his belt. The officer isn't wearing his customary sport coat today, just a white polo shirt bearing the city of Sunrise logo over black pants. It's too damn hot for a jacket, so he left it in the car.

Cindy opens the double mahogany doors before Octavio can knock. "Can I help you?" she asks, surprising the sergeant.

"Yes," he responds, clearing his throat from the lingering effects of a mild cold. "I'm Sergeant Octavio. New York police and the FBI contacted us regarding your husband's incident in Manhattan. Is he here? May I come in to speak with you both?"

"Um, yes, okay," says Ken, joining Cindy. "Sure, come on in."

When Octavio enters, Cindy asks if he wants coffee. "Oh. Yes, I'll have a cup," he says. "Black, please."

Ken directs the officer to a breakfast nook off the kitchen. "What's this about?" he asks, bidding Octavio to take a seat as Cindy brings a cup of steaming coffee and a plate of guava bread to the table and sits down next to Ken.

Blunt as a shotgun blast, the straight-talking officer gets right to the point. "Lieutenant Jack Stenhouse from New York wants me to tell you that Serge Kaspin hasn't given up on either of you. He said Mr. Kaspin called him and warned that you're both in his sights."

Cindy gasps and reaches for Ken's uninjured hand.

"We're committed to protecting our citizens," continues Octavio, "so we'll be setting up surveillance units to monitor your house 24/7 as long as the threat lasts. We also notified Fort Lauderdale police to watch your business on Las Olas Boulevard. In addition, the FBI will be contacting you to lend their assistance as well. You must be very important people."

"I should have killed that fucker when I had the chance!"

grouses Cindy angrily.

The sergeant flashes her a look. "I'm gonna pretend I didn't hear that," he says. Then he fishes in his pocket for business cards. "Please call if you see anything suspicious or out of the ordinary. Unmarked vehicles will be following you as you go about your daily lives, so don't be alarmed about that."

"How are we gonna know whether it's the police or someone else?" asks Ken.

"We'll call you every morning with the make and model of each day's car. Let us know immediately if you see anyone else around."

"Um, okay," says Ken.

"Are there any other questions?"

Ken looks at Cindy. "Well… No, I don't think so," he says. "Thanks for stopping by."

"All right. That's it for now," says the sergeant, rising to leave.

Cindy stands along with him. "I'll walk you to the door," she says.

As the sergeant steps out of the door, Cindy follows, closing the door softly behind her. "Have you heard about the Patriot Guard?" she asks quietly.

"Yes," says Octavio. "They're a paramilitary group desperate to cause chaos in the country so their issues are heard."

"That's right. They're ex-mercenaries armed with military-grade weapons. They've already attacked a police precinct in New York and would have no qualms attacking you, either."

"Yes, thanks for your concern. The FBI and Homeland Security already warned us about them. Please be careful, Mrs. Rodriguez. Those guys have a special interest in you so you're not safe as long as they're running around. We'll do our best to protect you, but you must be constantly on alert."

After spending seven-and-a-half-hours in a cramped airline seat, John Burley is tired but eager to see his wife, which is making the wait for his luggage at Brussels Airport baggage claim more intolerable than usual. He and the other one-hundred-some passengers are sullen and silent, many of them staring at the carousel, willing it to move.

When it looks like he'll be there a while, John starts people-watching to keep himself from going crazy. Immediately, he notices a family with two young children running circles around their weary parents. *I hope those kids slept on the plane*, he thinks, feeling sorry for the traveling couple.

Shifting his gaze away from the children's antics, he soon spots a man in the crowd who seems to be searching for someone. The guy is noticeable among the generally conservatively dressed passengers. He's wearing a Hawaiian flowered shirt, worn jeans, Tony Lamas boots, and a NY Yankees baseball cap.

Wow, that guy looks completely out-of-place in his American getup, he thinks. Then, his luggage appears on the rotating belt, and he puts that thought out of his mind.

While John yanks his suitcase off the carousel, the man in the NY Yankees cap walks up to him. "Can I help with that?" he asks.

John steadies his bag on the floor and studies the stranger. For a moment, he seems confused. Then, his eyes widen in recognition. "Frank Sansone? Holy cow! What the hell are you doin' here, man? I thought you retired a while ago! How the hell are ya?"

"Doin' well, buddy, doin' well. Yeah, I tried to retire, but they wouldn't let me. So now, I'm assigned here."

"You're livin' in Brussels? Must be great!"

"Ah, it's not bad. I'm okay as long as I can wear my American threads. They're kinda stuffy here."

"Well, it's good to see ya, man."

"Yeah, you, too. Let's go. I have a car outside."

On the way to the terminal door, Sansone brings John up to date. "That Kaspin character stirred up some shit, didn't he? We contacted your wife and put you both up in a house in Zemst, a small town about seventeen kilometers north of here. I'll be staying there with you, and the local authorities and the FBI will keep watch over us as well. Ah, here we are," he says when a BMW comes into view.

John tosses his luggage into the back, then slides into the passenger seat. "Thanks for picking me up," he says.

"No prob, buddy. It's a pleasure to talk American English!" Frank puts his key into the ignition, then stops and turns to John. "I just hafta ask, did someone force your wife to marry you?"

"What?" asks John, rattled by the off-the-wall question. "What the fuck—"

"Don't get all defensive!" says Frank, laughing at John's expression. "You're a lucky man! You married up, my boy! I give your lady a solid ten!"

When Jack and Jacob arrive in Kansas City, they check into the Fairfield Inn down the road from the famous penitentiary, then take advantage of the hotel's complimentary breakfast buffet.

The seating area is quiet, as most of the hotel's guests have already eaten and left for the day. Many of them are relatives of military personnel at Fort Leavenworth Army Base, or they're visiting inmates at the prison.

Jacob grabs the last fruit cup and gets a cup of coffee. Then he joins Jack, who's wolfing down a couple of waffles.

"We got half an hour before they'll allow us to see Anderson," he states, as he places his breakfast on the table. "His appeal was denied last night, so he may be more anxious to talk today. It'll help if we can get him a Get out of Death Card."

Jack raises a brow. "You're not serious, are you? That guy wanted to take out most of Manhattan!"

"I know, but if we need leverage, that might be just the thing to loosen his tongue."

"Shit. I thought I knew you, FBI man, but then you say something that throws me for a loop."

Jacob rolls his eyes, then digs into his fruit cup, unconcerned by Jack's comment.

Across the table, Jack watches his friend eat, mystified by Jacob's willingness to go easy on Anderson. *Should I confront him about this or let it go?* he asks himself, going over the pros and cons.

Ultimately, he decides not to say anything that could jeopardize their relationship. Instead, he changes the subject. "You got anything new on Kaspin's whereabouts?"

"No. They didn't find anything at his house; he must have swept it clean before he left. But my gut tells me he's still somewhere in North Carolina. I don't think he'll go far from there. He seems to like the area for some reason."

The men finish eating in silence, each one deep in thought. Then Jacob downs the last of his coffee and gathers up his trash.

"Come on, let's get this over with," he tells Jack. "By the time we get through the prison security hoopla, they'll have Anderson waiting for us."

CHAPTER THIRTEEN

Former Marine Colonel Sam Anderson doesn't get many visitors, so he's surprised when correctional officers move him into one of the meeting rooms.

"They'll be here soon," says the guard, snapping Anderson's shackles shut at the ankles and placing his hands in handcuffs.

Anderson jokes, "You gonna heat up some coffee for my guests?"

The unsmiling man ignores the question and leaves, only to be replaced by another who takes up a watchful position by the door.

"Sheesh. No sense of humor around here," mumbles the prisoner, wriggling his feet to test the strength of the restraints.

Turning around as far as he can, he asks, "How long before they get here…" Then his eyes shift to the door, opening to admit Jack and Jacob. "Well, well, well," he says wryly. "Speak of the devils, and you arrive just like that!"

No one comments except the sentinel, who says, "You got fifteen minutes." Then he exits the room, closing the door behind him.

Jack and Jacob sit opposite Anderson at a metal table under a camera staring down at them from the ceiling.

"Those khakis compliment your complexion," comments Jack, eyeing the universal federal inmate uniform of matching pants and shirt.

"It'll do," shrugs Anderson. "I asked the guards to

prepare coffee for you, but I guess they forgot."

Jacob leads off the questioning. "Do you know why we're here, Anderson?"

"I have no fuckin' idea, G-man. Did you come to say goodbye?"

"Maybe. But before we do, I'm gonna give you one last chance to avoid the firing squad."

Anderson smirks. "They don't use firing squads anymore, G-man. Don't you know that?"

"Funny," responds Jacob with a roll of his eyes. "It was an expression, and I don't care how they execute you when the time comes. We're here to ask about Serge Kaspin."

Sam leans back in his chair and stares at the ceiling as a mocking snicker escapes from his lips. "Don't you guys get tired of asking the same questions? I already said all I'm gonna say. What makes you think I'll tell you clowns anything new?"

"They denied your appeal yesterday, and your execution is set for two weeks from today. So maybe we can help you avoid that stainless-steel ride."

Anderson grins. "I'm impressed. Where'd you pick up the prison slang?"

Jacob doesn't answer, so Anderson shakes his head and smirks. "We're all gonna die, G-man, but unlike most, I know when it's gonna happen. You two could get hit by a garbage truck heading out of here today, and it'd be a total surprise. Listen, I got no incentive to tell you squat. Life in this hellhole is worse than dying, so I'm happy to be rid of it."

Jacob looks thoughtful. Cautiously, he asks, "If we can reduce your sentence, would that loosen up your tongue?"

Jack looks at Jacob with wide-eyed wonder. "You're not gonna do it, are you? You wanna let this scumbag off with a reduced sentence?!"

The FBI agent quickly turns to Jack with a 'shut your

trap' look that silences him, and Sam notices. "Fuck this shit!" he shouts. "I don't believe a word you said! Guard! Get me the fuck out of here!"

Jacob shoots Jack another warning look, then holds out his hands to Sam. "Wait, c'mon, look. That was... Just hold on!" he urges, desperate to save the interview.

"Nothin' doin'!" shouts Anderson as two prison officials burst into the room. "You guys got the next two weeks to come up with an exceptionally compelling incentive for me to help you, or I'm gone for good! Ta-ta, fuckers!" he yells while the officials disengage his shackles and lead him out.

Jack stares at Assante. "You can reduce his sentence?!"

"I'm gonna put in a genuine effort. But you may have screwed us, Stenhouse!"

Early morning is a pleasant time to be up and about in the Smokies. It's usually quiet and still, except for the soothing sounds of woodland critters waking from their nighttime slumbers.

Serge Kaspin enjoys this time of day. He does his best thinking with only a cup of coffee and the rustling leaves to keep him company. However, today, he's conferring with Colonel Powel about their next steps.

Serge has settled into his new digs at the end of a winding dirt driveway nestled in a forest, and he asked Powell to move in with him. Things are moving quickly, and they have a lot to discuss. The house they're in now is a modest 3/2 ranch with a two-car garage and a large metal building resembling a Quonset hut behind the house. This house is one of several that Kaspin owns in North Carolina, and he's used the hut before to hold meetings of the entire Patriot Guard.

Serge has already told Colonel Powell that Anderson lost

his appeal. "His execution is scheduled for two weeks from now, so that'll be a good time to stir up some shit. Now what have you heard about Burley and Rodriguez?"

"Only them?" retorts Powell. "Aren't you worried about Gomez, too?"

Serge chuckles, but it's a mirthless sound without humor. "I'm sure we haven't heard the last from him, or from Stenhouse and that jerk from the FBI, for that matter. We'll just have to pick them off whenever they rear their ugly heads. Let's concentrate on the other two for now."

"You're the boss," replies Powell. "So to answer your question, our assets in Belgium report that John Burley and his wife, Sylvia, are being closely watched by law enforcement — local police, CIA, and FBI. Right now, all we know is that they're somewhere south of Antwerp. Our intel should become more solid within a few days. As for Cindy, she's at her home in South Florida with her husband. They only have local police guarding them, so it may be easier to get to her."

"Hmm. Then I guess you need to go to South Florida. I want you to handle that yourself. Meanwhile, I need to find a different hideout. This one is good, but the Charlotte FBI office is too close, and all of our people know about this place. I'm thinking about something out of the ordinary, something unique. Somewhere no one they interrogate would know about."

"You have a place in mind?"

"Yes, I do, and I'll look into it while you're in Florida. Don't be surprised if we go back in time at my new place."

"'Go back in time?' What does that mean?"

"You'll see."

After visiting Sam Anderson, Jack returned to New York,

and he's now staring at the whiteboard at his desk, where he's keeping track of everything they know so far about their case. He placed a photo of Serge Kaspin at the top, and along the left are photos of all the others involved: Elena Guerra, Vicky Simpson, Didi, Russell Holden, Cindy and Ken Rodriguez, Allison Giancarlo, Hector Gomez, and John and Sylvia Burley. A photo of Sam Anderson is on the right, and under Kaspin are pictures of his home in Charlotte and his cabin on the Tuckasegee.

Jack zeroes in on the photo of his wife, and his eyes become watery. *Ah, babe, I miss you so much,* he thinks sadly, just as two people move to the front of the board. "What the fuck do you guys want?" he asks gruffly, trying to disguise his misery.

Gomez takes in a breath, sorry to be interrupting. "Uh, we just want to know what happened with Anderson."

"Oh," says Jack, hoping they didn't notice his sorrow. "The fucker said he's not sorry about his sentence. But then again, he may be interested in canceling his execution if we give him something worthwhile. We got two weeks to come up with a carrot he'll jump at."

"Figures," says Gomez. "Are the feds in on this reprieve?"

"Assante's gonna try to work it out, so I guess we'll be going back to Kansas soon."

Jack yawns and stretches his neck side-to-side. "Walk with me to the coffee station; I need some fuel."

Jack pours a cup of six-hour-old coffee into his mug and asks the others if they want some.

"No," they reply, knowing how it's probably going to taste.

"What's going on with Burley and the Rodriguezes?" asks Jack.

Hector says, "John and Sylvia are at a cottage south of Antwerp. Belgian police and an old friend of yours are guarding them there."

Jack arches a brow. "An old friend of mine?"

"Yeah. Frank Sansone."

Jack crinkles his nose and spits a mouthful of coffee into his cup. "Holy shit, this coffee is awful! But did you say, Sansone? I thought that guy retired!"

"It's Sansone, all right," confirms Hector. "He says hi."

"Well, all *right*!" says Jack, pleased at hearing the name of a familiar CIA operative he worked with a few years ago. "That means Burley's got one of the best at his side! Hey, how about Cindy and Ken?"

Gomez smiles. "You told me to contact Sergeant Octavio, right?"

"Right..." hesitates Jack, unsure of where Gomez is going.

"Well, this may sound like we're arranging family reunions, but they put Octavio in charge of protecting the Rodriguezes."

Jack's face lights up with pleasure. "He's a good guy, too, and he was a great help when I was still in Florida! Hey, does Assante know Cindy and Ken are back home?"

"Of course I do," hails a voice somewhere behind them. "The feds know everything!"

At that, the homicide crew bursts out laughing, along with Jacob, who claps Jack on the back when he draws near. "What's goin' on, boys?" he asks, looking around at their friendly faces.

"We were talking about protecting Ken and Cindy from Kaspin. Sunrise police are on it, but without your help, they're sure to be outgunned."

Jacob pulls a photograph out of a manila envelope and hands it to Jack. "This is Kaspin's second-in-command, Colonel George 'Patton' Powell. He's a former Marine and a complete badass. We already sent that photo to Octavio."

Jack studies the colonel's face. "Can I have this?" he asks.

"Be my guest," snickers Jacob. "I know how you old-timers like visual aids."

The others struggle to suppress laughter at Jack's expense while he ignores them and adds the photo to the whiteboard. "Any response to Anderson's request?"

"Nothing yet. The attorney general will let me know if he wants to make a deal. My gut says we'll be back in Kansas shortly."

Jack didn't drink any of his coffee, so he rolls his shoulders tiredly. "Well, while you're at it, you better get help out to Sunrise police, or we may have to deal with two more dead bodies."

"We're on it," responds Jacob, confident that he's covered everything. "On another note, we believe Kaspin's still in western North Carolina, so we put assets on the ground in the area. We're gonna smoke that bastard out of his hidey hole!"

"But will you find him before innocent people die?" asks Gomez, chiming into the conversation.

Striding up to the group, James Ruiz adds, "That includes your assets on the ground."

Jack nods in agreement. "And remember, the mob is out there looking for him, too."

The men stare at each other in silence, each of them considering the scale of the case before them. And to make matters worse, Captain Conrad adds to the tension.

"Gentlemen!" he shouts from his doorway. "We need to talk! Get in here, all of you!"

Ken and Cindy Rodriguez are on their way out of the house.

"We're going to be busy for the next ten days," says Ken, walking toward the couple's SUV in the driveway of their South Florida home.

"I know," replies Cindy, hitting the car's remote to open the doors. Ken is still in therapy, so she's doing all the driving while he recuperates.

"Man, it's hot," she says, turning the car on to crank the air conditioner up as soon as possible.

As she backs out of the driveway, the couple waves to the Sunrise police officer in the cruiser in front of their house, then Cindy points the car toward Artchop's office and gallery in downtown Fort Lauderdale.

"Is the unmarked following us?" asks Ken, trying to see if he can spot it in the passenger side mirror.

"Yeah, I see him," replies Cindy after a quick check in the rearview.

Ken has been ruminating on everything they need to do to prepare for their next event, hoping he's covered it all. "Miami Swim Week is big for us," he says. "I hope we can get it all done in time."

"We always do," says Cindy, turning onto Flamingo Road for the trip south.

As the SUV and the unmarked approach Sawgrass Mills, a technician working on a streetlight takes multiple pictures of them from a bucket twenty-five feet above the road. Then he makes a call.

Captain Conrad closes the door after Jacob, Jack, Hector, and James file in. They take seats at the conference table around a chair occupied by someone they don't know.

"Hi," says Hector, sitting down closest to the unfamiliar person. "We haven't met. I'm Hector Gomez."

The woman smiles and nods hello.

Conrad introduces the team, then the stranger. "Gentlemen, I'd like you to meet CIA Field Agent Samantha Waring. She was sent here to update us on what they're doing to protect John and his wife in Belgium."

Samantha, a brunette with long flowing hair, opens a folder and pulls out a typed sheet of paper. "Mr. and Mrs. Burley are currently at a house in a town called Zemst, a small farming community. We chose that location because it's rural and quiet, so any out-of-the-ordinary activity will stand out and be noticed by local law enforcement and our onsite agents. We're working with FBI agents based in Brussels and Antwerp, and the Belgian federal police are coordinating our activities with the locals. We're confident that any attempts to harm John or Sylvia will be dealt with swiftly and decisively."

Jack raises a hand like a schoolboy to get the agent's attention.

"Yes?" she responds with an amused grin.

"Look," he says gruffly. "Over the past few years, we've had several run-ins with Serge Kaspin and his crew, and we know how vindictive he can be. Do you really think he gives a damn about whether or not the people of Belgium know his guys are there or that you've put a lot of agents in the field? How can you be sure that what you're doing will keep our friends safe? From what we've seen of your operations, many of us have a less-than-stellar opinion of the competence of your agents. So as for me, the only saving grace in your plan is that Frank Sansone is on your team. And I assume you've armed John Burley... Right?"

For a moment, Jack's outburst silences Waring, but she recovers handily. "Lieutenant, we are aware of your past criticisms of government involvement in criminal cases, so I'm not surprised by your assessment of the situation. However, to answer your question, yes, Detective Burley is armed, and I agree that Frank Sansone is one of the best."

Jack opens his mouth to speak again, but Samantha holds up a hand. "If you don't mind, I'd like to conclude this meeting sometime today. But I'm willing to discuss your concerns further if you like. Say tonight, at dinner?"

Jack stares at the CIA agent, imagining what's underneath the tight pinstripe business jacket and knee-length skirt. While he does, the men at the table roll their eyes and shake their heads. Every one of them is awed by Jack's uncanny ability to garner attention from just about every woman he meets, without even trying.

Jack smothers a smile and looks to Conrad for his reaction. But Conrad is too busy gaping at Samantha's invitation. So Jack just goes for it.

"Well, there are a few issues I'm still unclear about. So, if you're buyin', I'm eatin'."

Samantha grins and places the typed sheet of paper back in the folder. Then, an uncomfortable silence follows, bringing Conrad back to the task at hand.

"All right," he states loudly, "that's enough of that. I have some things to share with all of you."

As eyes shift away from Jack and Samantha, he declares, "First, the FBI is sending additional agents to southern Florida because we feel the Rodriguezes will be the next target. They're easier to get at than John and Sylvia, and Ken has a big event coming up in Miami. It's the same type of fashion show as the one he was shot at in New York."

"Hey, boss," interjects Gomez. "I want to be part of the team down there. I think I should be there if Kaspin tries something."

Conrad shakes his head. "We're short of Homicide personnel up here, Detective. So I need you to partner with Ruiz while Jack and Assante work the Anderson angle."

"What? No!" shouts Gomez, jumping out of his chair. "I

want to look that fuck in the eye! I have a score to settle with that bastard!"

"I know how you feel, but—"

Gomez stops his boss mid-sentence. His face is flushed, and his fists are balled at his side, a highly unusual sight for the normally even-tempered man. "Try to stop me!" he shouts. "I'll hand in my badge if you leave me out of this!"

The people around the table stare in open-mouthed shock as Gomez storms to the door and jerks it open.

"Not the damn glass!" screams Conrad. He's seen this behavior before and cringes, fearing the worst for his oft-broken door. "Hold on, Gomez! Hold the fuck up!" cuts in Conrad angrily. "I have something else to tell you all, so cool your jets!"

Conrad sighs and rubs a hand over his tired eyes. Then, looking at Samantha, he states, "I'm not sure you heard yet, but the police in Cherokee, North Carolina, pulled a black Cadillac sedan out of a ditch with two Mafia goons inside, both shot in the head."

"Shit!" growls Jack. "Seems Lucchese's also on Kaspin's trail, and Kaspin got the upper hand on him again!"

Samantha refers back to her report. "We've already sent a forensic team to the house where Gomez was held, so we'll be in the area."

Gomez perks up with an idea, then fixes his eyes on Conrad. "Well, if I can't go to Florida, I'm goin' back to North Carolina! I know that house!"

"I already told you you're not goin' anywhere," reiterates Conrad sternly.

Hector is now incensed. Grabbing the door handle, he shouts, "Try and stop me!" and storms out, slamming the door shut.

The onlookers gasp as decorative glass shatters into tiny

pieces all over the floor.

"Holy shit!" murmur some of them, flabbergasted by Gomez's passion.

The room becomes deathly quiet. Those who know the captain fully expect him to explode at any moment, and they're unsure of what will come next.

All of them, except Jack, that is. "That was awesome!" he snorts, slapping a knee exuberantly. Jack knows how much the broken door angers the captain, and he's glad he's not the one who did it this time.

"Fuck this!" shouts Conrad, kicking the chair next to him so hard that it careens into his desk. Shouting through the closed door, he roars at his defiant employee, "That's comin' out of your pay, Gomez!! I'm not footing the bill for it this time!!"

Everyone remains quiet but Jack, so Conrad shoots him an angry look. "I swear I didn't teach him that," he declares, wiping away tears from laughing so hard.

Then Jack catches sight of Samantha, gaping at all of them.

"We're a pretty passionate bunch," he says, dismissing the strain in the room. "So, what time are you treating me for dinner tonight?"

Later that evening, the lobby buzzer rings while Jack is getting ready for his dinner with the CIA field agent. He's not expecting anyone, so he's puzzled about who could be downstairs.

"Who is this?" he asks curtly, annoyed by the interruption.

"Hi, it's Samantha. I got your address from the captain, and I thought I'd pick you up tonight. Hope you don't mind."

"Oh, um, okay. Can you wait a minute? No sense coming up here. I'll be down in a flash."

Soon after, Jack is sitting in Samantha's rental car. "How often are you in New York?" he asks conversationally.

"I don't come a lot, but when I do, I like to go to a little place that makes the best eggplant parm. I hope you like it."

Jack becomes alert when Samantha turns down a familiar street. "Hey, see that building over there?" he points. "That's Kaspin's work!"

Jack is calling Samantha's attention to a building undergoing extensive repairs, but Samantha isn't taking her eyes off the road. "Can't look now," she says. "I'm trying to find a parking spot. What did he do?"

"He blew up mob boss Vito Lucchese's restaurant while Vito and his son, Michael, were in it. Michael survived, but Vito didn't, and I can't say I'm sorry about that."

Samantha raises a brow and glances at Jack, then turns back to the road without comment.

She passes the next intersection, then stops when a car enters the road in front of her. "Oooo, lucky me," she says, easing her rental into the vacant space.

Samantha gathers her purse while Jack climbs out and walks around the car to open the driver's side door. "Thanks," she says, slinking out of the car and straightening her skirt. "The place we're going to isn't far."

At a small bistro, Samantha flips her hair back while Jack once again holds the door open. "I made a reservation, so we shouldn't have to wait."

Inside, Samantha gives her name to the hostess. "Ah, yes," says the woman, double-checking her reservation list. "Please follow me."

The hostess grabs a couple of menus and leads them to a small corner table, the only empty one in the restaurant.

Jack pulls Samantha's chair out, then sits down facing the door. "Must be a popular place," he comments over the chatter of multiple languages and clanking dishes.

Soon, a waiter brings a complimentary basket of garlic bread and an unexpected bottle of Asti Spumante.

"What's this?" asks Samantha. "We didn't order anything."

The waiter points to a man grinning at them from a barstool. "It's from the gentleman at the bar."

Jack's brows arch in surprise. "You gotta be kidding," he says. "That's Michael Lucchese. Excuse me while I go over there to talk to him."

While Jack walks to the bar, Samantha picks up the menu, even though she knows what she's going to order.

"You heal well," says Jack. "Thanks for the bottle."

Michael accepts Jack's outstretched hand. "You're welcome. You on a date, Lieutenant?"

Jack turns around to look at Samantha. "No, not really," he says, but then quickly adds, "Well, maybe. She's a fed."

"I know," responds Michael, grinning mischievously. "But you ever hear of tribade, buddy?" he laughs.

Michael and the passing bartender crack up at Jack's blank look.

"What's the joke?" asks Jack, scowling at the men's amusement at his expense.

"Ha, I love it!" taunts Michael, thoroughly enjoying Jack's agitation. "Your fed is on the opposite team, man!"

Jack turns again to look at Samantha. "Really? How do you know—"

"I know lots of things, Lieutenant," jeers Michael, raising his glass in a toast. "You'd be surprised by all the things I know."

"Huh. Well, thanks for telling me," says Jack,

disappointed by how his night is going.

Michael is relishing having the upper hand. "And here's something else I know, officer," he says, clearly enjoying a sense of superiority over his adversary. "I'm in charge of our crew now, may my dad rest in peace. And one of the first things I did was to order a hit on our boy, Kaspin. So, here's to me!" Michael raises his glass again, confident that he'll come out ahead. "Let the best man win!"

Jack isn't impressed by the mobster's bluster. "I wouldn't plan a party yet, Mikey," he sneers. "We heard about your guys' carelessness in Cherokee, going into that ditch and all. Maybe you should train your men better; whaddya think?" As the grin slips off Michael's face, Jack adds, "Oh, and thanks again for the bottle of Asti. We're really gonna enjoy it!"

When Jack rejoins his "date," Samantha looks guarded. "What was he laughing at?" she asks warily.

Jack rolls his eyes up to the ceiling. "Oh, it's nothing," he dismisses Samantha's concern. "The joke's on me, I guess."

But Samantha knows something's up. "Come on," she says, leaning in. "I'm a big girl. Did he say something I should know about?"

Jack hesitates, then leans in as well. "Okay, yeah. He said, 'tribade,' and I didn't know what it meant. But it seems you bat for the other team."

"Oh, that?" replies Samantha, straightening up and pouring Asti into their glasses. "That bit seems to rattle a lot of people, but I'm used to it by now." Samantha clinks her glass to Jack's. "Well, now that we got that over with, did he say anything else I should know?"

Jack is impressed by Samantha's resilience. *This woman's one tough cookie*, he opines admirably. Then aloud, he says, "He told me he put a contract out on Kaspin and was pretty proud of it. But his demeanor quickly changed when I told him we knew about his dead men in Cherokee."

"Huh. That's it?"

"Yeah."

"Okay. So now, we can get down to dinner," says Samantha, putting her menu aside. "I know what I'm getting; how about you?"

"Uh, how's the calamari here?"

"It's good, if you like that kind of thing."

When the waiter returns, the pair gives him their orders, and Samantha adds a special one. "See that redhead alone at the end of the bar?" she asks him. "I want you to bring her another of whatever she's drinking."

When the waiter leaves, Jack turns to look. "Whoo-hoo, you got good taste," he says approvingly.

Samantha watches the waiter place a drink in front of the woman, then point back at her, and she sighs when the woman smiles at her. "I do have good taste, don't I?" she says dreamily. "Um, you okay taking an Uber home, Jack? I hope to be busy later. Oh, that's unless you want to join us?"

"Ah, uh, no thanks. I think I'm gonna pass."

Jack leans back in his chair, surprised at himself for turning Samantha down. *I must be getting old,* he muses silently. *I can't believe I turned that offer down!*

The next morning falls hard. Jack walks past the construction crew finishing their final repairs to the First and heads to his desk. He's dressed in his usual sports jacket, jeans, button-down shirt with no tie, Tony Lamas, and mirrored sunglasses, with a Coke in one hand and a black coffee in the other.

Beyond Jack's desk, Gomez walks out of Conrad's office, gently closing the now plywood-covered door. When he comes closer to Jack, he covetously eyes Jack's favorite hangover remedies. "Wow, that must have been some date last night," he says enviously.

"Tribade," replies Jack, trying to laugh without having his head explode. "If you don't know what it is, Google it. I just drank too much."

Behind them, Jacob Assante walks through a crowd of victims and suspects toward Jack's desk. "Rough night?" he asks when he sees Jack's condition. "How'd you navigate through this maze without spilling anything?"

"Fuck you," mouths Jack, then winces and takes a drink of coffee.

"You don't look too good," says Jacob, "but I know it's not something you're unfamiliar with. So I'll get on with today's business."

"You do that," mumbles Jack, wincing again.

Jacob takes a minute to assess Jack's situation, then shrugs. "All righty then. I hope you can clear up the cobwebs soon because we're heading back to Kansas today. The AG is willing to reduce Anderson's sentence for information on Kaspin."

Jack pinches the bridge of his nose and sighs. "We better hurry and get the guy because the mob put a contract on him."

Gomez overhears the conversation and butts in. "Hey, don't forget that I want a piece of that shit! The Mafia better not screw it up for me! I just reminded Conrad that I'm going to North Carolina with or without his approval!"

James Ruiz sits down at his desk as Jack and Jacob exchange looks. "What did I miss?" he asks, looking from one to the other.

CHAPTER FOURTEEN

Twenty-four hours later, Stenhouse and Assante are back at Leavenworth in the same interrogation room as before. This time, Sam Anderson isn't already there, so while they wait, they pass the time chatting about mundane things.

A short time later, the steel door creaks open, and two guards lead Sam in, then shackle his feet to the floor. Following them in, a young professional in a fashionable skinny suit puts his briefcase on the table and takes a seat.

"I'm Kevin Langdon," he says, adjusting his tie. "My client is willing to cooperate as long as the federal government takes the death penalty and life in prison off the table."

"Really," retorts Jacob. "That depends entirely on Mr. Anderson's testimony and whether we determine that what he says is sufficient enough to reduce his sentence."

Jack catches Anderson's eye. "Tell us what you know," he says, adding his two cents, "and we'll decide whether you deserve to be rewarded."

Sam's mouth twitches in anger. He knows these two are holding all the cards, and he's not happy. "I have to talk to my lawyer," he says, leaning over to confer with Langdon.

While the men talk, Jack and Jacob watch their expressions and suspect the conversation isn't going well. Their suspicion is confirmed when Sam straightens and turns to them.

"I'll only talk if you agree to my demands up front," he states, cocky as hell. The prisoner is naively assuming the law enforcement officers need him and won't be able to refuse his demand.

However, Jacob shakes his head. "You think you got this all sewn up?"

"Yeah. Don't I?" asks Sam, a trace of doubt flitting across his face. The former Army colonel was known for his brilliant tactical moves and isn't used to being upstaged by a mere civilian, a young one at that.

"I don't think you understand," explains Jacob. "We don't have time for this nonsense; we're not negotiating a labor contract here. Here's what the AG agreed to: he'll exchange your execution for life only if your information is valuable. And if it's better than that, he'll reduce your sentence even further. Now, you can take that as it is or have your last meal next week. Your choice."

Sam looks at his lawyer, then turns to Jacob and Stenhouse. "You're a couple of shits, you know that?" he says, throwing out a line he's been thinking about since their last meeting. "So, Kaspin's eyes and ears are everywhere — from Congress to state and foreign governments. He has dirt on a lot of important people, so they're not gonna act against him. However, you guys did one thing right. Your raids on the Guard lowered his ranks of followers considerably, but you didn't get all of them. There are still remnant groups across the country keeping Kaspin's ideas alive."

Jacob has a question. "Who's working with him now that you're in prison? Who else does he trust to lead those groups?"

"I heard his new second-in-command is Marine Colonel George Powell. That man is a badass, so I wouldn't fuck with him if I were you."

"Oh, he's worse than you?" asks Jack in his characteristically sarcastic manner.

Sam knows the cop is baiting him, so he keeps his anger in check and directs his response to Jacob.

"Kaspin is nuts, a psycho, and if he got his nuke, he'd use it. So, I did whatever he asked, but I also hoped the mob would cook his ass." Then, shifting his eyes to Jack, he adds, "Because I knew you wouldn't do shit."

Jacob splutters, "He already got his nuke! An EMP device is a nuclear weapon! When we stopped you, you were trying to detonate it over a densely populated area! So don't tell us Kaspin is the only psycho here!"

"Yeah, I know. But Kaspin really wants a full-on nuclear bomb. The EMP was just a candy-ass substitute. He has big plans, you know. He had an agent in Interpol working on getting him a small one, so you better hope that's no longer on his radar."

Sam stops and holds Jacob's gaze. "And that's it. So, we got a deal here?"

"What about morals, Anderson? You were going to drop a bomb on innocent people, for God's sake!"

"All in the name of liberty, G-man."

Jack is furious and can't take anymore. With his hands balled into fists, he shouts, "Fuckin' shit! If I could, I'd punch you straight to hell, you bastard!"

Alarmed by the sudden turn in the conversation, Attorney Langdon stretches his arms across the table to keep Jack away from his client. "Calm down!" he shouts at Stenhouse.

"Where's Kaspin now?" asks Jacob.

"How the fuck would I know?" shrugs Anderson. "He has properties near Charlotte, Bryson City, and Cherokee, but he could be anywhere in the world. He's compromised operatives in the CIA, Interpol, and even the FBI."

"You have any names?"

"Um, let me think," says Anderson, happy they need him again. "Yeah… There's a guy in the FBI, an Agent York. Thomas, I think," he grins, looking smugly at Jacob. "He's out of D.C. Is that good enough for you, G-man?"

Jacob narrows his eyes. "It's good, but if you can come up with the name of that Interpol officer who's trying to get that nuke, I can assure you there's a good chance you'll get out of here. Right now, I can give you twenty-five years, with possible parole in fifteen."

Sam leans back. "York knows a lot, and I'm sure of that. So how about fifteen, parole in ten? And if you get more names out of York, I go free with a new identity."

Jacob glances at Jack, then turns to Sam's lawyer. "That could work. I'll pass it on to the AG, and he'll contact you, Mr. Langdon."

With nods all around, Jacob and Jack stand and walk to the door.

"We're ready to go," calls Jack, rapping on the heavy metal.

In the hallway outside, Jacob looks grim. "I know York," he says, his mouth set in a thin line. "He was my boss in D.C. before he moved me to New York. I never liked that fucker. There was something about him…"

Jack catches a fleeting glimpse of Maria, Jacob's late sister, in the agent's determined expression. "He was your boss? Don't that take the cake! But that means you'll be gunning for him, right? Just make sure to call me when you're set to confront him. I'm gonna be right at your side when you wring his neck."

Interpol Agent Claude LaGrange has been posted to Russia for the past two years. He's been there long enough to know better, but when he's alone at night, he still gets uneasy feelings that any minute, Soviet agents of the past will jump out of the shadows and grab him just for being there. In the wee hours of the morning, thoughts that Moscow is haunted by the ghosts of czars and the sounds of ancient balalaikas won't leave him alone.

Tonight, as Claude enters a dark alleyway behind a bar near Red Square, he shivers against the cold. But still, he stops to listen for those nonexistent footfalls. "I have to stop thinking like this," he mutters, pulling the collar of his heavy coat closer. LaGrange wouldn't have chosen this location for his meeting, but his supplier insisted on it, so he has to make the best of it.

While the agent waits for his eyes to adjust to the darkness, a Mercedes van with its headlights off emerges from the gloom and stops a few feet away from him.

This vehicle is unfamiliar to me, he thinks. *Better wait to see who it is.*

When it seems that he and those in the car have sized each other up long enough, a tall man with a ragged scar across his left eye steps out of the vehicle.

"Yuri?" asks Claude, squinting against the bright light of a flashlight shining on his face.

"Da. You have money?"

"Only if I see the weapon. I will transfer your money if it is what I ordered."

Yuri walks to the back of the van and opens the door so Claude can look inside.

"This is portable?" asks LaGrange, staring in disbelief at a four-by-two-foot-long aluminum case with heavy-duty wheels and a telescoping handle.

"This is real world, not movie," replies Yuri in a thick Russian accent. "You want small thermonuclear device? This is it. You don't like, we sell to someone else."

Claude sighs and takes out his phone. With a few clicks, he accesses a foreign bank account, then hits "Submit." After the transfer goes through, he shows the confirmation to the Russian.

Assured that his money is on the way, Yuri motions to two associates waiting in the warmth of the van. "Where is car?" he asks Claude. "I hope it has large cargo area."

Working together, the two Russians lower the large case to the ground, then wheel it to the SUV Claude parked at the entrance to the alley. Grunting heavily, they load it into Claude's car, then all three Russians pile back into their vehicle and leave the alley without saying another word.

Claude is happy to see them go. *That is all for czars and balalaikas tonight*, he mutters into the darkness.

No one was surprised when Hector and Captain Conrad were called into the inspector's office after Hector's outburst at Conrad's meeting. The team expected this, so it didn't come as a surprise. However, they became concerned when Hector started packing up some personal items.

"You still employed here?" asks Sergeant Ruiz anxiously.

"Yeah, for now," replies Gomez, picking up items to put in a box. "I'm taking three weeks of my vacation time."

"How mad was he?"

Hector stops what he's doing to look at James. "You're not gonna believe this. Rawlings stood up for me! He jumped down Conrad's throat and basically told him to get out from behind his desk and do some real police work!"

"Holy shit! Are you serious?"

"Yeah. It was awesome! You're gonna hafta work with someone else till I get back."

Ruiz's face drops. "Aw fuck! How am I gonna get along without your pretty face?"

Gomez grins and whistles a cheerful tune while throwing things into the box.

"You think this is funny? We're just getting into the

swing of things, and now you're leaving?"

"Chill, Ruiz. I'm going on vacation. I'll be back before you know it."

"You better be. I don't want to have to break in a new partner! Where you goin'?"

Gomez closes the box without responding.

Serge Kaspin clicks on his buzzing phone while a young massage therapist tries her best to finish his "morning therapy."

"Good," he replies to the caller, breathing a little heavily. "When will it be delivered? Great. I'll give you a new destination next week."

Kaspin ends the call, then looks down at the top of the "therapist's" head. "That's good," he sighs. "Keep it goin', babe."

Jacob puts down his phone, then gulps water from a reusable bottle he filled in the terminal. "My mouth gets dry on planes," he explains. "Don't you want something to drink?"

"Nah. I'm okay," says Jack.

"Well, it seems your CIA friend Samantha Waring called my office, and on her advice, they took Agent York into custody. He's in a holding cell in our D.C. facility."

"What a gal!" responds Jack, applauding this new development. "That makes it much easier for us. I wasn't looking forward to confronting him in his office."

"Me neither," replies Jacob gratefully. "Waring's proving to be a fountain of good intel. She also said a Russian general sold a portable nuke to a foreign buyer. The CIA knows that guy's been selling Russian technology and military equipment for a while, so they've been keeping tabs on his bank account and phone records. However, they don't know who the buyer is yet."

"You think it's Kaspin?"

"That wouldn't surprise me. The CIA's going to try to apprehend that general, but if they get caught, our government will disavow any knowledge of their actions."

Jack smirks. "That's cheesy, Jacob. You sound like that old TV show."

Jacob's mouth curves into a smile. "I thought you'd like that."

"You think York knows anything about the nuke?"

"Could be."

"Any ideas on how it'll get here?"

"I've been thinking about that. It can't come through legit points of entry, so if I were going to do it, I'd bring it across the Canadian border. Their security isn't as tough as ours, and there's hardly anyone watching most of that border."

Jack shakes his head. "Beauty, eh?"

By the time their private jet lands at Dulles International Airport, it's early evening. So instead of going directly to the FBI office, they check in at their hotel.

"Shouldn't we talk to York first?" asks Jack.

"We can interview him in the morning. I'm sure they already introduced him to intense interrogation, so let's relax tonight."

"Suits me fine," replies Jack. "I can use this time to catch up with Mark and Sharon.

In his room, Jack chats with his son and mother-in-law, then stretches to get some kinks out of his back.

"Ugh. Still a little stiff from the plane ride," he grunts, then looks at his watch. "Hmm, it's too soon for bed, so I guess I'll go down to the bar."

Though the bar is crowded, Jack instantly spots Jacob sitting in a club chair. "Hey," he says, catching the FBI agent's eye. "Mind if I join you?"

Jacob points to a chair across from him. "Have a seat. You want one?" he asks, indicating a pint of Guinness on a low table between them.

Jack lifts a brow. "Huh, I can't believe how much you resemble your sister. That was her favorite beer. She was good people, Jacob."

When Jack receives his own glass, the men toast deceased loved ones.

"You know," says Jacob, looking off into the distance. "Sometimes I feel she's right behind me, telling me what to do, like when we were kids. Did you know she's memorialized on the Wall of Honor at the FBI Academy? That's where they remember agents who gave their lives in the line of duty. I could never look at it when I was there. Every time I walked past, it reminded me she's no longer here."

Jack nods. "She talks to me, too. I can still see her lying on that street."

Following this exchange, the men turn somber and drink their beers in silence. Then Jack sighs and puts his empty glass on the table. "This is bullshit!" he exclaims. "We can't let ourselves get into a funk! We got work to do!"

Jacob tilts his head to the side and stares into his beer. "I got a bad feeling," he says glumly. "That northern border is so porous, anything can get through. I don't know why the country isn't talking about erecting a wall up there, as well as at the southern border."

Before Jack can respond, the men notice a young woman winking at Jacob from the bar.

Jack grins and leans toward his pal. "That one looks ready for action," he whispers. "You better act now, bub. But let me give you a word of caution. Before things get too far, be sure she has all her female parts. You never know."

Jacob laughs heartily. "What are you gonna do if I get lucky?"

"Me? I'm goin' back to my room before I get into trouble. I'm gettin' too old for this dance, and I miss my wife."

Jack looks toward the bar again. "Jacob, my man, if you don't do something I'd do, I'll have no choice but to classify you as a complete idiot."

Hector feels strange being back at Kaspin's cabin on the river, even if an FBI forensics team is there this time.

"Can I go inside?" he asks of the first agent he sees.

"Yeah, just put on booties and gloves."

Pleased to be given free rein to roam around, Gomez looks into every room in the house where he was held captive. But it's completely empty now, except for faint but noticeable odors of Lysol and bleach. "Sheesh," he mutters, disappointed but not surprised. "This place has been stripped clean down to the floorboards."

Gomez expected the mercenary to be too efficient and calculating to leave anything behind. Even so, he's disgusted that he's right. Still, even if the place is bare, he's happy the FBI team is carefully scouring the interior and the grounds.

After inspecting the top floor, Hector heads down to the makeshift brig, hoping there's some evidence he was there.

"Crap. This is empty, too," he says, dismayed that this area has also been cleaned thoroughly. There's no cot, no bedding, and none of the extra clothes they gave him.

"Hi," says a forensic technician, poking his head into the room. "Okay if I sweep for evidence?"

"Be my guest," Hector replies. "Mind if I watch?"

"No prob," says the tech.

The technician turns on a portable UV light, then uses it to scan the entire room, starting at the back. The area is small, but the tech is meticulous, so it takes a while for him to return to the doorway.

Hector is disappointed the forensic specialist hasn't found anything. He's about to leave when the man's expression changes. "Gotcha!" he says when a slight glow appears near the floor.

Hector leans close. "Looks like they missed a spot," he gloats. "Guess I'll leave you to it."

Outside the room, Gomez opens the exterior door. "Ahh," he murmurs, inhaling the fresh mountain air in the cool of the early evening. "If I didn't know better, I'd think this was just a great vacation cabin."

Gomez walks along the dirt road to retrace the steps he took during his escape and notices something sparkling through a tangle of Kudzu crawling up a tree. Bending down, he moves the vines away and picks up a gold-tone gambling token.

"Oooo, what do we have here?" he mutters, turning it over in his hand. "Harrah's Cherokee Casino? Let's get you to the techies."

Back inside, the FBI forensics analyst is still working in the "brig."

"Hey, I found this outside," says Hector, handing the token to the analyst. "Check it out, would ya?"

"Sure thing, Detective. Let's see if there are any prints."

The tech sifts a fine powder over the coin, revealing several fingerprint whorls. "Well, there's a couple here. Let's hope they're not yours. By the way, I found another spot with the light."

Hector gives the man a thumbs up, then heads up the stairs to speak with Joyce Clinger, FBI special agent in charge. She's on the phone, but Hector thinks his discovery is important enough to get her attention.

"I found a casino chip from Harrah's Casino," he says, ignoring her angry glare. "There are a couple of prints on it, so I thought you should know."

The agent cuts her call short and scowls at Hector. "I was on the phone, bub."

"Yeah, I know," he replies, grinning like a kid caught with his hand in the cookie jar.

"So what's so important about it?" she asks, sizing up the guy in front of her.

"It could be significant. Kaspin likes to gamble, so maybe the casino is worth checking out."

"Hmm. You may be right. You know, Cherokee isn't far from here, so you wanna take a ride?"

"Sure. I've seen as much of this place as I want to. Lead the way, Special Agent."

Hector follows the federal investigator to her car, watching her backside sway as she walks. *This woman is fit!* He can't help noticing how her slacks cling to every curve. *I wonder how I can get some of that? Might be a fun way to end the day!*

Hector takes his time surveying the rest of her and runs through some tried and true pickup lines. Then he stops, realizing what he's doing. *Whoa! I know she's cute and all, but these thoughts sound more like Stenhouse than me!*

Even though it's a weeknight, the Cherokee casino is packed full of people, every one of them hoping to hit it big.

"Are you a gambler?" asks Clinger, holding the handle of

a soft-sided briefcase.

Hector shakes his head. "Nah, I'll dabble, but nothing serious. I don't see the point. All I do is hand over my hard-earned money for no return. I never win."

"I don't win either," responds Joyce. "But I like the possibility."

Joyce and Hector show their credentials at the information desk. Then they're escorted up a circular stairway.

"Excuse me, Mr. Cardel," says their escort, knocking at the door of the casino manager. "The FBI is here."

"Oh?" says a graying man, turning away from a sizeable bulletproof glass window overlooking the happenings below. "Have a seat," he tells the pair, motioning to the chairs in front of his desk.

The casino business is George Cardel's life. Born in Nevada, he likes to tell people that the Vegas Strip's neon lights dazzled him so much as a kid that he had no choice but to make it his career. He worked his way through every job he could, and through hard work and perseverance, eventually reached his goal of managing his beloved Caesar's Palace. Now George is ready to retire and is spending his last few years in Cherokee overseeing their operations.

"How can I help you?" he asks.

"Mr. Cardel, I'm FBI Special Agent Joyce Clinger, and I'm here with NYPD Detective Hector Gomez. We're here to speak with you about a customer. But first, can you tell me the significance of a golden casino chip?"

"Of course, Special Agent. But let's move to the better chairs."

Cardel walks around his desk to lead them to a grouping of comfortable leather chairs surrounding a small table. "Would you like something to drink? Coffee, water, tea?"

"I'm fine," says Joyce, looking at Hector.

"Nothing for me," he says.

"Okay," continues Cardel. "The gold chip is for special players, our heavy hitters, if you will. It allows them access to our VIP room."

"I see," says Joyce, pulling a photo from her briefcase and laying it on the table. "Is this man one of your heavy hitters?"

George leans forward to take a closer look. "Yes, that's Mr. Kaspin. He comes here often. But we haven't seen him in a week or so. Is he all right?"

Joyce takes the picture back. "He's under investigation right now. Do you have any information on him? A current address or phone number? Perhaps an email address?"

Mr. Cardel looks at Detective Gomez, then back at Agent Clinger. "You surprise me, Agent. You're FBI, so you should know a warrant is needed for that information. But I'm going to bend the rules today. Let me make a phone call; I'll have our Financial Department hand over what data we have. It shouldn't take long." Cardel starts to walk to his desk, then stops and turns around. "On second thought, I'll get it myself. Press the green button on my desk if you want food or drinks brought up while you wait. It's on the house."

Cardel closes the door, leaving the officers alone in his office. "The guy seems a little too trusting, don't you think?" asks Joyce suspiciously.

"Yeah, we should be careful," replies Gomez, walking to the window over the casino. "Look at all those people!" he declares, marveling at the hundreds of players intently concentrating on placing bets on every machine and table. When Joyce joins him, he says, "We may get some banking or credit card info today, but nothing else. Kaspin's not stupid."

Joyce has a different opinion about their prey. "He was stupid enough to make himself stand out here, wasn't he? It's his ego. Men like him don't want to be in the background.

Sooner or later, that's what's gonna give him away."

George Cardel returns with credit card information and the address to Kaspin's cabin. "This is all we have," he says, handing a sheet of paper to Clinger.

Gomez isn't satisfied, so he tries a different tack. "Can we talk to the employees who work in the VIP room?"

Cardel goes to his desk to issue a couple of orders. Then he says, "We hold special poker tournaments in the VIP room, and today's events don't start till ten. So I asked the dealer and pit boss to come up here. There's only one of each assigned to the room. We rotate security guards outside the door, but they're strictly ordered not to interact with the guests."

"Thanks," says Gomez.

"No problem. But I'm sorry that I have to leave you both again. There's a nightly task in our counting room that I can't miss. So if you finish questioning my people before I return, just let yourselves out."

"That's very generous of you," says Joyce.

"I'm happy to cooperate. Now please excuse me. If there's anything else we can do to help your investigation, just contact me. Here's my card."

Joyce and Hector return to their seats around the table just as a young woman and a brawny bald man enter the room.

Gomez notices that the man has no neck and appears annoyed, and the young woman looks nervous. Neither of them is eager to enter, so Joyce waves them over. "Hello, I'm FBI Agent Clinger, and this is NYPD Detective Gomez. Please have a seat. We need to speak with you about one of the casino's VIP patrons."

The two amble over to the chair grouping, taking seats next to each other.

"May we have your names and job titles, please?" asks Joyce.

The woman answers with her eyes on the floor. "I'm Charlene Wilson, VIP Room dealer."

"Thank you," Joyce responds pleasantly, noting the woman's reaction. "And you?" she asks, turning to the man.

"My name is Kal Raindancer," he states, cricking his invisible neck, which announces its presence with a loud snap. "I'm the VIP Room pit boss, and I also work security."

Joyce hands the photo of Kaspin to Charlene. "Do you recognize this man?"

"Yes, this is Mr. Kaspin. He's a regular and a good tipper."

"Has he shared any personal information with you? Where he lives, and so on?"

Charlene looks exceptionally nervous. "Ah, well, no. No," she declares.

Kal doesn't like the question's effect on his dealer, so he quickly explains, "The casino has a strict policy of no fraternizing with customers. So neither of us has any personal information on Mr. Kaspin or any other players. However, I can tell you that he's a heavy better and a heavy loser."

Hector leans over to Joyce, who then looks up at the cameras in the ceiling.

"Okay," she says, smiling at the casino employees. "Thank you for talking with us today. Can you find Mr. Cardel and ask him to come back, please? We'll wait here."

Both Kal and Charlene rise, but Joyce quickly motions to Charlene. "Miss Wilson, can you remain behind for just a minute? I have a few more questions for you."

Kal gives his dealer a meaningful look, then leaves the room, and Charlene retakes her seat.

Several long minutes later, George Cardel breezes in, and Joyce takes him aside for a private talk.

"Mr. Cardel, this room is monitored, but we need privacy when we conduct our interviews. Is there anywhere in the casino where there are no cameras or microphones?"

George leads her to a door on the opposite side of the office and opens it to reveal his private living quarters.

"This is my home away from home. I sometimes work a later shift and sleep here instead of driving at night. You can use this area. There's no surveillance here. Please close the door when you leave. I have to get back to business."

Cardel leaves them alone again, and Joyce is grateful. "Thank you," she says to his retreating back. "I appreciate your cooperation."

Joyce turns to the young woman when the outer office door clicks closed. "Miss Wilson, please follow us into this private area so we can talk without being observed."

George's living quarters is a small studio apartment with a sofa and chairs, a kitchenette, and a small bathroom. There is no bed, so the couch must fold out.

While Joyce and Hector sit on the couch, Charlene sits in a chair.

"Miss Wilson," says Hector, "we've noticed that you've been nervous ever since you arrived, and we want to assure you that we're only here to gather information about one of your customers. If there's anything you've withheld because you knew you were being observed, now is the time to let us know. Is there something you'd like to tell us?"

Charlene is staring at the floor again, taking deep breaths to calm herself. "If my boss finds out I've said anything to you, he'll fire me on the spot."

Joyce sympathizes but presses on. "Nothing you tell us will get back to him," she responds reassuringly. "You can trust us."

Charlene's face is pale, and her upper lip is trembling. But it seems like she wants to reveal something, so the officers wait patiently. Finally, the woman's back straightens, and she looks directly into Joyce's eyes. "I swear it was only one time!"

"That's all right," soothes Joyce. "Please go on."

"Ummm… Mr. Kaspin invited me to a private party. He asked me to be the dealer for a high-stakes poker game."

Joyce is intrigued. "Where was the party?" she asks.

"It was at a nice place on a river."

"Was it a cabin in a town called Bryson City?"

"Yeah."

Joyce nods and makes a notation on a pad. "What can you tell us about the people at the game?"

Charlene sighs. "There were some men in uniforms and camouflage apparel. He called one of them Colonel. And there was someone else there, a man with a French accent."

Joyce casts a sidelong glance at Gomez, then rummages through folders in her briefcase, stopping at a thick dossier. Pulling it out, she removes a cover card to hide confidential information, then shows a photo to Charlene. "Is this the Frenchman?"

Charlene nods affirmatively.

"Can I see that?" asks Hector.

Joyce hands the photo to Gomez, then turns to the dealer. "Thank you," she tells Charlene. "You've been a great help. Please remember that what you've told us is private and won't be released to anyone. However, don't be alarmed if we ask for your assistance again. Just to clear up some details."

"I understand," says Charlene. "Can I go now?"

"Yes, and thanks again."

Charlene is only too eager to leave. She jumps out of her chair and exits the room as if it were on fire, eliciting concerned looks from Hector and Joyce.

"That woman is way too upset," notes Hector. "There must be more to her story."

"Could be," Joyce responds, reaching for her briefcase.

Nodding toward the photo in Hector's hands, she asks, "Do you know who that is?"

"No, but I guess you're gonna tell me."

"Yeah. It's Interpol Agent Claude LaGrange. Our mole."

CHAPTER FIFTEEN

Estonian Prime Minister Olev Lepik, a holdover from the Soviet Union, is excited and hopeful. His country's discovery of a novel way to produce a lithium alternative has granted him a place at the upcoming G20 Summit in Quebec City.

Since the breakthrough, the world's leaders have shown a heightened interest in Estonia, even to the point of personally requesting his presence at the summit. Rather than being flattered, however, the prime minister is wise enough to know that the only reason he's invited is because of the innovative technology. He understands that the G20 leaders will do whatever is necessary to prevent it from falling out of their hands.

Regardless, Lepik has a deathly fear of flying and was unsure of how he would get to that coveted meeting. He knew it would be an honor to represent Estonia through the European Union but couldn't figure out a way to get there — until an aide offered a plan. The adviser recommended that Lepik persuade the government to provide the official yacht for his journey from the country's capital of Tallinn to the Canadian province of Quebec.

Though an ocean crossing would take an extraordinary amount of time, Lepik's superiors agreed to the plan because Olev assured them that he would keep up with his work during his voyage. Modern technology and virtual meetings are the accepted standards nowadays; they work even on ships at sea. However, because of the length of travel, Olev must leave within days if he is to arrive for the start of the summit.

Olev scratches his head as he prepares another draft of

his speech. He's been agonizing over what he wants to say for several days, knowing it needs to be perfect. So a knock at his door is a welcome interruption.

"Mr. Prime Minister," announces his assistant, "you have a visitor from Russia. He says he is General Sergei Mednikov, an old friend."

Olev cocks an inquisitive brow at the assistant while the man waits for a reply.

"Mednikov? The name sounds familiar… Let me think… Ah, yes, I remember a Colonel Mednikov. He was stationed here just before we declared independence. Send him in, Villem."

Seconds later, a tall man dressed in a military uniform pushes past the assistant, and Olev gasps involuntarily, not because he recognizes him but because of a ghastly scar across the man's eye and forehead.

Sergei Mednikov ignores the reaction and extends a hand. "Olev Lepik, you have come a long way from security chief!" he says pleasantly. "I was delighted to hear of your nomination, and I am sorry I did not congratulate you all those years ago."

Seeing his old friend again evokes pleasant memories in Olev, but he's wary of him. A general in the Russian government holds many powers, some of which are best kept unknown, and an unexpected visit could be cause for concern.

"Mednikov! It seems you have risen to a position of high authority as well! I remember that all you could talk about was getting that star, and here you are! It is good to see you, my friend. What can I do for you?"

Sergei stares through a slit in the scar covering his eye. "It is good that you remember when we were younger men. Do you recall how I helped you move your private bank accounts out of Moscow?" When Olev's face turns ashen, Sergei knows he remembers. "Now it is time for you to help me. I need you to transport a package to Canada. I know you are going there by ship."

Summers in the Washington, D.C., area are brutal. The hot and muggy climate in that former coastal floodplain forces residents, workers, and visitors to make it a daily habit to search for the best ways to beat the heat.

True to form, the temperature is already approaching ninety when Jack and Jacob meet in their hotel lobby. The night before, they planned to walk to FBI headquarters since it's close by, but when they stepped outside, they quickly changed their minds. Rather than risking sweat-stained shirts, Jacob hired a driver from a ride-hailing company.

At the entrance to the J. Edgar Hoover Building, Jacob thanks the driver, then both men scurry from one air-conditioned shelter to another, their professional outfits of sports jackets and ties incompatible with the heat.

Jack clears the security scanners first and waits for Jacob to do the same. When they're permitted entry, Jack asks, "Where's the Wall of Honor? I want to see Maria's name up there."

Jacob winces at the question. "It's not here. I told you it's at the Academy, remember?"

"Oh, yeah, that's right. I was hoping to see it. Oh, well. Just do me a favor, will ya? Never do anything to disgrace her name. Always do your sister proud."

"You don't have to remind me of that, Jack. I think about her all the time."

Jacob leads the way to a set of turnstiles, where he slips his ID into a slot that allows them passage to a bank of elevators. "We need to go down to a lower level. That's where they keep the detainees for questioning."

"I'll go wherever you say," states Jack. "I'm sure you can't wait till we confront that bastard of a boss."

"Um, I've been thinking," says Jacob. "He's gonna assume that I'll be the one to question him first, but I'm gonna let you take the lead. You okay with that?"

"I'm in," says Jack.

Later that day, it's already nighttime in a different part of the world when a black Embraer Legacy 500 business jet lands on a crudely made airstrip on the outskirts of Langa, a village in northern Estonia. At the side of the strip, a Ural-4320, painted black to evade nighttime detection, waits for the jet to taxi closer.

When the Legacy 500 stops, Interpol Agent Claude LaGrange exits and gestures back to three men dressed in fatigues, helmets, and dark tactical facemasks. Responding to the summons, they carry a transfer case from the plane to the 6x6 vehicle. Then LaGrange reboards the plane, and it takes off.

On the ground, the truck drives to a secluded cove on Lahepere Bay near Kersalu, while high above, LaGrange uses the aircraft's satellite phone to detail his plan to his contact.

"The package is on its way. I contracted with a group that owns an underwater vehicle to bring it to the Port of Tallinn. At the port, my men will load it onto the yacht of the prime minister, and he will bring it into Canada. They will not search the ship because of his diplomatic immunity, so it will be safe. I will contact you again when it arrives in Quebec City."

FBI Supervisory Special Agent Thomas York was foolish enough to think this day would never come. He believed his position in the FBI was high enough to make him untouchable. Therefore, he became careless.

While York waits for his interrogators, he considers his options, thinking through several scenarios and discarding each one until he finally concedes that the pickings are slim to none. Reluctantly, he settles back to await his fate.

The normally well-groomed FBI supervisor is unshaven and disheveled, and he's still wearing the suit he wore to work — now a wrinkled mess. This adds to York's anxiety, causing him to shake his legs against his shackles.

Suddenly, the click that unlocks the electronic door rings loudly in Thomas' ears. His future depends on what happens next, and he knows it.

When the door swishes open, Jack and Jacob enter, and both hear a sharp intake of breath when Jacob's former boss recognizes him.

No longer beholden to the older man, Jacob greets him informally. "Hello, Thomas," he says casually. "This is an odd place to meet, don't you think?"

York arches a brow at a thick folder that Jack places on the table.

Following his line of sight, Jack sneers. "Yes," he says, patting the folder, "this is all about you. Looks like you're the winner of today's prize. So let's get started."

Jacob interrupts, "Supervisor... Uh, Mr. York, this is NYPD Lieutenant Jack Stenhouse. He's assisting us in this investigation."

"Right," says Jack, opening the folder. "We have reliable information that shows you have a long-term working relationship with a pretty bad guy and a group he founded, namely, Serge Kaspin and the Patriot Guard. Would you care to explain yourself?"

Unsurprisingly, York declares firmly, "I want to speak to my lawyer."

"How did I know you'd say that?" asks Jack, boring holes into the man's eyes. "But it's interesting since you haven't been charged with anything yet. So, I'll tell you what. Fuck off, FBI bureaucrat. How about that? Now, do you know Serge Kaspin or not? And what do you know about a small nuclear device?"

York merely repeats his demand, so Jacob reaches over and grabs a sheet of paper from the folder. Handing it to his former boss, he says, "This is a list of calls you made to known associates of Serge Kaspin. The unidentified number is the same one Kaspin used to call Lieutenant Stenhouse."

While York looks over the list, Jacob explains, "You may be wondering why an NYPD lieutenant is here, so I'll save you the trouble of asking. He's here because he has skin in this game. You see, Kaspin was responsible for his wife's death, and he's pretty angry about that. So I'm afraid the guy won't let up until you answer him."

Slowly and deliberately, Jack reaches into a pocket and takes out a blackjack that he lays on the table. "I don't have a phone book at my disposal, but Agent Assante's case file will work just fine," he tells York, looking meaningfully at the blackjack. "You're about my age, so I'm gonna assume you know what I can do with that stick and a thick folder. So I'll ask you again. How do you know Serge Kaspin, and what's the skinny on the nuke?"

York tries his best to hide a sudden, nervous twitch. "You can't do anything to me. There are cameras and microphones all over the place."

Jack cocks his head to the side. Then he stands up and moves his chair to the corner of the room. Using the chair as a stepstool, he reaches up and disconnects the camera. Then he waves at the two-way mirror. "Oooo, looks like our observers are on a coffee break." When Jack sits back down, he smacks the table with the blackjack, leaving a dent.

"You're next," he says.

Thomas York has been behind a desk for several years and isn't keen on pain, so he pales, inhales deeply, and holds up his hands. "Okay, okay. I met Kaspin when he was schmoozing around D.C. with Black Horizon. He approached me at a party; said he wanted an inside man in the Bureau and that he'd pay me more than a couple of years' annual salary. I needed the money, so I said yes."

"You willingly went to work with an internationally known weapons dealer?" asks Jacob incredulously.

"I didn't know what his deal was, and I didn't check. But if he was going to spread money around, I wanted some."

Jack shakes his head cynically. "It's always the money," he declares scornfully.

Jacob asks, "What about the nuke?"

"I'm surprised you know about it."

Jack is exasperated. "Just answer the question, York."

"Yeah, okay. When Kaspin branched out into selling military weapons to finance his, um, 'legacy,' he asked me to help him find one. By that time, I was in deep, so I contacted a guy I worked with at Interpol."

Jack's ears prick up when he hears the more familiar name of the International Criminal Police Organization. "Which guy did you deal with?" he asks.

"An agent named Claude LaGrange."

Jacob is astonished. "How did you convince an Interpol agent to get a nuke?"

"I worked with him a couple of times and knew he had a gambling habit. The guy was neck-deep in debt. He loved the tables in Monaco and went there and everywhere else he could as often as possible. So I had something on him, and I used it. I told LaGrange that Kaspin wanted to buy surplus military hardware from Russia, and he said he knew of a general who sold weapons on the side."

Jacob gasps. "You swore an oath to defend this country against all enemies, York! How could you do that?!"

Jack shoots him a sidelong glance. "It's the money," he states disdainfully.

York looks off into the distance while Jacob focuses on the table to try to calm down.

Sitting nearby, Jack isn't ready to quit yet. "Did Kaspin tell you why he wanted the nuke?"

"I didn't want to know why. But I overheard him telling someone that he wants to take revenge on every person and agency that foiled his last attempt at a coup against the United States."

Looking up sharply, Jacob exclaims, "I don't believe this! You were my supervisor at the Federal Bureau of Investigation! I'll admit now that I thought you were an asshole, but I never believed you could betray our country!"

York's eye twitches, and he sighs heavily. "Before I knew it, things escalated and got out of hand, and I was stuck. But there is something I can tell you. Kaspin made that deal last week, and I was supposed to keep him informed if we found out anything about it."

"Did you get back to him?"

"No."

Jacob thinks quickly. "All right, that's good. Let's tell him what the Bureau 'knows.' It just won't be the correct info."

York looks at Jacob and Jack and nods wearily, sealing the deal.

With nothing more to discuss, Jack grabs the folder and the blackjack and rises from his chair. "Oh, man, it would have been so much fun," he says, tapping York's temple with the heavy club.

Parked in a chair, Serge Kaspin frantically pushes buttons to beat the invisible player in his favorite video game.

"Ah! Just one more, and I win!" he says, concentrating on every detail on the screen.

"Um, sorry to interrupt you," apologizes Colonel Powell.

"Not now, Powell!" shouts Kaspin, his eyes glued to the game.

"Um, I think you'll want to hear this."

Serge sighs and puts down the controller. "Your timing is deplorable, Powell! I was just about to put that guy down! What's so important?"

"We have information from York. He said they assigned more agents to protect Burley and Rodriguez, so it's not going to be as easy as we thought."

Kaspin exhales noisily. "Crap," he moans, lamenting the extra work this latest wrinkle will have on his scheme for getting even. "Nothing's going the way I thought it would. Well, we'll just have to find a way around this."

Serge reaches for the controller again, then stops because Powell hasn't moved. "Anything else?" he asks irritably.

"You should also know that Hector Gomez and the FBI are sniffing around your cabin. I can't imagine they found anything because we cleaned it pretty thoroughly."

"You better be right about that," grunts Kaspin. "Did those snoops say anything about our deal with LaGrange?"

"No; York says they haven't mentioned it."

"Ha. That means they don't know what we're up to yet. We better leave town now and go dark before they get lucky."

Focused on the conversation, Serge turns the game off. "Keep in touch with our guys in Belgium and Florida, and while you're doing that, get your ass up to Quebec. Our package is set to arrive in two weeks, and I need you to bring it over the border. I've been checking on how things work up there, and I think the Carbury/Goodlands crossing is good. There's an unguarded strip of land near Souris, North Dakota, and it's unpaved, so you'll need a heavy-duty off-road vehicle."

"Do you have one of those? I'll need it pretty quickly."

Kaspin smiles. "Take a look in the hut. I bought a Joint Light Tactical Vehicle a couple of months ago, and it was delivered this morning. Familiarize yourself with it because you're going to drive it to Canada. I have a contact in the RCMP, a guy named Constable Nelson. He knows you're coming and has your number. He'll get in touch with you next week."

"Excellent," replies Powell. "Semper Fi, boss!"

CHAPTER SIXTEEN

Ken Rodriguez's Artchop Gallery is on a well-traveled thoroughfare lined with stately palm trees, popular restaurants, high-end boutiques, and Fort Lauderdale's famous Riverside Hotel. The storefront is positioned to overlook the daily jaunts of tourists and their Ferraris soaking in the Florida sunshine. The gallery is Ken's pride and joy. It's full of collage art, movie posters, and book cover designs that Ken and his staff of artists have created over the years.

The shooting in New York caused Artchop to miss the fashion event in Los Angeles, so Cindy is busy booking new shows and filling orders. While she works in the back office, Ken is out front, mingling with the stream of people stopping in to admire his work. The pain in his shoulder is better, but he still favors that side and tires easily.

Just outside, a Fort Lauderdale police officer watches the crowd from an unmarked POS sedan. Ken and Cindy are still in danger, and the New York team wants to keep them safe.

It's late morning, and the summertime heat is beginning to ooze through the window overlooking the street, so Ken excuses himself from the customers. "Take a look around," he tells them. "It's that time of day, and it's getting warm in here."

While the shoppers move on, Ken walks toward the wall holding the controls for the retractable awnings over the gallery's window. Looking onto the street, he presses the button to swing the sunshade out, thinking, *Busy day*, and hoping for some sales.

Just then, a Range Rover passes his location, and all hell breaks loose.

"Holy shi—" he shouts when gunfire rings out, killing the police officer out front and piercing the gallery window.

As .223 projectiles shatter the glass, Ken lunges toward the closest customers and drags them to the floor. "Stay down!" he shouts, covering them as best he can.

When the shooting stops, everyone starts screaming.

"Cindy!" Ken calls out to his wife.

"I'm okay!" she yells back from under the relative safety of her desk.

"Is anyone hit?" asks Ken, rising slowly to his feet.

"I'm bleeding!" cries a man, crumpled on the floor beneath ruined artwork.

"I'm calling 911!" shouts Ken, turning toward the street as sirens wail in the distance.

Within minutes, the gallery fills with police, EMTs, and firefighters, and Ken points out the man who was shot. "Take care of him first!" he shouts. Then he runs to the office to find his wife.

"Where are you?" he asks worriedly.

"Under here," she replies, peeking out from under the desk.

"Are you okay?"

"I, I think so," she stammers. "What about you?"

"I'm okay, but one of the customers was hit, and a lot of my artwork is ruined."

"Oh, my god," moans Cindy. "I'm so sorry, Kenny. Kaspin just won't quit! We hafta get better protection!"

Jacob gets a call about the incident on Las Olas while he and Jack are waiting for their flight home at BWI.

"What is it?" asks Jack when he sees a look of disgust on

his colleague's face.

"Kaspin hit the Rodriguez's."

"Fuck! Where'd he find them?"

"At their gallery in Fort Lauderdale. The officer on surveillance was killed, and a customer was transported to the hospital for treatment."

"So Ken and Cindy are okay?"

"Yeah, looks like it. Homeland Security and local authorities are currently in a car chase on I-95. They're pursuing a white Range Rover believed to be involved in the attack."

Jack looks off into the distance with his deadly sniper stare. "I'm gonna kill that fucker," he growls.

"Well, you're gonna hafta catch him first," responds Jacob. "He's mighty slippery."

While the pair boards their plane, pursuit vehicles and police choppers trail the Range Rover as it weaves through a stream of traffic on northbound I-95.

When traffic thins near Boca Raton Airport, a small, publicly owned aviation facility, a state trooper driving a confiscated Z28 decides to make a NASCAR move. When the Range Rover passes him at ninety-five miles an hour, he bumps it gently with his car and causes the Range Rover to spin around, then flip into the air and tumble down the highway before bursting into flames.

The pursuers scramble to reach the burning car to get the driver out but exploding cartridges from a cache of weapons stored in the trunk stop them. All they can do is look on helplessly as it burns.

And just like that, another shitshow from sunny Florida hits the national news cycles.

When Jack returns home, he pours a cold Guinness and turns on the TV to relax. Flipping through the channels, the ten o'clock news reports about the chaos on Las Olas catch his attention, so he stops to watch, mesmerized by the debacle that could only come from his hometown.

While a reporter drones on, he glances at his favorite photo of Didi on the wall near the TV. "Here's to you, babe," he says, raising his glass to her memory.

Jack drinks somberly, then impulsively throws the glass into the fireplace.

With a deep sigh, he turns off the TV and stands, cracking his neck. "You're an idiot, you know that?" he asks himself, looking at the slivers of glass strewn about the unlit hearth. "Now you're gonna hafta clean that up."

Jack stares at the mess in the fireplace for a second, then shakes his head and sighs again. "Fuck it. It's gonna hafta wait. I'm goin' to bed."

After Agent Clinger and Hector ended their interview with Charlene Wilson, the VIP room dealer, Clinger didn't feel like driving back. "Do you mind if we stay somewhere overnight and leave in the morning? I know we didn't plan on this, but I've slept in my clothes before. What do you think?"

"It's okay with me," replies Hector. "Government's paying, I presume?"

"Yeah, I got you covered."

The pair books separate rooms in a town not far from the casino, then turn in for the night. Neither of them is happy with the day's results. They didn't get anything actionable from the casino employees, so they feel their impromptu trip was a bust.

Hector makes a couple of calls, then undresses down to his skivvies and climbs into bed, hoping for a good rest. But all he does is toss and turn. After an hour of restlessness, he dresses again and goes down to the lounge.

"Can't sleep, either?" calls Joyce when she sees him enter the room.

Hector rubs his chin stubble. "Nah, too hyped up, I guess. You, too?"

"Yeah. C'mon," she says, taking Hector's arm.

At ten o'clock, the lobby bar is deserted but still open, which suits them just fine.

Joyce says, "I chose this hotel because it's one of the few that serve liquor around here."

"Thank God for that!" responds Hector, climbing onto a bar stool. "Good thing this isn't a dry county."

The bartender, a young college kid, greets them cheerfully, happy for the company. "Hi, what'll it be?" he asks, placing cocktail napkins in front of them.

"Bring us a couple of beers and a plate of fried pickles," says Hector, looking over a short menu at the counter.

Joyce starts fishing for personal information when the kid leaves to fill the order. "So, how long have you been a cop?" she asks, fidgeting with her napkin.

"Oh, it's going on ten years now," answers Hector, surprised at how long it's been. "I joined after I left the Navy. How about you?"

"Five years for me. I was in D.C. for four years, then last year, they sent me to Charlotte."

"D.C., huh?" asks Hector. "I know I'm taking a chance here, but did you happen to know an agent named Maria Assante?"

Joyce is silent for a moment. "Yeah, I knew Maria. She was a great agent and a good friend. I was devastated when she died."

Clinger's ringing phone interrupts further conversation, and she moves to a table to answer it.

While Joyce is taking the call, Hector picks at the pickles the bartender places in front of him.

Not a minute later, Joyce bounds back to the bar and grabs her beer. "Drink up," she tells Gomez. "We're going back to Cherokee. My office got an address for Kaspin's house, and we're going to follow some agents there."

Joyce and Hector are trailing behind an FBI Swat team to the address they were given.

"Where the heck are we?" remarks Hector as their car bumps down a dirt road.

"I don't know... Oh, that must be it," responds Joyce, spying a modest 3/2 ranch with a two-car garage and a large metal building rising from the surrounding forest.

"Hey, you think he's here?" Joyce asks when she sees two pickup trucks in front of the metal building.

"We can only hope," replies Hector.

Before they get too close, both drivers cut their lights and engines and roll up to the house as silently as possible. Then the assault team splits up, some approaching the front of the house while the rest go around the back.

"Here, take these," says a SWAT officer, holding out two Kevlar vests to Gomez and Clinger.

"Thanks," says Joyce. "We'll join the team at the front."

At a prearranged time, both groups break through the doors and enter the house to hear loud snoring from the bedrooms.

"Must have been a party here," whispers Joyce, pointing to several empty liquor bottles strewn about the living room floor. "Let's look around."

The two bedrooms hold one man each, both snoring up a storm. Neither sleeper stirs while the team searches for their target in every room.

When they're certain he's not on the premises, they enter the bedrooms to handcuff the men. Then they drag them to the living room sofa.

Hector is frustrated that, once again, his prey has slipped through his fingers. Grabbing one of the semi-awake men, he bends down and holds his face two inches from his. "Where the hell is Serge Kaspin?" he bellows.

The young man, dressed only in dark blue briefs, is scared shitless. "I, I don't know, man!" he stammers. "We're the only ones here!"

With anger written all over his face, Hector turns to the second man, but he starts talking before Hector can get a word out.

"Hey, man!" the guy says, hoping to stave off the stranger's wrath. "We're new here! We just joined this militia! Colonel Powell brought us here and told us to keep the place safe, but he didn't say why! He just drove off in some heavy-duty military truck he took from the building outside! Who's Kaspin? We don't know who that is!"

"Are you part of the Patriot Guard?" asks Joyce.

"Yeah," responds the first man. "What's the problem?"

Joyce points to the two men. "Take them outside," she tells the officers. Then she motions to Hector. "Let's take a look in that Quonset hut."

While one assault team escorts the two losers to the MRAP, Clinger and Gomez follow the other team to the metal building.

"It's locked," says an officer. "Stand back while we break down the door."

When the team is inside, they turn on the interior lights, and gasp.

"Holy shit!" they exclaim, spotting a timer attached to plastic explosives perched on a small table. "We got a bomb!" they yell. "Get out! Get out!"

The four-person team, including Clinger and Gomez, run from the hut as fast as they can. However, they're only thirty feet away when the bomb explodes. The blast knocks all of them down and hurls large sections of wood and metal all around them.

Rolling around, Hector searches for Agent Clinger amid the dust and debris. "Shit!" he exclaims when he spots her pinned under a section of corrugated metal. The loud ringing in his ears prevents him from hearing himself yelling, but he shouts out anyway.

The SWAT officers rise to their feet, rushing to lift the metal sheeting off Clinger. When she's free, they inspect her for injuries but find none.

"She's out cold!" an officer tells Hector. "I don't know why she's unresponsive!"

Hector still can't hear anything, so he points to his ears and shakes his head no.

Jack slept well for the first time in many months, so he wakes early and heads right into the office, forgoing his customary first cup of coffee.

He parks in his usual spot, then steps out of the car, the summer heat gripping him like a vise. "Crap, too hot for this," he mutters, folding his sport jacket over an arm instead of putting it on before leaving the parking lot.

Whooooee, he whistles quietly, admiring the newly repaired façade of the building. "Looks good," he remarks to an officer passing him hurriedly.

"Too hot to chat!" the officer mutters, rushing for the coolness of the office.

Jack flicks a bead of sweat from his temple and follows the officer inside. "It's hotter here than Florida," he remarks, watching the officer wipe a handkerchief across the back of his neck.

The trip up to Jack's office is never long enough to prepare him for the mass confusion he knows he'll find when the doors open. No matter how long he's been a cop, the tense dance between victims, pimps, and perps on his floor never fails to jolt his senses. "Buckle up, buttercup," he mutters to himself as a kind of mantra to steel himself for another day's work.

Jack looks around while he walks to Homicide. It must have been a wild weekend, as the place is more crowded than usual.

When he nears his department, he sees Jacob sitting at his desk, with Sergeant Ruiz hovering nearby. "Fuck," he sighs, seeing their long faces. "Back in a minute," he calls out, steering around them for the coffee machine to delay the onset of bad news for as long as possible.

Finally, his coffee is poured, and there's nowhere else to turn. So he reluctantly shuffles toward his desk. "What happened? Someone toss you two out of bed today?" he asks, hoping to lighten the mood.

Jacob isn't feeling cheerful. "Kaspin struck again," he states glumly. "Gomez joined an FBI raid on Kaspin's house in Cherokee, but it was booby-trapped, and it went off. A special agent is in the hospital with broken ribs and a concussion, and Gomez temporarily lost his hearing. He'll be in later."

"You gotta be kidding!" moans Jack. "That guy can't

catch a break! Did they get Kaspin, at least?"

Jacob glares at Jack, his brows knitting together in astonishment. "You think I'd be in this kind of mood if we got Kaspin?"

Jack takes a sip of coffee and changes the subject. "Any news on the nuke?"

Worry lines form across Jacob's forehead, and he sighs heavily. "Chatter in Russia over the past forty-eight hours leads us to believe the purchase was completed. Interpol, the CIA, the FBI, and local police are watching all exits out of the country. But," he pauses, "the EU wants to involve NATO. They're vowing to send military resources to all the airports and seaports across Europe. There's a shit storm brewing over there. They don't want us to blame them if that device gets here."

Jack shakes his head. "Serge is no idiot. He won't use normal channels to bring that weapon here, so it'd be useless to check the usual exits. They'd be wasting their time."

No one says anything, so Jack asks, "What's going on with the Burleys?"

Jacob's eyes light up. "That's the only bright spot," he responds, vacating Jack's chair. "They're under 24/7 surveillance with armed guards all around. Kaspin won't get near them."

Ruiz gasps, and with a raised brow, looks at Jack, then turns derisively to Jacob. "How can you be sure they're safe after all that's happened, including what you just told us about the nuke? If there's anything we're sure about, it's that Kaspin can get to anyone! No one's immune to his tactics, not even your guards over there!"

"Just the guys I want to see," says Captain Conrad, unaware of the accusation Ruiz just landed. Grabbing a chair, he sits down heavily, with a case file on his lap. "Did you tell them?" he asks Jacob.

Jacob nods.

"Then you know we're currently at a standstill. Without anything more to go on, the best we can hope for is a major screw-up on Kaspin's part or someone seeing something and reporting it."

"Captain—" begins Jack.

"Let me finish," scowls Conrad. "The FBI and the CIA have evaluated the situation, and they believe the nuke will come here through Canada."

"Oh, shit!" frowns Jack. "Our border with them is a sieve!"

Conrad agrees. "I know. But it's out of our hands. The feds are handling it now, so I need you and Ruiz to return to your regular duties. We're short on personnel, and you're needed here for now. Jack, I know you're heavily invested in this, so I promise you'll be involved when the time comes. For now, I'm assigning Detective Gomez to work with Agent Assante on this angle. We need you elsewhere."

Conrad hands the case file to Stenhouse. "The sniper rifle used in the fashion show shooting at Castle Clinton came from this pawn shop in Chinatown. Vito Lucchese told us the owner does after-hours business in this type of shit. The shop is in the Fifth Precinct's jurisdiction, so we're teaming up with them."

Conrad sees surprised looks from Jack and the others, so he adds, "Keep that info about Lucchese on the down low, boys. Vito's working with us to catch Kaspin, but he doesn't want anyone to know." To Jacob, he says, "His guys in Canada will be in touch with you. Come to my office if you have any questions."

Jack opens the file and glances through it. "I know this guy," he says, holding up a photo. "His name has come up before. I think Vice and ATF are trying to build a case against him, so I'll turn this over to Sergeant Denali. Vice can bring him in for questioning."

Jack closes the file while Conrad digs in his pocket for his buzzing cell phone.

"Yeah?" he says. Listening intently, his eyes widen by the minute. "You gotta be shitting me!" he shouts, then shoves the phone back into his pocket.

Knowing there are eyes on him, he sighs heavily. "Fuckin' disaster!" he gripes. "Fuck that, Stenhouse. Our pawn shop owner is dead. The wife found him in his office with a bullet hole in his head. Jack, go down there with Ruiz and tell the guys at the Fifth what we know about him. Just make sure to leave Lucchese out of it."

CHAPTER SEVENTEEN

Jack runs into a sea of blue lights and yellow tape when he turns onto Canal Street. He parks his red beast next to a pack of patrol cars and puts a blue light on his dash. Then he and James flash their badges and duck under the yellow tape to walk up to the pawn shop.

"Here are some booties," says James, handing a pair to Jack.

Inside the crime scene, they thread their way through a crowd of uniformed police toward Detective Raymond English of the Fifth Precinct.

Raymond, a seasoned veteran and a hardass, scowls at the officers as they approach. They're in his jurisdiction, and he's not happy about it.

"What the hell is the First doing at my crime scene? We got this covered," he snarls and turns his back on them.

Unintimidated, Jack turns the man around and stands nose-to-nose with him. "Good morning to you, too," he snarls right back. "We got skin in this one. The rifle used by our Clinton Castle shooter came from your victim."

Detective English frowns but backs down. "The guy's name was Alfonso Chang. He was shot through the forehead with what appears to be a .45. Most of his brain matter is on the wall behind his desk. We're reviewing security tapes but there's no clear info on the killer."

Jack opens his mouth to speak, but English won't let him. "We did find something that may interest you, though. Come with me."

The detective leads Stenhouse and Ruiz into Chang's

office, where he points to a dark passageway behind a false shelving unit.

"Clever. Where does it lead?" asks Jack.

"Only one way to find out, right?" replies English. "Now watch your step," he points to the top of a narrow stairwell. "Use your flashlights."

At the bottom, the guys from the First gape at floor-to-ceiling racks filled with RPGs, missile launchers, grenades, sniper rifles, and automatic weapons of all makes and models.

Ruiz whistles in disbelief. "Geez! This guy knew what he was doing! Was he preparing for the apocalypse?"

"We believe the attackers in Little Italy and the one at your precinct got their weapons here."

"No kidding!" declares Ruiz. "I bet he earned a pretty penny from all this."

"Well, I hope he spent it all because he's not taking any of it where he's going," remarks Jack, still looking around at the amount of firepower stored in the hidden room.

"My guys found a laptop upstairs and a small floor safe," says Detective English. "I'll let you know what we find."

Jack heads to a rack holding a Barrett M82 .50 cal. sniper rifle. "I gotta get me one of these," he says, admiring the handling of the shoulder-fired weapon.

Just then, a couple of ATF and FBI agents enter the room, and one of them makes a beeline for Jack.

"I'll take that," he says, lifting the rifle out of Jack's hands.

Jack fakes a smile. "Let's get going," he says to Ruiz.

Outside, Jack's hackles go up when he spots a man in a silk suit standing next to his beloved Road Runner.

"Who are you?" he asks suspiciously.

"Mr. Lucchese wants to speak to you."

Jack turns, scouring the area for the mobster. Focusing on a black Bentley parked about one hundred yards away, he replies, "All right," and motions for Ruiz to follow.

At the Bentley, the suit holds his arm up to block Ruiz from going any further. "Only Stenhouse," he says, opening the back door.

Jack climbs into the car, and the door closes behind him.

"Hello, Michael," he says curtly. "Do you know something about this shooting?"

"No, I do not," replies the new Mafia chief, smoothing down an expensive tie over his expansive belly.

The motion draws Jack's eye to the neckwear's luxurious fabric. "Nice-looking tie," he comments.

"Thank you. Perhaps you could afford something like this if you were in a different line of business."

Jack chuckles. "What do you want to talk about, Michael?"

"Ah. *Va bene*. No small talk. Let us get down to business, then. I suspect you already know that this shooting is the work of 'our friend.' So I want to remind you that I have ordered my men to remove him from our list of problems."

"You're gonna remove him, huh?" grins Jack. "I remember you told me about the contract. But I also recall that your dad tried that already, and it didn't work out too well."

"Ah, yes. But I will not make the same mistake. What I intend to do now will have no impact on your investigation or on any others conducted by our government. If we find Kaspin first, well, better for you."

"Um—"

Michael pats Jack's hand. "No need to thank me. We know what he has planned and that he has obtained a nuclear device. I will let you know where that device is when we find it so you can remove it safely. However, we will not let you know when we locate him."

"Michael, you said you'd help—"

"I will help, and I will give you information, but only what I want you to know. He is not in Cherokee, but he is still somewhere in North Carolina. Now, I wish you a good day, Lieutenant. Remember to spend time with your son. *La famiglia è prima.* Family comes first."

Michael motions to the driver, who signals the man outside to open the door.

When Jack is free of the car, the goon slips into the front passenger seat, and the Bentley takes off, leaving Jack and Ruiz standing at the curb.

"What was that about?" asks James.

"Michael is serious about going after Kaspin. If they find him first, they're gonna make him disappear, and it may be permanent this time. They also know about the nuke. I don't know how they found out, but they're gonna help us find it."

"Oh? That's nice of them," scowls Ruiz. "I guess they don't want it around anymore than we do. If they were vaporized, I suspect it would put a serious crimp in their business plans."

CIA Agent Frank Sansone is having a hard time with Sylvia Burley at the safe house in Zemst. He's had to warn her repeatedly not to leave the house, but she's going stir-crazy, constantly whining about how she hates being cooped up. Her favorite argument is, "Haven't you been telling me about all the people protecting us outside? Why are they there if not to keep us safe?"

Sylvia is good at pestering, so after a particularly irritating session, Frank finally relents. "Okay!" he declares, throwing his hands up in surrender. "You can go out, but only with John, and you have to stay under the trees close to the house! And I'm going with you both!"

Elated, Sylvia throws her arms around the CIA agent. "Thank you, thank you, Frank!" she gushes. "You're the best!"

But John knows the risks and is worried. To get his wife's attention, he holds her by the shoulders and looks into her eyes. "Sylvia, we must absolutely stay under the trees. If you don't agree to that, we're not going to step one foot out of this house!"

"I know," she says, moving away from her husband. Grabbing a sweater, she asks, "Can we go now?"

John sighs and looks at Frank.

"Yeah," says Frank reluctantly. "Let me alert the guys."

Moving to another room, the CIA agent initiates a flurry of communications between himself and the officers from the Belgium government stationed in inconspicuous places around the house and on surrounding rooftops. Naturally, they're not pleased, but they defer to the CIA operative.

"All right, let's go," says Frank after getting everyone onboard. "But take it slow. And don't get too far ahead of me."

Sylvia is elated to be out in the sunshine. "Isn't it a glorious day!" she raves, carried away by the freshness of the air, the cool wind blowing through her hair, and the sounds of nature. Stooping down, she picks a few wildflowers growing haphazardly along the roadway and holds them out to John.

"Yeah, it's nice to be out, but we can't take too long," he replies. John is too nervous to be as carefree as Sylvia.

To make light of John's concern, Sylvia smiles alluringly and grabs her husband's arm. Then she fairly skips through a small apple orchard adjacent to their lodgings off Linterpoortenlaan, a two-lane road on the outskirts of town.

As promised, the couple is not alone on their stroll. Frank Sansone is walking behind them while others are watching intently from their rooftop posts.

Not long into their walk, a government officer scanning the trees along the couple's path freezes when a flash of light catches his eye. To zero in on it, he points his riflescope in that direction and adjusts the focus. "*Godverdomme*," he mutters, spotting a dark figure huddled among a tangle of branches. Concentrating on his target, he inhales slowly, then holds his breath and fires, hitting his objective squarely in the chest.

The instant Frank hears the thud of a body falling to the ground, he sweeps his gun around and shouts, "Get down!"

He needn't have bothered, though. John had already pulled his wife down and was also looking for the source of the problem.

Without delay, armed guards converge on the location given to them by the shooter. Using their radios, they inform each other that there's one man on the ground bleeding heavily from the chest.

"Everyone, report in!" orders Frank. "Are there any others?"

One by one, each officer declares his area clear.

Slowly, Frank rises from his crouched position. Then he turns to stare daggers at Sylvia. "Are you satisfied?!" he asks her angrily. "No more strolls, Mrs. Burley! Get back inside! NOW!"

Jack is hungry when he arrives at work, so he coerces James into eating breakfast at a popular eatery near police headquarters. Jack says he's tired of eating the same thing at home every day, and James is only too happy to step out of the department's madness for a while.

"Jacob's gonna meet us there," Jack says on the way.

While they wait for Jacob, the waiter comes by to take their orders.

"Should we wait?" asks James.

"Nah, let's order. I don't know when Jacob will get here."

Though the place is busy, it doesn't take long for their meals to arrive, so they dig in.

"Man, I'm hungry today," says Jack, chewing on a large piece of bacon. When he finishes, he lifts his cup and gazes out the window. "What do you think?" he asks, setting James up for one of his favorite questions. "How many of these people walking by do you think are hiding something or have broken the law one way or another?"

James stabs a forkful of eggs. "Geez, that's dark," he replies, chewing them thoughtfully.

"I know, but I've seen so many weird things on this job that I don't have much trust in humanity anymore."

"Huh. I know what you mean. It can get to you, so I've learned to let it go. The minute I step into my apartment, I lock up my firearm and go into 'me' mode. If I don't, I'll go crazy."

Jack rubs his chin. "That's good. I'll have to try that. Meanwhile, where's Jacob? He should have been here by now."

As if calling up the devil, Jack's phone rings, and he answers it quickly. "Jacob, where the hell are you?"

"York tried to commit suicide, so I'm going back to D.C. I'll be in touch as soon as I can."

"Goddam it!" grunts Jack, hanging up with a dark expression.

"What now?" asks James.

"Assante's former boss tried to kill himself, so he's on his way to D.C."

"Hell's bells! Does it ever end? That's another thing I'm gonna hafta shut off when I get home."

James picks up the bill the server left on the table. "I got this," he tells Jack, rising from his seat. "You can get the next one."

While Ruiz pays the cashier, Jack finishes his coffee as his phone rings again. "Stenhouse," he answers, then listens as a fellow officer describes a surprising find.

"Are you fuckin' kidding me?" he responds, shocked by what he's just heard. "Fuckin' A! You bet I'll be there!"

Jack pockets his phone and slides out of the booth. "Jimbo!" he calls. "We gotta go!" At the pay station, he grabs his pal's shoulder and turns him toward the door.

"What is it?" asks James, pushing his wallet and the receipt into his pocket.

"Someone placed a dead body on a bench overlooking the Lady of the Harbor! And there's a note pinned to it, addressed to me!"

Ruiz stares at Jack, not believing what he's heard. "Holy crap! She's back?!"

While the pair speeds to the crime scene, Andrea Singletary sits in a small room, staring at the ceiling. She's alone, but she doesn't mind. In fact, she prefers it that way. Most people bother her.

As if replying to a silent question, she nods and cackles happily, the sinister sound escaping from deep within. Highly pleased with her thought, she holds her arms tightly across her chest and rocks back and forth to a mysterious rhythm only she can hear.

Heavy traffic makes the trip from the restaurant almost forty minutes long, and Jack is beside himself with frustration. Because the vehicles ahead are moving too slowly for his taste, he periodically speeds up, then brakes to slow down, compelling James to grip his armrest tightly.

At last, he pulls into Battery Park, but that doesn't make him slow down. The flashing blue lights and distinctive "beep-beep" of his Road Runner force walkers, bikers, and joggers to turn aside in a hurry as he barrels toward them on the pedestrian walkways.

"Watch out!" James shouts, nervously pointing out the obvious as Jack weaves around a mother and baby.

Curses and raised middle fingers greet the Road Runner's passage, but Jack doesn't care. His sole focus is the body on the bench, and he won't let anything stop him from getting there as soon as possible.

At the crime scene, the young officer who discovered the body is still putting up a yellow tape barricade when Jack skids to a stop.

"Where is it?" he asks, leaping out of his vehicle.

"Over there," she says, pointing to a park bench facing the harbor. "I'm the one who discovered the body. Forensics and the M.E. have just arrived."

James follows closely as Jack makes a beeline for the waterside.

Without breaking stride, Jack asks, "You got gloves?"

"Yeah," responds James, handing him a pair.

Stenhouse snaps the gloves on when he arrives at the bench. The corpse is of a young woman, positioned to make it appear that her clouded eyes are looking out at the Statue of Liberty. She's wearing jeans and a hoodie, but no shoes, as her feet are nowhere to be found.

Jack removes the note pinned to the hoodie and shudders as he reads. *Detective Stenhouse, sunlight ebbs from lifeless limbs, and Jack's breath numbs the dew.*

Ruiz glances over Jack's shoulder at the note. "What the hell does that mean?" he asks. James is a relatively new addition to Homicide, so he's unfamiliar with the details of the old case.

Jack merely grunts and hands the note to a CSI officer. Then he abruptly leaves the scene, followed by James, who struggles to keep up.

"Where are you going?" asks James, annoyed by having to run again.

"*I'm* going to the First. *You're* going to the Joint Terrorism Task Force. Allison's no longer in charge there, so I need you to be my eyes and ears."

"Okay; you gonna drop me off there?"

"No. Get one of the uniforms to take you. I'm gonna be busy."

Thirty minutes later, Jack is at the First, requesting the records of the Saturnalian Killer case from a grizzled officer manning the desk of the Records Department.

"Whoa, that's an oldie but a goodie," the cop comments while he types the name of the case into his computer. "I'll send it over," he says, returning to other work.

Up in Homicide, Jack steps around a maintenance man replacing the glass in Captain Conrad's door. "Got a minute?" he asks the captain, barging into the office without knocking.

Conrad takes one look at Jack's expression and grows pale. "Yeah," he says. "But let's talk at your desk. It's too noisy in here."

Jack drops heavily into his chair as Conrad rolls an empty one over from an unoccupied desk.

"What's up?" asks Conrad. He tries to sound cheerful; however, he suspects Jack's news isn't good.

Jack drops his head and sighs. "We got a copycat killer, boss. A body was staged at Battery Park like the ones the Saturnalian Killer posed to get our attention."

For a minute, Conrad looks puzzled, then his face darkens. "Oh, now I remember. You handled that one right after you arrived here from Florida."

"That's the one," replies Jack. "The body is female; could be a hooker. The M.E. will give a final report, but it looks like she's been dead for a while. And get this — she has no feet, and she's partially frozen in this heat! There was also a note, just like before."

"Frozen, and with a note, huh? Didn't the Saturnalian killer use a freezer for the victims and quote some poem?"

"Yeah. It's the same one."

Conrad's eyes widen. "Jack, that was years ago! As far as I know, Singletary is still being treated at The Haven. That's a minimum-security facility, but still. If she got out, they'd let us know."

"Yeah, well. Someone out there must remember her and admire her work. I don't know about the missing feet, though. That's something new. Anyway, I sent Ruiz to JTTF to get a copy of the CCTV footage from Battery Park. As soon as he gets here, we're heading upstate."

Conrad rubs his temples as if trying to relieve a migraine. "Who the hell could be behind this copycat shit? It happened so long ago."

Jack shakes his head. "Maybe someone ran across Singletary at the hospital and got interested in her story. Or maybe it's a relative or a friend who's just as loopy as she is."

"Fuck. We don't need this right now. The FBI is still on our case about the nuke business."

"Any news on Kaspin?"

"No. We still don't know where he is, but a hitman with connections to him targeted the Burleys."

"Shit! Are they okay?"

"Yeah. Brussels police took out the sniper, and Sansone's

beating himself up about allowing them to go outside the safe house. He said Sylvia's been demanding fresh air, and he caved in. Said he'd chain her to a post if she makes even one peep again about being cooped up."

As if they'd planned it beforehand, Ruiz and Gomez arrive at the First's elevator at the same time.

James studies Hector closely. "Are you okay?" he asks, referring to the explosion in Cherokee.

Gomez focuses on James' mouth to understand what he's saying.

"Yeah, it's just my ears. You might say the blast was a little loud. I never thought I'd be happy to be back on the floor, but I'm honestly looking forward to the nut jobs up there."

Hector looks up to see what floor the elevator's on, then gets a twinkle in his eye. "Speaking of nut jobs," he asks, "how do you like working with Stenhouse?"

"Ah, Stenhouse," says James, turning his eyes skyward as if calling on divine intervention. "He's a hard act to follow, but I'm learning a lot. Hey, did you hear the latest?"

Ruiz brings Gomez up to speed about the copycat killer while they ride up to Homicide.

"Stenhouse must be shitting his pants," says Gomez as the elevator spits them out onto their floor.

Jack beckons James as soon as he sees him. "Jimbo!" he calls out urgently. "Did you get what we need?"

Ruiz's mouth curves upward. "This what you're looking for?" he asks, dangling a flash drive from a finger.

"Good man! Let's use your computer," declares Jack, moving to James' desk.

Obediently, Ruiz sits down, and after a few keystrokes, queues up the security tape.

"Fast forward until we see something," instructs Jack.

While they study the fast-moving images, nothing appears near an empty bench overlooking the Hudson but squirrels and blowing leaves.

Gomez joins them at the small screen. "Anything yet?" he asks.

"Nothing; it's dark. Timestamp says about three a.m."

Suddenly, a figure appears. "Stop it there!" orders Jack. "Rewind it a few seconds, then run it at normal speed."

As the recording advances, a figure dressed in a hooded sweatshirt comes into the frame pushing a wheelchair holding something wrapped in a heavy blanket. The wheelchair pusher stops at the bench, removes the blanket, then lifts an unresponsive body out of the chair. The figure places the body on the bench and arranges its limbs, making it appear to be looking out at the river.

"That's creepy," says James.

Over James' shoulder, Hector complains, "It's too dark and the hood is too low to see the guy's face."

The group studies the screen until the unknown figure walks off with the now-empty wheelchair.

"What did you guys catch from the footage?" asks Jack, rubbing his lower back after bending to watch the small laptop screen. The strain has aggravated a recurring ache.

"Our suspect is a man," says Ruiz, shutting down the computer and removing the drive.

"What makes you say that?" asks Jack.

"By the way he handled the body. He lifted it as easily as if it were a rag doll. Oh, and he has large feet."

Jack smirks at the rag doll reference. "Huh. Anything else?"

"Prints are a no-go," responds Gomez. "He was wearing gloves. And he has a bad leg."

"Right, I got that, too," responds Jack. "So, we're looking for a strong man with a bad leg. The leg may be causing him some pain because he was limping pretty badly and was using the wheelchair for balance. Look, we're gonna hafta talk to the doc treating Andrea Singletary, so before you got here, I called the mental hospital and made an appointment. The doc's name is Emily Santice. She said she has time to meet with us today. It's an hour's drive up there, so I wanna leave now. Hector, I'm gonna take Jimbo on this one. Go home and rest; you've been through a lot lately."

CHAPTER EIGHTEEN

The summer heat seems to have escaped the lush countryside and sculptured grounds of The Haven, New York-Presbyterian Hospital's Westchester Division psychiatric unit.

"Check out the temp," says James, pointing to the car's outside temperature reading as Jack drives down the facility's long winding drive. "It went down as soon as you turned into the entrance."

"Huh," responds Jack. "Guess the trees are doing their work. But look at this place! It seems more like an all-inclusive resort than a hospital!" he exclaims. "What the fuck? Nice place for a convicted loony to do time!"

A small visitor's lot comes into view ahead, so Jack points his car in that direction and parks.

As they amble up to the door, he nudges James' arm. "Look at the windows; they're reinforced," he comments, taking in the two-story brick structure with a gabled roof. "They're thick, like the impact-resistant hurricane windows back home. No one's smashing *them* to get out!"

At the entrance, the pair stops in front of a call box mounted on the wall, and Jack pushes the button. "NYPD officers Stenhouse and Ruiz are here for an appointment with Dr. Santice," he states, hoping someone is listening on the other end.

In response, a loud clack sounds, and double doors swish open to admit the men into a small, enclosed area with another set of doors directly in front of them.

"Now what?" asks James. "Are we stuck in here?"

A minute later, these doors also slide open, and the men

step into a hotel-like lobby.

"Nice," mutters James under his breath.

The lobby is decorated with high-quality carpets and comfortable lounge chairs staged along with colorful paintings and artificial plants that please the eye. The area is quiet, with only a reception desk and an armed guard behind a thick glass window.

The receptionist passes a ledger and a pen through an opening at the bottom of the glass barrier. "Please sign your names here."

The men fill out the requested information, then take two ID badges the guard pushes through the window.

"Hey, how'd you get our photos?" asks Jack, surprised that both badges sport pictures of both men.

"A camera in the vestibule takes visitor photos while you wait there. Have a seat, gentlemen. Dr. Santice knows you're here."

As they clip on their badges, a section of wall behind the desk suddenly opens, and a woman in a white lab coat breezes through a concealed door, instantly catching Jack's eye.

"Holy crap!" he mumbles to James while goosebumps form on his arms. "She looks a lot like Didi, except for her boobs!"

"Hello," says the woman, extending a hand. "I'm Dr. Santice. Welcome to The Haven."

Jack can't speak. He's too flustered to reply; it looks like he's staring at his late wife.

"Is something wrong?" the woman asks, turning to James for an answer.

"Ah, no," responds Jack, recovering from his brief scare. "You look just like… Well, never mind. Hi," he says, pumping the woman's hand. "I'm Lieutenant Stenhouse."

James waits for Jack to introduce him to the doctor, but

he doesn't, so he leans forward to do it himself. "Hello, I'm Sergeant Ruiz. Can we talk in private?"

"Yes, of course," replies the doctor. "Come this way."

Dr. Santice leads the officers through the hardly noticeable door into a typically antiseptic hospital setting.

"Hey, why the hidden door?" ask the men simultaneously.

Santice chuckles. "I was curious about it, too, so I asked. They said the builders wanted a calming space in the lobby for agitated people before they were admitted. They didn't want them to get any more riled up than they may already have been when they arrived here."

"So what happens when they get into this part?" asks Jack.

"They're okay. We give them something in the lobby to relax them."

The group passes several offices, then stops at a door at the end of the hall.

"Here we are," says Santice, motioning them into her office.

James leans close as he passes the doctor. "Please excuse my partner," he whispers. "You look just like his late wife."

Dr. Santice closes the door. Then she circles a large wooden desk and sits. "This is my business office. I meet visitors here, but I conduct patient sessions inside our facility."

As Stenhouse and Ruiz seat themselves, Santice flips open the cover of a thick file lying in the center of the desk.

"Before we begin, I'd like to extend condolences to you, Lieutenant, on the passing of your wife. Now, what do you need to know about my patient? Your call seemed urgent."

Jack is curious to know how the doctor learned about Didi but lets it slide so they can get on with business.

"Earlier today," he begins, "an NYPD officer discovered

a body at Battery Park with the same M.O. as the Saturnalian Killer from a few years ago. The body was partially frozen, and there was a note, similar to the ones your patient, Andrea Singletary, left on her victims. If we can, we'd like to speak with her, and we also need to see her visitor logs."

James raises a finger to interject, "We also need to know if anyone besides you or the staff has contact with her."

Dr. Santice leans back in her chair. "That's terrible news," she says, reacting to the finding of another dead body. "But Ms. Singletary has had no visitors in all the years she's been here. No one has come to visit her, and the only ones who've interacted with her are staff members. I understand that you need to question her, but I assure you that she hasn't left our facility. And in any case, you won't get anything out of her because she doesn't exist in our world."

This curious statement piques Jack's interest. "What exactly does that mean, doctor?"

Santice takes in a deep breath. "Before Ms. Singletary was transferred here, she was diagnosed with dissociative identity disorder, also known as DID. You may know it as multiple personality disorder. This is a mental health condition in which a person manifests two or more separate personalities."

James asks, "Like that old movie with Sally Field?"

"Yes, exactly, *Sybil*," says Dr. Singletary. "When Andrea got here, her dominant personality was Cronos. But he's been gone for about a year, along with Andrea. She now manifests an older lady she calls Rebecca. We've tried multiple therapies and procedures to bring Andrea back, but Rebecca is the only personality that communicates with us now."

Jack is concerned about the change. "Is Rebecca violent?"

"No, she's a harmless character who likes to knit and sit in the garden. As far as we can tell, she has no memory of Andrea or Cronos or anything that happened before she appeared in Andrea's mind. 'Rebecca' is in her room now, and you can speak with her if you like. Our patients don't react well to unfamiliar people invading their safe spaces, so I'll have to go with you. But only one of you can go in. I'll give you a lab coat to ease her concerns."

While the doctor fetches a white coat from a small closet, Jack stares at her rear end. Leaning over, he covers his mouth and whispers to James, "It's a fucking ghost, but with smaller tits."

Though Jack tried to be quiet, his voice carried, and the doctor heard him. Glancing down at her chest, she shrugs, then turns around and holds out the lab coat.

"Which one of you will do the interview?"

"That'll be me," says Jack, removing his sports jacket and putting on the lab coat.

"All right. Sergeant, you can either stay here or wait in the lobby."

"Oh. I'll take the lobby, thanks. Down the hall, right?"

"Right. You'll be more comfortable there."

Jack drapes his jacket over one of the chairs. "Lead the way," he says to the doctor waiting for him in the doorway.

"By the way," she says playfully, "in case you'd like to know, I'm a C cup."

Jack glances you know where, and winks at the doctor.

"Call me Emily," she says, then turns and enters the hallway.

At the end of another corridor, Dr. Santice stops in front of a security panel. "This is the entrance to our facility," she says, placing her palm on the pad.

When the lock disengages, she pushes the door open onto a resort-like setting similar to the lobby instead of the utilitarian area they came from.

The doctor points out various features while an orderly

delivers food to the rooms.

Jack asks, "No dining hall here?"

"There's a very nice dining area, but some of our clients aren't suited to mixing with other people, so they eat in their rooms."

The doctor stops at a door marked 'Rebecca's Room.'

"This is where Andrea lives," she says. "She insisted we change the door sign to Rebecca, so we complied."

The doctor pushes the door open, announcing herself in a cheery voice. "Hello, Rebecca! I brought you a visitor! His name is Dr. Stenhouse; he's from the city. May we sit down?"

Rebecca/Andrea barely looks up from her knitting.

The doctor tries again. "I love that blanket! Isn't it pretty, Dr. Stenhouse?" she asks, turning to Jack to urge him to participate in the charade.

Jack is surprised but complies. "Yes, it's lovely! You seem to have a knack for knitting."

"Rebecca," continues Santice. "Dr. Stenhouse has a patient just like you, and he would like to ask you a few questions. Is that okay?"

'Rebecca' looks up at Jack with a face so devoid of expression that he's taken aback, and for a minute, doesn't know what to do. He turns to Emily for assistance, but she simply gives him an encouraging smile.

Jack is there to do a job, so he puts the same smile on his face and plunges ahead.

"May I ask you a few questions?" he asks kindly.

The patient seems agitated, but she nods hesitantly and puts down her knitting.

Dr. Santice jumps in to protect her patient. "You know you don't have to answer anything you don't want to."

Rebecca shifts her eyes to the doctor and responds in a mature, reserved voice. "That's all right, Dr. Santice. It's just that I'm not used to receiving guests."

Sensing an opening, Jack assures the patient he won't take much of her time. Then he states, "I'd like to ask you about two names you may have heard of. Can you recall anyone named Andrea or Cronos? Do those names mean anything to you?"

Rebecca looks down at her hands. "Andrea was my daughter," she responds quietly. "She died, you know. But I don't know anyone named Cronos. Who is he?"

Jack glances at Emily, but she seems shocked. So he quickly tries to distract Rebecca from her physician's odd reaction. "Well, Dr. Santice can speak with you about that," he says. "It was nice to meet you today."

Rebecca looks up at him, and Jack notices that her face is flushed, with tiny beads of perspiration forming on her upper lip. "Thank you," she says quietly.

Dr. Santice looks at her patient curiously, then ushers Jack out of the door. "We'll talk in my office," she says, leading Jack back through the security door as the orderly watches them leave.

Jack holds his tongue until they get back into Santice's office. But once he's there, he unleashes on her and doesn't care if he's being offensive.

Spinning around to face the doctor, he throws his hands in the air and barks, "You have to be kidding me! You're a professional! Can't you see that she's playing you like a fiddle?"

The doctor's expression instantly changes from concern to irritation. "Whatever do you mean, Lieutenant? I don't like your tone. And why in the world did you mention her name or that god-awful Cronos personality? I told you that in confidence!"

Jack shakes his head, not believing what he's hearing. "I already knew about the Cronos character, remember? And didn't you see that she was nervous? She started sweating as soon as I mentioned Cronos! I don't know what kind of therapy you provide here, but I'm sure she's enjoying her little charade and her three squares a day!"

Now Dr. Santice is angry. "Wait just a minute, Lieutenant! I've been treating Andrea ever since she got here, and I can tell you that she's completely locked inside her own head! How can you tell me you know what's happening with her after only speaking with her for five minutes!"

Jack is confident in his assessment but doesn't want to argue, so he changes his approach. "Listen, I need a list of all hospital personnel who interact with Andrea in any capacity. That includes housekeepers, maintenance, nurses, doctors, aides, whoever comes into contact with her in any way. And I'm going to petition the court to have her transferred to a maximum-security facility. This place is too comfy for her."

Dr. Santice is still upset, but she knows that Andrea has committed heinous crimes. "If that's what you want to do," she says, "I won't interfere. Andrea is stable at the moment, and if she's moved, I could still treat her in a different facility. But I'll have you know that I'm not at all happy about this!"

"I understand," says Jack. "But my intuition is usually spot-on, and based on what I remember about Andrea Singletary and how she operates, she wouldn't have any trouble fooling you or anyone else!"

The doctor sighs and sits down heavily at her desk. "That's the first time in a long time she's acknowledged having any thoughts about Andrea or even mentioned Cronos!"

Dr. Santice extends her fingers and rests her chin on them. "Our facility has another building that's more secure. I'll make all the arrangements for her to move there; no need to get the courts involved."

Jack is pleased. A court order would take time, and this will be quicker. "Thank you," he says. "Now, how about those names?"

"Give me thirty minutes," says Santice. "You can wait here, or you can go to the lobby. There's a small refreshment area in the corner."

Jack removes the lab coat and grabs his sports jacket. "I'll join Sergeant Ruiz out there. Here's my card. Don't hesitate to call me if she slips up again and says anything more about Cronos or anything else."

Emily takes Jack's card and gives him one of hers. "You can also call me, Lieutenant. I know I got pretty upset, but I assure you that I'll do everything I can to get to the bottom of this. I wouldn't mind working more closely with you," she adds, tossing back her hair flirtatiously.

Jack stops to fill up his beast on the return trip to the First.

"You need gas already?" asks James, looking up from a stack of personnel files on his lap. "You filled up this morning."

"I know, but seven mpg doesn't get me very far."

"Ha! That's exactly why I drive a compact car," retorts James, returning to the files.

Jack sticks his head into the driver's side door while he works the pump. "Why don't we split up those files? You take some, and I'll take the rest. That way, we can go over them more thoroughly. According to Emily...uh, Dr. Santice... all of those people have interacted with Andrea at one time or another. We can compare notes in the morning."

Jack arrives at work bright and early the next morning despite reviewing the personnel files late into the night. None of them struck a note with him, so while he drinks a second cup of coffee, he remembers Dr. Santice's business card. Pulling it out of his wallet, he stares at it long and hard, then sighs and opens his desk drawer to search for a magnetic clasp.

"Where the hell are those things when you need one?" he mutters, pushing aside paper clips, pens, and miscellaneous slips of forgotten paper. Finally, he finds what he's looking for stuck to the side of the drawer. "Ah, there you are!" he mutters, holding up the clasp triumphantly. Grabbing the business card, he inserts it into the clasp's jaws and then sticks the magnet to the side of the metal cabinet next to his desk. Jack is staring at the card again when Ruiz breezes by, heading for the coffee station.

The previous evening, James reviewed his share of the files, then watched TV late into the night. So he really needs his pick-me-up and isn't happy when he hears Jack shout, "Oh, fuck! Forget that coffee, Ruiz! We got another body, and this one is missing its legs! This is bullshit! Is this gonna be another nut job like the Saturnalian Killer?"

On their way to the elevator, the men meet Captain Conrad and Detective Gomez coming on shift.

"Whoa, what's goin' on?" asks Conrad, just missing being run down by Jack.

"We got a legless body floating in the East River! Gomez, come with us! Captain, can you do me a favor?"

"What do you need?"

"Call Assante. We should get the FBI involved. This may be another serial killer!"

A quick trip to the Brooklyn Bridge brings Stenhouse and Gomez to the old Fulton Fish Market. In the parking area, they stand silently beside the car to wait for Sergeant Ruiz, who was following them in an unmarked sedan.

When he joins them, Jack throws his shoulders back and

inhales deeply. "All right," he says, steeling himself for what they're about to find beyond the line of yellow tape. "Let's get it over with."

"I'm not looking forward to this either," remarks Gomez somberly. "But at least we're not freezing our asses off this time."

Jack's head snaps around just as the men step onto a grassy area. "Geez! I thought that was Maria for a second!" he says, catching sight of an official-looking black SUV turning into the parking lot. "This case is bringing back too many bad memories."

"That's Jacob," says Hector, spotting Maria's brother at the wheel.

When the special agent joins them, the men pass under the barricade, then watch as an NYPD harbor unit pulls a woman's legless body onto their boat to bring it ashore.

Jack turns to Ruiz. "We're gonna need to look at the security footage from around the building, so I'm gonna put you in charge of that. Then, you can go to JTTF to get the footage from the other cams along the river."

"Sure," says James, happy to get to work.

Jack turns to Jacob. "I have an idea, but you may not like it."

"Why?"

"I was thinking that, just for shits and giggles, you and Gomez could check out the old meat packing house Cronos used."

"Huh. I see where you're going with this. That's a good idea."

"Great. Meanwhile, I'll accompany the body to the M.E."

"All right," says Jacob. "But before we split up, you should know that everything has gone cold on Kaspin. There are no leads, not even from Lucchese."

Jack is disappointed but not surprised. "What about LaGrange? Anything on him?"

"No, we're still working with Interpol to track him down. The only thing we know for sure is that he was last seen in Estonia. We're fairly sure he hasn't left that country yet."

When the victim's body is placed on the pavement, Jack puts on Nitrile gloves to look at it closer before the M.E. arrives.

"She seems young," comments Jacob.

"Yeah. Probably in her late teens or early twenties."

Jack turns the woman's head. "There's a bruise here," he says, examining a discolored area on her left temple. "Could be blunt force trauma."

Then he looks over both arms. Finding nothing there, he moves on to where her legs should be. "Sheesh," he says, trying not to divert his eyes. "These are clean cuts."

When Jack finishes his brief exam, he stands and snaps off his gloves. "It looks to me like the legs were removed postmortem. But the M.E. is the one who needs to say that for sure."

Gomez is disgusted. "Fuckin' bastard who did this should be hanged," he grumbles disapprovingly. "I know I shouldn't say that, but it's just so awful."

"I have a sick feeling that Andrea Singletary knows about this," says Jack.

Gomez replies, "Maybe you should talk to Dr. Santice again."

"Yeah. Maybe I should."

CHAPTER NINETEEN

Love Valley, a small North Carolina community about two hours north of Charlotte, was created in 1954 to look like an old western town. To this day, the streets are dirty and dusty, with only horses and horse-drawn carriages allowed inside town limits. As horses are the primary means of getting around, hitching posts and wooden water troughs are found throughout the downtown area, maintaining the Old West charm, along with occasional wooden sidewalks attached to certain establishments. The quaint municipality looks like a movie set for a TV western, which suits full-time residents just fine. Aside from the summer tourist season that brings in hundreds, the simplicity and quiet of the valley are what the residents like best.

This leisurely atmosphere is what also attracted Serge Kaspin. When Love Valley turned up in his research for a new location, he liked it so much that he purchased a cabin in the surrounding hills. But since the town is small, he knew he couldn't remain hidden, so to blend in with the locals, he also bought a business.

The hotel Serge bought was well-established but had become too much for its elderly owner. When Serge snapped it up, he planned to add a small restaurant to the lower level and rename it the Horseshoe Saloon and Hotel.

The tourist season was already in full swing when Serge moved there, so he let his underlings handle the day-to-day remodeling of his project. For Serge, that venture is only a diversion. His main concern still revolves around taking revenge on the United States government.

Across the Atlantic, Prime Minister Olev Lepik is enjoying his trip to Canada. The crew on his yacht *Phoenix* is making the long journey delightful, even though he's had to work most of the time. If the weather cooperates, the captain estimates that the ship should reach Canada in ten days, so Lepik is starting to review his schedule for the important meeting.

Interpol operative Claude LaGrange is also on his way to the summit. He arrived early at Tallinn Airport, Estonia's major link to the world, to catch a connecting flight to Canada through Paris. He has much to do in Quebec City, so getting there before the summit should give him enough time to accomplish what he needs to get done.

Today, the airport is busy, which LaGrange considers a good thing. He believes the more people there are, the less he'll be noticed. Still, he periodically checks his surroundings for unusual activity.

On the other hand, while the extra crowds are good in one way, they're also slowing the check-in process at the Nordica desk, and that's not a good thing.

When LaGrange's turn finally comes, he bounds up to the clerk and presents his credentials with a smile. "Nice day for flying," he says, hoping to appear as just another happy traveler.

However, the clerk suddenly appears nervous. He looks at LaGrange's ID, glances at the agent's face, then nods ever so slightly and turns away, unexpectedly engrossed in his computer screen.

Claude notices the odd reaction. But before he can do anything about it, a dapper gentleman, accompanied by two uniformed police officers, appears at his side.

"You are under arrest," says the man with a French

accent.

Claude's stomach drops. He realizes he's been made and briefly considers resisting. But with so many people around, he knows it would be foolish. So instead, he holds his head high and allows himself to be led out of the airport.

At the morgue, Jack heads down a long dim hallway, remembering a similar trip he made years ago at the Fort Lauderdale morgue with Didi on his arm. *Why do I keep thinking about her like this?* he grumbles, then dismisses the unwelcome thought while pushing aside the facility's swinging doors.

"Howdy, Doc," he cheerfully greets Medical Examiner Dr. Jennifer Stark. Jack has been in the morgue so many times that he can easily overlook the fact that the woman is standing in front of possible victims of another copycat killer. Two naked corpses are lying on adjoining metal tables, waiting for the M.E. to determine their causes of death.

Jennifer lifts her face shield to talk to Jack. "You arrived just in time. I'm about to begin my examinations."

"Oh, goody," Jack responds sarcastically. "You know how I love watching you cut into dead people."

The doctor scowls while buttoning up her lab coat and snapping on surgical gloves. "If you want to join me, you can grab a pair of goggles and gloves from that desk over there."

"Nah, I'm good," says Jack, stepping closer to the table Jennifer is about to work from.

With a shrug of indifference, the doctor begins by examining the arms of one victim and doing the same with the other one. "Well, it's obvious that both of them were heavy drug users, and I'd guess it was heroin."

The doctor inspects both chests and buttocks, then

moves down to the legs and studies the stumps on each body. "In my opinion, the killer removed the limbs with exceptionally clean cuts after the victims died. All the legs were severed at the joints, almost like boning a chicken."

Dr. Stark grabs a clipboard, flips through the pages, then turns to Jack. "The woman from Battery Park was partially frozen, and I don't have a time of death yet. But the woman from this morning was killed sometime during the night. I'd say around one a.m."

Dr. Stark walks over to a lab table, then hands Jack an evidence bag holding a piece of paper. "I found that on the corpse on the bench. It appears to be part of the same poem that Andrea Singletary, aka Cronos, left on her victims."

"I saw this, too," he says, reading through the plastic, *Winter's grey will take its toll on the unsuspecting few.*

Stark tells Jack that she sent the clothes to Forensics and that she'll need an internal to determine the first victim's cause of death. However, she believes the second one's skull trauma may be what killed her. Then she asks, "You want to stay while I do the internals? I wouldn't mind the company. There's popcorn in the vending machine."

Jack laughs. "I like your style, Doc, but I'll pass. I guess I'll go back to the precinct now. Forensics is gonna need this note."

"Suit yourself," Stark replies, pulling forward a table filled with surgical equipment.

With one look at the sharp instruments, Jack turns on his heel, hoping to leave before the doctor begins her craft. However, he barely makes it through the doors before the sound of a buzzing surgical saw reaches his ears. "I'll never understand how such an attractive woman can work with dead bodies all day," he mutters, quickening his pace to leave the gloomy facility.

Days after the shooting, Ken and Cindy Rodriguez start cleaning up their gallery. Their first tasks were to board up the broken windowpanes and order impact-resistant windows. Now, they're working with a local crew putting up new drywall. Because there's so much to do, Ken removed his sling and is also helping them mud the walls.

To pay for the damage their insurance won't cover, Cindy has been holed up in their office all day, making deals and setting up new fashion shows. So when she rushes out into the gallery, Ken turns and stares at her from his position high up on the scaffolding.

"What's up?" he asks.

Cindy is beaming. "I just signed us up with a TV shopping network, and they already sent the contract to the lawyer! We're gonna meet with him this evening! Kenny, if all goes well, we're gonna be in phat city!"

Back at the First, Stenhouse is surprised to see a familiar face from Fort Lauderdale in the forensics lab.

"What the hell are you doing here?" he asks, pointing at technician John Lennon.

John looks up from a microscope. "I'd shake your hand, but I'm a little occupied right now," he replies, leaning down again to peer through the eyepieces.

Jack can't resist getting in a dig. "What happened?" he asks sarcastically. "Did you miss me so much that you had to follow me all the way up here?"

"You wish," responds John, not looking up from his work. "Inspector Rawlings met with Captain Jeffers while he was on vacation. You remember the sunny days in Fort

Lauderdale, don't you?"

"Rawlings went on vacation? I thought he was a workaholic."

"Guess not. Apparently, your precinct needs help, and Rawlings heard about my stellar credentials. So, here I am. He made me an offer I couldn't pass up."

"Stellar, huh?" laughs Stenhouse. "Did you lie on the interview?"

"Same old Stenhouse," chides John.

Jack smiles. "So, when did you get here?"

Finally, John straightens up. "Last week. Oh, hey, sorry about Didi, man. Real bummer. That must be hard on you, with the little one, and all."

Jack swallows and looks away, so John changes the subject. "You have something for me?"

"Yeah," responds Jack, relieved to have something different to think about. "This was on our victim at Battery Park," he says, holding out the bagged note from Dr. Stark's morgue. "See what you can find on it, will ya?"

John takes the bag and places it on his lab table. "I did a preliminary check of the clothes from both victims and found similar hair strands that don't match either body. We're running a DNA test, so I'll let you know what we find."

"Okay. Anything else?"

"We ID'd both victims. Here, I'll show you."

John brings up two sets of criminal records on his computer. "Both of them have priors on drug and prostitution charges, so I ordered their files from Records. They should be here soon. You can wait, or I can send them up to your desk."

"Um, just send me the files. But call me if you get any good DNA results.

Jack turns to leave, then stops and swivels his head around. "Hey, good to see ya, man. And I really mean that."

"Well, this is one place we can knock off our list," says Gomez when he pulls up to the site of the old meat-packing plant used by Andrea/Cronos.

"Sheesh; there's nothing left," agrees Jacob as demolition crews haul off twisted pieces of concrete and metal from the scene of some of the city's most grisly crimes. "So what do you want to do now?" he asks Hector. "Feel like taking a ride up to The Haven instead?"

"Yeah, we could do that," replies Hector, putting the car into reverse.

When they arrive at The Haven, Jacob looks around the tastefully decorated lobby of the behavioral center treating Andrea Singletary. "Seems Jack was right," he declares. "This doesn't look like a hospital at all. Singletary was supposed to be transferred to a maximum-security psychiatric facility, and I've never seen one of those look this nice."

"Guess money talks," replies Gomez, keeping one eye on an attractive woman approaching them.

"Hello, I'm Dr. Santice," says the woman, holding out a hand. "Where's Lieutenant Stenhouse? I thought he'd be with you."

Jacob stifles a grin. "The lieutenant is investigating another victim. I'm FBI Special Agent Assante, and this is NYPD Detective Gomez. We're working with the lieutenant on the case he talked to you about, and we're here to speak with Ms. Singletary."

"Oh. Well, I don't know if that will be possible. Unfortunately, we had a setback last night, so she may not be responsive." When the men look disappointed, she adds, "However, if you still want to try, she's in our maximum-security facility."

Hector and Jacob look at each other, trying to decide what to do. Then Jacob nods and says, "I think we'd like to try. Can you take us to her?"

"Yes, of course. Please follow me. We'll need to ride over there in one of our carts. It's a long walk, and the weather has been pretty hot lately."

On the way through a security door out to a courtyard, Jacob says, "isn't this whole place maximum-security?"

"Oh, no," replies Santice, climbing aboard a golf cart. "We only put our most difficult patients there. The rest of the campus is a regular hospital."

"Ready?" she asks, starting the cart, then driving it along a winding trail toward an unusual-looking edifice shielded by trees and low shrubs.

"Wow, where's the moat?" asks Gomez, looking up at a red brick facade with narrow slits for windows and guard towers along the roof.

The doctor leaves the cart in front of the door, then leads the men through another secure entrance, this one manned by armed guards at a metal detector.

"More security?" asks Hector.

"Yes. There are thirty-five patients here, and we don't take any chances with them. Most of them have violent anti-social tendencies."

The men fill small baskets at the metal detector with their weapons, extra clips, badges, and the usual items TSA requires when going through airport screening. Then, at the other end, they retrieve their belongings and follow Santice through another security door she accesses with a retinal scan.

"Sophisticated," mumbles Jacob while they wait for the door to open.

Once inside, Dr. Santice turns toward the men. "As I said, Andrea Singletary has regressed to her original state. You may be able to talk to her, but it would likely be Cronos who responds."

Jacob looks down an antiseptic prison corridor. "Do any of the support personnel from the other facility work here as well?"

Santice shakes her head. "Oh, no, not with these patients. They need specialized care. Come on; I'll bring you to Ms. Singletary's quarters."

Halfway down the corridor, Dr. Santice stops in front of one of many metal doors fitted with a small access panel for transferring food and other items. To the left of the door is a large monitor that enables the staff to look into the room without opening the door.

Santice pushes a button. Then an image of Andrea appears on the screen. She's sitting on her bed, staring at the ceiling.

"Ms. Singletary," says the doctor, pressing another button, "there are a couple of visitors here who would like to speak with you."

For a long moment, it doesn't seem that Andrea heard the doctor. But then she stands and slowly approaches the monitor inside her cell. "Why did you say that?" she asks in a voice devoid of emotion. "You know Rhea isn't here. Who is asking about her?"

Jacob steps in front of the monitor so Andrea can see him. "My name is Special Agent Jacob Assante. I'm with the FBI." Jacob shifts position to make room for Hector, then says, "Detective Gomez from NYPD is here as well. We need to ask you some questions."

Andrea's eyes narrow into dark slits as she studies the images on the monitor. Then she laughs hauntingly and cocks her head to one side. "Interesting," she says. "I'm Cronos, and I remember an agent named Maria Assante. Are you her brother?"

"Yes," replies Jacob.

Andrea's eyes light up, then darken again. "Neither of you concern me. But, if you want Saturn's children to stop dying, I suggest you get Jack Stenhouse up here. I'll speak to no one except him. Besides," she says with a malicious grin, "Dr. Santice likes him. Hahahahaha."

Andrea's expression grows blank, and her eyes take on a distant look. Then she turns around, walks back to her bed, and sits down, looking up at the ceiling again and refusing to answer any more questions.

Flushed with embarrassment, Dr. Santice turns off the monitor.

Jacob is amused. "I won't ask about that last comment," he states, "but I guess Jack is going to have to make another trip up here."

Hector walks alongside Jacob while they follow the doctor out of the facility. "Seriously?" he mouths to Jacob. "Stenhouse, again?!" Neither man can understand women's strong attraction to the guy they work with every day.

When forensic tech John Lennon shows up at Jack's desk, he's carrying two files.

"Here ya go. Happy reading," he says, tossing the folders onto a pile of papers. "Hey, whatcha got there?" he asks, catching a glimpse of the name on a large box taking up most of the space on the desk.

"Oh, I'm reviewing the file from the Saturnalian Killer case."

"Right," states Lennon, understanding the possible connection to the latest victims. "Say, you still got that Road Runner?"

"Yeah, she's my first 'baby.' My other one, the flesh and

blood one, is with his grandma right now."

Lennon smiles. "You must be happy to have someone who can take over your legacy one day."

Jack clamps his mouth shut and looks away, giving John a strong hint that the conversation is over.

"Um," the technician says, self-consciously shifting his weight from one foot to the other. "I'll notify you as soon as we get more info." Then he turns on his heel and leaves.

Jack watches John retreat to the comfort of his lab. "If Mark becomes a cop, I'll beat his ass," he mumbles. "I don't care how old I am or how old he is." Then he sighs and shoves all the folders into the box for the Saturnalian Killer.

Hefting the carton onto one shoulder, he heads to Captain Conrad's office and peeks in through the open door. "I'm taking these files home with me," he calls out. "When Assante and Gomez get back, can you tell them to come to my place? Ask them to bring beer and pizza, too. Ciao!"

Conrad rolls his eyes but agrees to pass Jack's message on.

Later that night, an entire pepperoni pie and a half case of Guinness are finished in a flash.

"I'm still hungry," says Jack, flipping open the top of the second pizza box. "Oooo, extra cheese," he says, grabbing a slice and cracking open another cold one.

"You guys remember Sandy Harris?" he asks. "She was one of the hookers we busted in the Cronos case."

"Yeah," they mumble between chewing and swallowing.

"Well, she started a halfway house in Soho where they rescue girls to get them out of the sex trade. So I'm thinking she may have known our two victims, or maybe one of her rescues knew them."

Hector asks, "What are their names again?"

"Lisa Palmer and Julianna Colon."

Jacob grabs another beer and a slice. "I'll check on Ms. Harris," he says, taking a bite out of his fourth helping. "You're gonna be busy going upstate to talk to Cronos." Jacob chews, then gulps from his beer to help him swallow. "But don't go there alone, Jack," he says with a grin. "Take Gomez with you."

Jack shoots him a look. "I don't need any help—" he starts saying until a loud guffaw interrupts him.

"You're gonna need a chaperone!" laughs Jacob loudly, slapping one hand on the table. "That doctor's got a serious case of the hots for your ass, buddy!"

CHAPTER TWENTY

The next morning, another summer day breaks with the sun peeking through dark storm clouds, heralding another wave of thunderstorms.

"Gonna be dismal," remarks Jack, turning on his headlights.

Hector looks up at the dreary sky. "You really think Cronos is back?"

"That's what Jacob said. I'm not lookin' forward to today."

While the men drive to The Haven, Jacob Assante turns onto Spring Street to look for the building where Sandy Harris operates her rescue center.

"That must be it," he mutters, spotting a characterless brick structure on the other side of the street.

Like many other places in the Big Apple, getting a convenient parking spot anywhere near here will be as impractical as finding hens' teeth. So Jacob doesn't hold out much hope as he cruises slowly down the street.

"Shit! No parking allowed? That figures!" he shouts, cursing an unwelcome road sign. "All right, then, fuck it!" he says. "I'm gonna do a Stenhouse!"

Jacob pulls his vehicle up onto the sidewalk like he's seen Jack do countless times. "If he can do it, so can I!" After turning off the engine, he exits the vehicle with two folders held under one arm.

"Geez," he mumbles when a police cruiser with blue lights flashing pulls up alongside him. "Hello, Officer," he says, flashing his FBI badge through the cruiser's open window. "I won't be long. I'm on Federal business."

The officer studies the badge, glares at him, and drives off, even though the street's apartment dwellers are trying to catch her attention. They aren't happy about Jacob's parking technique and want her to do something about it.

Jacob knows they're upset, but he tells himself that he's entitled to a bit of leeway and weaves around them to cross the street, hoping none of them makes a move to stop him.

"It shouldn't be this difficult to do my work," he mutters, rechecking the business name above the door of the address he's looking for.

Several years ago, prostitute Sandy Harris radically changed her life when street friends fell victim to the horrific crimes committed by Andrea Singletary as her Cronos personality. She tried to escape the life before but had never been able to until that case, which jarred her to her core. The murders frightened her and her other friends, and she vowed to do whatever she could for everyone on the street. Knowing she couldn't do it alone, she sought financial help from wealthy acquaintances — some say her ex-clients — and purchased an old hotel.

Jacob strains to pull open the rusting door of the building, now a rescue center. Nestled between two large potted plants, a woman dressed modestly in a button-down blouse and jeans sits behind a reception desk that's seen better days. Looking up from a magazine. she says in a gravelly voice, "Welcome to New Beginnings. My name is Jackie. How can I help you?" The woman is young, but hard edges are present in her voice and demeanor.

"I'm FBI Agent Assante," says Jacob, presenting his credentials. "I'd like to speak with Sandy Harris, please."

"Uh," stammers the woman, unaccustomed to dealing with law enforcement without her hands in handcuffs. "Sandy's busy right now. She's, um, interviewing a new resident. Uh, have a seat. I'll tell her you're here."

Jacob arches a brow. He doesn't remember seeing a place to sit, so he looks around questioningly.

Jackie understands his confusion. "In there," she says, pointing to a small room off the lobby.

Jacob gets a root beer in a snack area with metal tables and chairs, cheap paintings, and two vending machines. Then he sits at a corner table facing the door. His visit is unscheduled, so he settles down for a long wait. He doesn't know when Sandy will be able to see him.

Fortunately, it doesn't take long. By the time he's halfway through his drink, a tall, buxom woman with care lines etched into her carefully made-up face breezes into the room. "Hello," she says, extending a manicured hand. "I'm Sandy. What can I do for you?"

Jacob stands. "Can we talk in private?"

"This is as good a place as any," replies Sandy, pulling out a chair. "No one will be using this room till noon or so."

"Okay," Jacob says, resuming his seat. Opening his folders, he slides two crime scene photos in front of Sandy. "Do you recognize either of these women? They were murdered a few days ago."

Sandy leans over to take a closer look while Jacob explains, "We know you were active in the life when the Saturnalian killer was around, and these murders are similar. We're investigating them as possible copycat crimes."

The reformed streetwalker inhales a ragged breath and looks up at Jacob through glistening eyes. It's shocking that the sickening crimes she remembers so vividly could be happening again.

Sandy blinks and looks at the photos again. "I knew her,"

she says, pointing at Lisa Palmer. "She interviewed here but never took the leap out. You really think there's a sicko out there doing it again?"

"Could be," replies Jacob. "Can you tell me where Lisa worked? Someone from the same track may be able to shed light on her killer."

"Yeah. I'm pretty sure she hung out at an old dive bar called the Rusty Anchor. It's on the Brooklyn side of the bridge. Lots of dockworkers go there to get their rocks off. It's not a friendly place."

"What about this other photo?"

"I don't know her."

"Okay," says Jacob, shoving the photos back into their folders. "You've given me a start. Here's my card. Please call me if you think of anything else that could help."

Sandy tosses back her long hair. "I'll keep it in mind. But hey," she says, looking at Jacob thoughtfully. "I know you're FBI, but maybe you can tell me... Is Jack Stenhouse still at the First?"

Jacob knows where this is going. "Yeah, he's still there. As a matter of fact, he's in charge of this investigation."

Sandy's smile is serious. "You know, that man saved my life. He busted me in a sting operation a while ago, and that's what led to my recovery, and this place." Sandy extends an arm to encompass the entire rescue center. "Tell him I said hi. And could you let him know I'd like to see him again? You know, to say thank you."

Jacob sighs but says, "No problem. I'll let him know."

Back outside, Assante curses when he sees his car. "Fuckin' shit!!" he exclaims, walking around the vehicle to examine several deep scratches on the side and rear. "This never happens to Stenhouse!!"

When Dr. Santice strolls through the concealed door in The Haven lobby, Jack has to suppress a whistle. Though the mental health professional is wearing a traditional white lab coat, it's obvious that her tight black leather skirt and white blouse, unbuttoned just a little, were designed to draw his attention.

"Welcome back," she says, smiling a little too widely for a professional visit. "It's nice to see you again."

Sitting beside Jack, Hector rolls his eyes when he sees him looking just where Emily hoped he would.

Eventually, Jack's eyes shift upward. "Good afternoon," he replies, trying to keep things serious. "A colleague told me Cronos Theopolis wants to speak with me."

Dr. Santice grins and wraps her arm around Jack's, urging him out of his seat. "Come with me, Lieutenant. Let's not keep Cronos waiting."

In the courtyard, the doctor climbs into the golf cart and slaps the seat next to her to show Jack where he should sit. Relegated to third place, Hector slips into the back for the quick ride to the secure building at the rear of the hospital campus.

Inside the maximum-security entrance, Santice empties her pockets into a tray. "Things are tight here," she explains before going through the security protocols ahead of Jack and Hector. After all of them pass through, the doctor leads them to Andrea's room.

On the way, an orderly pushing a supply cart captures Jack's attention. Something seems off, so he stops to watch. But the man isn't doing anything suspicious; he's only walking down the hall, whistling an unfamiliar tune.

"You ready?" asks Dr. Santice when Jack catches up.

"I guess so," he replies, looking back down the hall.

Dr. Santice hits a button on the monitor next to the door to show the inside of Andrea's room.

"What's she doing?" asks Hector, seeing Andrea pacing round and round.

"That's what she does most of the time," says Santice. "It seems to calm her."

The room is barely furnished with a plastic-covered mattress, no bed covers, and a stainless-steel combination sink and toilet. There is no shower, no TV or chair, and no window.

"That looks dreary as hell," comments Jack. "Do they eat in there, too?"

"Yes, we pass their trays through this opening, and they eat at their beds."

Jack looks at Andrea. "Can I talk to her?"

"Yes, this button enables two-way conversations.

Jack reaches out and presses the button. "Cronos, it's Jack Stenhouse. You wanted to talk to me, so here I am."

Inside the room, Andrea stops abruptly and peers at the monitor with dark eyes. Then she emits a maniacal cackle that makes Jack and Hector shudder. They remember that haunting sound, not at all fondly.

Cronos raises his chin defiantly. "I suppose you have seen my children by now. How are you, old friend?"

Jack recoils from the notion that Cronos considers him a friend. "Look, we're not buddies, all right? I'd like nothing better than to keep you locked up here with no visitors for the rest of your life. But things have been happening again, and I think you have something to do with them. So, tell me, Cronos, what do you know about the city's newest murders?"

The personality Andrea calls Cronos sits on the edge of the bed and begins to massage her breasts. "I can't get used to these things. They feel nice, though. Stenhouse, winter's grey will take its toll again, but you already know that. All you need is right in front of you. Do you like what you see?"

Andrea, aka Cronos, reaches into her waistband and starts to masturbate, so Dr. Santice quickly shuts off the monitor. "Sorry about that," she says to the men as loud laughter seeps through the door.

Jack looks at the doctor. "Do you tape your interactions with her?"

"Um, yes, that's standard procedure here. We ask our patients to sign a form acknowledging that their sessions will be recorded for later review. That's so we can recall everything that was said."

"Then I'll need to see your recordings for the past two weeks."

The doctor suddenly stiffens. "That's privileged information, Lieutenant. You know I can't release that information without a warrant. It's controlled by HIPAA privacy laws."

That's all Jack needs to hear. Standing nose-to-nose with Santice, he growls, "So much for your sexy flirting implying cooperation. I'll get that warrant, and then I'll be back, all within twenty-four hours. And if I think any of those tapes are missing, or were altered in any way, I'll arrest you for tampering with evidence and impeding my investigation. No need to drive us back. We'll walk to the parking lot. See you tomorrow, Doctor."

Dr. Santice opens her mouth to speak but thinks better of it and clamps it shut. Instead, she accompanies them to the exit and lets them out without a word.

"What the hell happened back there?" asks Hector as they walk the path to the parking area.

Jack shakes his head. "I'm not sure. She could just be protecting her rights and her patient's rights, but there could also be something she's not telling us. Cronos said it's right before our eyes."

"We gotta get that warrant," says Hector, turning around when he doesn't see Jack beside him anymore.

"What is it?" he asks.

"Someone here is killing for Cronos, and I'm gonna find that fucker."

Hector widens his eyes. "You got a hunch?"

"Yeah, something isn't right."

The men continue in silence, each absorbed by his own thoughts. When they emerge from the courtyard, Hector returns to old business.

"What's the latest on Kaspin?"

"Nothing!" replies Jack irritably. "Assante says they think he's still in North Carolina, and they're still looking for that Interpol agent who's helping him. But he probably already has the nuke by now, and who the fuck knows where that is!"

When they reach Jack's car, his cell phone rings as he sticks his keys into the door. "Stenhouse," he answers, instantly recognizing the voice. "Speaking of the devil," he says, listening to the caller. "You did?" he says, looking directly at Hector. "That's great! Thanks!"

Hector watches Jack's face light up. "He must have heard us talking about him! That was Assante. They caught the guy from Interpol — Claude LaGrange — trying to leave Estonia. They're transporting the asshole to Lyon. Assante's going there, and he wants you to go with him."

"Lyon? That's in France, right?"

"Yeah. You got a problem with that?"

"Heck, no! I've never been to France," says Hector, his eyes lighting up with anticipation. "But you think the Captain will let me go?"

"Don't worry; I'll convince him."

"I sure hope so," replies Hector. "Oh, but what about Cronos? This is starting to get interesting."

"I'll get Jimbo to help me with that fucker."

Hector grins merrily. "So, I'm goin' to France? *Au revoir, Monsieur*," he adds, doing a little jig and tipping Jack an imaginary hat.

Stenhouse laughs and good-naturedly shoves Hector in the arm. Then they both enter the red beast, and Jack heads south after giving his trademark sign, two quick beeps of his horn.

CHAPTER TWENTY-ONE

The following day, Jack drives Hector to the airport before going to work.

"Hey, boss," he says, taking a seat in front of Captain Conrad's desk. "I need your help."

Conrad looks up, his brow arching in surprise. Stenhouse doesn't ask for help often, but when he does, it's for a good reason. "What's going on, Jack?"

"The doctor at The Haven won't release the recordings of her sessions with Singletary. She wants a warrant first."

"So? Ever hear of HIPAA laws?"

"I know. But I got a bad feeling about this. Can you rush a warrant request through? I don't want to give anyone time to destroy evidence."

Conrad cricks his neck. "You think that's a possibility?"

Jack narrows his eyes. "My shit-o-meter is sky-high right now. I get the feeling that someone at that hospital is sympathetic to Singletary or Cronos, or whatever she's calling herself. She or he, I don't know how to refer to her, said things are there, right before our eyes. So I want to be cautious. Oh, and, by the way, Gomez is going to France with Assante."

Conrad picks up his phone. "Yeah, I know. He called to let me know he won't be in for a while. Very responsible of him," Conrad says, looking squarely at Jack. "Now, let me get to work on your warrant."

Confident that his request will go through, Jack heads down to Forensics, where his favorite 'Beatle' works. Unfortunately, John Lennon isn't at his desk, pouring over some minuscule piece of data.

"Hey, where's the Beatle?" he asks a technician.

Glancing over his shoulder, the tech says, "He went to see a man about a horse."

To wait, Jack sits down at John's workstation, and starts looking at the various articles of clothing scattered around the table.

"Don't touch anything!" orders John, upset that Jack is sitting at his desk.

Startled by the sharp command, Jack jumps off the chair. "Not guilty, your honor!" he shouts, raising his hands high.

John takes the seat vacated by Jack. "I could do without the sarcasm," he says, suppressing a grin.

Jack nods at the clothing. "Find anything useful with all that?"

"Well, I found a couple of hairs. One is a dye job, an auburn color, and the other is naturally black. Neither matches the victims, so we're waiting on DNA. We do have info on semen, though. We got samples from both bodies, and they're the same, but we don't know who it's from yet. We're doing further analysis on that."

Jack's internal light bulb turns on, shining like a beacon in the night. "I got the name of a bar where one of our victims worked, so I'm gonna head over there with Jimbo. I'm also getting a warrant for the recordings of some of Andrea Singletary's treatment sessions. When I get them, I need you to go over them with a fine-tooth comb."

"What are you looking for?"

"I want to know if they've been tampered with in any way."

"Okay. What are you thinking?"

"I don't want to talk about it yet. But I do have some ideas about who our copycat could be. I just need to confirm my suspicions."

Back in Homicide, Sergeant Ruiz shows Jack another flash drive he got from JTTF. "They got a hit near the Brooklyn Bridge. A dark figure with a duffel bag walks to the river, exits from view, and returns fifteen minutes later without the bag."

Jack takes the drive and heads back to the elevator. "Gotta bring it to Forensics so I can look at it."

"Forensics?" asks Ruiz, quickening his pace to catch up with Jack. "Ya know, you could see it on my laptop, or if you just get your own laptop like everyone else in the twenty-first century, we wouldn't hafta run around like this."

Jack doesn't respond. However, at the elevator, he holds the door back as if to allow James to enter. Then, just as the sergeant gets there, he releases the door and flashes James the bird as the door closes on him.

Ruiz whines to the closed door, "Come on, Jack! What are you, twelve?" Then, with a sigh and a roll of his eyes, he heads back to his desk.

Later, when Jack returns to the floor, Ruiz takes one look at him and smirks. "Hey, I know it pays to advertise, but your flag is at half-mast."

Jack looks down and closes his open zipper. "I was in a hurry," he shrugs. "Look, we need to go to Brooklyn. Lisa Palmer hooked at a bar called the Rusty Anchor, and I bet the other one worked there as well. You ready to go?"

"Yeah, nothin' goin' on here."

"Okay, then let's roll, amigo."

It's well known that The Rusty Anchor isn't safe for

strangers after dark, and it's not much better during the day. But since it's located near the Red Hook Container Terminal, it's become a convenient hangout for dock workers.

Jack parks his baby a block from the bar and asks passing police officers to watch it. "Will do," they say, admiring the beast. "You don't see many of them around anymore," says the older of the two.

"That's why I want you to keep an eye on it," winks Jack.

It's late afternoon, and a loud industrial whistle from the terminal signals a shift change. "The ladies should be coming out now," says Jack.

When they near the bar, a heavily made-up woman inhaling from a vape pen approaches them. "Hey, you guys wanna party?" she asks, striking a suggestive pose in the shade of a building while the dimming sun casts ugly shadows. Over many years, she's learned to use the gloom of the sun dipping below the Manhattan skyline to disguise imperfections from her hard life.

Jack stares at the girl with the weathered face, then waves her into the bar. "We'll question her inside," he tells James in a low voice.

Inside The Rusty Anchor, the place looks like an old pirate galleon, with gas lamps, fishing nets hanging from the ceiling, and wooden everything. The floor creaks under the trio's feet as they head to a small booth.

"I'll get us some drinks," says Jack, leaving for the bar.

At the well-worn counter, he tries to get the bartender's attention, but the man ignores him. "Hey, paying customer here!" he shouts, waving a hand over his head.

The bartender finishes ringing up a customer, then sidles over to Jack. The man is a dead ringer for Popeye, the cartoon character with muscular forearms, tattoos, and a half-closed eye. All he needs is a corncob pipe.

"We don't get cops here," says "Popeye," coughing deeply.

The smoke-filled air of the bar, mixed with stale beer and cheap cologne, causes Jack to cough as well.

He isn't surprised the guy pegged him for a cop, so he gets down to business. Pointing over his shoulder, he says, "See that girl over there? A couple of her friends were murdered recently." Holding up the post-mortem photos of Lisa and Julianna, he asks, "Have you seen either of these ladies here?"

The squinty eye opens wide. "Yeah. They come by from time to time. Who killed them?"

Jack shoves the pictures back into his suit pocket. "I was hoping you could shed some light on that. Do you remember anyone they hooked up with?"

The old man purses his lips. "You gonna buy something, or you just wanna waste my time?"

Jack shakes his head. "Two beers and a Coke for the lady."

Popeye closes that famous eye. "That'll be forty bucks. Twenty for the drinks and twenty for the info."

Jack squints back at the bartender. "I'll give you ten bucks, and if I like the info, I'll give you ten more. You gonna cooperate, matey, or should I shut down this fine establishment for human trafficking?"

The old barkeep laughs, a coarse, raspy sound caused by too much booze and smoke. Moving away, he gets the drink order, then nods toward the girl sitting in the booth with Ruiz. "Ask her. She knows who those two hooked up with. She went off with the same guy. I don't have a name, but I'll know him if I see him."

Jack takes the drinks and leaves another ten. "I'll be back."

When a bunch of dock workers enter the bar, they stare at the unfamiliar faces.

Jack sets the drinks on the table and hands the two grisly photos to the hooker. "Do you know them?"

The girl's eyes widen as she stares at the photos of the dead women. "What happened?!"

Ruiz says, "They were murdered. But I'm sure you've seen things like this before."

Jack gathers up the photos. "Popeye up there seems to think that you and those women hooked up with the same guy."

The hooker looks irritated. "You know, I'm losing money here," she says, glancing around at potential customers.

Jack sighs. "Look, Miss, be thankful that we're in Homicide, not Vice, so we're not here to bust you. However, we could always make an exception. Talk to us or walk out in cuffs. Your choice."

The girl sips her soda while playing suggestively with the straw. "Yeah, there was this creepy guy. He comes in here a lot. Doesn't say much; just pays, gets his rocks off, and leaves."

Jack leans in. "What else about this creep?"

The girl continues to suck on the straw until there's nothing left in her glass. Then she looks up at Jack. "He limps, and there's a tattoo of an anchor on his left hand."

Jack wasn't expecting this to be so easy, but he needs confirmation to be sure. "I want you to come down to the station to look at some photos. I promise to get you back here before eight tonight. You know, before you get busy."

The hooker agrees, sensing that she can trust the two cops to bring her back.

As the three walk down Pierrepoint to Jack's car, Ruiz tries to get more information out of her. "So, what's your name?" he asks kindly.

The young woman, white and blonde, looks off into the distance. "Name's Laura, Laura Langston."

"How old are you?"

Laura snorts. "How old do you think I am?"

Ruiz looks at her haggard face. "Not sure; that's why I asked."

"Huh. I'm nineteen, asshole."

"Nineteen, huh? How long you been in this line of work?"

Laura sighs. "Two years. My stepdad kicked me out when I didn't want to give him head."

Jack inhales to prevent himself from cursing. "What about your mom?"

Laura frowns deeply. "She's on heroin, so she doesn't give a shit about me."

When they reach the First, Laura complains in the elevator up to Homicide. "Hey, I'm doin' you guys a favor, but I'm losing money bein' here. This better not take long."

Jack ignores the girl's bullshit and points her to his whiteboard. "Straight down the aisle. The desk near the board with the photos on it."

The streetwalker struts her stuff, stopping at Jack's desk. "Now, what?"

Jack fumbles through some files for the one he wants. "Here it is," he says, holding up a photograph.

"That's the creep," she says, tossing her hair back with a shrug. "Gimpy leg and small dick."

Jack smiles and returns the photo he received from The Haven's personnel office to his folder. "Stay here for a minute," he tells her. Then he crooks his finger at Ruiz and pulls him a few feet away.

"What do you remember from that footage you got from JTTF?"

"Huh. The guy had a limp. And a tattoo."

Jack smiles again. "We got a house call to make. But before we do that, see that the girl gets a ride back to Brooklyn."

When James returns from arranging the informant's

transportation back to the bar, he and Stenhouse head up to an address in Yonkers.

Irving Shotley, a wounded Vietnam veteran, prepares for a night out after eating another lonely dinner at home. While he dresses, he wonders for the umpteenth time if he should start looking for a more accessible apartment. He'd rather stay where he is, but his limp is getting worse, and he's finding it harder to climb the stairs. "Damn shrapnel," he says, rubbing his old leg wound before stepping into a freshly drycleaned pair of pants.

Downstairs, Stenhouse and Ruiz climb up two flights, then stop in front of 201. Ruiz rings the bell, and both men put their hands on their Glocks.

Inside the apartment, Irving is at the kitchen sink, washing the last of his dinner dishes. He's a bit of a neatnik and wants everything tidy when he returns home.

"Who the hell is that?" he asks himself when his doorbell rings. "Who's there?" he yells, poking his head toward the door.

"NYPD!" answers Jack, tensing for whatever may come next.

Surprised by that response, Irving turns off the faucet and dries his hands on a dishtowel. Then he looks through the peephole. "You have ID?" he asks, cautious about opening the door to strangers.

Jack holds up his badge and ID while Ruiz does the same. Then they stand back as locks and chains are unlatched.

Irving peers cautiously around the edge of the slightly opened door. "What can I do for you?" he asks.

Jack removes his hand from his weapon. "Can we come in, Mr. Shotley? We want to talk to you about Andrea

Singletary."

Irving is puzzled. "Um…Andrea Singletary? Uh, yeah, okay. Come in."

Irving leads the officers to a small living room, both men noticing his limp and anchor tattoo.

"What do you need from me?" asks Irving, offering chairs to the two officers and sitting down opposite them. "I only know her through work."

Jack proceeds with caution. "We hope we're not disturbing you, sir."

"Not really, but I was just getting ready to go out."

James takes in what he can see of the small apartment. "You have a big night planned?" he asks.

"Uh, well, I live alone, so I like to get out once in a while."

Jack brings the conversation back on track. "Mr. Shotley, we know you work at The Haven and that you have access to the patients there. We're particularly interested in one of them, Andrea Singletary. How much contact do you have with her? Do you talk to her at all?"

Irving's brows arch high on his forehead. "Not really. I bring her magazines and stuff and straighten up her room, but we're not supposed to interact with the patients. I do my job and leave."

"Thanks," says Ruiz. "Now, what can you tell us about the Rusty Anchor?"

Irving's breath quickens. "What do you mean?" he asks hesitantly. "I mean, I've been there. Is that a problem?"

Jack stands. "Mr. Irving, you've been identified as a suspect in the murders of Lisa Palmer and Julianna Colon. Please stand, sir. We're going to handcuff you and bring you down to the station for further questioning."

Jack slips on the cuffs, and Ruiz reads his rights while Irving protests. "Wait, wait!" he cries. "What did I do? I didn't kill anyone!"

Irving watches Jack take the two photos out of his pocket. "These are the women, Mr. Shotley. Ring a bell?"

Shotley's eyes narrow at the sight of the dead bodies, but he still denies being involved. "Holy crap, they're dead?" he cries. "I don't know anything about that! I didn't have anything to do with it! What the fuck, guys? I knew them, but I didn't kill them!"

Claude LaGrange is being held in a small concrete cell in the basement of Interpol headquarters in Lyon, France. The building on Quai Charles de Gaulle overlooks the Rhone River, but Charles can't see the view. It's dark, and he can't sleep, so he paces his nine-square meter cell, unaware of the Airbus heading to Paris that will add another chapter to his life.

The flight to Paris isn't the end of Hector's and Jacob's trip. Hector wasn't pleased when Jacob told him they'd have to transfer to another plane to get to Lyon.

"That's another hour in the air!" he complains. "After layovers and other folderal, that will add up to close to eleven hours of traveling time!"

"Tell me about it," yawns Jacob. "Try to rest. I want to get to our hotel in Lyon by seven a.m. That way, we can try to get a little more sleep before we have to start work."

Hector is in a whining mood. "By that time, we'll have been awake for over twenty-four hours."

"Yeah. That's why I'm gonna try to sleep now. So can you shut up for a while?"

Hector stops and looks out of the window. "Sorry to be such a crank. But the good thing is that we'll be in France, right?"

Hector looks over at Jacob for his reply, but there is none.

The FBI agent is now wearing noise-canceling headphones, and his eyes are closed tightly.

As it often happens when they're on a case, Stenhouse and Ruiz are working overtime this evening. So, even though it's late, they're taking Mr. Shotley to the station.

At the First, James asks for a crack at Shotley, but Jack overrules him. So Ruiz resigns himself to observing the questioning through the two-way mirror connecting the interrogation room to a room next door.

When Jack begins, Ruiz watches Shotley fidget in his chair. "The guy's nervous as hell," he mutters.

Initially, Irving answers Jack's questions easily, but he seems to clam up when John Lennon enters the interrogation room.

Jack wonders what's happening until he sees Irving looking at a small glass tube and a long cotton swab in John's hands. To explain, he says, "You keep saying you've done nothing wrong and want to cooperate, so my tech's gonna take a swab of your inner cheek for DNA."

"Oh," says Irving, rocking back and forth in his chair. "Um… I think I need a lawyer. I do want to help, but I still think I want a lawyer."

John looks to Jack for direction, but Jack is staring at Shotley, who's glancing from the test tube to Jack and back again.

When there is no further conversation, Shotley breaks the silence. "Um, I guess it's okay," he says. "I haven't done anything wrong except paying for sex, so… I guess you can do the test."

John takes the sample and leaves the room as quietly as he arrived. Then Jack resumes the interview. "When was the last time you saw those women?"

Irving closes his eyes to think. "I saw Lisa a couple of nights ago. We hooked up in the bar's bathroom, and then I left. I screwed Julianna a few days before that. Same scenario. If you want to arrest me for using a prostitute, then go for it. But I didn't kill anyone. And you know what? That's all I'm gonna say. I want a lawyer now."

Jack gets up and goes out the door, leaving Irving alone in the room. He goes into the adjoining room to talk to Ruiz.

"Whaddya think?" he asks the sergeant as Captain Conrad opens the door and peeks his head in.

"Well, we can charge him with a misdemeanor, and he'll post bail and go home."

"Or," says Jack, waving Conrad in, "we could hold him for twenty-four hours and hope we get a positive ID from that surveillance footage. The DNA sample won't matter if it matches the vics 'cause it'll just prove he had sex with them. Captain," he says, turning to Conrad, "he requested a lawyer, but I don't know; I don't think he killed them. My shit-o-meter isn't registering anything right now."

Conrad looks through the mirror at Shotley. "Let's wait to see what the video says. We can put him in Holding and keep him there till morning. If Forensics doesn't get conclusive evidence from the video, we'll release him to his lawyer."

James pipes up, "What about the misdemeanor charge?"

"Not worth the trouble," replies Conrad. "Go home, you two. I'll let Shotley know he's gonna be our guest overnight. Tomorrow, he can call an attorney or have one assigned to him."

At three in the morning, the Big Apple is quieter but still noisy. The city is never completely asleep, and Jack is among those who are awake.

Pacing his loft, he stops to stare at the flickering lights across the darkened cityscape, eyeing the occasional vehicle flowing through its veins. Jack is lonely; he misses his family. He's desperate to hold his wife and hear her infectious laugh, and he longs to play with his son. At this time of night, he's even sentimental about his mother-in-law, whom he knows is taking good care of Mark.

With a deep sigh, he turns and looks at the empty bourbon bottle on the coffee table, wondering if he should open a fresh one. Then he blinks.

"What the hell are you doin'?" he mutters angrily, exhaling the breath he didn't know he was holding. "That's not gonna solve anything."

Grabbing the empty bottle, he throws it in the trash and heads to bed, desperate for the oblivion of sleep.

In an Interpol interrogation room in Lyon, Jacob, and Hector guzzle cups of black coffee while they wait for Claude LaGrange.

"I'm sooo tired," moans Hector, holding a hand over a yawn.

Jacob lets out his breath with a loud whine. "I hope he doesn't give us any trouble," he says, not bothering to disguise his weariness.

The wait makes it hard for the men to keep their eyes open. So when Claude is finally led into the room, they sit up straight and try to perk up.

The normally sophisticated Interpol officer is shackled and haggard looking. His hair is uncombed, his silk shirt and suit pants are disheveled, and he needs a shave. This isn't the image he likes to portray, and he's not happy.

As Claude sits down, a second man slips into the room and takes a seat, slapping a folder onto the table. "I am *Inspecteur* Renaud Passereau," the new arrival tells the Americans. "Monsieur LaGrange is one of my subordinates and a disgrace to my unit. Therefore, I will lead the questioning. I know of your interest in his activities. *Alors*, you may ask questions as well."

Hector and Jacob exchange glances but say nothing. They are no longer on their home turf, so they know they need to be flexible.

"*Puis-je avoir un café?*" Claude asks his superior, licking his lips.

"*Non*," Renaud replies, shaking his head firmly. "I will not interpret for you. We will speak English. Now, tell us how you came to know the mercenary, Serge Kaspin."

Claude widens his eyes to project an air of innocence. However, the corners of his mouth curve upward at the same time, an involuntary contradiction indicating devious thinking. "Who?" he asks in a heavy accent. "I do not know this person."

"Right," mutters Hector, angrily balling his fists at the obvious deception. He's tired and in no mood for playing games. So, skipping the niceties of international relations, he jumps right into the conversation. "We know you played poker with Serge Kaspin in the states, and we have records of your telephone conversations with him. So cut the bullshit, okay?"

LaGrange merely shrugs, further angering Hector. So with a deep scowl, he leans forward, saying, "You wanna play hardball? Okay, then, how about this? Does the name General Sergei Mednikov ring a bell?"

Hector's gambit pays off, as this name triggers something in Claude, and he blanches.

This reaction infuriates the inspector. Adding fuel to the smoldering fire, he reaches into his folder, removes a sheet of paper, and waves it in front of his subordinate. "We have your travel itineraries, Claude. Did you think you could hide everything from us?" The inspector removes his glasses from the top of his head and continues, "You recently departed from France for the United States. You returned to France one week later and then went to Estonia."

The inspector returns his glasses to his head and asks, "How is Mednikov these days? I have heard that he has been selling interesting items to top-quality customers."

Claude looks down at the table, then brings his head up and looks the inspector in the eye. "I will not speak any longer. I wish to have an attorney present."

Renaud's face darkens, and his eyes grow cold. "You are not in the kind and generous United States of America now, Claude," he says slowly. "Here, we do not give all kinds of freedoms to satisfy your every need. Now, listen to me. The CIA has confirmed our suspicion that General Mednikov has made a deal to sell a portable nuclear device. So, Claude, you have a decision to make. You can tell us what we need to know right now, or I can hand you over to the CIA. As you are aware, they have particular ways of holding serious conversations."

"*Va te faire foutre, inspecteur,*" replies Claude. "*Je vais rien dire de plus.*"

Renaud scowls and translates for the Americans. "He will not say anything else."

Jacob rises from his chair with both palms on the table. Then he moves next to Claude. Leaning close to his ear, he whispers, "*Vous parlerez immédiatement, ou vous mourrez. C'est ton choix.*" Straightening, he waits for a response, but the Interpol officer only clamps his mouth shut and crosses his arms over his chest.

Jacob sighs. "If that's your decision, we'll move on to the next phase." Then, tossing his head at Hector, he marches to the door, and the others follow.

Outside the room, a cold chill and musty odor permeate the corridor.

"Ugh, it's drafty down here," says Hector.

"*Oui.* That is because we are below the Rhone River," explains the inspector.

Jacob turns to Passereau. "CIA officer Samantha Waring is in Belgium right now. She's working this case with us and will handle the transfer."

Renaud's gaze is on the concrete floor. "I am sorry about the failure of one of our own," he says. "I will continue to interrogate Monsieur LaGrange until you take over. I know the tactics the CIA uses, and I fear he may not live through them."

Assante nods. "That's exactly what I told him." Then he turns to Hector. "We'll stay in Lyon until Waring takes custody."

CHAPTER TWENTY-TWO

After last night's binge, Jack needs a third cup of coffee to focus on a growing pile of paperwork. With bloodshot eyes, he purses his lips, cricks his neck, and runs a hand over the stubble he didn't have the energy to shave off.

"Damn coffee isn't working," he mutters, catching the attention of Ruiz passing by.

"What?" asks the sergeant, stopping to raise a brow. "Ah, shit!" he says, noting Jack's red eyes. "What the hell happened to you? Close your damn peepers before you bleed to death!"

"Wish I could," replies Jack, tiredly placing a hand on the paperwork. "This mound of unfinished casework is busting my ass. I'm seriously thinking of getting out of this shit."

"Whoa, hold on just a minute, Stenhouse! You're not thinking of leaving the force just because of a little paperwork, are you? Snap out of it!"

"It's just not the same anymore, ya know? I used to look forward to coming here. But now, not so much."

Jack glances down at his watch, then looks up as someone else appears beside his desk.

"Hey," greets John Lennon, slumping down in an empty chair with a loud yawn.

"No sleep, either?" asks Jack.

"No, I was working on the CCTV footage all night." John rolls his chair closer. "I got good news and bad news."

Jack narrows his eyes, waiting for John to explain. He isn't in the mood for riddles.

"Hmm. No shit today?" asks John. "I thought I'd get

a thank you for slaving away all night on your case, but whatever. So...the figure by the river isn't Shotley."

Jack is now wide awake. "What the fuck?" he exclaims.

"It's a woman with auburn-colored hair. At first, she's limping on her right leg, but when she reappears, she's limping on her left."

"Oh, crap," says Jack, rubbing his chin at the shit he's going to get from Ruiz for bringing Shotley in. "Hey, Jimbo!" he calls out. "Don't say a fucking word, but bring your laptop over here, will ya?"

Ruiz places his laptop on Jack's desk and enters his password. Then he turns it around so Jack can access it.

After a quick internet search, Jack turns the screen toward Lennon. "Is this the woman?"

The meticulous forensic technician takes his time looking at the photo. Then, he leans back with a slow smile. "Yeah, that's her. Yikes."

Ruiz peeks over John's shoulder. "No shit!" he exclaims, his jaw dropping to the floor. "We gotta get a warrant!"

Jack's back in business. "Let's do that," he says, "and then we gotta go back upstate. But first, I gotta take a piss. Too much coffee."

On the way back from the restroom, he stops at Conrad's office.

"So you brought the wrong guy in?" frowns Conrad. "I heard the commotion out there."

"Looks that way. I'll get Shotley released. Meanwhile, can you get us a search warrant?"

"Yeah, who's it for?"

"Emily Santice."

"You're kidding."

"Nope. Lennon just recognized her in the Battery Park video. We gotta search her house."

"Right. Bring some uniformed guys with you, and CSI."

"Gotcha. I'll give this one to Ruiz."

At his desk, Jack phones Holding to release Shotley. Then he walks over to James. "Hey, Jim—"

"Yeah, I know, we're goin' out."

Jack shakes his head. "We're goin' out, all right, but not together. I'm goin' back to The Haven, and when the warrant comes through, you're gonna do a search of the doctor's house. Take CSI and some uniforms with you. I'll catch up with you later."

Jack checks his pants on the way to the elevator. "Thank God," he breathes, relieved that he remembered to close the zipper.

In the North Atlantic, the sleek, turbine-powered ship named *Phoenix* is cruising over the vast blue sea at over seven knots.

"We are making good time; the ocean has been friendly so far," the captain tells Olev Lepik when he joins him on the bridge. "If it keeps up like this, we should reach the St. Lawrence River in three days."

Lepik is pleased. "Then we will arrive in Quebec City earlier than planned. That is very good."

The Estonian prime minister remains on the bridge, staring at the calm waters while thinking about his upcoming meetings. "I appreciate your seamanship," he tells the captain. "And that of your crew, of course," he adds. Then he turns away from the large window overlooking the ocean. "I will leave things in your capable hands."

As soon as his only passenger is out of earshot, the captain activates his satellite phone.

"We expect to arrive in seventy-two hours," he declares.

"Yes, I understand, Colonel."

When Dr. Santice passes through the concealed door in The Haven lobby, Jack notices that although all the buttons of her lab coat are fastened, no clothing is peeking out from under it, only cleavage.

Flirtatiously, the doctor flips a stray piece of her red hair away from her eyes. "Good morning, Lieutenant. It's so nice to see you again," she coos.

Jack isn't impressed. He's wise to the doctor's tricks, so with some effort, he refrains from glancing at her breasts and instead gives her his famous, cold sniper stare. "Hello," he declares dully. "I need to see Singletary."

Santice pouts at the lack of warmth from the usually personable man. However, her mood changes an instant later. "Oh?" she says, batting her eyes with a coquettish tilt of her head. "You haven't come to see me today? I'm hurt, Lieutenant." Then she takes Jack's arm and leads him outside, giggling like a schoolgirl.

Jack steals a glance at Santice while she drives them to the other building, wondering what she's up to. However, painful memories threaten to surface, so he closes his eyes to shut them out. He still can't get over how much Emily looks like Didi. It's unnerving.

The pair follows security protocols at the outer building, then walks to Andrea's door.

There, Jack stops to face the doctor. "I want to go inside alone today. I don't want you in there with me. I don't want you to influence her in any way."

Santice sighs heavily. "I don't know what you think I'm doing. I don't have any sway over her. I'm her doctor, that's all," she contends, hoping that will change Jack's mind.

Jack is adamant. "I need to be alone with her. It won't take long."

Santice is frowning. "What's going on? I don't know what will happen if I'm not in there. Andrea has never been alone with a visitor before, so I don't know how she'll react...or which of her personalities will respond to you. I must insist—"

Jack holds up a hand. "This is going to happen, Doctor, with or without your consent. So shall we get on with it? I really don't want to get the D.A. or a judge involved, and I'm not leaving here before I speak to Andrea without anyone else in the room. Of course, you can always watch us on the monitor."

Santice huffs but activates the comm button. *You bet I'll watch*, she thinks, then gets her patient's attention.

"Andrea, it's Doctor Santice. How are you today?" she asks soothingly. Andrea looks up at the screen mounted on the wall but says nothing. "Lieutenant Stenhouse is here, and he's going to come in and speak with you." Andrea's eyes shift to the floor. "I'll be outside the door while he comes inside. I'll be watching on the monitor, so if you want my help, you only have to say so."

As if she were considering her options, Andrea tilts her head to the ceiling, then smiles and turns to the camera. "That will be lovely," she responds sweetly.

Dr. Santice is stunned. She hasn't heard the voice Andrea replied with in a while, and it startles her. Cutting off the audio, she moves away from the monitor so Andrea can't see her. Then she turns to Jack somewhat resentfully. "The personality who responded was Andrea. It seems that just by being here, your presence has made the breakthrough I haven't been able to achieve through established professional methods."

"Really?" Jack responds, noting bitterness in the doctor's voice.

With a sigh of resignation, Santice activates the

electronic latch, admitting Jack into the confines of Andrea's cell.

"Hello, how are you?" he asks, noting that Andrea appears frail, like she's lost a lot of weight.

Andrea grins and extends a hand in welcome, which Jack returns with a smile of his own.

Oof, she's got a powerful grip for someone confined so long, he thinks, hoping she'll let go of his hand soon. However, Andrea continues her grip, looking deep into Jack's eyes. *When you gonna let go?*

When the woman finally breaks contact, Jack flexes his fingers to ensure blood is still flowing. *Not sure what just happened, but I got a job to do, so better get on with it.*

Leaning close so the doctor won't hear, he whispers into Andrea's ear. "Santice is the killer, right?"

Andrea smiles from ear to ear. "Sunlight ebbs from lifeless limbs as Jack's breath numbs the dew," she responds.

The pair stands there for a long moment, looking at each other in silence until something shifts within Andrea. As if someone flipped a switch, her body language changes, and she lowers her head to stare at her visitor through hooded eyes.

"Well played," she declares in a vastly different voice. "Well played."

Jack turns to the monitor. "Open the door," he mouths, and Santice presses the buzzer to let him out. Behind him, Cronos laughs loudly.

As soon as Jack clears the door, he makes a beeline for the building's exit, leaving Santice speechless at the monitor.

"Coming, Doctor?" he calls over his shoulder when he realizes she hasn't moved from Andrea's doorway.

"Uh, yes," she answers, turning off the monitor before following Jack out of the building.

At the golf cart, Jack faces the doctor. "Dr. Emily Santice," he says, "you're under arrest for the murders of Lisa Palmer and Julianna Colon."

Remarkably, the doctor neither struggles nor protests as Jack cuffs her and recites the Miranda warning. Strangely, the doctor merely snickers. Her only comment while Jack drives the golf cart to the parking area is, "I don't need an attorney. They're only for losers."

At his car, Jack pulls the doctor out of the cart and puts her in the back seat of his Road Runner. Standing outside, he clicks his contacts while keeping an eye on his prisoner. "I just arrested Santice," he tells Ruiz. "Where are you now?"

"We're in Nyack, near her house. I'll text you the address."

"Sweet. We'll meet you there."

Thankfully, the ride to Santice's home is uneventful. Jack expected something, anything, from the doctor, but all she does is stare out the window, humming a tune he doesn't recognize.

At last, he pulls into the drive of a large Tudor house where police vehicles have already gathered.

Jack gives two quick beeps to announce his presence, then escorts the doctor to the door.

"Any trouble on the way?" asks Ruiz, standing in the doorway.

"No," he responds, tugging at the doctor's arm to force her to walk up her front steps.

For some reason, Santice doesn't want to enter her house, so Ruiz grabs her other arm, and the two officers drag her in.

Over the doctor's head, Ruiz says, "You're not gonna believe what we found."

The sergeant leads the pair to the den/office, where they find CSI technicians poring over photos of the victims stapled to the walls and newspaper clippings of the Saturnalian Killer case strewn across the desk.

"Whoa," mutters Jack.

Dr. Santice puffs out her chest. "Glorious, isn't it?" she asks, looking at her collection with pride.

Jack has no words for her, but his disgust registers on his face.

"This is nothing," says Ruiz. "You should see the basement. I'll stay here with her."

Jack sighs heavily and leaves to find the entrance to the lower level.

Down a short hallway, wooden floors creak under his feet as he passes several rooms, each with modern furnishings and somber wall paintings.

Coming upon an open door, he asks, "This the cellar?"

"Yeah," responds a nearby forensic tech without looking up from his work.

At the bottom of the stairs, Jack stops to survey his surroundings in the dim light supplied by a single hanging fixture and a couple of casement windows high on the wall. The area gives off a slightly damp smell, reminding Jack of the times he played in the basement of relatives in New Jersey when he was a youngster. Their basements were filled with "stuff," while this one is empty. He sees nothing on the poured concrete floor but an oil furnace, a water heater, a washer and dryer, and a small utility sink.

From upstairs, a voice calls out, "Check out the room in the back."

"Gotcha," replies Jack, heading for a door he can barely see in the shadows.

As he nears the room, sounds of activity tell him there

are people hard at work inside, which he confirms as soon as he opens the door.

"Holy smoke!" he exclaims, causing John Lennon to look over at him from a large floor freezer next to a metal table.

John waves a hand over the unit and waits for the detective to get close. "Looks familiar, don't it?" he asks, moving aside so Jack can peer in.

Inside the icebox are several frozen body parts and a complete body, all wrapped in heavy plastic sheeting.

Jack lets out the breath he was holding in anticipation of what he was going to see. "We gotta put a stop to this," he mutters, looking away. Patting John's arm, he says, "I don't envy you, buddy. Send your report as soon as you're done."

Back upstairs, Jack finds Ruiz in the living room holding onto Emily Santice, who is rocking back and forth on her heels with a faraway look.

Spotting Jack, she focuses on him and crows, "Oh, Cronos is so proud of me! I love him sooo much!" Then the distant look returns, and she resumes her rhythmic rocking.

Jack purses his lips and lets his gaze shift to Ruiz. "Bring her in. I'll do all the bullshit paperwork." Then he turns and practically runs to the front door, wanting to distance himself from the demented doctor.

"Nooooo! Don't leave me, Jack!" calls Emily, lunging forward so hard that Ruiz has to struggle to bring her under control. "Nooooo! Aaaaaargh!" she shrieks with a howl so deep that it carries out to Jack as he sprints to his ride.

With the Road Runner in gear, the beast's 400 horses grab onto its rear wheels, and the power of its screeching tires, together with Jack's two quick beeps, are just the things he needs to erase the sound of Emily shrieking from his mind.

Later that evening, Jack is still at work when most of the Big Apple's roadways become as clogged as lifelong bacon connoisseurs.

"Here you go," he says, dropping a stack of paperwork onto Captain Conrad's desk. "This closes the case against Emily Santice. I owe Lennon a steak dinner for identifying her from the video and noticing she was faking a limp. Ruiz is processing her, so I did his paperwork as well. That doctor is one fucked-up lady."

Conrad leans back in his chair, looking at the paperwork. "Listen," he says. "Now that that's over, you need some time off. This case brought back a lot of memories for you."

Jack pulls a chair forward and takes a seat. "You know I can't do that, boss. There's still unfinished business out there. What's the latest with Kaspin and the nuke?"

Conrad shakes his head at his lieutenant. "You're a stubborn son of a gun, Stenhouse. So, Assante says Interpol is transferring LaGrange to the CIA. He's not talking, so…"

"Where's the nuke?"

"They still think it was in Estonia at one time, but they don't know where it is now."

"And Kaspin?"

"Nothing new. Still in North Carolina, as far as we know. All we can do is hope the CIA gets more out of LaGrange."

Jack wrinkles his nose at the lack of forward movement. "Have you heard anything from Giancarlo or Burley? Are they okay?"

"Well, we got good news there," reports Conrad. "Allison is coming along fine. She regained most of her mobility and strength, but there's still some leg weakness. She's pissed that she's gonna have a permanent limp, but she's happy she can walk at all."

Jack grunts. "That fuckin' Guard did a number on her."

"And we won't forget it," Conrad replies, more firmly than necessary. "As for the Burleys, they'll remain sequestered until Kaspin's dead or in prison. Sansone has them locked up tighter than a drum."

The two are silent for a moment, then Conrad shares more good info. "Oh, hey! Did you hear Burley's gonna be a father?"

"Yeah! Can you imagine that? I never thought he'd go that route."

"Well, that's what happens when a guy and a gal are confined together in a small place."

"Tell me about it," replies Jack, slapping a leg. "Good for him."

The men laugh until Jack turns serious. "You know, Captain, you're right about a break. I used to like this job, but now, not so much. I gotta do some heavy thinkin'." Using the armrests as leverage, he lifts himself out of the chair and walks toward the door.

Before he can disappear into the madness of the Homicide Department, Conrad stops him. "Do what you need to do to clear your head. It'll be good for you."

Jack gives his boss a peace sign — a full one this time. Then he snakes his way to the elevator through the typical dregs of society that constantly surround him at work.

From inside the packed elevator, he stares out at the sea of humanity and inhumanity as the door slowly closes, trapping him inside with the very wrongdoers he no longer wants to associate with.

It's now one in the morning at Lyon International

Airport, where Jacob and Hector are waiting for their flight back to New York. They're heading home because they transferred control of LaGrange to the CIA, so they no longer have access to him.

Gomez hands Jacob a bag of chips and lowers himself into the seat next to Assante. "I picked up some snacks."

"Thanks," says Assante, grabbing the bag with one hand and reaching for his ringing phone with the other.

The FBI agent listens, mumbles his assent, and hangs up. Then he tears open the snack bag.

"What?" asks Hector, intrigued by the non-existent conversation.

"That was Agent Waring. Looks like we'll be heading to Langley after we land in New York. That's where they're bringing LaGrange."

Hector draws in a deep breath, then lets it out slowly. "More air travel and no sleep. Sometimes, this job sucks."

"Yeah, but you got to go to France, right?"

Hector sniffs. "Some trip. I barely knew I was there."

CHAPTER TWENTY-THREE

Serge Kaspin's second-in-command has settled into a small B&B not far from downtown Quebec City. He arrived in the city earlier than necessary to make sure everything was ready for the arrival of the *Phoenix* at the Port of Quebec Marina. He also wanted to be sure he was there when it docked. The colonel is counting on everything going as planned. Kaspin insisted he be on his way to Souris, North Dakota within the week.

The colonel receives the call he'd been expecting just as he starts his first day in the unfamiliar city.

"Wonderful," he says, pleased with his planning. That was the last piece he needed to complete his preparations, so now he can be a tourist for the next few days.

Colonel Powell tucks a shirt into his jeans, layers a Blue Jays jersey over it, and dons a matching cap. Then he grabs his jacket and goes outside to wait for the ride-hailing service he booked.

The previous day, it was after sundown when Powell drove the armored Joint Light Tactical Vehicle (JLTV) Kaspin gave him over the Canadian border, and when he arrived at the inn, it was late. He was tired, so he didn't take time to consider where he parked; he just wanted to climb into a soft bed. However, the light of day marks its location as much too conspicuous, so before he leaves, he moves it behind the inn, where it won't be visible from the street.

The B&B the colonel chose is a quaint, three-story former home with a large, wraparound porch with a nicely landscaped row of azalea and juniper bushes. The inn's short driveway is also attractively bordered by native plants sloping gently down a slight hill to kiss the street.

Powell returns to the front of the inn just as his phone dings with a notification that his ride is about to arrive. Soon, a silver Corolla pulls up and parks at the end of the drive.

"Mr. Powell?" asks the young woman, exiting the car with a wave.

The colonel answers, "Yes," and hurries down the drive to climb into the back.

"Where to, sir?" asks the woman.

"I'm not sure. I'm new to the area, and I'd like to see the sights. What's interesting around here?"

Jack is lost in thought this morning. He's alone, sitting in the dining room of the Maryland safe house, staring absently out of the window while he waits for the others to wake up. *This is a great location,* he muses, happy the FBI moved his family here. *I'm so glad I changed my mind about coming this weekend.* Then he recalls Mark's reaction to seeing him enter the house, and he knows the price of his last-minute ticket was worth more than gold.

While Jack sips his first cup of the day, he wonders if he could get used to a quieter life. There are no traffic noises here, no car horns, no sunlight bouncing off high-rise buildings. And he's even seeing nature. While his coffee was brewing, he was delighted to catch sight of a mother deer jumping over the backyard fence with her fawn. *What a sight!* he said to himself as he brought his coffee into the dining room. He was just sorry that Mark wasn't awake to see it with him.

The deer are still grazing in the backyard while he finishes his wake-up brew. *We'd never see this in the city!* he's said to himself more than once this morning.

Jack listens for movement from upstairs, but the house is still quiet. So he goes into the kitchen for another cup. While he's pouring, the deer family disappears into the woods, and he finally hears footsteps creeping down the stairs.

"Thanks for not waking me too early," says Hector, wolfing down a generous helping of waffles at the hotel's complimentary buffet breakfast. "That extra sleep sure kickstarted me. What time do we have to be at Langley?"

"We should get going now," replies Jacob, checking his Bulova as he downs a glass of cranberry juice. "The CIA building isn't far, but traffic around there is a bear."

With Mark strapped securely into his stroller, Jack and Sharon take their time meandering through the throngs of people packing the area along Baltimore's Inner Harbor. They're in no hurry this morning — something that Sharon has had to remind Jack of several times already. It's hard for the career cop to relax; he isn't used to having downtime. But he wants to try — for Mark's sake and his own.

At Sharon's suggestion, the family is on the way to the National Aquarium. Jack's mother-in-law told him how much Mark enjoys looking at picture books of the ocean and its marine life, so Jack leaped at the chance to give his son the experience of seeing real ocean creatures.

Near the museum entrance, they come upon the USS *Torsk*, a World War II submarine docked along the Harbor Bridge Walk.

"Oooo, a submarine! I've never seen one before," states Sharon. "I wonder what it's like inside."

Jack grins halfheartedly. "It's no big deal, really. You can go in if you like. I'll wait here with Mark."

Seeing Jack's lukewarm expression, Sharon suddenly remembers the terrifying experience he had a few years ago while investigating the case involving former President Howard Burris. When Didi told her about it, she was grateful Jack survived the ordeal.

"Oh, I'm so sorry I suggested coming here today," she apologizes. "You want to go home?"

"No, Ma," Jack responds with a genuine smile this time. "I always wanted to see the aquarium. But I've had my fill of that sub. It reminds me too much of how I almost drowned here."

"That's all right, honey. I don't have to see it today. I was just curious."

Before they reach the museum, Mark falls asleep, so Sharon stops the stroller to adjust his jacket. Jack can't help staring at the sub while she fusses with the baby. *I don't think I ever want to set foot in one of those cans again*, he thinks, recalling the case they dubbed Blue Falcon and how a garbage truck plowed into his POS sedan and sent him and an FBI special agent deep into the murky water.

For Jacob and Hector, going through security at "the Company" was like passing through a TSA line on steroids. It was no walk in the park, even with the men's law enforcement and federal identification documents readily available.

After the screening, they're led to a small room with only metal and plastic chairs for comfort. There are no tables or windows in this holding area, only glaring fluorescent lighting and four walls with nothing hanging on them to look at.

To bide the time, Hector stares at the black and white

linoleum floor, absently watching a stink bug scurry from one side of the room to the other. Casting a sidelong glance at Jacob, he notes that the FBI special agent is also gazing at the intruder. "I guess it had the appropriate security clearance," he says, ridiculing the excessive length of time it's taking the CIA to grant them admission to their inner sanctum.

While the men continue to wait, they try not to fidget, presuming they're being watched. But their patience is wearing thin.

At long last, an interior door opens, admitting a woman dressed in a one-piece jumpsuit with her long hair tucked under a CIA baseball cap.

Field Agent Samantha Waring greets the men with firm handshakes. "I see the FBI and NYPD are early risers."

"Good to see you," says Hector. "You look ready for your 'talk' today," he says, eying her protective garb.

Samantha chuckles. "I hope our Interpol asshole is ready for me as well. Follow me, gentlemen."

The peace officers pass through a series of doors and corridors, then enter a small alcove with just enough space for an elevator monitored by an armed security guard.

Samantha nods at the man and swipes her badge at a wall reader. Instantly, a low whoosh signals the door sliding open, revealing a cylindrical, chrome-plated interior.

Neither Jacob nor Hector has seen a tube-shaped elevator before, and they're impressed.

"Guess this is an example of taxpayer funding," comments Hector, entering the car ahead of the others.

When they're all inside, Samantha pushes a button, and the car descends. At first, the downward motion is slow. Then it speeds up considerably, continuing at this rate far longer than the visitors think possible.

"Where the hell are we going…China?" asks Hector with

a sidelong glance at Samantha.

Equally confused, Jacob quips, "Now I know what my money feels like when I go to the bank drive-up."

Samantha chuckles at her visitors' inexperience, keeping an eye on the controls as the cylinder slows to a crawl. When it stops, the doors open with another whoosh.

"This way," the CIA agent tells them as she walks down another hallway to a steel door guarded by men with automatic weapons. Passing them without comment, Samantha walks up to another security panel and puts her eye up to it. Immediately, lights flash and turn green, and the door snaps open with a clank.

"After you," says Jacob, unsure of what he's going to see.

Filing in, the men instantly spot Claude LaGrange. The Interpol traitor's eyes are closed, and his head hangs down to his chest inside an austere cell bordered by inch-thick bars.

Hector is stunned by the man's condition. "Sheesh," he mutters. "Is he alive?"

"Yes," responds Waring.

Claude's arms and legs are fastened to a stainless-steel, high-backed apparatus positioned above a drain in the concrete floor. The man is a mess. His hair is disheveled, and he's only partially clothed — a white T-shirt covers his chest, but his lower half is bare.

What the hell is he sitting on? wonders Hector, studying the contraption under LaGrange. It resembles a toilet more than a chair.

Alongside Claude, a stainless-steel worktable holds various paraphernalia, including a closed attaché case and a long firehose connected to a valve on the wall.

Hector and Jacob try to conceal their reactions, but their shock is evident.

"You guys ain't kiddin'," says Hector, watching

Samantha enter the cell after another retinal scan.

When the door snaps shut, she walks over to the table near Claude and looks over the devices arranged neatly on its polished surface. Then, with a determined expression, she reaches into the pocket of her one-piece outfit and removes a pair of gloves. With loud snaps, she puts each one on, knowing the sharp sounds will help to awaken Claude from his stupor.

When he lifts his head, she smiles at him. "Welcome back," she says, grabbing the hose from the metal table. Pointing it at the prisoner, she widens her stance, then pulls back on the lever attached to the nozzle to release a powerful stream of icy water that strikes Claude in the middle of his chest.

The pressure from the hose makes Claude jerk and stiffen, and the ice-cold water in the frigid, 45-degree room rapidly drops his core temperature. Sputtering and shaking, he tries his best to get the water out of his eyes and nose, but it's useless. It just keeps coming at him.

Claude shivers and shakes uncontrollably but doesn't make a sound. To the onlookers, it seems he knows what to expect, so this must have happened before.

After a while, Samantha releases the lever and drops the hose. "Now that your morning shower is over, do you care for some hot coffee?" she asks, her voice colored with undisguised hostility.

Claude lifts his chin, defiant against the agent's onslaught. *Te faire enculer, salope!* he shouts, flinging a common French curse at his torturer.

Samantha is determined to get the information she wants. "You know this will end if you just tell us where that nuclear device is," she retorts wearily.

Claude responds by leaning back and letting loose a stream of piss in Samantha's direction. But because the room is so cold, it doesn't go far.

"Wow is that the best you can do?" she sneers, resting her hands on her hips to consider her next move.

Smiling wryly, she glances in Jacob's and Hector's direction in a flash of inspiration. Then, leaning close to her target, she blows gently into his ear while simultaneously releasing the lock on the chair. This causes the chair holding Claude to fall backward onto the concrete with a thud.

"Where's the nuke?" she asks, once again voicing the million-dollar question.

This time, Claude replies in a mixture of French and English. "Fuck off, *putain!*" he exclaims. Then he lets loose a burst of spittle that Samantha jumps back to avoid.

Claude's continued defiance angers Hector. "Wrong answer!" he shouts, rushing toward the bars and grabbing them tightly.

Samantha raises an appreciative brow, then takes a bath towel and a leather strap from the metal table. She soaks the towel in cold water from the hose, then straps Claude's head to the chair back and places the towel over his face.

Now, Hector's eyes widen. What he knows is coming next is too much, even for him, but he can't seem to make a sound.

"Here we go," says Samantha, pointing the nozzle at Claude's face to waterboard the hapless fool.

For what seems like forever, Claude struggles against the restraints, trying to get at least a small amount of air. But he can't.

Just before he goes limp, Samantha lifts the towel and waits for him to fill his lungs. Then she repeats the process.

Claude is petrified that he won't survive the torture. Every time the towel comes off, he inhales as deeply as he can and fights against the straps tying him down. His fear is so great that his body responds by loosening certain muscles. As a result, with his bladder previously emptied, his bowel is the one to go.

When Samantha sees the water washing feces into the floor drain, she halts the onslaught and removes the towel.

"That wasn't very nice of you," she says, wrinkling her nose at the smell. "But you must feel better now. So are you going to tell me?" Outside the cell, Assante and Gomez turn away, coughing at the stench.

Despite everything, Claude still won't respond to Samantha's question. Frustrated and tired, she grabs the back of the chair and lifts it upright, clicking it into place. Then she walks around to face Claude.

"Where's the nuke?" she asks again.

Claude is still breathing heavily, trying to take in as much air as possible. "I…do not…know…what…you are…talking about," he stammers. "What nuke?"

The man's stubbornness exasperates Samantha. "Really?" she sighs, knowing she's going to have to increase the pressure to get him to reveal what he knows.

On the table, an attaché case sits next to a rheostat, a resistor used to control electrical current. Samantha removes a set of jumper cables from the case and uncoils them slowly, making sure Claude sees them.

Watching Claude's eyes, she asks, "You know what these are for? No? Well, you're about to find out, unless you want to answer the question now."

Claude sets his mouth in a hard line and turns his head in the other direction, further irritating Samantha.

Shaking her head in disbelief, she attaches the cable to a terminal on the rheostat and turns a dial.

When a low hum fills the cell, Samantha holds one cable clamp in her left hand and the other in her right. Touching them together, she makes a connection creating sparks that crackle and cause Claude to whip his head around in fear.

"What the fuck?" yells Hector, never having seen this level of torture before and hoping to stop it.

Hector's outburst does stop Samantha for a moment. She turns her head to look at him but then lifts a shoulder dismissively and bends down to clamp the red terminal to the shackles on one of Claude's wrists.

Straightening up, she holds the black terminal aloft, looking Claude right in the eyes. "You know what I'm going to ask, so now's the time to answer—"

"That's enough!" shouts Jacob loudly, halting Samantha's hand in midair. "You have to stop! This is too much!"

Claude looks expectantly from Jacob to his torturer, hoping against hope that the lawman's protest works. But Samantha isn't moved.

"Aww, is the pussy FBI agent upset?" she coos, holding Jacob's gaze while she forces the black clamp against Claude's torso with one hand.

The men's expletives at the brazen act are lost amid Claude's screams. However, the horror on their faces is unmistakable, so Samantha relents.

"All right," she says, calmly removing the clamp while Claude's head drops onto his chest, and he breathes heavily. "That's enough for now. We'll meet again in about an hour. That should give you enough time to think about the dial on that rheostat," she tells him. "And just so you know, that was its lowest setting."

Leaving the red clamp attached to Claude's wrist restraint, Samantha drops the black one and walks to the cell door to scan her eye again.

Outside the bars, she removes her gloves and puts them in her pocket. She seems utterly unaffected by the torment she just inflicted on a fellow human being.

"I'm starved," she whines to the men. "You two have

breakfast?"

When there's no response, she pushes the com button on the wall. "Beam me up, Scotty," she says, "there's no intelligent life down here." Then, after another quick eye scan, the door unlocks.

As it swings open, she turns to the men and removes her CIA baseball cap, shaking her head to release her long hair.

"Coming, boys?" she asks, strolling out of the room housing Claude's torture cell.

Stuck in place, Hector and Jacob exchange silent glances, neither managing a reply. They're stunned by what they've seen Samantha do and don't know how to react.

United by their uncertain feelings, they turn to look back at Claude, then follow Samantha out, flinching when the heavy door clanks shut.

CHAPTER TWENTY-FOUR

It's now Monday morning, and as preparations continue for Friday's G20 Summit in Quebec City, Jack sits at his desk in New York, recharged and reenergized better than that stupid bunny.

His recent trip to Maryland did wonders for him. However, thoughts of his son and his late wife are now running around in his mind. He's becoming increasingly aware of how much he'd rather be with Mark than stuck in this dingy office.

Closing his eyes, he contemplates a future watching Mark grow up, and soon, a smile appears at the imaginary scenes he conjures of an idyllic life. So engrossed is he in his fantasies that he doesn't hear Gomez, Ruiz, and Assante trying to enter his little world.

The group stands at Jack's desk for a long moment, puzzled by his enigmatic grin and faraway expression.

They stay there, uncertain about what to do, until Hector finally mouths, "*Is he sleeping?*" Not sure, they merely shrug back.

To get Jack's attention, Hector fakes a sneeze, and the smile instantly leaves Jack's face. He snaps to, with his eyes flying open in surprise. "Warn a guy, would ya?" he growls, noting the bodies around his desk. "What the fuck?"

"Sorry," apologizes Hector, straddling a chair as if it were a prostitute. "Where were you?"

Jack blinks into focus. "None of your business," he grunts. "You got anything on Kaspin? Tell me you guys solved that problem and it's all gone now."

Hector sighs. "From your lips to God's ears. All we have is LaGrange being tortured by the CIA and giving up nothing. But he better talk quick because the way they're going, they're likely to kill the fucker."

Hector describes what he saw at the CIA office while Jacob goes over to the coffee station to pour himself a cup. But the pot is now two hours old, and when he tastes it, it's nasty.

"How the hell do you guys drink this swill?" he asks, trying to make it more palatable with healthy amounts of sugar and creamer. Not surprisingly, this fix doesn't work, so he leaves the cup there and walks back to the group.

"Kaspin disappeared," he tells them. "The Bureau is interrogating Guard members again, but they don't have much of anything new to say. However, we do know that Colonel Powell drove out of the state in an armored JLTV and was last seen outside Albany. But that trail has also gone cold."

Jack turns his head to relieve pressure in his neck, a sensation that seems to occur when his internal light bulb turns on. "Just for shits and giggles, why don't we send a picture of the Colonel and that vehicle to the Canadian border guards?"

Ruiz cocks his head. "You think he went to Canada?"

Jack lifts an ambivalent shoulder. "Fuck if I know; it's just a hunch. There's no harm in checking it out, right? That northern border has so many holes in it that it's a likely place for the bad guys to bring a nuke into the country."

With grunts of agreement, the men disperse to complete other duties, leaving Jack alone again. Swiveling his chair around to face his desk, he looks at the increasing pile of paperwork. "Crap, this stuff won't complete itself," he mutters, wondering whether he should tackle it now or let it go for another day.

Just then, his cell phone rings, relieving him of making that decision. But first, he looks at the call screen. *Who the hell is this?* he wonders, not recognizing the number. For a split second, he dithers between answering it and dismissing it. But the former wins, and he slides his finger over the answer button.

"Stenhouse," he says. Then, "Thanks," and hangs up.

Rising from his desk, he marches into Captain Conrad's office with a bit of news. "Hey, boss," he says, not waiting for an invitation to speak. "I just got a call from Mike Lucchese. Turns out, Colonel Powell is in Canada."

It took a bit of searching, but in the end, Colonel Powell was relieved to find a tugboat captain at the Port of Quebec who was eager to make extra cash off the books. He last talked to the tug owner months ago, so today, he will meet him face-to-face. He's hoping the man has done what he asked. The colonel won't accept slipups; everything must be on schedule. If there are any problems at all, he will cancel this arrangement.

At five minutes to ten, Powell stops in front of a receptionist in a weather-beaten building. The woman sitting behind a glass partition at a low counter is on the phone, so while he waits for her attention, he uses the time to gain insight into the man he's about to meet.

The waiting area is bleak and uninviting, with only photographs of tugboats hung on a wall for decoration. Instantly, he surmises, *This guy is struggling. That's why he was so agreeable. Now I can be sure he will do whatever I ask; he must be desperate.* The captain's research showed this company to be one of the area's lesser-used ones, and now he sees his information was accurate.

The woman finally hangs up the phone with a broad smile for her rare customer. *"Bonjour, comment puis-je vous aider?"* she asks politely.

"Bonjour," replies George, hoping this meeting won't be difficult. "That's all the French I know. Do you speak English?"

The smile that adorned the Canadian's face fades slightly. "Oui, monsieur. I speak English."

"Great," responds George, disregarding the woman's mild look of contempt. "My name is George Powell, and I'm here to see Louis Garnier. I have an eleven o'clock appointment."

"Ah, one moment, please," she says, looking at her computer. "Ah, yes, I see you are on his calendar. I will let him know you are here."

Turning away, she reaches for the phone, and speaking in rapid French, says something that George hopes is only announcing his arrival.

Seconds later, a short man with a receding hairline enters the foyer, making a beeline straight for him. "Bonjour, Mr. Powell," he says, pumping George's hand enthusiastically with nicotine-stained fingers. "Good morning. Please come in."

With an expansive gesture belying the threadbare office conditions, Louis Garnier leads George through a small work area with several unoccupied desks, then opens a door at the back of the room. "Here we are," he says. "Please sit."

While George takes one of the only available chairs, he notes that this room is just as drab as the lobby. The only concession to adornment here is a Canadian flag hanging from a pole in the corner and a well-used filing cabinet under a small window covered by cheap blinds.

"The *Phoenix* arrived last evening," says Louis, sitting behind a desk littered with papers and a half-full ashtray. "I guided it to the slip myself. It is on Rue Dalhousie, and I made sure to keep it off our logs. Officially, your ship is not here. You can see it out of my window. It is the large blue vessel there, with no other ships nearby."

Powell stands to gaze between the slats of the dirty

blinds, then returns to his chair. "When do I get my package?"

"Ah, yes," nods Louis, understanding that his visitor wants to get to the point. "There is a cocktail party for the G20 attendees tonight, which the press says the prime minister will attend. I assume you want to make the transfer before then?" To the colonel's nod, he says, "Alors, to ensure the discretion you require, I have encouraged the captain and crew to leave the ship unattended for a certain length of time." Louis pauses to emphasize his next words. "It is not an easy feat to get a ship's crew to leave their vessel, but what I have done will give you privacy."

The tug owner watches his visitor intently, hoping he will appreciate the extra time and effort he put into the business deal and reward him for it. But Powell's expression is neutral, so he expands his explanation. "I have provided them several enticing entertainment opportunities, and I have offered my services to watch the ship while they are gone."

Louis continues to study Powell's face, but there is still no recognition of his efforts, so with a deep sigh, he says, "*Eh bien*. We can make the transfer with no interference if you come before eleven. Your package for my money, *d'accord*?"

At last, Powell reacts. Rising from his chair, he grins slightly and offers a hand. "*C'est bon*," he states, concealing his pleasure with a mask of studied indifference.

For Stenhouse and his crew, an unusual lull in the frenzy of activities at the First Precinct takes the men by surprise. Nothing in the city seems to be breaking loose at the moment, so they're enjoying the temporary respite.

While it's quiet, Assante returns to his office in the Federal Building. He tells them he wants to wait there for an update from Agent Waring at Langley, but the guys know he's happy to skip out for a while. At the same time, Gomez and

Ruiz head out for a long lunch. They invite Jack, but he takes a raincheck to reevaluate the open cases piling up on his desk.

Fifteen minutes into his review, Jack's stomach rumbles, so he gets up to buy something from the vending machines. In the break room, he stuffs a couple of dollar bills into the drink dispenser, pulls out a soda, then tries his luck on a bag of chips from the snack machine. When his choice gets stuck at the end of the display rod, he curses more loudly than the malfunction calls for and grabs the sides of the machine, shaking it violently. His disappointment at not receiving what he wants seems to have hit a raw nerve, releasing a host of pent-up frustrations and emotions that Jack wasn't aware he'd kept bottled up. In the process, the chips fall into the receiving area, along with two candy bars that somehow join in on the fun.

Pleased with his extra prizes, he grabs his bounty while the captain looks on from the doorway. "You know, you broke two machines doing that," he tells his lieutenant.

Jack shrugs while peeling the wrapper off one of the candy bars. "I guess you think I give a shit about the delicacy of vending machines."

"Yeah, well, repairing them costs money," says Conrad. Then he adds, "maybe you'll give a shit about this. Assante called. Seems LaGrange is dead."

Jack rolls his eyes and bites into the Snickers bar he didn't pay for. "So, fuck. They killed him after all, and I bet they didn't get any information, either… Did they?"

Conrad snorts. "The nuke is heading to Canada by ship, and then somehow, it'll make its way to Kaspin. That's all they got. LaGrange never said when or where it would be arriving. By the way, in case you're interested, the CIA claims it was a heart attack."

Jack smirks. "Yeah, high voltages will do that. Look, did you send photos of Colonel Powell and his JLTV to the

Canadian authorities? Powell is probably up there to bring that nuke back to Kaspin. So I was thinking… Let's let him do that. We can keep tabs on him, then bag all the players at the same time."

Conrad agrees. "I was thinking the same thing."

Jack finishes the last of the candy bar and throws away the wrapper. "When Gomez and Ruiz return from lunch, I'm gonna ask Hector to go up to Canada with the FBI. He can report back to us before Jacob gets the okay to share his intel. They need to be there yesterday, and they're gonna hafta cast a wide net."

It's almost two-thirty when Hector and James return to work, and Jack gives each of them a cold stare.

"What's wrong with you?" asks Hector, belching after an especially full meal.

"I'm glad you blockheads finally decided to come back. LaGrange was offed by the CIA."

Hector chuckles while rubbing his belly. "No surprise there. They put him through shit, and shit he did."

Jack rolls his eyes at Hector's crudeness while simultaneously stifling a secret grin. With mock seriousness, he asks, "Are you trying to steal my thunder? I thought I was the only one around here with such a foul mouth."

Hector beams proudly as Jack continues, "Claude said the nuke is headed to Canada by ship. So Hector, I want you to head over to Assante's office. You and he are going up there to poke around; one of you to Montreal and the other to Quebec City. Look for Powel at all the ports in your area. But don't engage with him. We want to track him back to Kaspin so we can pick them both up at the same time. Meanwhile, Ruiz, you're gonna stay with me. We hafta be ready to keep a close eye on Powell as soon as he hits the states."

Jack says, "One more thing," while Hector pulls his keys out of his pocket. "I'm sure he's on it, but remind Jacob to check Interpol for ships leaving Estonia for Canada over the last three weeks. Maybe something will pop up."

"Will do," responds Hector. "We really need a break in this case. Let's hope we get one."

Jacob is making travel arrangements for himself and Gomez when Hector knocks on the side of his cubicle.

"Geez," says Hector, squeezing into the small space around Jacob's desk. "Was the janitor's closet taken?"

I'm on hold, mouths Jacob, flashing Hector the bird at the slight. When he gets the relevant information, he writes it down and ends the call.

"Guess you heard about LaGrange," says Jacob, tearing his notes from a pad. "Fucking Langley spooks got overzealous."

Hector shoots him a glance. "You mean Waring? That chick is sick."

Jacob looks down at the paper. "You're going to Quebec City, and I'm going to Montreal. We need to concentrate on the ports along the Saint Lawrence for all the ships coming in from Estonia. That's where LaGrange took possession of the weapon, so those are the ships we need to look for. While we're doing that, other agents overseas will look for General Mednikov. We know he's been trafficking military hardware out of Russia."

"Good deal," responds Hector. "When's my flight?"

Jacob refers back to his notes. "You leave at four. You're on United out of JFK. Mine leaves at 5:15 on Air Canada, also from JFK. RCMP officers will meet us in Canada."

Hector draws in a breath and lets it out slowly. "When we find Powell, Stenhouse intends to track him to Kaspin, and he's not the only one. I'm determined to get my own piece of that shithead."

Hector catches sight of a framed photograph of Jacob's sister, Maria. Picking it up, he stares at it for a long moment, then shakes his head and sets it back down. "She was legit," he mutters.

"Yeah," replies Jacob, stuffing his notes into a pocket. "Now, as Jack would say…"

"Let's roll!" holler both men.

CHAPTER TWENTY-FIVE

After retrieving his luggage at Quebec City's Jean Lesage International Airport, Hector looks around the baggage area for the officer he's supposed to meet. In time, he spots an exceptionally tall man holding a sign with his name.

"Um, I'm Detective Gomez," he says, approaching the sign-holder hesitantly.

Hector is wary because he was told an RCMP officer would meet him, and this man isn't what he expected. To be fair, his only reference to Canadian law enforcement is an old American cartoon series called Dudley Do-Right, about a Royal Canadian Mounted Policeman in a bright red jacket and poufy pants. But this man is wearing a business suit.

The stranger turns, looking down at the shorter man standing next to him. "I am RCMP Inspector Owen Donnell," he says, lowering the sign. "Welcome to Quebec City. My car is parked outside."

On the way to the car, Donnell notices Hector pulling his collar tight around his neck. "Yes, it is much cooler here," he says. "It will reach the fifties Fahrenheit in the evenings and the high seventies during the day. Oh, and before you ask, we only wear red jackets on formal occasions."

Hector laughs while he climbs into the passenger seat, and Owen starts the engine.

"We set you up at a hotel near our headquarters," Owen says, backing out of the parking spot. "We received photos and a dossier on George Powell. Tomorrow, I will pick you up at the hotel around eight to bring you to the office."

"Sounds good," says Hector.

Owen adds, "But we checked port records, and there are no cargo ships due here from Estonia. However, one is docked in Montreal."

When Owen's peripheral vision catches Hector shaking his head and rolling his eyes, he casts a sidelong glance at the American officer. Hector is wishing that he, instead of Jacob, had gone to Montreal. But he keeps that thought to himself, so Owen turns back to the road.

"Did you have dinner?" he asks.

"No, only some crackers on the plane."

"Well, then, let me take you to a great steak restaurant."

While the Canadian drives Hector to a popular hangout near the Quebec City airport, Jacob arrives at Montréal–Trudeau International Airport and starts looking for the person who was sent to meet him.

Before long, a woman approaches him from within a crowd of travelers. "Are you Jacob Assante?"

"Yes," he responds. "Are you with the RCMP?"

The woman extends her hand. "Oui. I am Emma Bouchard."

Jacob tries not to look like a dumbstruck teenager while he shakes the Canadian's hand. "Hi," he stammers. "Uh, don't take this wrong, but you're the best-looking cop I've seen in a long time. It's nice to meet you."

Emma cocks her head to the side, trying to size up the blunt American. "Thank you, I think," she replies. "I do not know why you are surprised, but there are women in the RCMP. Many of us, including me, are stationed in the big cities, and I am grateful for that since I grew up in Montreal and am not at all a country girl."

Jacob looks away, knowing he sounded like an ass.

Emma ignores his discomfort. "I thought we could swing by the office of CBSA, the Canada Border Services Agency. It will not take long. They have information on the JLTV you are looking for. After that, I will bring you to your hotel. There is a restaurant there, so I will buy you a meal if you are hungry."

A short time later, the two officers are inside a dark computer room with multiple workstations and several HD video monitors fastened to a wall. Emma sits at an empty station and hits a few keys. Then she points to a large monitor at the end of the wall.

"You are looking at a black JLTV entering Canada at the Champlain, New York Border Crossing about a week ago. The vehicle is registered to Black Horizon, LLC in North Carolina, USA. Now, I have one other item of interest for you. Please follow me."

Emma escorts Jacob out of the computer room into an area with desks and chairs lined up one after the other. Weaving through them, she stops at a cluttered desk at the rear, where she removes a sheet of paper from a manila folder.

"Earlier today, an Estonian freighter docked at our port here in Montreal. We quarantined it and posted armed guards at the pier. Our preliminary check showed a spike in radiation, giving us hope that we had found the correct vessel. However, a subsequent review of the manifest revealed medical supplies and testing equipment on board, which could have been the reason for the spike. Of course, we will do a proper search, but that will not be until morning."

"Oh, ah, that's good," responds Jacob, lost for a moment in Emma's blue-green eyes. "Um, I'm pretty hungry. Are you ready for dinner? We can discuss your plan for tomorrow while we eat."

"Okay, sure," says Emma, wondering why Jacob is staring at her so intently. "We can go to your hotel now."

"Thanks," Jacob replies, following Emma out of the room. Behind her, he asks, "Um, will you also pick me up at the hotel in the morning?"

Emma's lips curl upward, secretly pleased by the American's question. "Actually, I was planning to have one of my fellow officers do that. But I suppose I could do it instead."

At 10:45 that night, Colonel Powell backs the JLTV up to a pier along the Rue Dalhousie. The marina appears deserted and gloomy at this late hour, bathed in long shadows cast by the only illumination — a few dim lights from the *Phoenix*.

Powell turns off the engine, then approaches the yacht, aware of the lonely sound of water slapping against the vessel with the incoming tide. *I wouldn't be here if I didn't have to be*, he tells himself, quickening his steps in the darkness.

Above him, a lone figure watches from a walkway leading from the ship to the dock.

"Do you have my money?" calls tugboat captain Louis Garnier when Powell is within earshot.

Powell looks up as he ascends the gangway. "You'll get it when I get my package," he responds, reaching Garnier in record time. Under cover of darkness, anyone could be out there watching, so the quicker they make the transfer, the better.

Powell is a cautious man. His attention to detail has served him well through years of strict military discipline, multiple combat tours, and now, the unpredictable demands of Serge Kaspin.

"Come aboard," says Garnier, beckoning the colonel to move quicker. The tugboat captain also wants to get this over with, as his job and his company are on the line if he's caught. "It will take both of us to move the case. It is not large, but it is heavy."

The men take a freight elevator down to a storage room on a lower deck, where brass fittings and teakwood floors show off the owner's wealth.

Louis points to an aluminum case standing upright on heavy-duty wheels, hidden among the ship's provisions and the prime minister's belongings.

George looks at it with an arched brow. "If that thing weighs so much, how did you get it down here?" he asks suspiciously.

Louis clasps his fingers together, cracking his knuckles. "It was hard work, *mon ami. Ainsi*, you pull, and I will push."

George extends a telescoping handle, then struggles to tilt the case on its wheels. When it's balanced, Louis sets it into motion, and it rolls smoothly, despite its weight.

On the trip back to the elevator, George has a troubling thought about the next phase of the move. Turning his head, he looks back at Louis without stopping. "This thing must weigh a couple of hundred pounds. How are we gonna get it into my truck?"

"No problem," grunts Louis, pushing it into the elevator. "The difficult part is not getting the case into your truck; it is taking it down the gangplank. We will have to control it well, for it will want to overtake us down the ramp."

Though the night is cool, the men are overheated and sweaty when they reach the dock.

"Wait here," says Louis, breathless from the strain of curbing the heavy weapon's momentum down to the pier.

"Don't take long," says Powell, uneasy about being out in the open with Serge Kaspin's nuke.

Louis disappears into the darkness and returns minutes later, the quiet hum of an electronic motor announcing his presence.

Ah, that's how he's gonna do it, observes George as a yellow forklift materializes out of the gloom.

While Powell watches, Louis guides the twin forks of the machine under the case, then steps down from the cab.

"You will need to help me," he says, leaning a shoulder into the case.

Working together, the men tilt the heavy container onto the forklift. When it's in place, Louis drives it to the JLTV.

"I'll get the doors," says the colonel, sprinting ahead to unlock the vehicle.

Louis eases the forklift up to the truck's cargo area, then slides the case in, noting how its weight lowers the vehicle a tad before it levels itself hydraulically.

George is thankful the weapon is no longer out in the open. Locking the doors shut, he walks around to the front and retrieves a briefcase from the passenger seat.

"Here you are," he says, holding it out in front of him while Garnier clicks the latches open to check the contents.

The captain licks his lips at his good fortune. "Very good, mon ami," he declares.

"You can count it if you like," snickers the colonel, holding the briefcase in his outstretched arms.

Louis' eyes dart rapidly over Powell's face. The colonel's remark is worrying, so he backs up a few steps to search for signs of treachery. However, the promise of reward is too tempting to ignore. Stepping forward again, he closes the lid and snaps the locks shut. "I am going to trust you," he declares, taking the briefcase from Powell. "Is there no honor among thieves? Safe travels, my friend."

With that, Louis tucks the briefcase under an arm and quickly climbs back into the forklift. Then he and the machine disappear back into the darkness.

The colonel waits until he can no longer hear the forklift

in the distance. Then he pats the side of the JLTV and boards the vehicle. He'll spend the rest of the night at the B&B, then leave Quebec City in the morning. His next destination is North Dakota. After that, North Carolina.

On a brisk, forty-five-degree morning, Hector sits at a small metal desk at the local office of the RCMP, watching Inspector Donnell search files on his desktop. When he finds the one on Serge Kaspin, he stops and shuffles through some paperwork on his desk.

"It looks like we have information on the JLTV," he tells Hector. "And it says here that a ship from Estonia docked at the marina thirty-six hours ago."

Hector's ears prick up. "What do you know about the ship?"

Owen refers to the paper in his hand. "A yacht called the *Phoenix* brought the prime minister of Estonia here. He's going to attend the G20 Summit later this week. The ship is docked at a private berth."

Owen turns back to his computer and clicks a few keys. "*Euh*, a surveillance video of the pier shows activity near the yacht late last night. It is dark, but you can make out two men removing a case from the yacht. They load it into a large vehicle, then the vehicle leaves. Here, take a look." Owen restarts the video and swings the monitor around so Hector can see it.

"That's a JLTV!" says Hector excitedly. "It must be Powell and the nuke!"

Donnell lifts another sheet from his desk. "This is the transcript of a transmission sent to us from Interpol. It says a Russian general named Mednikov was apprehended after selling a nuclear device. They believe it is the one Serge Kaspin bought."

"Yes!" shouts Hector, happy about the good news. "Looks like we're finally closing in on those fuckers!"

"It seems so. We are also working with the municipal police force to find George Powell. We assume he is staying near the port, so they are checking hotels and other lodgings in the area. As for the JLTV, surveillance cameras show it entering Canada at the Champlain, New York border crossing."

Hector springs out of his chair. "That makes sense. Our last visual on it was near Albany."

Hector walks over to a window to think. "Can we get on that yacht? Can we talk to the prime minister?"

Donnell shakes his head. "That could take some time, if it is allowed at all. Our government would need to be involved. Diplomatic immunity, you know?"

Hector rubs his forehead irritably. "We don't have fucking time! Powell is probably on his way back to the States right now!"

"We are doing our best. We cannot—"

Hector stops Owen with a raised hand. "Look, I'm gonna check out that yacht. We need to know if the nuke was on it. Will you come with me?"

Donnell sighs deeply. "You Americans are very reckless, but I like that. So, I will go with you, American. Just let me tell my superior what we are doing."

"Will he let you know if they find Powell?"

"Yes, I will ask him to keep me informed."

Hector watches Owen enter his superintendent's office, then listens to the familiar sounds of muffled yelling behind the closed door. "Just like the First," he mutters. "Doesn't matter where you are; there's always bullshit."

When the loud noises subside, Owen exits and slams the door, then stomps over to his desk and shuts down his computer, muttering in French the entire time. Hector knows the inspector is cursing because of his tone of voice and the French word "*merde*," repeated several times.

Fishing his keys from a pocket, Owen grumbles, "Let us go now, before I do something I will regret."

Hector nods. "I know what you mean. I'm right behind ya, pal."

It's chilly outside when Colonel Powell begins his trip to Winnipeg, his first stop on the way to delivering Serge's nuke.

The colonel's electronic mapping system points him to the fastest route, estimating it will take twenty-seven hours on the Trans-Canada Highway. But Powell knows he'll spend much longer than that on the road. The automated system assumes ideal conditions and no stops along the way, and he and the vehicle will need fuel at regular intervals. The JLTV isn't great on gas under the best of circumstances, and with the extra weight it's carrying now, he expects to be stopping more often than usual.

In planning his route, Powell decided to drive straight through to Winnipeg, stopping only at truck stops to grab quick meals, gas up, and rest. To minimize detection, he wants to avoid hotels as much as possible, so he'll sleep in the truck. The only room he intends to book is in Winnipeg because he knows he'll need a proper rest by then. After that, he'll drive to North Dakota, his first stop in the U.S. on his way to Kaspin's hideout.

Halfway to the marina, Hector gazes at traffic on the opposite side of the road and can't believe his eyes. Traveling in the opposite direction is a black JLTV heading away from the port.

"Shit! That's Powell!" shouts Hector, shaking Donnell's shoulder for emphasis. "Turn around! We have to follow him!"

Donnell catches only a fleeting glimpse of the vehicle Hector points to, but because the American insists, he executes a quick maneuver to get over into the right lane.

To get out of the way of the crazy driver, the morning traffic screeches and swerves around them, leaving Hector holding onto the dashboard.

"We have to get on his tail! He's going to Kaspin!" claims Hector, urging the Canadian to speed up.

Donnell is incredulous. "You want me to follow him to North Carolina? That is ridiculous! Moreover, he is traveling west, not south!"

Hector smirks at the inspector. "The U.S.-Canadian border is mostly unguarded, so I'm sure he's heading for a remote access point where he can cross undetected. Somewhere west of all the major cities." Then Hector takes out his cell phone and opens his contact list.

Still driving to catch up, Donnell shakes his head at Hector's optimism. "That would be a very long trip, American, and when the traffic thins, he will surely detect us. I will let everyone know where he is and radio for backup and air surveillance. However, if my superiors decide to end this chase, there will be nothing more I can do."

Hector waits for his call to go through. When it's answered, he says, "Jacob, I need assistance from the Bureau. I'm with RCMP Inspector Donnell; we're following Powell and the nuke. Use my cell signal for our coordinates."

Jacob is elated. "You got him?" he cries.

"Yeah!" replies Hector enthusiastically.

"Good work, Gomez! I'll get on it right away! We're gonna need cooperation from the Canucks, though. By the way, there was nothing on the ship here."

"Do whatever you need to do, buddy! I'm not gonna let him out of my sight!"

The trip from Quebec City to Winnipeg is a 2500 km trek, a long journey for Colonel Powell, but he knows it's urgent. To emphasize its importance, Kaspin keeps calling, demanding updates, and constantly reminding Powell that he won't tolerate slowdowns. The colonel knows he's going to have to push himself. Time is of the essence. The JLTV isn't comfy, and his bones are going to ache, but he's going to have to finish his mission quickly.

Powell's first break will be at a truck stop near Hearst, about 1300 km from the marina. He intends to top off his tank there, get some food, and spend the night in the truck.

Gomez and Donnell have no idea how George Powell plans to get to North Carolina. However, both are committed to following him all the way through Canada — providing RCMP superiors agree to allow the inspector to remain on the case.

When the colonel turns off the highway at Route 117 to make a fuel and pee stop, Jacob and Emma Bouchard follow Hector's directions to join the pursuit.

Assante and Bouchard keep an eye on Powell from another pump while he puts gas in his truck. Powell doesn't know either of them, so their presence nearby isn't an issue. However, the colonel met Gomez when Kaspin held him at his mountain cabin, so Hector asks Donnell to park at a restaurant next to the gas station.

Knowing it'll take a while to fill up the armored vehicle, Emma gets snacks from the station's convenience store while Assante tops off his tank. When she comes out, Powell is still gassing up.

"Let's get on the road," says Jacob. "We can wait for him along the highway, so he doesn't think we're following him out of the station."

A short way from the gas station, Assante reenters the road just after Powell passes them, with Gomez and Donnell some distance behind them. The two unmarked police vehicles are now the colonel's (as yet) undetected shadows.

CHAPTER TWENTY-SIX

When Powell first mapped out his journey, he seriously considered driving straight through to Winnipeg. But then he thought better of it. He knew he could do it if he were younger, but now that he's older — and hopefully wiser — he understands that his mature body will no longer allow that strain. Furthermore, he's a realist. He knows that driving a JLTV is nothing like driving a Cadillac.

Nevertheless, as much as he intended to rest often, his military tenacity took over, and he ended up pushing himself — hard. When he started to doze off, even after being fortified by gallons of Tim Hortons coffee, he was surprised to find that he had been on the road for seventeen hours.

This won't do! he scowled, and immediately started looking for a place to bed down for the night. *I don't want to get a room yet, but I can't do anymore driving today.*

Gomez, Donnell, Assante, and Bouchard are all in the same condition, so they're relieved when they see Powell turn into the parking lot of a small motor lodge in the city of Longlac.

"Keep your distance," warns Hector in the lead car. "There's a gas station up the road. Turn in there."

The temperature is now a chilly thirty-four degrees Fahrenheit, and the Canadian coffee from the station's minimart is a welcome purchase.

While they drink their Timmies, as the Canadians refer to their omnipresent Tim Hortons coffee, Jacob stares out the window toward the inn and the large JLTV parked in front of it. "That place is small, so even if there are enough rooms available, it's too risky for all of us to stay there. So I have a suggestion. Owen and Emma can try to get a room as a couple, while Hector and I sleep in the car. We can take turns monitoring Powell's activity. This way, you guys will be refreshed and ready to drive in the morning and we can take turns catching up on sleep if we need to."

Owen looks to Emma for approval, and when she nods, he says, "Okay. I will let you know if we get a room."

Fifteen minutes later, Hector clicks on an incoming call.

"We are in," says Owen. "We are three doors down from the colonel."

"Excellent. I'm going to get something for us to eat from the minimart. I saw a display with prepackaged sandwiches. I hope they're edible. What are you guys going to do about food?"

"Emma is going to drive over to the minimart."

Before Hector leaves the car, Jacob tells him to buy a couple of deodorants and some aftershave. "Who knows when we'll get a warm shower? Just make sure to get different scents of aftershave. We may be sharing the same 'bed' tonight, but I don't want to smell like you, too."

"Funny," replies Hector.

When the detective returns, they eat cold sandwiches and packaged donuts in the car, downed by more coffee. Then Jacob tries to sleep while Hector takes the first watch. It's going to be a long night.

Longlac, Ontario, is in the eastern third of the vast Canadian countryside, far from the hustle and bustle of Quebec City and Montreal. Instead of tall buildings crowded together, rolling hills and forests fill the surrounding landscape as far as the eye can see. It would be a pretty area to explore if there was time.

It's early, and Hector is on the last watch. He's been staring at the colonel's room for so long that the slightest movement catches his eye. "Hey," he says, poking Jacob, snoring softly in the next seat. "He's leaving."

Jacob sits up, blinking sleep from his eyes in time to see the door opening and George Powell walking to the office.

Minutes later, their target backs his JLTV out of its parking spot and heads for the gas station to feed the beast.

Hector calls Donnell to wake them up but finds they're already awake. "I'm dropping off the room key now," says Owen. "Emma's waiting in the car."

Powell fills his tank, then turns back onto the Trans-Canada highway, followed a safe distance behind by the two RCMP officers. Meanwhile, Jacob, always cautious, waits a few more moments before he and Hector join the chase. There is sparse traffic on this stretch of highway, so the group keeps well behind the colonel.

"Check in with HQ," says Owen, glancing at Emma. "They need to know we're on the move again."

None of the officers knows where they're headed, but they're determined to keep up the chase to find out.

Back in Manhattan, Jack is on his second coffee when he hears his name bellowed from Conrad's office.

"Why doesn't he ever use the fucking phone?" he mutters, rising from his seat to answer his boss' summons.

Holding onto his coffee, Jack walks through a maze of people and desks, then pokes his head into Conrad's world. "Don't you ever use the phone?" he asks irritably. "What's up?"

Conrad motions for Jack to sit down. "Gomez and Assante are following Colonel Powell through western Ontario with a couple of RCMP officers. None of them know what he's up to, but it doesn't appear that he's heading to the U.S."

"Then where the hell's he going?" grumbles Jack, stroking his chin thoughtfully. "Why the hell is he still in Canada?"

"We don't know that yet, but I have more. The RCMP questioned the prime minister of Estonia in Quebec City, and he said he allowed General Mednikov to load a large case onto his yacht as a political favor and doesn't know what was in it."

"Ha. Of course, he'd say *that*," Jack responds, sarcastic as usual. "Did they check it out?"

"Yeah. He allowed them to board the vessel, but the case wasn't there. However, they found traces of radiation in one of the storerooms."

"Bingo."

"Yup. They also arrested one of the guys in that surveillance video from the marina. His name is Louis Garnier, and he's a tugboat captain there. Garnier says Powell paid him to take the package off the ship, and during the transfer, he mentioned Serge Kaspin."

"Oooo, I'm liking this so far," says Jack, rubbing his hands together gleefully.

"This is good, too," says Conrad, picking up a sheet of paper. "The feds have finally made progress with the Patriot Guard members they've been holding. One of them says he'll talk, but he wants immunity from prosecution. They'll let us know if they get anything solid."

Jack leans forward, fixing his boss with a direct stare. "I've been thinking about Powell," he says, "and there's only one reason he'd be driving such a heavy-duty vehicle over such a long distance. It can't be comfortable, so he must be planning to go off-road somewhere. If he's still going west, he's far from the major cities by now and in sparsely populated areas."

"So maybe he's not going to North Carolina," posits

Conrad. "Maybe he's going out on his own somewhere else."

Jack stops to think, then shakes his head. "Nah, I still think he's headed for Kaspin. I've always thought he'd cross the border in some remote region, far away from paved roads. Maybe near North Dakota or Montana. And if that happens, our shadows won't be able to follow him in their POS sedans."

"They have air surveillance on him," considers Conrad.

"Yeah, but the Canucks won't fly across the border, so we're gonna have to hope Jacob can line up some U.S. flyboys for us."

"There's always that Guard member," offers Conrad hopefully. "If he can give us more intel, maybe we can keep better track of Powell when he crosses over."

"Yeah, there's always that," concurs Jack. "But I've been studying maps, and I'm willing to bet that North Dakota is where he'll cross. There are several border stations in that area, but it's remote and pretty uninhabited. The good thing for us is that Minot Air Force Base is also there. It's about an hour from the Canadian border."

"So? Why is that significant?" Conrad isn't following Jack's line of thinking.

"I want to plant myself at that base with some FBI agents. Then, if Powell does go through that section, we could deploy more quickly from there, than here."

Captain Conrad gives Jack a blank stare. "I see what you're getting at, Stenhouse, but that's only a hunch. You have no solid facts to back it up."

"I know—"

"BUT," says Conrad, raising a hand to stop Jack. "I'll pass your theory on to Rawlings. If he agrees with your assessment, he can get the ball rolling for you to stay at that base until this is done."

"He'll agree," Jack states, confident that his hunch is the

best they have to go on right now.

As the long drive drags on, Hector begins to notice a certain odor assaulting his nose. "Jacob, my man," he says, taking his eyes off the road for a second. "You're beginning to ripen. Put on more cologne, will ya?"

Jacob rubs the side of his nose with his middle finger. "You sure it isn't you? Next time, we better be the ones to get the hotel room. If we don't, they're gonna have to burn this car when we're done with it."

At nearly eleven that night, Powell and his shadows spot bright lights in the distance.

"Major city coming up," says Jacob, rousing Hector from a short nap.

The lights are from Winnipeg, the capital city of Manitoba province, the region's largest metropolitan area. With a population of over 700,000, the city is situated only seventy miles from the U.S. border.

"He's pulling off here," notes Hector, sitting up straighter to see better.

The cars take their time following the JLTV as it lumbers into the grounds of a hotel. To remain undetected, they circle the parking lot until Powell disappears inside. When he's gone, they find spots at the rear where they can still keep the truck in sight.

When Powell reappears, he moves the truck, and it disappears behind the hotel.

"Let's go in," says Jacob, gesturing to the RCMP officers sitting in the car next to him.

It's a brisk twenty-nine degrees when the men exit the warmth of their cars, but the cold doesn't faze the Canadians.

"I guess the weather reports are right," says Jacob, shivering inside his buttoned-up coat. "That early polar vortex must be on the way."

Inside the lobby, Owen Donnell approaches the front desk with his badge and ID.

"Hello," he cordially greets the clerk. "I am Officer Donnell, and this is Officer Bouchard," indicating Emma standing beside him. "The other men with me are associates from the United States. All of us are tracking a suspect, a man who just checked in, a Mr. George Powell."

"Oh," responds the clerk. She's not surprised, which leads the officers to believe this isn't the first time she's had to respond to a law enforcement request. "Let me get my manager to help you."

The woman leaves the counter for an office in the rear, and the group hears muffled voices. Soon after, a middle-aged man approaches them with a smile. "Good evening. I am the manager here. Is there a problem?"

"Not at all," replies Owen, looking at the man's name tag. "Antoine Pelletier? I was informing your employee that we are following a man who just checked in."

"I see," says Antoine, his hands poised over a computer keyboard. "His name, please?"

"George Powell."

Antoine hits a few keys, then looks up. "Yes, Mr. George Powell. We assigned him to Room 215. It is around back, in our auxiliary building."

Owen smiles his thanks, then says, "We do not have reservations, but we are going to need two rooms for as long as Mr. Powell is here."

Antoine turns back to the computer for a quick check of

available accommodations. "I am sorry, but there is only one room open. It is the honeymoon suite, on the fifth floor of this main building. It is large enough for four, however, with a king-size bed and a couch. We can also supply a roll-up bed. Because you are with the RCMP, I can offer a reduced rate."

Owen turns to the others. "Any objections to sharing a room?"

All of them hesitate for a moment. Then Jacob shrugs, and the others nod.

"We will take it," says Owen, turning back to the manager. "Please inform all staff on every shift that they need to call our room if they see Mr. Powell leaving the hotel or checking out. This includes the housekeeping staff. We need to be kept aware of his activity. Naturally, our presence here should not be mentioned to Mr. Powell or any of your other guests."

"I understand," replies Pelletier. "I will just need a credit card to finalize the reservation."

Hearing the request, Jacob steps forward to offer his credit card. "I'm U.S. FBI Special Agent Assante. I'll pay for the room."

Antoine finishes the check-in, then hands electronic keys to Jacob and asks him to sign in. "One of our porters will bring a portable bed to your room. It is Suite 521. You can access it via the elevator. Is there anything else I can assist you with?"

"Nothing at this time," responds Jacob, taking back his credit card. "Thank you for your cooperation."

Minutes later, the group is huddled together inside the elevator. All of them are tired, so none of them has anything to say. At least until Emma voices what everyone's thinking.

"Someone needs a shower."

As silence returns, each person wonders if she meant them. Then, when the elevator stops with a gentle bump, they leave the confining space as quickly as possible.

At the door of the honeymoon suite, Owen and Emma pop inside, but Hector stops, blocking Jacob's way.

"You waiting for a personal invitation?" asks the FBI agent, confused by the silly grin plastered on Hector's face.

Hector's smile widens until it involves his entire appearance. "I'm waiting for you to carry me over the threshold, Special Agent," he teases, doing his best to mimic an eager bride.

"Oh, for cryin' out loud," huffs Jacob, wrinkling his nose at the thought. Then he shoves the detective aside and marches around him, moving as far away from him as possible.

As everyone laughs at the joke, their tensions ease, and they start scrambling for first dibs on the shower.

When the order is decided, a knock on the door reveals the porter with the roller bed, and the new hot topic becomes which sleeping arrangements they'll agree to.

The group at the Winnipeg hotel isn't alone in settling into an unusual arrangement for the night. Five hours south of them, the latest development in the case has Jack exiting the backseat of a car in the driveway of Colonel Whitley Yearwood, commander of Minot AFB. The Air Force base is the home of the 5th Bomb Wing and the 91st Missile Wing of the Air Force Global Strike Command. Therefore, this base commander is in charge of many of the nation's B52 bombers, missiles, and ICBMs that are always ready to defend our country at a moment's notice.

This evening, Jack will stay in the colonel's guestroom until proper quarters are available for him and the other officers arriving over the next couple of days.

Jack is more than a little awed by his proximity to so much of the country's firepower. Just one hundred yards from the commander's modest ranch, he spotted a large sign indicating a field of ICBMs.

"Shit," he muttered under his breath as he approached the house where the six-foot-six commander was waiting for his guest. The light from inside emphasized the commander's height as he stood in his doorway. "This is gonna be interesting."

CHAPTER TWENTY-SEVEN

Early the next morning, Emma took over one of the stools behind the front desk. To appear as if she were one of the staff, she put on the same blue polo shirt as the hotel's desk clerk over the top she wore the day before. She told the clerk she wouldn't be a bother but needed to observe the hotel's comings and goings and watch for signs of Powell.

To pass the time, she talked a little with the clerk to find out if they could trust him if she weren't there, and it's a good thing she did. The youth doesn't seem very motivated. He confided that the only reason he took this job was to earn extra beer money while he attends the local college, and that he only does the bare minimum until each shift ends.

The rest of the time is pretty boring. Emma watches guests entering and exiting the main doors and going in and out of the elevator. But none are George Powell, and she thinks about returning to the room. However, a low rumble outside changes her mind.

Shit, it's Powell, she mumbles, putting herself on high alert.

To avoid the cold, the colonel dashes into the hotel and approaches the desk while rubbing his hands together.

"Hi," says the clerk. "How can I help you?"

"I want to check out. Here's my key."

While the clerk processes George's bill, Emma uses the phone in the office to call the honeymoon suite. "He's checking out," she hisses, hanging up quickly.

At the counter, Emma hears the clerk say, "Thank you for your stay, Mr. Powell. But before you go, you should know that you are entitled to partake of our free continental breakfast right there in our lobby."

Emma peeks out the door to see George looking over his shoulder at the breakfast bar.

"Oh, yeah," he says. "I could use some coffee and maybe a muffin. Thanks."

During that exchange, Emma pops back into the office and pulls off the polo shirt. Now, while George waits for his receipt, she leaves the office and walks around the counter, hoping George is too occupied to notice her.

Without a coat, she exits the hotel, shivering as she unlocks the car she and Owen are driving and starts the engine to warm up.

"Where the hell are they?" she mutters, anxiously watching the door. "I hope I will not have to leave them here. I do not want to tail him on my own."

When George finishes capping his coffee cup, he grabs a packaged muffin and walks toward the door just as the rest of the crew enters the lobby.

"There he is," whispers Hector, pointing at Powell's back.

Without breaking stride, Jacob tosses their room key at the desk clerk. "We're checking out," he tells the young man.

Outside, Donnell sprints toward his running car with Emma's coat dangling from his hand. "See you later, eh?" he calls back to the Americans.

Emma is poised to back the car out as soon as Owen throws himself and the coat inside. "He's already on the move," she says as Owen closes the door.

In the other car, Gomez and Assante join the procession, lagging behind as much as they dare without losing sight of the target vehicle.

Powell turns southwest, then stops at a gas station sharing the same lot as a large grocery store. While the locals gawk at the unusual black vehicle, Powell removes the gas cap and starts to pump, trying to seem oblivious to the French comments thrown his way.

The station isn't large, so Bouchard pulls her car into the farthest pump while Jacob parks closer to the store. He also needs gas, but he'll have to fill up after Powell leaves and catch up later.

Fortunately, Powell seems to have let his guard down. He hasn't detected them yet; he's still unaware he's being followed.

Earlier that morning, well before the day's activities began in Winnipeg, base commander Colonel Yearwood pounded on Jack's door. "You're on military time now!" he called out. "Get your ass out of bed!"

Jack's eyes flew open at the noise; the commander's steady thumping roused him out of a deep sleep. *What time is it?* he wondered, shaking his head groggily.

It wasn't even light out, but there was no chance of him sleeping any longer. So Jack unwillingly sprang out of bed and began fumbling for the light switch. When his toe bumped the corner of the night table, he squealed like a stuck pig.

At the door, Yearwood chuckled loudly at Jack's ripe verbiage. "Now that I know you're up, get moving! It's already 0530 hours, and I'm leaving at 0600, whether you're ready or not. I suggest you pick up the pace, Officer! It's a long fucking walk to where we set up an office for you!"

Jack sighed and ran into the bathroom. *No time for a shave*, he muttered, turning on the water for a military shower. When he was finished, he dressed and flew into the kitchen in record time.

Colonel Yearwood was on his third cup of coffee when

Jack skidded into the room.

"I'm impressed," he said. "Scrambled eggs and bacon are on the stove. You still got fifteen minutes before we go, so eat up. When you're done, put your dishes in the sink. My lovely wife will clean up later."

While Jack scooped food onto a plate, Yearwood studied the civilian who suddenly turned up at his doorstep.

"Tell me why the hell you're on my base," he barked at Jack's back. "I heard the military version. Now, I want the real shit!"

Jack brought his breakfast to a small table and sat down across from his host.

"Well, first, I want to thank you for your hospitality. I know civilians aren't usually allowed access to this facility, so I appreciate you giving us permission to be here."

"Ha," scoffed Yearwood. "I follow orders. Get to it, man," he barked.

Jack swallowed a mouthful of bacon, then washed it down with a healthy gulp of coffee. "Our people have been following a domestic terrorist traveling through Canada with a portable nuclear device. He's been going west for a while, and we think he's going to cross into the U.S. somewhere near here. He's part of a terror group we've had our eyes on for a while. We want to capture this guy with the nuke and also his asshole of a boss before they can activate the bomb. *That* is the real shit, Colonel."

While Jack finished the rest of his breakfast, Yearwood looked at him hard, trying to digest what he said.

Finally, he seemed to accept Jack's account. "Well, you're in the right place, son," he said. "We're in the business of deterrence here, so we should be able to help. Besides, I'm doing your Inspector Rawlings a favor. He was my CO in Kuwait, and he saved my ass more than once."

Jack lifted a brow in surprise. He didn't know Rawlings

was in the military.

"We set up a command center for you and your companions," continued Yearwood. "And you also have access to a unit of the National Guard. So, now, who's this asshole you're chasing?"

Concerned about the time, Jack gulped down the rest of his coffee. "I can't believe you know the inspector. Small world, right?" Instead of acknowledging the comment, Yearwood merely pinned him with dark eyes, so he returned to the topic at hand. "Umm… The asshole with the nuke is a guy named George Powell. He's a colonel, a former Marine. His boss is Serge Kaspin, a mercenary, and an international arms dealer."

"Kaspin? That Black Horizon spook? I thought he was dead!'

Jack sat back and cricked his neck, while in Canada, the rest of his crew was just waking up. "So did we," he replied dismally.

Like clockwork, the colonel's staff car arrived right on time, and the men headed out the door. Jack stowed his overnight bag in the trunk, then hopped in the back with the colonel, and they sped off, passing missile fields and a line of B-52H Stratofortress bombers.

"Amazing, aren't they?" declared Yearwood when he noticed Jack's admiration for America's military power. "You're looking at just some of what your tax dollars pay for."

Jack nodded, keeping his eyes on the passing armaments. "I knew we were well equipped. "It's so impressive to see them up close."

While researching this trip, Powell found a little-used dirt road before the border crossing at Carbury-Goodlands. It goes through a sparsely populated area dotted with farmland, the main reason he's driving the JLTV. His plan is to breach the border unnoticed by authorities by cutting through rural homesteads and open plains.

At eleven o'clock that morning, Powell and his shadows turn onto Provincial Trunk Highway 21, about sixty-seven miles north of the U.S.-Canadian border near North Dakota.

When Powell turns south, Hector and Jacob go on high alert.

"He's getting ready to cross into the United States," declares Hector as Jacob nods. "If I were him, I'd turn off the main road somewhere around here and go over the border in a secluded area."

"That's what I'd do," says Jacob. "But if he does that, how the hell are we gonna follow him off the main road? He has a heavy-duty truck, while our vehicles are only light passenger cars."

"Maybe we won't have to follow him offroad. The RCMP has air cover, right? I don't know if they're still following us, but if we give them our location, they should be able to take over."

Hector's phone has been quiet for a while, so when it rings, he grabs it quickly. "It's Stenhouse," he announces, putting the call on speaker. "What's up, Jack?"

"Hey. I'm at Minot Air Force Base in North Dakota with Homeland Security and a unit from the National Guard. Where's Powell?"

"He's heading south on Highway 21, about three miles north of the border. We're pretty sure he's gonna turn off this road and cross the border somewhere overland. We'll follow as far as we can, but our sedans won't hunt."

"Gotcha. Stay on the line and give me your coordinates when he turns off. Then continue south. We'll stop Powell when he crosses over."

Hector shoots Jacob a sidelong glance. "You got eyes in

the sky?"

"Yeah. Make sure your coordinates are accurate."

"Okay, but how are we gonna find Kaspin if you stop him now? I thought we were gonna let him lead us to North Carolina."

"No need," states Jack. "The FBI came through. They got one of the Guard members to turn, so we know where Kaspin is. After we nab Powell, we're gonna mount an assault on Kaspin's location. He's in a town called Love Valley. Can you believe that shit? They're gonna send undercover guys in to scope it out and verify he's there. Then, we'll drive in with the JLTV."

Hector snorts. "That cold-blooded killer's in Love Valley? Don't that beat all."

"We gotta do this smart," continues Jack. "We don't want to put civilians in jeopardy. So keep me posted, all right? I'm leaving soon to get closer to the border. When we have a better idea of where he's crossing over, we're gonna use some heavy-duty military vehicles to set up a roadblock. Powell's toast."

It's nearly noon when Serge Kaspin ends a phone conversation with Colonel Powell. The colonel's report is good, so he's all smiles as he tends to lunchtime visitors at his saloon.

The mercenary is actually enjoying his role as a tavern owner in this small town. Part of the charm of his new role is the uniform he gets to wear — a plain white shirt with arm garters, striped pants, and a fake handlebar mustache. The outfit lets him lose himself in another character, and that pleases him.

Kaspin serves up laughs and beer at a long wooden bar while employees dressed as saloon girls wait tables and a piano player fills the room with old-timey music. The tavern's menu is plain American fare: burgers, franks, beans, and fries, with mac and cheese for the kids and apple pie for dessert. Kaspin aims to keep things simple. "No need to invite trouble," he tells himself when he rejects other ideas that would make him stand out from the crowd.

At his temporary office, Jack notifies the FBI about Hector's suspicion that Powell would go offroad, and in turn, they inform the CBSA and the RCMP.

This latest information causes the Canadians to reevaluate their options. They already have a drone up, but they don't want their guys to lose the ground advantage. So after some discussion, they settle on sending a Humvee to rendezvous with Donnell and Bouchard.

Pleased by the confidence of their superiors, Donnell lets Jacob know they're going to swap their sedan for an offroad vehicle.

"Hey, that's great!" replies Jacob, equally gratified that their efforts won't end without seeing Powell arrested. "Now we can continue to track him! I can't wait to get that bastard! Okay if we leave our car here and hitch a ride with you?"

As all of them climb into the Humvee, a Canadian drone operator reports that Powell is slowing down near a hard-packed road less than three miles from the U.S. border.

"Let's get him!" exclaims Hector, eager to get on the way again.

Assante clicks on Jack's contact number. "Good news, buddy!" he declares happily. "The RCMP supplied us with a Humvee, so we're still in pursuit! I texted you the coordinates of where he turned off the main road. This is farm country, and we're heading west. I'll keep this line open to update you as we go."

The Humvee is now on a lonely country road, and it and the JLTV are the only two vehicles in sight.

"Uh oh," says Emma Bouchard. "With no other traffic around, we're more exposed on this road. I hope he doesn't spot us."

Too late. Powell finally notices the clouds of dust thrown up by the Humvee behind him.

What the fuck? he asks himself, checking and rechecking his mirrors. He hopes he's just being paranoid, but the vehicle keeps coming. *Shit! I gotta lose that bastard!*

Up ahead, Powell spots a dirt track leading into a field and makes a sharp turn there, sending the JLTV bouncing over gullies, creeks, and open plains, past homesteads, grain silos, and farming equipment in various states of use and repair.

Behind him, the Humvee follows Powell's dust cloud while Bouchard gets the latest information from the drone operator.

After a particularly harrowing ride through the uneven terrain, Bouchard grabs Jacob's phone to update Jack. "We are within one hundred meters of the border," she reports. "Our drone sees a small farm on a narrow road on the U.S. side. Several military vehicles are near there, about one-hundred-fifty meters to the east."

Jack passes the information to his Minot AFB partners, who move their heavy-duty vehicles into position, blocking the road on all sides, including well into the low shrubs along both shoulders.

National Guardsmen and police sharpshooters also take up positions nearby. They're waiting for the target to cross over 'the Slash,' a twenty-foot-wide area kept clear of all vegetation that marks the border with our northern neighbor.

For the crew in the Humvee, the last leg of the pursuit is the hardest. The pursuers get knocked around in their seats every time the vehicle hits holes or rocks.

"My kidneys are sure getting a workout!" calls Jacob, holding tightly onto a roof strap.

"This is awful!" grumbles Emma Bouchard. "I'm gonna hafta see my dentist after this! My fillings are about to pop out!"

Ahead of them, Powell is determined to outrun his chasers. *Just a little farther!* he mutters, bearing down on the accelerator to reach the border, where he believes his trackers will give up the chase.

Unfortunately for him, as soon as he passes through the barren section of land not far from the city limits of Souris, shots ring out, and he knows he has more to worry about than one Humvee.

With the gas pedal to the floor, Powell turns onto the unpaved road the drone spotted while keeping an eye on the Humvee looming larger and larger in his rearview mirror.

When he focuses back on the road, the sight up ahead turns his stomach. Blocking his way is a line of heavy vehicles, police sedans, and a truck with a large disc pointed in his direction.

"Holy shit!" he yells, swerving to miss a deep hole in the rutted road. Feeling around the passenger seat, he searches blindly for his phone and grabs it to make a desperate call to Kaspin. However, the call refuses to go through. "Damn it!" he shouts, throwing the phone onto the seat and pulling the JLTV away from another hole.

For a split second, Powell considers running the roadblock. But just as quickly, he knows he wouldn't make it through. So instead, he steps on the brake, coasts to within inches of an eight-wheel drive military truck, and shuts down the engine.

Defeated, he leans out of his window with both hands extended. "You win!" he calls out to a police officer and a couple of National Guardsmen approaching him with their weapons pointed at his head.

RCMP Inspector Donnell parks his Humvee at the rear of the JLTV to block a retreat.

"Keep those hands visible, and don't make any sudden moves!" barks Stenhouse as the Canadians join him.

Powell puts his hands in his lap while a Guardsman opens the driver's door.

"Don't do anything stupid," warns Jack, "or it'll be your last mistake. Step out of the vehicle, nice and slow."

"Cool your jets," grunts Powell. "My mama didn't raise no fool. I'm comin' out."

The instant Powell steps out of the JLTV, the Guardsmen grab his arms, and Jack cuffs his wrists.

"It's over, asshole," growls Jack. "We know where Kaspin is, and you're gonna help us arrest him." Then he turns to the Guardsmen. "Get this fucker outta my sight."

As they walk Powell away, Jacob opens the back of the JLTV while a crowd forms around him. All of them want to get a look at the weapon they've been tracking.

"Whooee, look at the size of that thing!"

Hector is amazed. "Fuck! That's one motherfucker of a bomb! Can you imagine the damage it would cause?"

"I don't wanna think about it," grunts Jacob. "I'm too happy the chase is over!"

Jack brings the conversation back on track. "So here's what we're gonna do now. We're gonna regroup at Minot, then head out from there."

"What about this?" asks Hector, pointing at the bomb.

"The military will dispose of it."

Hector turns to the Canadian law enforcement officers instrumental in Powell's capture. "Guys, I wanna thank you both for all your help. We couldn't have gotten this far without you!"

"It was our pleasure," Owen responds. "I am happy to have had a hand in protecting your country!"

The Americans smile amiably, knowing there's much truth in Owen's comment.

Emma adds, "Next time you visit Canada, I hope you won't be in such a rush!"

The group turns when they hear a loud engine bearing down on them.

"What the fuck you guys doin' roarin' down my road?" shouts an irate farmer behind the wheel of a battered Chevy pickup. Flinging his door open, he stomps up to them with a tricked-out AR slung over his shoulder. "You need help identifying private land?!"

Jacob raises his hands and approaches the old sodbuster with a polite, "Sorry about the hoopla. I'm an FBI Special Agent; all of us here just caught a terrorist who was planning a large attack in the country. Your road helped us stop a bomber, and we thank you for letting us use it."

The farmer spits a large wad of tobacco at Assante's feet. "I don't give a good goddamn who you are, sonny. I'll shoot you or anyone else who enters my land again."

Spinning on a well-worn heel, the farmer climbs back into his truck and leans his elbow out the window. "Hey, sonny! Thanks for catching that bastard!" he shouts, speeding back in the opposite direction.

Bouchard sidles up to Jacob while he watches the retreating pickup. "Damn, that guy was more dangerous than your target!" she grins. "Hell, if all Americans are that ornery, who in their right mind would ever try to take over your country?"

Jacob smiles proudly. "That's our Second Amendment in action!"

Around four p.m., Kaspin begins preparing the saloon for the dinner crowd. Checking the dining room, he sees a lone couple eating burgers at one of the tables and crooks a finger to call over a Patriot Guard member posing as a waiter.

"Watch those two; they're cops," he orders while he washes beer mugs. "I can smell 'em a mile away. Get friendly with them and tell me if they say anything I need to know."

Kaspin calls Powell for a status update, but it goes directly to voice mail. "Hmm," he says to himself. "He must be out in the boonies without a signal. Guess I'll try again in the morning."

The waiter peeks his head into the kitchen. "They didn't say anything, boss. They just asked about the town and said they liked the saloon. They wanted to compliment the owner in person, but I said you were getting ready for the dinner rush. So they just paid the bill and left."

Kaspin looks at his henchman. "They paid cash, didn't they?" The man nods, confirming his suspicion. "Figures," he says. "No way to trace them."

After his arrest, George Powell is treated as a military war criminal because of his membership in Serge Kaspin's Patriot Guard. They put him in the stockade at Minot AFB and are now trotting him out of his cell for interrogation by Stenhouse and a Homeland Security officer.

It's early evening, about 1800 hours, and George is tired from his lengthy trip and resulting capture. With shackled hands and feet, he shuffles into a base interrogation room in an orange jumpsuit, signifying his status as a maximum-security prisoner.

Powell takes a seat in a metal chair opposite Jack and Homeland Security Officer Richard Sosa while an Air Force corrections officer secures his leg shackles to the floor.

Before the prisoner arrived, Jack had time to talk to the Homeland officer and was gratified to learn that Richard has made a career out of the DHS. That alone made him confident the man would be a good partner, but his bald head, six-foot height, and muscular physique helped cement that image.

Powell eyes the men in front of him. "So, no lawyer for me, I guess," he declares matter-of-factly.

Jack gives the former Marine colonel his sniper stare. "You're lucky we didn't shoot you on sight. But you should know that's not entirely off the table yet."

Powell studies his adversary. "Noted," he states. "So what now?"

"In the morning, a National Guard C-130 will transport us and your vehicle to Charlotte. From there, we'll drive to Love Valley. That's where your boss is, right?"

Powell purses his lips with a heavy sigh. "Why are you asking if you already know that?"

"Just to piss you off."

"I see," says Powell, wrinkling his nose as if there was an unpleasant odor in the room. "Have you considered that flying me and the JLTV to Charlotte would make me get there too soon? I'm supposed to be driving there."

Jack pins the colonel with a smug look. "We already thought of that. We calculate that you would have reached Love Valley around nine tomorrow night, factoring in the usual food, fuel, and rest stops. So if you waited to drive in until that little town shut down, we figure you'd be talking to Kaspin by ten at the latest."

"Clever," says George. "So?"

"Well, if you help us nab him, it'll be very useful at your

trial. Providing you have one."

George leans forward, looking squarely at Richard, then at Jack. "What do you mean — help?"

The Homeland officer says, "We want you to keep contacting Kaspin, just as you've been doing all along. He left a message on your phone, so we want you to return it. We'll tell you what to say."

George sucks in a breath, trying to decide whether to cooperate or not, and Richard sees his hesitation. "As you can imagine," he says, "we're going to raid his position with or without you. So if you're thinking of warning him or refusing to help, your military guards are authorized to use deadly force against you at any point. Do I make myself clear?"

"And I'll shoot you myself if I have to," contends Jack.

George wrinkles his nose again. "Yeah, I got it."

CHAPTER TWENTY-EIGHT

George Powell watches with growing unease as his JLTV is driven into a grey C-130 Hercules military plane. It's a crisp summer morning in North Dakota, but George doesn't notice. His thoughts are centered on his upcoming betrayal of Serge Kaspin and how he hopes it will ensure his own survival.

Beside him, Homeland Security Officer Sosa hands Powell a cell phone. "Check in with Kaspin and be careful what you say. Remember that you have to sound calm and confident. Put it on speaker."

Powell's military guard unshackles George's hands to let him make the call. Then they wait for Kaspin to answer.

"Mornin'," says George. "I'll be there tonight, around ten or so. Everything's going well."

"Where are y—?" they hear Kaspin ask, but George ends the call before Kaspin can finish.

"Why the hell did you hang up on him?" Sosa asks angrily. "You tryin' to pull something over on us?"

"No, I just got nervous," Powell responds, handing the phone back to the officer. "You want me to call him back?"

Richard sighs. "No. Let's leave it at that." Then he motions for the guard to re-handcuff Powell. "Get him on the Herc."

On the other end of the line, Serge pulls the phone from his ear and stares at it, wondering why the colonel didn't continue the conversation. *Must be driving*, he reasons, watching a chipmunk scurry out of the swinging doors in the empty saloon. "Don't ya love it when a plan comes together?" he asks the critter before it disappears behind a box.

During operating hours, no vehicles are permitted in the Old West tourist town of Love Valley, so the law enforcement offensive will have to take place after all the visitors leave.

To wait for nightfall, the authorities choose a campground outside the nearby village of Union Grove, an old mill town with less than two thousand residents. Union Grove is so small that it has no police department of its own, just a tiny auxiliary office staffed by officers from the larger city of Statesville.

The following morning, the sounds of FBI and Homeland Security vehicles pulling into the Union Grove police parking lot bring the Statesville officers outside to see what's happening. Among them is an older man with a prominent beer belly, wearing a Smokey the Bear hat and mirrored sunglasses.

Sauntering over to one of the Suburbans, he removes his glasses to address an agent exiting the vehicle.

"What do we have here?" drawls Smokey, eyeing the caravan assembled in his lot. "You guys Feds?"

"Yes," replies Cory Randolph, a by-the-book officer from Chicago. We're FBI and Homeland Security."

Smokey cocks an inquisitive brow. "What the hell are the Feds doin' in my town?"

Agent Randolph looks down at the policeman's nametag so he can address him properly and extends his hand. "Chief Long, I'm FBI Field Agent Cory Randolph."

Long stares at the hand, asking again, "What the hell are you doin' here?"

Though Agent Randolph would love to jump down the guy's throat, he forces a smile instead, asking politely, "Can we go inside to talk?"

Police Chief Danny Long looks at the caravan and then back at Randolph, who still has his hand out.

"Yeah," he says, shaking Cory's hand firmly. "Let's get this over with. I got some coffee inside, but not enough for your whole crew. There's a great place near here where you can get coffee and livermush." Long turns and walks into the building without checking to see if Randolph is behind him.

With a shrug for his team, the agent follows, wondering, *What the hell is livermush?*

The auxiliary office consists of two desks, one bathroom, a thirty-six-foot holding cell with a sink and a toilet, and a communications table with a police radio and desk supplies. It's a prefab building with paneled walls and a shabby floor.

Long removes his hat, exposing a head devoid of hair, and sits at his desk while Cory places a chair in front of it. Then Long picks up a Styrofoam cup, takes a sip, and lays the cup back down on the desk, saying, "Okay, Agent. Welcome to Union Grove. Now, why the hell are y'all here?"

Cory stares down the chief. "We're after a guy named Serge Kaspin. He's a terrorist who's taken up residence nearby. You know the town of Love Valley?"

"Yeah, I know Love Valley. It's a cute touristy place north of here; has an Old West vibe. There's a terrorist there?"

"Yes, he bought the town saloon. He thinks he's being clever, but we found him. We're going to raid his place tonight, after the tourists have left, and we're going to need your help."

Long shakes his head. "Shit. There are only two of us here. I can call for backup and get help from the State police."

"That's a good idea," says Randolph. "It may get messy."

"I hope you got a good plan. After hours, that town's locked up tighter than... Well, anyway, help yourself to some coffee. It's hot, but that's about it. Meanwhile, I'll give a shout-out for assistance. If you guys are hungry, the place I was talking about is just down Highway 21. It's called Dotty's. She makes the best grits and homemade livermush around here."

While Long calls in his request, Randolph gets himself a cup of coffee, adding lots of sugar and creamer just in case. However, he still shudders when he sips the gruel. "You were right; it is hot," he says charitably.

After Long makes the arrangements for reinforcements, Randolph returns to the parking lot to direct his men to the restaurant Long recommended.

"We're going to Dotty's," he tells an officer who appears beside him. "We're gonna get breakfast."

Long scratches his head, then dons his hat. "I'll join ya as soon as my assistant chief gets back. Shouldn't be more than a few minutes. Don't forget to try the livermush."

Randolph casts the officer a sidelong glance, then leans in. "What in heaven's name is livermush?"

When the chief overhears the question, his belly laugh fills the parking lot. "City fella, you are in for a treat!"

Later that afternoon, the C-130 taxies up to a private hanger off the main runway at Charlotte Douglas International Airport and opens its large rear door.

With a tight grip on Powell, Richard Sosa and Stenhouse exit the belly of the beast toward Jacob, Hector, and a contingent of federal agents awaiting their arrival.

When they reach the group, Richard removes Powell's handcuffs and hands him his phone.

"Make your check-in call, and don't do anything stupid this time."

Powell clicks on his saved contact. "Yeah, it's me. I'm outside of Indianapolis. What? No, everything's fine. I just needed to make a few more stops than I thought. Oh, it's this hunk of metal; it really loves diesel. Okay, right. See ya later."

He hands the phone back, and Richard re-shackles him. "Everything okay on his end?"

"Yeah. He wanted to know why it took so long for me to call. You heard what I said about the gas."

Jacob pulls Jack and Richard aside. "Let me fill you in on the latest. We're gonna stage at a town called Union Grove tonight. Unfortunately, they only have a small auxiliary police office, so the local chief had to call for backup."

"Where's Union Grove?" asks Jack.

"It's a little over an hour north of here and fifteen minutes from Love Valley. So we should get going now."

It's midafternoon when the law enforcement vehicles with George Powell rumble into Union Grove. As they pass, wide-eyed kids on bikes gawk at the FBI SWAT trucks and the large JLTV.

While they were waiting for them, the federal SWAT teams already in the town split up. Some are inside a small office with Chief Long, while others are at the nearby restaurant.

Long peeks out the door as Jack, Jacob, Richard, and Hector escort George Powell inside, where most of the team is sitting on the floor while Agent Randolph perches on one of the only chairs.

"Great," says Long, "more Yankees to create havoc. I'd offer you all a place to sit, but we don't have extra chairs. We're also out of coffee."

Cory Randolph stands to greet the new arrivals. "I'm FBI Special Agent Randolph," he tells them. "These men are one of two teams I assembled. The other is down the road, at a great little restaurant."

Jacob introduces himself and his posse, then turns his

attention to the chief. "Can we put our prisoner in lockdown till tonight?"

Long grabs a set of keys from a desk and walks over to a cell, unlocking the door and holding it open. When no one makes a move, he barks, "You need a personal invite? I ain't a goddamn doorman!"

Grabbing Powell's arm, Richard moves him into the cell, and Long locks it.

"Not to seem inhospitable," says Long, "but this office can't hold all of y'all till tonight. You can wait at Dotty's with the others, or there's an American Legion Hall about a block past her place. I'm a member, a veteran of the Gulf War, so I can open it up for ya. You can come back for your prisoner when you're ready. I go off duty at seven, but Billy Green, my assistant chief, has the night shift."

Long expects them to leave, so Jacob shrugs. "That would be great, Chief. We'll get out of your hair. The American Legion Hall sounds good." Jacob looks at the others in the room. "Any of you wanna go out for something to eat? I can bring something back here for our 'guest.' You want anything, Chief?"

"No, thanks," replies Chief Long. "My grub is hand-delivered when I'm in town. Dotty's the best; she knows what I like. Tell her you got a prisoner, and she'll send something over for him, too."

From the cell, Powell shouts, "Just don't send me any livermush!"

Outside the building, Jack turns to Jacob as they walk back to the cars. "Guess it's livermush for Powell. And no, I'm not ordering that shit for myself."

"Never had it, but I'm willing to try," says Jacob. "Listen, after we eat, we'll get the entire team together and wait at the American Legion Hall. After dark, we'll head over to the campground, where they left most of the vehicles for the raid."

The dinner crowd is sparse that evening. The usual tourists didn't materialize, so Serge has time to gather his crew of five men for a little talk.

"I got a twitchy feeling," he tells them. "It's just a hunch, but I want you on your toes tonight. Something's up; I don't know what. Arm yourselves but stay out of sight. If anything happens, it'll probably start after this fucking town shuts down."

It's only eight p.m., but Union Grove is quiet.

"Where the hell is everyone?" mumbles Cory, looking out a window of the Legion Hall.

Jacob walks over to share the window. "I guess that's small-town life. Oh, there's the chief."

Outside, Police Chief Long is approaching the hall in jeans and a Harley T-shirt.

Cory tuts his disapproval. "Pretty casual, isn't he?"

"Well, he said he was going off duty at seven. I guess nothing much happens around here."

Chief Long steps into the hall and spots Cory and Jacob at the window. "You leaving soon?" An unlit White Owl bobs up and down at every word. "I gotta lock this place up for the night."

"It's a little too early," answers Cory.

"Oh, okay. Anyway, I also came to let you know that I have two squads ready for the assault, one from my office and the other from State police. And by the way, I did some checking on your Kaspin prick. I can't believe a criminal of his caliber is in our neck of the woods. That guy's bad news! You gotta get that fucker out of here!"

"That's exactly what we plan to do. Just pray that he cooperates, and no one gets hurt."

Long stops to light his cigar. "I ran into some townsfolk who say he ain't alone over there. So watch your asses, boys. I'm headin' over to my office now, so keep in touch with me there. I'll lock up the hall later."

DHS Agent Sosa catches up with the Chief at the door. "I'll go with you. I want to bring Powell over here. We're gonna need him soon."

After Sosa and Long leave, the two undercover operatives who posed earlier as the couple at Serge's saloon arrive at the American Legion Hall.

"Good to see you," says Cory. "Jacob, these are agents from our Charlotte office, Mary Simpson and William Barry. They went undercover to check on Kaspin."

"Nice to meet you. What can you tell us?"

"Serge runs a quaint place called the Horseshoe Saloon and Hotel on Henry Martin Trail," says William. "It looks like the set of an old TV western."

Mary nods. "None of the roads in the town are paved, and all the structures are wooden. There are also raised walkways, hitching rails, and horse troughs. There's a general store, a bank, small shops, a livery stable, and the like. The town attracts tourists who want to see people dressed in period costumes interacting with them and staging gun fights. It looks like a cute place to spend an afternoon."

"Sounds interesting," agrees Jacob. "Except for the fact that a cold-blooded killer is walking around with all those guests. I can't imagine Kaspin blending in there. What did you find out about him?"

"He seems to have a crew of at least four. That's as many as we could identify; there could be more. It looks like they live on the second floor of the saloon. The 'hotel' part is just for show; they don't rent the rooms."

Mary cuts in with an observation. "Don't forget the dance hall in the bar area. We're not sure if the performers are also working with him."

"Yeah, they put on a couple of shows there."

"Sounds like you really poked around. So, we want to go in after ten," says Cory. "Can you verify that visitors will be gone by then?"

"Yeah, that's right. Some of the character actors said the town has usually cleared out long before that."

"Good. What about a way in?"

"There's a back entrance. I can show you on a map," says William, handing Jacob a brochure with the saloon circled in red. Pointing to a road at the rear, he says, "That's where delivery and garbage trucks come in, usually between four and five in the morning."

"Did you notice whether his men were armed?"

Mary laughs. "They're all armed. Ruger 45s, mostly, probably Vaqueros. It's an old west town, so everyone dresses the part. But I wouldn't be surprised if they also keep AR weapons out of sight somewhere."

Cory and Jacob turn to each other with anxious looks. Cory asks, "How well do you think they could defend the place?"

William takes a moment to consider his response. "There's a balcony over the saloon with windows facing the street. They could probably hold off an assault from there. I think a couple of the rooms open onto it. There's also a staircase inside the saloon and another one attached to the south side of the building."

Jacob has a final question. "Any other entrances besides the main door?"

"We saw one on the north side that looks like it goes to the kitchen. There's a large propane tank on that wall and a couple of garbage bins."

Cory draws in a deep breath and lets it out slowly. "Good work, you two. William, I want you in the JLTV with Powell and me. You can guide us in."

The backcountry roads of North Carolina are dark and quiet as the convoy travels from the staging campground to Love Valley. There are no streetlights around here. If it weren't for their headlights, the only illumination they'd have would be the weak flashes of fireflies zipping through the kudzu. High above, the night sky is a deep black, and if the travelers were interested, they could see the flash of an occasional meteorite and millions of stars.

It doesn't take long for the caravan to enter the main road toward the town, and those in the lead car turn off at the sign indicating a camping area. The plan is to stop there to regroup before launching the attack.

"Whoa, who's that?" asks Cory, pointing to a darkened black Suburban parked near the restrooms. "The manager said only a couple of customers are occupying spaces near the back."

Jack studies the vehicle. "It looks like Lucchese's men. Or maybe a hired hitman," he says, exiting the car with a hand on his holstered weapon. "I'll check it out."

Jacob mutters, "Shit," and follows him out of the JLTV.

While Jack and Jacob approach the vehicle — Jack on the driver's side and Jacob on the other — the rest of the SWAT team exits their vehicles with their weapons trained on the car.

Jack taps the tinted driver's side window. "Hello?"

The window lowers, revealing a well-built man dressed like a ninja.

Jack smiles at the getup. "Howdy, partner. You look out of place. But hey, we all got our thing, right?"

The man looks almost invisible in the dark, but Jack can see his eyes boring holes into him through his dark mask.

"Look," says Jack. "I know Lucchese paid you to be here, but look around; you're not needed. So, I'm gonna give you a professional courtesy tonight. I'm gonna allow you to drive away, no questions asked. But if you don't, I promise things won't go well. Capeesh, *amico*?"

Ever so slowly, the hitman shifts his eyes to his rearview mirror, spotting the men assembled behind him. Then he looks at Jacob standing on the other side of the car.

Turning back toward Jack, he responds in Italian without removing his mask. *"Bene, Tenente. Accetto tua offerta. Buona caccia."* Then the window ascends, and the SUV drives away from the campground.

Assante lowers his gun and stares at Jack. "What did he say?"

"I'm not sure, but I think it was something like, 'You're the best! Go get 'em, tiger!'"

Jacob snorts. "Yeah, right."

It's now 9:50, and Serge is rechecking his Rolex, even though he knows the time couldn't have changed much from when he last looked at it. Powell is supposed to call in ten minutes; he's anxious to know he's here.

On the dot of ten, his cell phone rings.

"Colonel Powell! So glad you made it!"

"Yes, sir. I'm entering the town now. I should be at your back door in five minutes. Make sure your guys know I'm coming."

Serge's face brightens. "Believe me, they know," he replies happily. "We've been expecting you."

Serge ends the call and looks around at his men, five of his best recruits from the Patriot Guard. All of them have 45s strapped to their hips, with one also carrying an M60 machine gun and the others gripping M4 rifles.

"I'll stay at the bar and wait for Powell," he tells them. "I want three of you up on the balcony, including you," he says, pointing at the man with the M60. "The rest of you go up to the rear windows. That bad feeling hasn't gone away, so I want to be prepared. If you see anything you don't like, tell me immediately. Did you check your headsets?"

"Yeah," they reply through a mixture of grunts and nods.

"Good. Don't fire unless I direct you to. But if I do, light this town up! I don't give a crap what happens to it."

CHAPTER TWENTY-NINE

It's time. Everyone from the assault team is concentrating on the upcoming raid. High above, the Constellation Orion seems to follow them as they move out of the campground.

The lead vehicle is the JLTV driven by Cory, with passengers William, Colonel George Powell, and Jack. The rest of the core team found places in the SWAT vehicles and the local and State police cruisers bringing up the rear.

Without the amenities of modern society, the Love Valley area is eerily quiet. The JLTV's headlight beams catch a raccoon crossing the road, but nothing else seems to be stirring in the darkness. Not that they could see anything beyond the lights, in any case. The team is edgy; anyone could be lying in wait for them, and they'd never know it.

At the sign announcing the entrance to the touristy town, the convoy slows down and stops.

"All right," announces Cory to his team in the other vehicles. "This road becomes Henry Mitchell Trail here, and the Horseshoe Saloon is on this road, so we're close. You know the drill."

The JLTV's passengers turn to watch the FBI MRAP turning off the road behind them and parking on the shoulder. Five black-outfitted commandos climb out and proceed into town on foot while the rest of the vehicles turn left onto similarly named Mitchell Trail Road.

Cory will keep the JLTV where it is until he receives word that everyone's in place.

When they're all set up, William directs him to an alley

beside the saloon. Cory parks there, but keeps the engine running. "I'm not gonna turn it off yet, in case we need to make a quick getaway."

Inside the saloon/hotel, Serge's headset awakens. "Sir, we got an assault team across the street at the dress shop," a voice crackles.

Behind the bar, Serge purses his lips. His intuition was correct; this isn't going to be easy. "Hold off," he instructs. "Powell must be here. I just heard the JLTV pull up. Wait for my command."

Outside, Cory decides to turn off the engine. Quietly, he tells his team, "This is it, folks. Stay alert. Anything can happen."

Jack swivels his head around, checking for movement outside the windows. Then he exits the JLTV. "It's clear," he says, waiting there for Hector and others to join him.

Cory trusts Jack's assessment. "I'm bringing Powell out," he announces.

Everyone on the team is wearing armored vests tonight except the prisoner, but the disgraced Marine colonel isn't complaining. He understands. He knew the risks when he signed up with Kaspin and is now resigned to whatever befalls him.

Cory keeps Powell close while he waits for Jack's signal to go in. When he gets it, he leads Powell into the saloon.

Unknown to any of them, Serge's men have been watching everything from above, including the movements of police and SWAT teams at the rear of the building. One of them notifies Serge. "Some coming in now; others at the back."

When the crew is inside the door, Cory unshackles Powell. "You go in ahead of us. We'll come in after we hear you talking to Kaspin."

Powell is sure Serge won't give up easily, but he's prepared to go along with Cory's order. Nevertheless, he can't resist scoffing at the agent's confidence. With a soft chuckle, he tells Special Agent Randolph, "You know you guys are in deep shit, right? I'm gonna enjoy watching you all go down!" Then he gives Cory the finger, steels himself for what he's certain will come next, and pushes open an interior door, continuing through the kitchen into a short hallway outside the dining area.

From his position behind the bar, Serge studies Powell as he approaches. The corrupt arms dealer was looking forward to congratulating the man who brought him his cherished acquisition, the suitcase-sized nuclear weapon he intends to use in his plot to reverse the country's move from the Constitution. However, something isn't right. The man Kaspin has been relying on all this time should be pleased that the next phase of their mission is about to begin. Instead, his face is filled with uncertainty.

Serge's mind circles around every scenario he can think of. *What could have happened? Why is Powell so nervous?* Reaching down, he places a hand on the barrel of the AA-12 automatic combat shotgun he propped against his leg for easy access. Then, he issues a command to his men.

"Open fire!" he shouts. "No mercy!"

At that exact moment, the SWAT commander announces to his team that they've been seen from the second story, and they also begin firing.

While all hell breaks loose outside, Serge aims at Powell. Shouting, "Traitor!" he takes his second-in-command apart with 12-gauge.

Serge's men fire from the front and back of the building, rattling the quiet night with rapid-weapon blasts.

Jack and his team sneak into the narrow hallway. "Fuck!" he shouts into the din. "The bastard has an automatic shotgun! Hector, Jacob, I have an idea! Come with me back into the kitchen! We're gonna try to outflank him! The rest of you, keep him busy!"

As the firefight continues inside and outside, the legendary gunfight at the O.K. Corral pops into Jack's mind. Ducking behind a shelf to avoid flying debris, he mutters, "That gunfight was nothin' compared to this!"

Low and slow, Jack leads Hector and Jacob through the kitchen, stopping only when he comes to a pair of swinging doors. Peering through a crack, he spots Serge ducking down behind the bar.

Outside, one of the SWAT teams neutralizes the men at the back windows. Then they head inside to stop the men on the front balcony.

Hidden by the bar, Serge searches for his extra box of ammo but can't find it among a host of splintered wood. Giving up, he reaches into his waistband and pulls out his 45, his last weapon of defense.

At that moment, the firefight stops, and Jack takes advantage of the silence. From his position at the swinging doors, he yells, "Serge Kaspin! It's over, man! No time like the present to turn yourself in!"

Serge sinks lower behind the bar. "Come on!" he shouts back. "Where's your sense of adventure, Stenhouse? Capturing me won't give you the revenge you're looking for! You know it won't bring your precious Didi back! So how about we meet face-to-face and handle this man-to-man?"

Hector is enraged by Kaspin's appeal to Jack's sense of honor. "Fuck you, Kaspin!" he roars, rushing past his fellow officer. "You gotta go through me first!"

Jack springs up from his crouching position, hollering at Hector to stop. But he crashes through the swinging doors and keeps going, pausing only when Serge stands up to meet him.

"Well, well, well," remarks Kaspin, his mouth contorting into a snarl. "It's the Navy Seal! Remember our video, Navy boy? I must admit I was highly disappointed when you left my house so suddenly a couple of months back. I'm insulted that you didn't like my hospitality. So whaddya wanna do now, Navy?"

Serge walks out from behind the bar, unbuckling his belt and holster and pushing at tables and chairs as he passes. Then he stops, drops the weapon to the wooden floor, and kicks it away.

Hector's eyes bore into his tormentor, but he says nothing.

"What's wrong?" asks Serge, nostrils flaring in anger. "Chicken?"

From Jack's vantage point, the mercenary looks like he's itching for a fight. But Jack won't have it. "What's all this macho shit?" he barks. "You're toast, Kaspin, and you know it!"

However, Hector has been waiting for this moment. With an eye on his adversary, he hands his Glock to Jacob and walks up to Serge, growling, "I'm not drugged and shoved into a cell now, am I, you wuss! I'm gonna beat your ass! Just like I did in Kandahar."

In a flash, the two men are on each other like white on rice. With arms flailing and legs kicking, the pair pummel each other for what seems like forever.

At one point, it appears that Hector is getting the upper hand. But Serge breaks free, grabs a mug from the bar, and smashes it on Hector's head, sending the detective crashing to the floor.

Elated by the win, Serge cricks his neck and looks around for Jack to continue the fight. But Jack is pointing his Glock at him.

"Ah, there you are, Stenhouse," declares Kaspin, raising a blood-splattered hand to wipe sweat from his eyes. "You gonna do it? You know you want to kill me, so what are you waitin' for? Are you chicken, too?"

Jack's eyes dart to two western leather holsters he

spotted earlier hanging on the wall near the bar. The elaborately tooled leather holds a pair of ornate Ruger 45 revolvers.

Unholstering his Glock, he removes his vest and hands it and the gun to Sosa. Then he walks over to the wall and removes the holsters and revolvers.

"What the fuck?" calls Jacob. "What the hell are you doin', man?"

Jack keeps his eyes on Kaspin. "It's all right," he says. "I gotta do this."

Jack throws one holster at Serge and straps on the other one. The western style fits low on his thigh, so he ties it in place and walks to the far end of the bar. Both men inspect their weapons.

By this time, all the assault team members and some locals still in town have gathered inside to watch the spectacle.

Kaspin looks around but can't see any of his men in the crowd. "Did you get them all?" he asks, a fleeting measure of respect taking him by surprise.

"Looks like it," replies Jack. "There's no one here to support you, Kaspin, so you still want to be a big man?"

While the two continue to talk smack, a pair of SWAT officers rush forward to drag the unconscious Gomez out of the way. "We'll fix him up," they whisper to Jack as they pass.

Thirty feet from Stenhouse, Serge watches Jack twirl his revolver around a finger. "You gonna play with that or shoot it?" he asks coldly.

Jack looks at the gun, then slowly inserts it into his holster. "You should know that this isn't my first standoff, Kaspin. Go ahead, draw."

Serge licks his lips and lowers his hand while Jack's eyes narrow into his sniper stare.

In a flash of movement, Kaspin goes for his weapon,

but Stenhouse has already drawn, and his gun is now cocked, pointed, and ready to fire.

The arms dealer's hand stops midair. "Holy shit, Stenhouse! You been practicing?"

Jack stares at him. "Go ahead, make my day."

Serge laughs mirthlessly at the movie reference and cocks his gun — a half-second too late to avoid the bullet that pierces his thigh.

With a loud groan, he crumbles to the floor, and a crimson pool begins to form around his leg. "Fuck, fuck, fuck!" he shouts. "Lucky shot, you bastard! I'm not done yet!" Turning on his good side, he lifts his weapon to fire, but Jack simply shoots it out of his hand. "Aargh!" he screams, now bleeding from his hand as well as his leg.

Jack re-holsters his Ruger. "Pick it up, Kaspin," he orders coldly. "I'm not done with you, either."

Serge refuses to give up. Crawling to the weapon, he grabs it and raises it in a shaky hand just as Jack draws and fires, placing a .45 slug into Serge's temple.

Unmoved by the mass of blood and tissue splattered on the floor, Jack twirls the Ruger again and re-holsters it. Then he walks around to the back of the bar. "Drinks are on Kaspin!" he calls to the onlookers.

But no one moves. Everyone is staring at the scene with their mouths open in shock.

"What the hell just happened?" asks Jacob, stepping toward his friend. "You just... What the hell happened, Jack?"

Stenhouse shrugs and pours himself a Jack Daniel's, neat. "I'm not just a pretty face, Jacob. Come on, drink up. There's more than enough here to go around."

Hector pushes through the swinging doors with a white bandage around his head.

"You okay, buddy?" asks Jack, holding out a drink.

"Yeah, but..." he replies, struck by the gruesome sight in front of him.

Jack shrugs and downs his drink, then pours himself another. "Hey, can someone rustle up some grub? Gunfights make me hungry."

Two days later, Jack watches his boss' face while he reads his report about the raid at Love Valley and the deaths of Kaspin and his men.

Conrad looks up. "And the nuke's been neutralized?"

"Yeah, the military took care of it."

The corners of Conrad's mouth curve upward, and he closes the folder. "I don't know if I approve of everything," he begins, but Jack doesn't let him finish.

"Before you say anything, I have something else to give you," he says, removing an envelope from his jacket pocket.

"What's that?" Conrad asks guardedly.

Jack looks at the envelope as if deciding what to do with it. Then, he hands it over. "It's been a wild ride," he says, "but I'm resigning from the First. This is my two weeks' notice."

Conrad backs away from Jack's outstretched hand. "You don't mean that," he insists, screwing up his face in a grimace. "You love police work! You were instrumental in catching Emily Santice! You just need to decompress!"

Jack drops the envelope onto the desk, but Conrad refuses to pick it up. "You're one of the best, Stenhouse. Why don't you take some time to think about this? Take your family on vacation. Didi's death left a deep mark on you, and I don't think you've recovered. Not that you could ever... I mean... I know you wanted to get revenge on Kaspin, but that's it? He's dead, and you're just gonna leave now? What the hell would you do instead of this? You're a cop, and a damned good one. A little too snarky for some, but that's never been a major issue for me. In fact, you may be one of the best cops I've ever worked with."

Jack's eyes light up. This is rare praise from his boss. Conrad has never acknowledged his skills to this degree before, and he's pleased to finally hear it. "I appreciate that," he says graciously, "but I don't need more time. I've been thinking about this for a while. No reflection on you, but there's too much PC in police work, too much bullshit, and too many suits running around for my taste. The last straw was when I had to send Sharon and Mark to Maryland. That was the beginning of the end for me. I never thought I'd say this, but the shit involved in everyday policework is out of my blood now."

Jack stands, shakes the captain's hand, then places his Glock and badge on the desk. "I'm keepin' the cuffs; I'll need them," his eyes twinkle with information he's not ready to reveal. "I'm gonna use a chunk of the vacation time I haven't used to bring Sharon and Mark home. I'll be back before my last day."

Conrad sighs. "What can I do to change your mind?"

"Nothing."

"Then I guess there's nothing left to say... If you're really sure about this."

"I'm sure."

The Homicide Department head forces a smile. "It's not gonna be the same around here without you, Stenhouse."

"I bet you say that to all the cops," says Jack, rolling his eyes to the ceiling. Then, he gets serious. "I know I'm gonna miss everyone here, but this is good for me. So... I'll be back in two weeks. And when I get back, you better give me a good sendoff! With a BIG cake!"

EPILOGUE

On Jack's last day at the First Precinct, Ken and Cindy Rodriguez are at home in Florida, happily preparing a room for their soon-to-be-born baby.

"Are you sure you're well enough to do this?" asks Ken.

Cindy pushes her husband's hand away from her paintbrush. "Oh, stop fussing," she says grumpily. "I can do this just fine. I'm not due for another month."

"I know, but you're so busy at the gallery, I thought you'd want to take it easy now."

"The gallery won't run itself," she replies, dipping the brush into a can of yellow paint. "Business is thriving, so there's lots to do."

Hesitating, she puts the brush down and walks over to her husband. "Kenny, I know I've said it before, but I'll be forever grateful that you're not holding those problems with Serge Kaspin against me. Especially since you got caught in the crossfire."

Ken brushes a stray hair from his wife's forehead. "I'm all healed now, and I love you too much to do anything else. I've put it in the past, and you should, too. Besides, we're going to be a real family now, so we have a lot more to think about! How cool is that?"

In New York, the going-away party for Stenhouse is about to begin in the station's rec room, but Jack hasn't made an appearance yet.

Captain Conrad isn't surprised. He thought this would happen; Jack is Jack, and there's no telling what he'll do at any given moment. However, there's still work to be done at the station, and they can't wait forever.

"Where the hell is he?" grumbles Inspector Rawlings.

"If I know him, he's planning a grand entrance," replies Conrad, just as noise near the door captures their attention.

"Hey, he's here!" exclaims some of those closest to the commotion.

Unexpectedly, the room falls silent.

With a lopsided grin, Jack Stenhouse stands in the doorway with his wife, Didi holding their son, Mark. Didi's mom, Sharon, stands behind them.

Astonished gasps fill the air as everyone clears a path for Jack and his family to the front, where a long table holds the special cake they planned for this occasion.

Jack states, "I've been looking forward to this," as he marches up to the cake. "I want a big piece of…"

Stopping in his tracks, he bursts out laughing. At the center of a frilly design of lacy multicolor frosting is the unmistakable image of a hand giving a one-finger salute.

Jack hoots, "You guys! This is perfect!" He laughs so hard that tears form in his eyes.

Looking on, Didi and Sharon find the decoration so hilarious that their equally side-splitting reactions threaten to make Mark cry.

"We held a contest!" declares Conrad, delighted by Jack's response to the department's efforts. The captain has to raise his voice loud enough to be heard over the crowd's guffaws. "And that design got the most votes!"

"I love it!" exclaims Jack, turning to his friends and colleagues packed tightly into the small room. As his eyes roam around, he spots Hector, John Burley, James Ruiz, John's very pregnant wife, Sylvia, and Jacob Assante. He also sees John Lennon from Forensics and many others he's worked with over the years.

"Didi!" calls someone from the back of the room. "Oh, my god! We thought you were dead!"

Jack looks through the crowd to see Allison Giancarlo fighting her way to the front. Her face is no longer drooping, and aside from a slight hitch in her gait, she looks as healthy as ever.

"You look great!" says Jack, hugging his ex-partner for a long time. "I'm so happy to see how well you recovered!"

"Yeah, but Didi's alive?! What the hell, Jack?!"

Listening in, Inspector Rawlings clears his throat to make an announcement.

"I know all of you are confused about seeing Jack's wife alive and well. So I guess I should explain. When Serge Kaspin blew up Didi's boutique, she was indeed injured and unconscious when fire rescue arrived, but not fatally, thank God. However, the team made an on-the-spot decision. Together, we conspired to use the blast to make Kaspin believe that he succeeded in getting his revenge against Jack so that when we moved the family away from the city, he'd have no need to seek them out. To that end, it was better for all of you to think Didi died in the blast."

"Ha! You did a great job making us believe that!" shouts someone in the crowd.

Another yells, "It sure was a nice funeral, Didi!"

Didi smiles and dips her head in a mock bow, holding onto Mark so he won't fall.

Inspector Rawlings waves his hands in the air for attention. "Okay, settle down, everyone! You got thirty minutes left to send Jack off before you hafta get back to work!"

The ensuing moans and groans of employees enjoying

the short respite in an otherwise stressful day force Rawlings to cut through the din again. "Let's slice up this cake and say goodbye to one of our own, a great detective and a good friend to many of you! As for me," he adds through scattered hoots and applause, "I know he's stepped out of line quite a few times…and kept our maintenance crew busy replacing window glass! But all-in-all, I'm gonna miss him!"

While the crowd roars with laughter at the reference to Jack's famous temper, the inspector asks, "Any words, detective?"

Jack cricks his neck like he always does. "I have nothing much to say, which I know is not like me. The only thing I really want to do is thank you for all the help you've given me, especially my crew! I had a blast working with all of you, and I wouldn't have lasted here as long as I did if I didn't get to see your hideous faces every day!" Amid more laughter, he adds, "But…you're not completely rid of me yet! I'll still be around; I'm gonna set up my own shingle as a P.I.! Now, let's dig into this cake!"

While Sharon distributes generous wedges to everyone who wants it, Jack walks over to Allison. "It's so great to see you, Ally! What have you been doing to keep yourself busy now that you're no longer working?"

"Well," she grins mysteriously, "I'm actually coming back! Because of you, the First needs a new Homicide lieutenant, so Rawlings called and asked if I wanted back in. Of course," she says, glancing at Hector and John Burley who have joined the conversation, "your babies are gonna need a new leader. So how could I refuse?"

Pretending to pout at Allison's jest, Gomez and Burley rub their middle fingers on the sides of their noses but chuckle just the same.

"So what are your plans?" asks Allison. "You're gonna become a P.I.?"

Jack straightens his back with pride. "You're lookin' at the future Jack Stenhouse, Private Investigator. As soon as I get my license, I'm gonna set up shop and do what I've always wanted to do — without the political correctness bullshit we've had to put up with for way too long!"

Outside precinct headquarters, Jack and his family head to his Road Runner, happy to start the next phase of their lives.

While Didi straps her son into his car seat, Jack waves at Sylvia and John Burley as they walk to a police sedan parked across the street. "Gonna miss you, Stenhouse!" calls John. Then he opens the door, and an explosion engulfs him, the sedan, and Sylvia in a fiery ball of fire.

With a burst of adrenaline, Jack leaps forward to cover his wife while Sharon cowers in the back seat.

As car and passengers burn, debris from the explosion flies in all directions, and police officers swarm out of the building like angry ants.

"KASPIN!" yells Jack, tears falling down his cheeks at the sight of losing his friends to the person he thought was out of their lives forever. "You harass us even from the grave?! What orders did you give the Patriot Guard? I thought we were done with this shit!!"

A NOTE FROM THE AUTHOR

I hope you enjoyed reading this novel as much as I enjoyed writing it. As a reader, you are the recipient of the hours and hours I spent organizing my thoughts into the story I wanted to create, then editing it into the form you see here. My goal is to entertain you and give you something to think about.

I'm fortunate that my muses never let me alone. They're always available with another interesting idea, making *Operation Retribution* the eleventh novel I've published to date. There are more to come; they only need to be edited, which takes more time than the actual writing.

The best way for me to know how my stories are received is by reading your reviews. Your thoughtful comments give me insights into how my stories affect my readers, and are an effective tool for piquing the interest of others.

Please post a brief note about your reactions at Amazon.com. This and all my books are listed on that site under my name.

Thank you, and happy reading!

Frank A. Ruffolo

Made in the USA
Columbia, SC
21 September 2023

23133307R00217